THE SEPARATIST

Gordon Snider

The Separatist

Helm Publishing

For information address:
Helm Publishing
3923 Seward Ave.
Rockford, IL 61108
815-398-4660
www.publishersdrive.com

ISBN 978-0-9792328-8-6

Printed in the United States of America

Other Books by Gordon Snider

Sigourney's Quest

Author's notes:

The Separatist is based on a Japanese custom where people hire such a specialist to end relationships. This might involve a spouse, a lover, a business partner, or any other kind of personal relationship. The idea is to create a situation that is so embarrassing to the "mark" that he or she will agree to severe the relationship without public displays of discord, publicity, or court proceedings. In the novel, Mr. Andersen says he is in the breakup business, and while such practices are unheard of in this country, they are still practiced in Japan. I found the concept so intriguing, it led me to write this novel.

While the concept of a separatist is very real, the Chinatown I describe in San Francisco is quite fanciful. It combines scenes and customs from the late 1800s, when this "city within a city" was called the haunt of the highbinders, to the present day. Unfortunately, if you wander down Chinatown's streets, you will not find the hidden alleys, opium dens, and curing sausages hanging from windows that I portray, but such scenes did exist once upon a time. And today's side streets *are* crowded with the sing-song voices and open markets selling fresh fish, vegetables, and other delicacies that I have described. It only takes a little imagination to picture the darker world described in the novel.

Since the story spans forty years of computer technology, it was necessary to carry Julia's world slightly into the future. However, The Separatist is meant to be a mystery/suspense novel, not science fiction, so I have deliberately left the time frame vague and have introduced only a few futuristic devices, such as electronic fences and laser guns. It was important that such contrivances not get in the way of the story.

However, writing about San Francisco has wetted my appetite for more, so another novel is planned, and this one *will* take place in the time of those uncharted alleyways and smoking dens that once made Chinatown such an intriguing and ominous place.

Dedication

To my loving wife, Fe, who lets me hide in "my cave" and write.

PROLOGUE

The two boys knew they were about to trespass, and that was the fun of it. They had slipped through the scratchy weeds and dry summer grass growing outside the perimeter of the Port of Oakland's shipping docks, and they now faced a series of large signs with bright, orange letters warning them they would be shocked by an invisible electronic fence if they ventured any closer. Shipping containers stacked as high as three-story buildings filled the yards beyond the perimeter, the result of a labor dispute that had shut down the port for the past five days, rendering the large cranes lining the waterfront lifeless. The air was electrified with anticipation as the boys studied the bold, angry letters on the signs. They already knew about the fence. In fact, the taller boy even knew how to make it visible.

"See," he whispered to his companion, "You just toss electrically charged particles like this." He produced a handful of dun-colored fragments with the consistency of sawdust from his pocket. "I snuck it from Dad's work lab. Watch." He slung the particles into the breeze, producing a brilliant barrier of streaming blue lights where the dust came in contact with the electronic beams.

"Wow," his companion exclaimed as he marveled at the shimmering display. "It's awesome, but how can we get around it?"

"There's no way you can get around it and if you touch it, you'll have burns on your skin for a week. You gotta go under it.

Follow me."

He crouched down and began running along the perimeter, keeping a safe distance between himself and the fiery barricade. Nothing moved beyond the fence, but the boy knew there were still watchmen and guard dogs to worry about. It was best to keep out of sight. They reached a depression where last winter's heavy storms had washed away enough top soil to reveal an old creek bed that had once drained into the bay. The taller boy produced a rusty shovel he had hidden in the nearby bushes and began digging.

"All we gotta do is dig down a coupla feet, and we can crawl under the fence. Here," he commanded, handing the shovel to his companion. "You dig while I keep an eye out for the guards." The smaller boy took the shovel without complaint and started pawing at the dirt. It was evident that he was used to taking orders from the taller boy, who now strode importantly back and forth watching the quiet docks with a keen eye.

It was more than just a warm August day, and sweat soon poured off the young digger, causing him to shrug the sticky shirt off his back and roll up his pants legs. Wiping his hands on his pants, he stood for a moment watching the grasshoppers jumping around him like playful dolphins. Nearby, two ground hogs chirped shrill warnings before scampering into the protection of their burrows. The earth smelled like old tires where the boy turned it, evidence of the chemicals and oil that had been spilled or dumped there in years past.

The boy was about to tell his friend he'd had enough when his shovel made an odd clinking sound. "Bobby, come 'ere. I think I found somethin'." He dug more carefully, feeling his way around the buried object.

"Aw, you just hit a rock," Bobby replied skeptically. "Keep diggin'."

Several pieces of bone slowly emerged from the soil. "It ain't no rock. It looks like fingers!"

Bobby raced over to have a look. When he saw the gnarled bones, he fell to his knees and started pushing the dirt away with his hands. More pieces of bone emerged, until they saw the skeletal remains of a claw-shaped hand.

"Maybe it's an animal," Bobby huffed, wiping his brow with his arm.

"Looks too big for an animal." The boy with the shovel frowned and shifted his weight like a runner at the start of a race. "I think we should get outa here."

"Go if you want to," Bobby replied, digging eagerly with his hands. "I wanna see more of this." The soil was still soft from the big storms that had flooded the area, and he quickly uncovered the long bones of an arm.

His companion shuffled his feet uncertainly at this new revelation, but Bobby seemed unperturbed. He continued with reckless abandon, until a pair of sunken eye sockets and two rows of grinning teeth suddenly emerged from the soil. This was too much even for Bobby, who scrambled to his feet with a yelp. The two boys gaped apprehensively at their find. The facial remains stared back at them with a ghoulish sneer that made them both shiver despite the heat. A hole was clearly visible in the skull's forehead.

"I bet the guy was shot," Bobby exclaimed.

"Maybe we should tell somebody," his friend responded.

Bobby didn't need any more encouragement. The two boys turned in unison and crashed through the grass like twin grass hoppers, jumping and running as fast as their young legs would carry them.

Detective Rodriguez stood beside his department's forensic expert and viewed the crime scene with a dark frown. The setting reminded him of photographs he'd seen of ancient burial sites in the Andes Mountains in Peru, and he thought about his original goal of becoming an archeologist. It had been a long time since he'd thought about his decision to drop out of college and join the police force, but watching the two men carefully brushing the remaining dirt away from the skeleton made him wonder where he would be now if he hadn't. Probably up in the Andes instead of standing here swatting away flies and looking at the remains of a dead man.

"Doesn't seem to be much doubt how he died," Rodriguez offered.

"A single bullet through the forehead would be my guess. The poor bastard knew what was coming. Been there a long time." His companion reached down and flicked a bit of dirt from the skeleton, which was completely uncovered now and lay on its back with one arm resting comfortably across its chest in the relaxed pose of someone napping.

"What's your estimate?"

"Thirty, maybe forty years."

"Great. That's just what I need. A goddamn murder that probably happened while I was still in diapers." Rodriguez looked behind him at the reporters milling about like expectant vultures just beyond the cordoned-off area. "What the hell am I supposed to tell *them*?"

"Say it's an ancient burial site. Incas or something like that."

Rodriguez barked a laugh. "You read my mind." His face grew serious. "Do you think you can find me something? This is the kind of thing that can stir up the public's imagination once the media get hold of it."

"Give me a day or so. We'll see."

Rodriguez was right about the media and the public's morbid fascination with a murder that took place before many of them were born. The newspapers played the story for all it was worth. The coroner's report didn't add much to what he had surmised at the crime scene. The victim was a man in his fifties, just under six feet. He'd been shot once through the head forty years ago, give or take a year. There were healed fractures of the left forearm and right index finger, indicating he had been in a fight or accident. Dental charts were being checked against missing persons, but it was difficult to track records back so many years. Computers and information systems had changed dramatically since the murder. All it took these days was a digital scanner plugged into a computer satellite link. He could have the information in five minutes. But forty years was a millennium in technological terms.

Finding out about this guy would take leg work and some luck.

Rodriguez sighed. He didn't like the feel of this one. Everything pointed to a professional hit, and his gut told him he was going to spend more time on the case than he wanted. He began to regret not becoming an archeologist.

CHAPTER ONE

The moment Julia saw the elderly gentleman in the tweed jacket walking through Washington Square Park, she thought of someone she had never known, her father. It was a strange connection, but the jacket rang a bell somewhere deep inside her. She could almost feel its scratchy fabric against her face.

Sunlight fell in uneven patterns through the surrounding trees, highlighting the old man's white mane with luminous drops of light. She could tell by his bearing that he refused to yield gracefully to his advancing age. The cane he held in his left hand went unused despite a perceptible limp, and he strode with purpose across Union Street to the entrance of the Fior d'Italia restaurant, where Julia sat at a window table observing his progress. He entered the restaurant with dignity, his head held high and his shoulders squared, ready to absorb an imaginary opponent's blow. Julia couldn't help smiling. He was an aging lion, but he wanted people to know he still had fight in him.

Once inside, however, he hesitated for just a heartbeat while he scanned the room with a wary eye. It was a subtle gesture but enough to betray a moment of uncertainty, a suggestion there might be some danger. None presented itself among the smartly tailored men and women who sat at the bar or occupied the handful of tables surrounding Julia. Their chatty voices echoed off the wood floors and high walls like cawing crows, but she was the only one who gave the new arrival more than a curious glance.

The maitre d' nodded familiarly to the man and, to Julia's surprise, led him towards her table. Was he the one who had called her? She stared at the old man with renewed interest. He looked robust despite his limp, and his face was remarkably handsome for someone who had very likely celebrated his eightieth birthday. On the phone, his voice had sounded younger. Perhaps, it was the hint of a British accent that had fooled her.

The old man eyed her in turn. What did he see, she wondered? She knew her skin was still smooth, although it had lost the lustrous purity of youth and yielded to the tiny lines and uneven elasticity that made their appearance in the early stages of aging. She had always considered herself more sensual than beautiful, with her full lips, oval face, long neck, and shoulder-length hair. She liked to portray a seductive charm, accentuated by careful grooming. Today, she wore a knee-length, black skirt and long-sleeved blouse to affirm the fact that she was a working woman who wanted to be recognized for her skills, not her femininity. She kept her smile polite, letting the stranger know that even though she had no idea why she was meeting him for lunch, she was conducting herself in a professional manner.

"I would recommend the veal, if you haven't ordered," he said without preamble as he sat down opposite her.

"I waited for you, Mr. Andersen." Her frank gaze betrayed a skepticism that poured off her with the intensity of an icy wind. He had given her little information when he called her at the San Francisco Chronicle, other than to say he had a story filled with greed, romance, and murder that would interest her.

A waiter hurried to their table before more could be said, and Mr. Andersen turned his full attention to him. "Arthur, we will both have the veal scaloppini, but let's begin with your special Caesar's salad and sourdough bread. And my usual refreshment. Would you like something to drink, Miss Rice?"

Her polite smile shifted to one of amusement at his

presumptive behavior in ordering for her. "No, thank you. I prefer not to drink while working."

"Do you think that is what we are doing, working?" His eyes danced with amusement of their own.

"I expect so, although I still do not know why I'm here." She returned to her professional smile.

"You are a journalist."

She nodded.

"I believe I can make use of you, and you of me. But not before I have had a sip of my scotch and a bite or two of this establishment's marvelous salad. In the meantime, I shall tell you about yourself, Miss Julia Rice."

She raised her eyebrows at this unexpected change in tack, prompting a smile of delight from Mr. Andersen, but she said nothing.

"You are thirty years old, unmarried, career comes first I suspect, love the city, frequent bars and restaurants shared by your colleagues and occasionally take one home with you, including a woman named Jackie." She opened her mouth to protest, but he waved his hand and continued. "You grew up in Irvine, California, and earned your degree in journalism at UCLA, but after your mother committed suicide, you left Orange County and landed a reporter's assignment here in San Francisco. Your career has been, shall we say, pedestrian? You have a comfortable, one-bedroom apartment in Laurel Heights, rarely cook and like white wines. Your credit cards are paid, but you spent more than you could afford on your car. A small concession to self-indulgence for your long hours at work, no doubt. You have no pets or permanent attachments at the moment, having recently ended an affair with your married boss. You have a preference for older men, due, perhaps, to the fact that you never knew your father. In many ways, you remind me of a woman we shall talk about, if you choose to continue our conversations beyond this lunch."

Anger exploded in short, painful bursts in Julia's chest at the stranger's assault on her private life. Her eyes twitched in disbelief. The old man had spied on her! Knew details about her parents she hadn't even confided to friends. Julia sat back in her chair, too shocked at first to move, then inhaled a gulp of air and rose from the table, signaling her intent to leave.

Mr. Andersen quickly raised his hand and touched her arm. "Please contain your anger for just a moment, until I explain myself." She stood there trembling with indignation, uncertain what to do.

"As I told you on the telephone, I have an unusual story that will interest you," he continued. "One involving romance, greed, murder, and political intrigue. All the elements for a good book, I should imagine. If you listen carefully and tell it correctly, it could change your career."

The words thundered in her ears, but she hardly heard them. His revelations into her private life so confounded her, she could not control the angry wildfire spreading across her face. Professionalism yielded to hostility. "Mr. Andersen, I don't know why you've shown so much interest in me or how you've managed to come by your information, but it smacks of invasion of privacy, and I don't like it. Good day." She turned to leave.

"There is one more thing, Miss Rice," he called after her. "I may be able to help you find your father." The words struck home with the force of a slap to the face, stopping Julia in her tracks. She paused in mid-step, her mind churning with confusion, then swung around and confronted him.

"What do you know about my father?" she demanded in a voice that betrayed more hope than anger.

"Only that he swindles people and keeps moving about the country to avoid unpleasant encounters with the law." Mr. Andersen gestured to her empty chair. "Please, sit down and hear what I have to propose. It will be worth a few minutes of your time."

Julia took a sharp breath and slumped back into her seat. "Do you know where he is?"

"No, but I have ways of looking for him. I shall be happy to pursue them while you work on my story."

Mr. Andersen unexpectedly pulled a handful of wrapped, mint

candies from his coat pocket and offered her one. The sudden gesture sparked poignant memories of a similar incident when she was a small child, and her earliest childhood memory popped into her mind. She was hanging upside down from what seemed a great height. Her only security was a hand gripping her by one bare foot. Blood was rushing to her head, and her upside-down world was spinning out of control. She heard herself screaming and gasping for breath while a man's laughter echoed in her ears. Then, a woman's voice shouted angrily, and Julia was magically lifted into the protective warmth of the man's arms. She couldn't remember his face, only the scratchy fabric of his jacket rubbing her cheek and the piece of candy he magically produced from his pocket.

Julia had grown up fearing anything higher than a stepping stool, and she blamed it on that incident. Whenever she looked down from an upper floor window, a bridge, or other high vantage point, her stomach plunged down an elevator shaft, and it took all her courage to keep from fainting.

Julia straightened her shoulders in an effort to rid herself of the memory and declined Mr. Andersen's offer of a mint with a shake of her head. He popped one into his mouth and returned the candy to his pocket. While he did so, she forced herself to meet the old man's gaze. His eyes reminded her of a fox's, watchful and clever, but were they the eyes of someone who wanted to do her harm? She didn't think so, and despite her anger, she couldn't rein in her curiosity about the mysterious man who smiled so benignly at her from across the table. She thought about the mints in his pocket, and the fuzzy image from her childhood returned. Was it a memory of her father? She had never been sure, but Mr. Andersen's reference to him had hypnotized her.

The waiter's timely arrival with the salads and Mr. Andersen's drink interrupted them, returning Julia's world to a sense of normalcy. The fire in her chest waned; the twitch in her facial muscles subsided. In a concession to the old man's spell, she put her hands in her lap, leaned back in her chair, and watched with fascination as the waiter placed an opened bottle of Glenlevit on the table along with a glass filled with ice. The waiter poured an inch of scotch and left the bottle.

Mr. Andersen twirled the golden liquid in his glass for nearly half-a-minute without tasting it, then took one sip and set the glass down. "Please, try your salad. You will find it delightful. They use real anchovies in it, something many restaurants no longer do. It gives just the right "bite" to complement the dressing."

A brief silence ensued as they both turned their attention to the salads. Mr. Andersen took a hearty mouthful; Julia nibbled. After her second bite, she returned her fork to the table and leaned forward. "Now that you've sampled your scotch and salad, I don't expect this conversation to go any further until I know who you are, and what this is about." The indignation in her voice told her she was still smarting from the spotlight-glare he had just beamed on her life.

Mr. Andersen's expression grew more serious. "That is what the story will do, tell you who I am. As for investigating your background, that's an old habit I'm afraid. It was how I made my living at one time. I had to know who I was dealing with. Who could I trust with my life?" He smiled once more, and she found herself drawn to him despite herself.

"There are some rules, however, that must be acknowledged before we begin. You cannot tell anyone what you are doing until we are finished. You can name the days and times for our meetings, since your schedule is much busier than mine, but I must insist on at least three times a week. I want to keep a flow to our dialogues, and time is of the essence. It is also best that we avoid such public places." He nodded towards the noisy room. Julia recognized the same wary look he had revealed when he first entered the restaurant. Was the fox the hunter or the hunted, she wondered?

"We can avoid prying eyes by meeting here." He handed her a slip of paper with an address on Telegraph Hill. It was less than a mile away. The idea of meeting him privately gave her pause. Could she trust him? "I have also prepared a contract that gives you full rights to publish what I am about to tell you. You will keep all income earned. I will give you documentation and sources to verify facts."

Julia marveled at his ability to control their conversation. Instinctively, she understood that he was doing so now. It was a problem of hers, yielding to the whims of older men, but she had never let herself succumb this easily. Mr. Andersen had slipped through her defenses without firing a shot.

She became aware of the steady hum of other voices around her. They echoed inside her head, and she glanced around the room in an effort to hide her vulnerability. The smell of steaming pasta and sautéed veal permeated the air. "Why are you doing this?" she finally asked.

"I wish to renew my acquaintance with an old adversary and bring him to account for his misdeeds. However, I cannot confront him directly. He is still very powerful. That's where you come in. As a wise man once said: the power of the pen is mightier than the sword. I want the truth to be published. It never mattered to me before, but as you get older your need for justice grows stronger. Some day you will know what I mean.

"It sounds like you want revenge, not justice." Julia eyed him with suspicion.

He shook his white mane, a melancholy smile playing on his lips. "Revenge is an ugly word, Miss Rice. If there *is* an element of revenge, it's for the woman in my story, not for me. She taught me one of life's great lessons . . . how to fly." He paused, and Julia gave him a quizzical look. Mr. Andersen continued. "To grab hold of the future, you must let go of your past. Revenge, self-recrimination, and lost love were all rooted in my past, but I learned to let them go. When you learn how to fly, it will set you free."

Julia had the feeling Mr. Andersen's words were meant for her as much as for himself, and she squirmed uncomfortably in her seat. Before she could reply, he removed a folded paper from his coat pocket.

"If we are to work together," he continued, "we should start at once. This week if possible. Here is the contract." He handed her a single sheet of paper which he had already signed and dated.

She was tempted to shove the contract back at him, just to see his reaction. Despite his charm, she wanted to refuse him. He had told her nothing about himself, and she found the way he tried to manipulate her infuriating. She was also in the middle of a story on the labor dispute currently taking place at the Oakland Port, giving her little time for a wild goose chase.

"I know you are reporting on the strike at the docks." His clear, blue eyes bore into hers with the precision of a dentist's drill. "There have been recent developments there that will interest you."

He knows everything about me, including my assignments. Julia's fingers twitched nervously at the edges of the contract. Twice, she tried to push the document away, but her hands refused to respond. His reference to the port strike and her father aroused her interest with maddening ease, and she knew she couldn't call his bluff. But it was more than that. There was something in his behavior that struck a cord deep inside her psyche. Memories of a scratchy jacket and wrapped candies made her shift uncomfortably in her chair. Julia had recalled these things before, but never with such clarity. She wanted to learn more about this man.

"I'll read the contract and deliver it to you at our first meeting," she said with defiance, as a way to reassert some control over the discussions.

"Agreed. Shall we say tomorrow afternoon? How does one o'clock suit you?" With that he drank his scotch, carefully laid a one hundred dollar bill on the table, and rose without touching any more of his food or waiting for her reply.

So much for letting me set the schedule, she thought as she watched him hobble from the room. She didn't know whether to be angry at the man's preposterous behavior or intrigued by his secrecy. In the end, it didn't matter. He had roused her curiosity, and she was determined to make some sense of today's encounter. Especially the comment about her father. Could he find him? That possibility was reason enough to meet Mr. Andersen again. She owed her mother that much. Mother. It had been awhile since Julia had thought of her, but as she nibbled her food, she did so now.

8

Julia grew up in a world surrounded by the hollyhocks, gingersnaps, and parma violets growing in her mother's nursery, Nature's Flowers. It was a cramped but orderly place, whose selection was limited to flowers standing in neat, potted rows along gravel pathways. The scent of blooming flowers permeated the place year 'round. Nature's Flowers was nothing like the enormous Westminster Nursery across town where a person could get just about any plant imaginable, including young trees and sod. Julia's mother never tried to compete with her larger rival. She said Westminster's was for people interested in landscaping; Nature's Flowers was for gardeners.

Everybody called her Gabriela, including Julia. It had always seemed the natural thing to do. "Mom" was too casual, "mother" too formal and "mommy" was out of the question. Her mother was too graceful and charming to be called mommy.

Her father had disappeared before Julia was two, leaving her with snapshot memories of perspiration odors, a scratchy jacket, and a large hand holding her upside down.. She had gradually come to accept a fatherless life as normal, although she often experienced bursts of jealousy towards friends whose fathers still lived with them. She would come home from school, lie on the bed, and try to summon up memories of her father. The best she could do was that vague image of a man with large hands, a scratchy jacket, and candy in his pocket. There were no photos of him in the house, and his face eluded her. He was a ghost who haunted her life.

Gabriela refused to talk about Julia's father. "Life isn't a bed of roses," was all she would say. They were brave words, but they couldn't hide the bleak moods that regularly descended upon her and caused her to wander about the house in a daze. Julia pretended these bouts of heavyheartedness were the result of a witch's spell, and she believed if she prayed hard enough, she could break it. Sometimes it took a day or more, but when Gabriela eventually felt better, Julia was always pleased to see that her prayers were working.

By the time Julia was six, her prayers had lost most of their potency, however, and it often took several days for Gabriela to rise from her depressions. During those spells, the drapes remained closed and the house dwelled in sadness. A woman named Mrs. Collins helped part-time at the nursery, and she took over at such times, keeping Nature's Flowers open for its loyal customers.

But a wintry day finally came when the prayers no longer worked. Gabriela took Seconal and was rushed to the emergency room. After that, she spent a year in a psychiatric hospital coming to grips with her severe depression, and Julia moved in with a childless neighborhood couple who had little understanding of a six year old girl's needs. Julia spent that year wondering about her father and praying for Gabriela's return.

When Julia left the Fior d'Italia restaurant, a brisk ocean breeze swept away her childhood memories and replaced them with the cunning face of Mr. Andersen, which floated through her consciousness like a wayward spirit looking for a place to land. Her mind buzzed with a disturbing gamut of questions. Who was this man who had so arrogantly intruded on her life? What had he been? A detective? FBI agent? Private investigator? Spy? He *knew* about her. About Jackie! He had spied on *her*! Yet, she had agreed to meet him again. Why? Because he'd mentioned her father and promised her a career-making story. He'd stirred up feelings she normally kept concealed from herself. He'd captivated her. But what did he want, and why had he spied on her?

Her nostrils flared in the chilled air as she thought about him. Something inside her warned Julia that working with this man was going to be a high wire act with no safety net, and she could already feel her stomach starting to tumble down the elevator shaft.

CHAPTER TWO

"We shall begin many years ago when I was hired by a woman named Mrs. Grant, to produce compromising evidence about her husband."

Mr. Andersen sat in a deep cushioned chair facing Julia in a living room devoid of plants, photographs, and other personal effects. He wore a seersucker suit that reminded her of an English gentleman on safari. A dormant odor filled the place, the kind of odor one associated with unopened tombs. Julia glanced at her surroundings and wondered if anyone really lived there.

She had arrived twenty minutes late, earning a slight frown of disapproval from her host, and now sat across from him on a sofa with notepad in hand and digital recorder by her side. The room was dimly lit by weak afternoon sunlight that struggled to penetrate the fog curling its way up Telegraph Hill towards Coit Tower, one of the city's many famous landmarks. The house was located halfway up the hill, and on a clearer day it would have commanded a dramatic view of the San Francisco skyline.

"You were a private detective, then?" she asked in response to his opening remark.

"Not a detective. I was a separatist." Mr. Andersen brushed some indecipherable lint from the sleeve of his coat with an air of haughtiness.

Julia gave him a quizzical look.

"A private detective merely follows people and documents what they do. A separatist prepares a web to entrap the subject. You will understand when I tell you about Arnold Grant." He closed his eyes and sat so quietly Julia thought he might have fallen asleep. When he spoke again, it was in a softer tone that drew her forward in her seat. She had the eerie feeling she was about to join him on an adventure, sharing his experiences as they occurred.

****

Arnold Grant was short, chubby and balding. He walked too fast and bobbed his head like an unhappy quail when he got nervous. He was bobbing it now as he stood at the corner of Columbus and Broadway in San Francisco's famous North Beach. I knew that meant trouble. Things weren't going as planned.

His wife for the past twenty-three years was just as short and round as he was. The first time she came to my office, her eyes flicked so rapidly between my face and her hands, I feared she would have a seizure. Arnold bobbed; she flicked. They must have made quite a pair when they were nervous together.

When she finally told me what she wanted, however, I was pleased to see a steely resolve creep into her composure. It was a good sign. It told me she had the "stuff" to see her plans through, whatever those plans might be.

"I want you to dig up something on my husband that I can use in court," she confided. Her flicking subsided.

"Why?" I asked bluntly. I wanted to know motivation. The wrong reason--for a woman it might be feeling abused or cheated--usually led to a messy situation filled with second thoughts and self-recriminations.

"I want out of my exhaustingly dull and tedious marriage," she responded matter-of-factly. "My husband recently inherited a rather large sum of money. Four million dollars to be exact. I want to divorce him and collect as much of that money as I can."

An excellent reply. Greed rarely led to self-doubts or cancelled plans.

"My fee is $50,000. Half now and the balance when I deliver the evidence." I looked her straight in the eye. Her head recoiled in turtle-like fashion at the cost of my services, but she didn't flick, another good sign.

After a moment's pause, she straightened her back and quickly touched her graying hair with the palm of her hand. "It'll take me a few days to get that much money together without alerting Arnold."

"Next Monday will be soon enough." I suppressed an urge to smile, not at the size of my fee, but in anticipation of a new assignment.

Fifty thousand dollars sounded like a lot of money, but things rarely went as planned. Many jobs ended up being a bargain for the client at that rate, and for a while, I thought that would be my fate with Arnold. I set my team, Carl and Patti, to work digging into his past. Carl was a computer genius and my second in command. When he wasn't "accessing" some data bank or tapping into a communications network, he helped me set up and run the field operations. He was also a good friend. Patti was my office manager, my alter ego and my anchor. She mothered me, scolded me, and gave me her famous "librarian look" whenever she thought I was about to do something she didn't approve of. At those moments, her stern looks reminded me of the ones I'd received as a child from librarians when I made too much noise. Patti coordinated the research and our operations.

They spent two weeks trolling Arnold's life for clues to a vulnerable underside, but there were none. He was a vice-president at a respectable company that manufactured tools and factory equipment. There were no accounting irregularities or business scandals to uncover. Arnold worked long hours, took saunas at his local club and went straight home to his wife. He didn't gamble or drink. He never chased women or rented dirty movies. I made it a strict rule never to let personal feelings enter into my relationship with a client, but I was beginning to have sympathy for Mrs. Grant. Arnold *did* lead an exhaustingly dull life.

But two days later, Carl wandered into my office, slouched cat-like in his favorite chair, and began twirling my razor-sharp, samurai-sword letter opener between his fingers. It was his "guess what I've found" pose, and whenever he assumed it, I stopped whatever I was doing and waited.

"Pornographic chat rooms," he announced without preamble.

"Our boy, Arnold?" I asked in amazement.

Carl nodded. "Some with very young girls."

After so many years in the business I shouldn't have been surprised, but I hadn't expected that from Arnold. "He's not so dull after all," I said with a smile and clapped my hands. Carl had found the key we needed to build our spidery web.

"Patti," I yelled to the outer office, "call Josephine. Tell her we've got work to do." Josephine was my best freelance associate. She was equal parts werewolf, sorceress, and siren. She would devour Arnold Grant.

Two days later, Josephine began casual conversations in Arnold's chat rooms. Nothing directed towards him, but lots of comments filled with beguiling little innuendos that soon had his attention. They started talking directly to each other, and Josephine slowly turned their conversations towards a personal encounter where Arnold could experience his fantasies firsthand. The trick was to let Arnold propose the rendezvous. Josephine kept dangling carrots and waited. A week later, Arnold suggested they meet.

Now, he was bobbing his head at the corner of Columbus and Broadway, just beyond the reach of my waiting spider. I observed Arnold from a second story window across the street. The intersection was alive with evening revelers and curiosity seekers who had ventured into North Beach to peek into the brightly lit strip clubs and sex stores that permeated the area. North Beach hadn't always been like that. Years ago, it had been famous for its jazz clubs and fine restaurants. The intervening years had not been kind to the neighborhood, but tourists still came to have a look and to spend their money, before escaping back to their hotels.

Arnold held the carnation Josephine suggested he bring to identify himself, but instead of turning onto Broadway and entering the Daisy Club, he shuffled his feet and hesitated. His courage was failing him, and if I didn't act fast, he would turn and run.

"Jossie, come in," I said urgently into my headpiece. Everyone on the team wore hidden communications gear during an operation.

"Where's our boy?" Josephine's voice crackled in my ear.

"He's about to turn tail on us. You'd better get out there and sweet talk him. Carl, are you hearing this?"

"Check. You want me to stall him?"

"Yes. Move into position."

I watched Carl stride across the street and stop beside Arnold just as our mark turned to leave. Carl was a big man in every sense of the word, and he literally blocked Arnold's retreat. He held up a street map and began asking Arnold for directions while he waited for Josephine to arrive. Moments later, Josephine emerged from Daisy's and approached the two. Carl strolled away, and Josephine took over.

"Put on the charm, Jossie," I exhorted under my breath. "Don't let him slip away."

Josephine was nearly as tall as Carl, which put her half-a-head taller than her quarry. She had to stoop slightly to bring him to eye level. This had the benefit of exposing her ample cleavage. Even from my lofty perch, I could see that Arnold was more entranced with Josephine's body than her smile, but it might take more than her physical charms to reel him in. Fortunately, we had prepared a contingency plan. Josephine began to act nervous and unsure of herself, putting Arnold in the position of reassuring *her*. Her experience as an actress in local theater productions worked wonders at times like this. Soon, she was holding his arm, and they were walking towards the club. They disappeared into the bright lights, and I exhaled the breath I had been holding.

"Get ready, everybody," I announced to the team, "Our mark has landed."

Arnold's fate was sealed. Josephine let him buy her drinks, then led him to a private room where cameras were ready to roll. There, she handed him off to one of the club's entertainers for a private show, and the hidden cameras silently recorded everything.

"Enjoy your date, Arnold," I whispered. "It's going to be an expensive one."

****

Julia shifted uncomfortably on the sofa. The old man's story twisted in her stomach with a piercing ache similar to the one she had felt at the restaurant when he exposed her life with such matter-of-fact precision. It smacked of devious behavior and violated her sense of fair play. She closed her notebook and looked accusingly at her storyteller. "You ruined that man's life."

"No, he ruined it. I merely provided the door for him to open. He would have found that door sooner or later, with or without my help."

"But you manipulated him." *Just as you manipulated me*, she thought ruefully. "You made it impossible for him *not* to fail. You destroyed him."

"A separatist destroys relationships, not people." He took a deep breath and paused, as if trying to think how best to explain himself. "I was in the breakup business. People came to me when they wanted to break up with someone: a boyfriend or girlfriend, a secret lover, a spouse, even a business partner. I was hired to do whatever it took to sever the relationship, personal or otherwise. It took many skills and a great deal of imagination to be a separatist. Operations were often quite complex. Extensive research was required. My field people played dozens of roles, everything from sexy women or men to business professionals to housewives. Even gangsters! My operations were clean. No violence, ugly publicity or courtroom theatrics. Evidence was gathered, and people quietly parted ways."

Julia turned off the recorder. "Why did you tell me about Arnold?" she asked at last. The story had shaken her. It made her wonder what sort of web this seemingly harmless old man was spinning for her.

"Because it leads to the main story. As you know, North Beach is adjacent to Chinatown, and unbeknownst to me, I was being observed, even as I did the same with Arnold. There is irony there, don't you see? The hunter becoming the hunted."

Silence. Mr. Andersen sat staring at Julia as if he had recounted all he could remember. A clock ticked somewhere in the room, overridden from time to time by the distant echo of a foghorn. He was manipulating her again, teasing her with hints of intrigue, perhaps danger, and as badly as she wanted to resist him, she felt compelled to continue. Chinatown was a subject very much on her mind at the moment.

"Why do you mention Chinatown? What bearing does it have on your story?"

"There were really two Chinatowns. One was filled with good restaurants, quaint shops, and fish markets that tourists visited. The other was cloaked in the mysterious haunts of opium dens, warlords, and deadly intrigues. The one masked the other, bringing respectability to a pernicious underworld. I was about to step into that other world and be consumed by it. All because I failed to follow the number one rule in my business."

"Which is . . . ?"

"Never become personally involved with your client or your mark."

More silence. Each time Mr. Andersen stopped telling his story, it was like a punctuation mark ending a sentence, a paragraph, a chapter. Inertia set in, and it required considerable energy to set things in motion again.

"What about my father?" she asked.

"That will take some time." He frowned and hesitated. "Perhaps we should continue this discussion the next time we meet," he said at last. "Otherwise, you will be late for your appointment."

Julia glanced around and spotted the ticking clock on the mantel. *Damn it, I am going to be late.* But it wasn't just the hour that bothered her. He *knew* she had an appointment, which meant he was still spying on her. She looked into his bright, unwavering eyes with the apprehension of a small animal being pursued by a shadow in the forest. She couldn't see the peril, but she knew it was close by. Just like a fox, he was keeping her off balance and on edge.

Julia grabbed her belongings and fled to the door in an effort to escape the vulnerable sensation that had so unexpectedly washed over her.

"You haven't signed the contract or proposed a schedule." Mr. Andersen rose from his chair to follow her. His voice was calm and reassuring. Julia wanted to flee and stay at the same time. She grasped the doorknob and turned it, determined not to be trapped into staying longer.

"I need to give your proposal some more thought. If I agree, I'll have it for you at our next meeting." She was suddenly unwilling to commit herself to this man. "I can return tomorrow, but it'll have to be in the morning. Nine o'clock."

He nodded. "By the way, I have a tip for you. The skeleton found near the docks belongs to a man named Parker. Patrick Parker."

His sudden revelation stopped her in her tracks, and she wheeled on him. "How do you know that?" she demanded.

He stared at her with those keen eyes but remained silent. She hesitated a moment longer, torn between the conflicting needs to learn more and to escape. She then ran out the door.

CHAPTER THREE

Traffic snarled at her, blocked her way, and forced her into side streets. The traffic was a multi-headed monster, a hydra with twelve angry jaws flashing their fangs. The monster knew she was behind schedule, knew she had stayed too long with the old man and was desperate to reach her next appointment before her informant panicked and fled.

Julia knew she was close to a major story, closer than she had ever been before. She had no idea how to re-contact the man whom she was rushing to meet, and it infuriated her that she had risked missing him because of her fascination with Mr. Andersen. It was his reference to Chinatown that had delayed her. It seemed an odd coincidence that he should raise the subject just when she was about to plunge into that district's murky backstreets herself.

But it was his knowledge about the skeleton that really spooked her. The police had been scratching their heads for weeks. Now, a complete stranger had appeared out of the blue and revealed the skeleton's identity. There was no way for him to know that, unless he was somehow involved in the murder. Well, she would have to deal with that later. Right now, all she wanted to do was keep her rendezvous.

Her informant, a dock worker named Romeo, had called her

regarding the dock strike. The International Longshore and Warehouse Union's contract had expired, and they were at loggerheads with the Pacific Maritime Association over work rules and wages. Dock workers had recently staged a walkout to demonstrate their anger, and a slowdown in work procedures was now in progress. Cranes were operating at half speed, and personnel were reporting to the wrong work sites. The result was a growing backlog of containers waiting to be loaded or unloaded. The shipping employers were threatening to retaliate with a lockout, but the President had ordered a temporary injunction. The docks were operating, but no one knew for how long.

Julia had been asked to cover the negotiations. It had seemed a routine assignment, until she received a phone call at her office one evening when she was working late.

"This Julia Rice?" a coarse, male voice queried.

"Who wants to know?" It was past nine, and Julia was uncomfortable getting a call at such a late hour. It meant somebody knew she was there, alone.

"You're the one talkin' to dock workers about the labor contract, right?"

Julia hesitated. She looked around, half expecting to see a co-worker having a little fun at her expense. The office was dead quiet and empty.

"I am," she said at last.

"There's more at stake than the contract," the voice confided.

"It seems pretty straight forward to me." Julia sat up straighter in her chair. Something in the caller's edgy voice told her to take him seriously. She listened intently to the background chatter she heard behind the caller. He was in a phone booth at a night club or bar.

"Not the contract." His voice chafed with irritation. "There's a smuggling operation goin' on with the blessing of the port bosses. Not just drugs. People too. Guy in Chinatown runs it. I got information that'll give you a helluva lot bigger story than work rules. But it'll cost you."

Julia was on her feet pacing back and forth in front of her

desk. A waterfall of questions tumbled through her head. What did he mean about smuggled people? Was her caller trustworthy, or just a crank? She wondered if he only wanted money, or something more. Buzz-saw noises hammered inside her head. She had to collect herself, collect her thoughts. *Take deep breaths*, she told herself. *Stay in control*. She began to think more rationally.

Her first thought was the caller's demand for money. It wasn't uncommon to get these requests, but she didn't want to promise anything until she knew who he was and what he had to offer. "Smuggling people isn't news. Illegal immigrants have been spirited into the country for decades."

"I'm not talkin' about immigrants. I'm talkin' slavery," the voice hissed. The unexpected word snapped at Julia's thoughts. Slavery was a hideous word, one filled with images of Africans chained to the hulls of wooden ships. But slavery hadn't existed for more than a hundred and fifty years.

"What are you talking about?" she asked in a hushed tone.

"I'm not saying more until I see some cash. You interested or not?" Anxiety crept into the man's voice. Julia worried he might hang up.

"If you've got worthwhile information, I can arrange something," she replied. "What's your name?"

The man hesitated. She could hear a woman squealing with laughter and a music system blaring a song that had been popular two years ago. "Romeo. My name's Romeo. Meet me day after tomorrow at the Buena Vista. Three o'clock. I'll be wearin' a Giants baseball cap. Bring a thousand dollars." The phone clicked and went dead.

Julia listened to the dial tone for several seconds. The Buena Vista. Why there of all places? The Buena Vista was the last place she wanted to go, but she had no choice. Not if she wanted to find out what Romeo was talking about. A thousand dollars was a lot of money. Her editor, Phillip, would never approve that amount unless it was a blockbuster story. Drug smuggling stories were old news, but if a connection could be made to the port authorities, it would be an intriguing development. Still not worth that kind of money. But people-smuggling was a different matter, especially if it involved some sort of servitude. She would have to know more. Whoever Romeo was, Julia hoped he knew what he was talking about. She intended to find out.

The Buena Vista, a colorful bar and restaurant located near Fisherman's Warf, was famous for its Irish Whiskies. It was a favorite hangout for tourists and locals alike, and Julia had spent more than one evening there socializing with fellow journalists. It was also where she had met Jackie, and she hadn't returned since they parted. Vivid memories of radiant smiles and glimmering eyes teased her when she entered the narrow bar, but she thrust them aside. Nostalgia would have to wait. She was late and desperate to find the man who called himself Romeo.

The place was surprisingly crowded for that time of day, forcing many to stand in the narrow aisle between the tables and bar. Their casual clothes and digital cameras told Julia it was mostly a tourist crowd. A steady buzz of voices filled the room, accompanied by the rich aroma of freshly brewed coffee. Glasses clinked as three men in aprons stood behind the broad, mahogany counter filling rows of transparent cups with whiskey, coffee, and cream. She moved impatiently through the throng looking for Romeo. Faces loomed in front of her, but they were the soft, clean faces of vacationers. None had the sun-hardened face of a dock worker. None wore a baseball cap. Julia's eyes raced across the room in snap-shot bursts, bounding from person to person while she continued to work her way through the crowd. At last, she spotted a man in his thirties sporting a goatee and Giants cap seated on a bar stool in the far corner of the room, and she exhaled the breath she had been holding since entering the place.

Julia moved towards him with a tentative smile. "Are you Romeo?" she asked over the room's din.

"You're late." Tense, dark eyes bore into hers. Despite being seated, his scowling face nearly met hers at eye level. He was clean-shaven, except for the goatee, but the uneven colors in his skin and the lines around his eyes spoke of long hours in the sun. If

22

Julia had to choose one word to sum him up, she would have said hard-boiled. He wore a short-sleeve shirt despite the chilly breeze blowing off the bay, revealing muscular arms that attested to years of physical labor. He made no effort to rise or to offer his seat.

"Sorry," she apologized. She could sense by the way he leaned forward on his stool that he was edgy and ready to take flight at the first hint of trouble. She didn't want to aggravate him further. "Is it all right to talk here?"

"You got my $1,000?"

Julia hoped he was bluffing on the amount and was ready to bargain. Her boss, Phillip, had set a limit for half that amount and wanted her to negotiate for less if she could.

"I can't go more than $500." Julia fidgeted and shifted her weight. She had never been very good at haggling over money.

"Then, you're just wastin' my time," he said angrily and started to rise from his seat. His manner told her he wasn't bluffing.

"Wait." She touched his arm. The sinewy texture of his skin reminded her of a thousand-year-old redwood tree, and she found the sensation oddly arousing. He sat back down and looked at her hand, which she quickly withdrew. His expression changed to one she knew all too well: a male who sensed the heat of a woman.

"Please try to work with me, Romeo. My editor will never authorize that kind of money. If I give you more, it'll have to come out of my own pocket."

"How much more?"

Julia tried to calculate how much more she thought she could squeeze out of Phillip if the story was good enough. "I'll give another $250. Seven-hundred-and-fifty total." She set a firm edge to her voice to let him know it was a final offer.

The man seated next to Romeo got up to leave, and she grabbed his stool. Now that they were both seated, she felt better about her chances of keeping him there.

"I'm takin' a hell-of-a chance, you know. Anybody finds out about this, and I could end up in the bay. Seven-fifty isn't much."

"It's all I've got. Five hundred now, and the rest when we're finished." She pulled a roll of cash from her purse and held it discretely under the bar. After a moment's hesitation, he took it and slipped it into his pocket.

"You can't use my name or tell anybody where you heard this."

She nodded eagerly and reached for her recorder. He grabbed her arm. "None o' that."

Her skin felt uncomfortably warm where he touched it. He held Julia's arm a moment longer than necessary and stared at her with a hunger that startled her. She pulled her arm away and returned the recorder to her purse.

"I'm not just doin' this for the money. What's goin' on isn't right. There's containers comin' in with Chinese women in 'em. Some are sold as prostitutes. Others work in sweatshops in Chinatown. Drugs come in with 'em, but, hell, that's nothin' new. It's the women that bother me. They're just kids, no more than teens. Some even younger. It's all controlled by a guy in Chinatown. He isn't one to fool with. Been runnin' drugs for years. The women are new, though." Romeo scanned the room as he spoke. His posture remained tense and alert.

The heat of his touch lingered on Julia's arm. She had to admit that his square jaw and broad features gave him a rugged appeal that she found attractive, but his animal-like ferocity frightened her. She was out of her depth with this man.

She forced her wandering thoughts back to the subject at hand. "Can you get me proof? Documentation, ship's logs, that sort of thing?"

"I can get you better than that." A hint of a smile softened his no-nonsense expression. "There's a woman in Chinatown who's involved in the operation. Wants out. She'll trade what she knows if you help her."

"Would she testify?"

"Maybe. You give her a new identify, that sort o' thing."

"Set up a meeting. Tell her if she can deliver what she promises, I'll see she gets the help she wants." Julia wasn't certain she could deliver on her promise, but she would have to try. Make contact first. That was the important thing. She would worry about the details later.

Romeo gave Julia a look that said he wouldn't mind spending the rest of the day with her, but she was all business again. She sensed this could be an important story, and she wasn't about to let a little testosterone complicate things. Besides, she suspected Romeo would be more than she could handle.

Not that she had ever been good at handling men. Phillip, in whose office she now waited, was a perfect case in point. Most women would have been attracted to his bold features, including a sculpted nose that strayed slightly to the left, his vampire-black hair, and his mustache dappled with grey. But not Julia. She had been drawn to him because he was in his forties and held a position of power over her. It didn't matter that he was married. In fact, that increased his charm. That and his ability to tap into her sexual desires with conductor-like precision.

Julia's fling with Phillip began the night she earned her first, front-page story. Not the lead column or headline, but a breakthrough nonetheless. Phillip had paid little personal attention to her until then, but that night he suggested they have a drink after work. "To celebrate your arrival to the front-page club," he said. They went to a bar not frequented by the newspaper's other reporters or staff. At first, she had been intimidated by Phillip. His manner towards her in the office had always been abrupt and off-handed. But after sharing a bottle of white wine together, Julia found Phillip more and more appealing, and when he reached across the table and touched the back of her hand with his fingers, sparks flew up her arm and into her head, where they flitted about like fireflies. It was a simple gesture, but it stirred her blood. They ended up in her bed, and Julia quickly discovered a healthy appetite for this self-important man.

"Sordid affair" was a term she came to understand intimately during their time together, but it didn't stop her from seeing him whenever she could. He would drop by her desk at noon to check on a story, raising the hairs on the nape of her neck with his tropical breath, then leave for lunch. She would follow ten minutes later, her heart pounding in a stormy sea of hunger, and meet him at a motel tucked away in a discreet location. Phillip would be waiting with a blue-ribbon spread of wines, cheeses, French bread, pickled herring, olives, and fruit. Once they had consumed the food, they consumed each other.

The most intense episodes, however, took place after work at her apartment, when Phillip told his wife he was working late. Unlike the mid-day affairs, when they dashed through their lovemaking, their evenings together grew steadily longer and more complex. It began with a simple role-playing game. One night, Phillip brought her a tight, leather skirt and black, lacey stockings, and gave her a brassy-red lipstick and heavy rouge to smear on her face. Julia was hesitant to place herself in the role of a prostitute, but when she donned the outfit and applied the makeup, she entered an out-of-body experience that stimulated her imagination and her body in unexpected ways. He paid her fifty dollars when they were done, then left before she could regain her composure or put on her clothing.

On another occasion, he brought silk ropes and tied her to the bedpost. Once he had bound her wrists, he tormented her with ice cubes. Bondage became more frequent, and hot candle wax and other mild forms of torture were added to the retinue. Julia enjoyed her steamy roles and submitted to Phillip's machinations with a gusto that startled her. But, she eventually realized their lovemaking had turned a corner and was racing down a darker street that alarmed her. She had become Phillip's sex slave, and each new episode drew Julia deeper into a world that both stimulated and repulsed her. Her sexual pleasures reached heights she had never imagined possible, but after Phillip was gone, she often pulled the covers over her head and lay in bed too ashamed to face herself. She began to experience skin rashes while waiting for Phillip and perspired so uncontrollably she would have to change her clothes before he arrived.

Julia thought about ending their relationship, but her courage failed her. It was Phillip who finally put a stop to it when his wife became suspicious. When Phillip told Julia he could no longer see her, she drooped like a sail in a dying wind. Her eyes smarted with so many tears, she could no longer see Phillip's face. He was abandoning her just like her father had. She was no good with men. They never stayed in her life. They came and they went, leaving a wretched empty space deep inside of her.

Yet, after Phillip was gone, she breathed a sigh of relief, and a sense of freedom swept over her. As badly as she had wanted him, she was thankful that she would no longer have to play out his fantasies. Her bouts of uncontrolled sweating stopped. The rashes disappeared.

It wasn't her first affair with a married man, and in many ways it characterized her problems with the opposite sex. She had always been attracted to powerful, older men. They usually were married or recently divorced. The married ones never expected to leave their families, and the recently divorced men were born-again schoolboys, delighting in their second chance to "play the field." The result had been a series of "sordid affairs" that left her feeling like an old Chevy in a used car lot when they were over. Great memories, but not really the kind of car to take home to mother.

"You have a father complex," a friend had once told her, "because you never knew your father." She had bristled at the suggestion, but she couldn't deny the Freudian implications of her attraction to these men. Unfortunately, such insights did her little good.

Phillip entered the office without apologizing for making Julia wait and turned on her. "Giving that informant money before he produces his witness was a dumb thing to do." His angry voice scattered her thoughts. "You'll probably never hear from him again." He hardly looked at her when he spoke, an irritating habit she had come to dislike intensely. Eye contact had never been one of his strong suits. Even when their naked bodies had been pressed together in a tangle of sweaty passion, his eyes had wandered to the floral mini-prints in the wallpaper above her bed.

"I didn't give him everything," Julia retorted defensively. "He'll call.   He *wants* that other $250." She tried to sound confident.

"Well, I can't cover the extra money. That's your problem." Phillip fiddled with his pen. "But if you can put the story together, I *will* promise the front page and a raise." He turned his attention to a paper in front of him, signaling the end of their meeting.

Julia returned to her desk and stared angrily at her computer screen. Dozens of voices chattered in the vast room. Phones rang. Someone dropped a coffee cup and swore. The room vibrated with a furious energy that tumbled over and over inside her head. When she thought about Phillip's callous behavior, her throat contracted into a scream that died on her lips. His indifference chafed her skin. She knew he had the money in his budget to cover her commitment to Romeo. Was his refusal just business, or was it his way of telling her not to expect any favoritism because they had been lovers? Either way, it was unfair, but there was nothing she could do about it. She needed the story. She would have to put up the additional money herself.

Her thoughts returned to Thomas Andersen. She didn't know which upset her more: being out $250 or knowing that Andersen was still spying on her. She could feel his eyes following her wherever she went. It was like living in a fish bowl with no place to hide. Well, two could play that game. She wasn't without resources of her own, and it was time to learn more about her mysterious storyteller.

She pulled up the databases in her computer and began cross-referencing the things she knew about Andersen: his name, approximate age, and current address. It wasn't much, she realized. In fact, she was amazed how little she had learned about him during their first two meetings. It wasn't like her to be so uninformed. She normally made it a point to build a profile on anyone she was investigating or interviewing, but she had allowed herself to be pulled along in the swift currents of intrigue and adventure promised by this stranger. He had been remarkably vague about himself, even as he began to reveal his past. She wondered if she would find anything on him at all.

It didn't take long for the computer to confirm her suspicions. There was no record of a Thomas Andersen. As far as the government and private databases were concerned, the man didn't exist: no social security number, credit history, property ownership, or driver's license. He didn't appear on society's radar screen.

The house where she had met him was owned by Collins & Russell Realtors. She called the company, but an administrative assistant told her there was no record of a renter at that address. As far as he could tell, the house was empty.

Frustrated, Julia entered Patrick Parker's name. She pulled up the police records and missing persons reports from forty years ago, but the data search drew a blank. She was used to tips not panning out, but this one disappointed her more than most. Julia had hoped for more substance this time. She was about to forget the whole thing, but she remembered the furrowed lines in Mr. Andersen's face when he spoke the name. There had been a note of sadness in his expression. Patrick Parker was someone he had known. He must be out there somewhere, hiding in cyberspace. She tried a new tack, searching all the obituaries in Francisco and the surrounding communities. Records that old were buried in dormant files; it would take some time to cross-reference them. She set the computer on auto search and began sifting through her mail and phone messages.

Every time the phone rang, she jumped in anticipation of hearing Romeo's sandpapery voice. She had to admit the animalism he'd displayed at the bar had gotten her attention. Not something she wanted to explore, but finding herself drawn to a man closer to her own age was encouraging. Maybe there's hope for me after all, she thought with a sigh.

An hour passed before the computer beeped, informing her that it had found a match. Julia looked at the screen in amazement. There he was, Patrick Parker, private investigator. That explained how Mr. Andersen knew him. They were in similar lines of work. He had died in a fiery, single-car accident, burned beyond recognition. No foul play was suspected, which explained the absence of a police record. There was no record of living relatives, so his body was cremated and consigned to the footnotes of history.

Questions spun around inside Julia's head. Was Mr. Andersen wrong about the identity of the skeleton? If not, how did Mr. Andersen know it was Patrick Parker, and who was cremated in the man's name?

It wouldn't take long to answer the first question. Julia called the Oakland Police Department and asked to speak to the detective on the case. After a considerable delay, a tired voice came on the line. "This is Detective Rodriguez. Can I help you?"

"Detective, this is Julia Rice with the San Francisco Chronicle. I'm calling about the skeleton found near the Oakland docks."

"I've got nothing new to report, Ms. Rice. Please don't waste my time with unnecessary phone calls." His irritable response betrayed frustration. She'd been in situations where an assignment turned up nothing but dead ends, and she knew just how he felt.

"I'm not calling to get information, Detective Rodriguez. I'm calling to give it."

A moment's silence.

"About what?" Irritation was now mixed with curiosity.

"I may know who your skeleton is."

More silence. She knew he was waiting for her to continue, but she didn't intend to show her hand that easily. His breathing pulsated in her ear.

"What do you want, Ms. Rice?" Irritation had regained the upper hand.

Good. He understood the information was going to cost him something. She ignored his sharp tone and continued, "A meeting and first call on future case developments."

More silence. More breathing. "Ms. Rice, if you withhold information, I'll have you thrown in jail." Another pause. "If you can help me, I'll be glad to work with you." His voice grew more agreeable. "Please, tell me what you've got. If it sticks, we'll talk."

Now Julia hesitated. Her whole body tingled with the excitement of landing a potential scoop, and she didn't want to lose it. Giving her information to Detective Rodriguez over the telephone meant putting her trust in someone she'd never met. She didn't like the idea, but she had little choice. The cat was already out of the bag, and his offer sounded genuine. She took a deep breath and proceeded.

"His name is Patrick Parker. He worked as a private investigator and allegedly died in a car accident around the time your forensics people say the murder took place. He was supposed to have been cremated, so there's no missing persons report, but if you can find his dental records, you might get a match."

Another silence. There was a distinct pattern to the detective's conversations. He always paused to digest new information before responding, the sign of a deliberate person who thought things through very carefully. Julia liked that.

"I'll be back in touch, Ms. Rice." There was a click followed by a dial tone. Her story was in his hands, and he was gone. All she could do now was to wait.

CHAPTER FOUR

Julia arrived at Mr. Andersen's the next morning with her game face on. It was time to flush the fox out of the forest, to find out who he was and why he thought the skeleton found near Oakland's docks was a private detective named Patrick Parker. But Andersen's warm greeting and noticeable limp--he was using his cane this morning--defused her combativeness. Julia hated to admit it, but the old man continued to mesmerize her.

"Welcome, Miss Rice. I've been looking forward to your visit. Come, sit with me in the living room. I've made coffee for you."

He waved his free hand towards the sofa, where Julia saw a pot of steaming coffee, cups, and sugar waiting for her on the table. She noted the absence of cream. He knew she only took sugar! She stared, nonplussed, at the delicate china cups and saucers as she considered Andersen's intrusions into her life, then shook her head and followed him into the main room. The room was comfortably furnished, but the absence of personal items was even more pronounced in the morning sunlight. No magazines, books, knick knacks or photographs. Nothing that spoke to the man's interests, background, or family. It was a Spartan setting that suggested impermanence. Yet, he looked quite at home, as if he'd lived there for years.

"I've done some checking of my own," she declared as she sat down and poured coffee for them both.

"I expected you would." Mr. Andersen settled back in his chair, cup and saucer in hand.

"There's no lease or rental agreement for this house. In fact, there's no record of you at all. Are you a ghost, Mr. Andersen?"

He chuckled. "A very good way of putting it. Sometimes it is better to remain . . . shall we say inconspicuous? More can be accomplished that way. I assure you I'm very real, but things are not always as they appear." He beamed a smile that told her he was enjoying their repartee. "The realtor who owns the house is an acquaintance of mine. He lets me use one of his vacancies from time to time, when I'm in town."

"Then you don't live here, in San Francisco I mean."

"Haven't for a long time, but we are getting ahead of ourselves. Much of what you want to know will reveal itself in my story. You must be a little patient, is all. However, I cannot continue without our contract. I trust you have brought it." His bushy eyebrows arched upwards in twin question marks.

Julia felt as if she were peering down a dark passage, unable to see where her commitment would take her, and that disturbed her. The mystery surrounding Mr. Andersen was unsettling. He had deftly parried her queries, leaving her questions about him unanswered. His intimate knowledge of her life was another concern. Could she trust someone who had spied on her, someone who had mined the inner depths of her personal relationships? She *had* signed the contract but kept it hidden in her purse. Once she handed it to him, there would be no turning back. Her only other choice was to decline his offer. Then, she would never know his tale or learn what happened in Chinatown. And if his promise was true, she could be throwing away the chance to report a story that reached far beyond the discovery of a skeleton named Patrick Parker. Her hands fidgeted with her purse while the silence between them wrapped itself around her in a thick fog. His eyes burned her skin while he waited patiently for her reply. She wanted to resist him, but there was a charisma about Mr. Andersen that made her think of magic spells. She knew he was weaving a spell on her.

Her resistance faded, and she slowly pulled the single piece of paper from her purse and handed it to him. As she did so, a small voice whispered that her life would never be the same again.

"Good," Mr. Andersen said with satisfaction. "Now, I suggest we get started before time zooms past us, and you are late for another appointment."

Julia's face flared with anger at his reference to yesterday, but he had already closed his eyes and leaned back in his chair.

****

After finishing with Arnold Grant, I joined Jossie, Carl and Patti for a little celebration at a local bar and returned to my office in a state of exultation. I always felt that way when I completed a contract. It was like climbing to the top of a mountain and seeing the world at your feet. There was finality about both endeavors that brought great satisfaction.

My euphoria was short lived, however. A white, #10 envelope had been slipped under the office's outer door with a very strange threat in it: *Death will come to you.* The letters had been cut out of a newspaper and pasted on a sheet of lined paper in a very careful fashion, suggesting an orderly mind. I stared at the queer phrase with alarm. It wasn't like a normal death threat at all, yet I could feel its sinister intent piercing through me.

I turned the note over to the police the next day. They dusted it for fingerprints but found nothing. The note dispelled my happy mood as I went about the day's business. I tried to convince myself it was just some prank, but it stuck to me like gum on the sole of my shoe.

The following evening, I was sitting at my desk still pondering the meaning of such a strange message, when an unexpected knock sounded on the outer door. It was past seven, and I wasn't expecting anyone. My first thought was the threatening letter. I didn't much care for guns, but I was licensed to carry one. I took it from my desk drawer and shoved it into my waistline behind my back. When I opened the door, I half-expected to find some demonic person wielding a knife. Instead, I came face-to-face with a Chinese man who looked far more menacing. Well, not quite face-to-face. He was a head taller than me, over six-and-a-half feet, with an uncharacteristically broad nose--the kind a boxer gets after too many punches in the ring--and a glowering stare that said he would just as soon kill me as look at me. This was not a man who wasted time making idle threats.

"My boss wants to hire you," he said without preamble. His voice sounded like a truck climbing a steep grade in low gear. We stared at each other while I tried to decide what to do. He had made no move to enter, and I wasn't sure I wanted him to. He was much bigger in the shoulders and forearms than me, and from the way he balanced his weight on his feet, I suspected he *had* been trained in the ring. He reminded me of one of those Godzilla monsters from an old horror movie. I decided to conduct our business in the hallway.

"Who's your boss, and why does he want to hire me?" As always, I was looking for motive.

"That's not important. You deal through me." His English was too good for him to be an immigrant. My guess was second or third generation.

"I only deal with the person hiring me, and I don't take an assignment before meeting him first." I held my breath, hoping Godzilla wouldn't take offense.

He hesitated. Clearly, my response had not been anticipated, and the man didn't know what to do.

"Tell you what," I continued. "I'll be in my office tomorrow. If your boss still wants my services, ask him to get in touch. I'm sure we can make accommodations that will be comfortable for us both." I closed the door and waited for him to break it down, but he walked away without uttering a word, and I didn't expect to hear from him again.

He returned the next day, however, sending Patti scurrying into my office with one of those library looks. I asked her to show him in.

"My boss will meet you tonight in front of your building," he announced once Patti had left.

"Why not in my office?" I countered.

Exasperation showed on the man's face, and I decided not to push the point. We agreed on nine o'clock downstairs.

I exited my building that evening at the appointed time just as a black limousine pulled to the curb. Godzilla got out of the driver's side and opened the rear door for me. It was dark inside the vehicle, and I hesitated. I didn't like surprises. When I entered a place, I wanted to know what waited for me. The words from the threatening note kept playing inside my head.

"Please join me," a pleasant Chinese voice beckoned from the interior. It didn't sound like the voice of someone about to murder me.

As I stepped into the car, a bright ceiling lamp clicked on, shining light in my face and blinding me. I tried to shield my eyes, but it did no good. The man who spoke to me was nothing more than a voice floating in the darkness beyond my pool of light.

"Forgive my circumspect behavior, but I have always shunned the spotlight." I admired the irony of his comment as I squinted into the brilliant light. But I admired his grasp of the English language even more. Circumspect was a big word for a Chinese man, even one riding in a limousine. The man was well educated. "You did a commendable job with Mr. Grant," he continued. "A very professional operation, one that lived up to your reputation."

I was shocked to realize he had observed my little drama. It implied that he had been watching me for some time. Spying was my game, and I didn't like him reversing the roles.

"Please do not be upset." He was a mind reader, as well. "I needed to be certain I was dealing with someone competent."

I noticed he said please a lot, and I wondered if he was really that polite. I suspected he wasn't. "What's your proposal?"

"There is a woman I have been seeing. I need her to disappear. I want you to see that it happens."

I wasn't sure what he meant by "disappear," but I didn't like

36

the sound of it. "I'm a separatist, not a murderer."

"I never want to see or hear from her again. How you arrange that is up to you." The voice was mild, almost serene.

"Why?" I was back to motivation.

"Does it matter?"

"Yes. I don't take cases unless I know why."

The voice breathed a sigh. "My assistant told me you could be difficult, but I suppose that is why you are so good. Very well. She has been my mistress. I now wish the relationship to end, and I cannot afford any public displays of . . . shall we say displeasure? No publicity. She must go quietly, or I will have to make other arrangements."

There was no mistaking the threat. If I couldn't do the job someone else would, and he wouldn't be as subtle. I thought seriously about getting out of the car and never looking back. I didn't want to know this man. He obviously moved in a world that was alien to mine. But the fate of the woman held me back. If I didn't take the job, who would, and at what cost to her?

"My only other requirement," he continued, "is that you make this assignment your personal responsibility and do not take any other jobs until you are finished. In return, I will double your normal fee. Here is a $50,000 deposit." A gloved hand appeared out of the darkness with a briefcase. My throat compressed at the size of his offer, and I nearly choked. One hundred thousand dollars could overcome a lot of doubts. After a moment's hesitation, I took the brief case. It weighed my hand down like an anchor. "The balance will be delivered when my conditions have been met. You have my word on it, and in Chinatown, a man's word is worth more than a written contract. Here is the information you need to get started." He handed me a large manila envelope.

"And if I want to speak to you?"

"I will be in touch. If it is necessary, you can leave a message for me at the Golden Moon restaurant."

Godzilla opened my door, indicating the interview was over. I stood on the sidewalk and watched the limousine blend into the evening traffic. There was no license plate or other identification on the car, nothing I could use to trace him.

I returned to my office and opened the manila envelope. There was a woman inside whose life might depend on me, and I was anxious to know who she was. Her name was Kathy Griffith. She was thirty-five, unmarried and worked as an accounting auditor and children's photographer. A small snapshot of her showed a hesitant smile, light brown hair pulled back in a ponytail and narrow lips that turned up impishly at the corners. The camera had caught her with her eyes half-closed, giving her face a dreamy quality. It was a face caught mid-way between merely pretty and Vogue-magazine beautiful.

I began following her the next day, while Carl and Patti sifted through public records and private databases. It didn't take long to begin building a profile on her. She worked part-time for an accounting firm in downtown San Francisco and spent the rest of her time on photographic assignments for magazines and private parties. She hadn't begun college until she was twenty-two but blazed through her undergraduate program in three years with a 3.85 grade average. She lived alone in a rented house near Golden Gate Park, where she spent her free time bicycling or sitting in one of the open meadows reading books. She didn't own a car, preferring to ride her bicycle to local destinations and cabs elsewhere. She owned a piano and could be heard playing Chopin most evenings before retiring. Her manner was open and friendly-- she greeted strangers in the park and addressed her neighbors on a first-name basis--but there were few real friends. Only one, an Emily Monroe, was close enough to share intimacies. She exuded warmth but shielded herself with a polite manner that kept people just beyond reach. Her favorite restaurant was the Fior d'Italia, where she maintained an open account.

She had dated an older man named Harry Webster for awhile, but an incident in the man's home involving considerable shouting and breaking glass had put an end to the relationship. Lately, she had spent some of her time in Chinatown and was rumored to be seeing a Chinese businessman reputed to have ties to the area's drug trade. No photos of him were available. However, a quick search by Patti turned up the name Liu Kwong. I could now put a name to my employer.

There was only one problem with our profile of Kathy Griffith. She didn't exist before she was twenty-one. We ran every search program available, including cross checks on related names, but found nothing. No birth certificate, school records, marriage license, newspaper articles, or dental charts. Nor could we locate parents or other relatives. Not even a distant cousin. Ms. Griffith left a trail filled with vitality and creative energy that stretched back for fourteen years, then disappeared into obscurity. Whoever she was before her twenty-first birthday, her name wasn't Kathy Griffith.

One more thing. She played poker every Saturday night at a card club in Chinatown.

This news jolted me with the force of a heroin dose shooting through my veins. I could feel my pulse rate rising sharply and my head spinning. Poker had nearly been the end of me a few years ago. I had been as addicted to it as any mainlining junkie waiting for his next fix. It had cost me my marriage, my job, and very nearly my sanity. I still broke into cold sweats when I thought about the odds of drawing a single card to a straight flush. Now, I was tailing a woman whose passion for the game could re-ignite mine. I knew only too well the labyrinth that awaited me if I pursued her there. I was standing on the edge of a precipice, uncertain whether to back away or leap. The first choice could cost the woman her life; the second could bring the downfall of mine.

****

Mr. Andersen's words faded into silence. When Julia saw he was finished, she looked at the clock on the mantel and was amazed to see how much time had passed. A quiet solitude hung between them.

"I believe it is time for you to go," he said at last.

She didn't know whether he was dismissing her or reminding her of her day's busy schedule: meetings, interviews, and deadlines that would push right into tomorrow. Her first priority was learning if Romeo had arranged the meeting as promised. She checked her satellite communicator for messages. There were none. She would contact the office as soon as she left.

"I can return tomorrow evening at seven." Julia's voice broke the heavy silence with the jolt of a gun shot. "Evenings will be best from now on."

He nodded but made no effort to rise. Exhaustion had pushed his shoulders back into the cushions of his chair. "Forgive my poor manners. I had not realized how much telling this story would tire me. I am like an old battery drained of my energy."

Julia leaned forward, surprised. Would he be able to continue? Would he want to? "Should I call before coming?" she asked apprehensively.

"No, no. I will be fine tomorrow." He waved his hand to emphasize his point.

She hoped so. She couldn't imagine stopping now. He had pulled her into his orbit, and she hungered to hear more.

Two messages were waiting on Julia's private line when she arrived at the office. The first was from Romeo. He left a phone number where he could be reached at the docks. She called him back and learned he had arranged a meeting with his informant for eleven o'clock the next morning at the lookout point on Twin Peaks. He said the woman's name was Li Chang. She worked for a Chinese warlord who had ruled the drug trade in Chinatown with impunity for years, thanks to important political ties to the port authorities and city hall. She claimed to have names, dates of payoffs, and delivery schedules, including those of the young women now being spirited into the country. In return for this information, Li Chang wanted enough money and security to begin a new life where she could never be found. She refused to go to the police for fear someone in the department would compromise her. There were too many ties between the local police and Chinatown. She wanted Julia to organize a meeting with someone she could trust.

Julia's second message was from Detective Rodriguez, and she wondered if *he* was such a man. She picked up the phone and dialed his number.

"It's time we met, Ms. Rice," he said without formality. "Can you come to my office this morning?"

"I'm on my way."

Julia flew out of the building and all but tackled the first cab she saw, forcing it to stop. She knew she was sitting on a story with headline potential. A series of stories, if Andersen's information was half as promising as it sounded. Nailing them down would earn her more than the raise Phillip had offered. It would put her in the upper echelon of journalism. But it wasn't the money or even the peer recognition that excited her as much as the knowledge she was about to uncover a one-of-a-kind story. It gave her an adrenaline rush much like the one Thomas Andersen described when he talked about poker.

Detective Rodriguez looked as weary as he had sounded on the telephone the first time Julia called. She'd expected to meet a man in a rumpled shirt with rolled-up sleeves, but he was neatly attired in a dark, wool suit and meticulously knotted red tie. He presented her with a neutral smile and watchful, protruding eyes that said he needed to know her better before becoming amicable. The eyes assessed her without apology. She wanted to return his stare but found her gaze slipping to the uneven patches in his dusky skin, which reminded her of a stained tablecloth. His black hair retained its lustrous sheen on top, but around his temples it had curdled to the color of sour milk. Age gave no quarter as it advanced across the detective's features.

The open room bellowed with debating voices and clamoring telephones, producing an air of controlled fury that crackled around them. Detective Rodriguez led Julia to a small office in the far corner. "Excuse the racket. Police work is a noisy business."

Julia gave him an amiable smile. "It sounds like a newspaper office. Makes me feel at home."

The detective ignored her overture and, once she was seated, got right to the point. "How did you know about Parker?" He stared at her with the intensity of an attorney cross examining a witness.

"Woman's intuition and a little legwork." She tried to sound casual but didn't pull it off. His question made her nervous. "Am I correct in assuming you found a dental match?"

He nodded and paused before continuing. "We're not stupid, Ms. Rice. We already checked police and missing records before you called. It was a careful search, but Parker's name didn't come up. It wasn't intuition or legwork that got you that name. You had a lead."

Julia fidgeted in her chair. The conversation wasn't going as she'd expected, and it put her on the defensive. She quickly flipped through her options. Revealing Mr. Andersen wasn't one of them. He would simply disappear, and she would lose her other story. But there was no point being flippant with this detective. He was too smart to be fooled by simplistic answers. Her best choice was honesty, see if he could be trusted. She might need his help with Li Chang.

"You're right detective. I was given Parker's name. But I can't reveal my source. I hope you'll respect that."

Rodriguez frowned at the piles of papers on his desk and adjusted his tie. "I have a lot of cases to handle. I don't need the burden of an unsolved murder from forty years ago. If you know something that would help and don't tell me, you'll make me very angry. You don't want to do that." He leveled his eyes at her, and she could see the glint of his implied threat in them.

"I'm being completely honest. His name is all I know so far. Frankly, I'm hoping you'll find something that will help me."

"Then, we understand each other." He stood up, indicating their conversation was over.

"There is one more thing, detective." Julia remained in her chair. "I may have an important lead on something much more current, involving a smuggling operation at the Oakland docks. It has nothing to do with my source on the skeleton, but if my informant decides to come forward, she'll need protection. Perhaps a new identity. Frankly, she's afraid of the police. Doesn't know if she can trust them. I need to know if I can trust you." Now, Julia leveled her gaze at Detective Rodriguez, who sat back down.

Once again, he paused, and she waited. "I'm not sure what you're implying, Ms. Rice, but the integrity of my department has never been questioned. If it ever is, I want to be the first to know about it." His look hardened, changing to a glare. Julia could have cooked a meal on the blaze in his eyes, but this time she refused to be intimidated or to look away. She met his gaze and held it. Then, she smiled.

"I believe you've answered my question, detective."

A hint of humor played at the corners of Rodriguez's mouth, and his eyes lost their heat. "We'll stay in touch."

"Count on it." Julia rose and shook his firm hand. She prayed she was right to trust her instincts about this man. Li Chang's life might hang in the balance.

Julia was determined not to be late for her meeting with Chang. She nervously watched the office clock while reviewing morning story lines, then left for her rendezvous on Twin Peaks promptly at ten, arriving at the hilltop well before eleven o'clock. Twin Peaks was a popular tourist spot where people gathered for spectacular vistas of San Francisco Bay. Today, an insistent fog bank pushed its way across the face of the peaks, obscuring the city's famous landmarks. The fog was accompanied by a chilly wind that forced the small bands of hardy visitors to pull their sweaters and jackets more tightly around them as they braved the elements. Julia sat in her car and waited. Most people spent only a few minutes exposed to the weather, before retreating to the warmth of their vehicles and heading back down the hill. None of them were Chinese.

Without the engine running, Julia's car was quickly becoming as cold as her surroundings, even without the wind. She rubbed her hands for warmth as she searched each approaching vehicle for some indication of Li Chang, but there was no sign of her. By the time half-a-dozen groups had come and gone, Julia sensed she wasn't coming at all. Something or someone had changed her mind. Disappointment mingled with frustration. She dreaded facing Phillip without something to show for her money. Had Romeo played her for a fool, after all? Julia didn't think so. She remembered the intensity in his eyes, the mixture of concern and sexual desire. Romeo wanted her and the money, but he wanted to stop the trade in human flesh, as well.

Julia waited another half-hour before giving up and returning to the office to call Romeo and to face Phillip.

Phillip gave Julia his I-told-you-so smirk and said nothing, making her blush with anger. She had already tried to reach Romeo, but he wasn't on the docks. Could he have taken her money and split? Phillip thought so, and Julia was beginning to wonder. All she could do was sit at her desk and wait. She tried to work on other stories, but her mind was as foggy as the view that morning on Twin Peaks. She had nearly given up hope, nearly decided to go to Phillip and admit defeat, when the phone snapped her from her depression.

"Li Chang's disappeared. Nobody knows nothin'," Romeo growled in her ear. His bravado didn't fool Julia. She could hear the uncertainty in his voice.

"What should we do?" she asked.

"Wait 'til you hear from me. I'll call soon as I hear somethin'."

"Wait . . . ." Julia wanted to keep Romeo talking, but a heavy click told her he was gone. Her promising day was sliding into oblivion.

Julia sat and pondered the strands of information that were slowly emerging. They formed a maze, a puzzle without answers. Patrick Parker, Kathy Griffith, Mr. Andersen: the names swirled around her like so many letters in an alphabet soup. Each held a key to the growing mystery. She had the uneasy feeling it was a mystery that was going to take her through many more twists and turns before it was solved, and she would have no choice but to let the currents carry her wherever they might lead.

Julia sighed and turned to her computer. She was tempted to

run a trace on Kathy's name, to see if any information turned up that Mr. Andersen hadn't told her, but something held her back. Digging into Kathy's past would be like starting a good novel, then turning to the last chapter to see how it ended. She was too intrigued by Mr. Andersen's story to ruin it now.

So, she performed another computer search, instead. It was a monthly ritual she called "searching for CONDAD." Julia's knowledge of her father was almost as sketchy as her information about Mr. Andersen. She had traced his life through his brief marriage to her mother and to his last known address in Arizona, where he had moved after he abandoned them. Police records connected him to a fraudulent land deal there, but he had left town before he could be interrogated and disappeared.

Julia had started computer-searching her father as soon as she learned how to use the newspaper's databases. She cross-checked his first name, Roger, and age, now fifty-seven, against con artists using land schemes to cheat people out of their money. It wasn't long before she stumbled across a police report from Oklahoma about a man fitting his description who used the name Roger Rose. He'd swindled over a hundred thousand dollars from unsuspecting investors by offering shares in a fictitious housing development. He had sent a dozen roses to each investor after they signed up. When she picked up his trail again, this time in El Paso, Texas, he'd changed his name to Roger Lily and sent lilies to his victims. Carnations and orchids popped up in police reports in Lincoln, Nebraska and Ogden, Utah. By the time she discovered each of these leads, however, it was as moldy as month-old bread. Her flower-giving father had long since slipped away and burrowed himself into the fabric of another unsuspecting community.

Julia remembered one spring, hope-is-in-the-air, heart-pumping day when she nearly caught up with the man who had never been more than a shadow falling across her life. She was checking on-line news stories when she stumbled across an advertisement in Portland, Oregon, for **POPPY LAND INVESTMENTS, ROGER POPPY, MANAGING PARTNER.** Julia stared at the copperplate gothic gold type. Her ears popped, and the room tilted just as it did when she looked down from her a height of more than a few feet. She felt herself tumbling into an emotional labyrinth with nothing to break her fall except the hard floor that rose up to meet her as she slid off her chair.

Julia regained her equilibrium and brushed away the helping hands of the office mates who had gathered around her. She slumped back into her chair and waited for the room to right itself, then rushed to Phillip's office to request an emergency leave for two days. She hadn't confided in him about her father, but she did so now. When she told him about her discovery in Oregon, he consented. She stopped at her apartment just long enough to fling a few personal items into an overnight bag, then raced to the airport in time to catch a non-stop flight to Portland.

CHAPTER FIVE

The first time Julia went looking for her father, she was still a month short of her seventh birthday. She remembered her aborted effort as clearly as yesterday's news. It happened while her mother was recovering in the psychiatric ward and she was living with their neighbors, the Howards. The Howards tried to make her feel at home, but they were a childless couple with little understanding of a young girl's needs. They expected her to act like an undersized adult, which meant she couldn't make noise or leave things around the house. Her room had to be tidied and the bed made each day. Dinners were suffocating in their silence, and her table manners had to be exemplary. Any misbehavior resulted in a "sit down" in the cellar, a scary-dark place filled with whispering shadows and the smell of rotting apples.

Her unhappy state made her think more and more about another whispery shadow, her father. Why, she wondered, couldn't she stay with him while her mother was gone? She hardly remembered him, of course, but it still seemed like a better alternative than the Howards. One day it dawned on her that he probably did not know about her mother's illness. All she had to do was get word to him somehow. Julia had once seen a hand-addressed envelope in her mother's bedroom from Phoenix,

Arizona, and she instinctively knew the jaunty handwriting was her father's. She decided to go looking for him there.

So, one spring morning when the sun overwhelmed the sky with brilliant light, Julia rose early, put on her nicest dress, and broke open her piggy bank. She wasn't sure how many quarters and dimes she had, but she thought it should be enough for a bus ticket to Phoenix. She crept past the house's ticking clocks, her knees trembling at the prospect of being discovered, and slipped out the front door. Julia walked with cool, deliberate steps to the sidewalk, but once she was out of sight, she ran all the way to the Greyhound station.

She was still panting from her exertion when she approached the ticket window, and she could feel beads of moisture sliding down her arms. She hesitated as she neared the window, fearful she wouldn't know what to say. An overweight woman with a big nose and black-rimmed glasses eyed her from behind the window's bars. Julia knew she had better look confident. She took a deep breath, squared her shoulders, and piled her money on the counter.

"I want to buy a ticket to Phoenix." She tried to sound firm in her request, but her confidence wilted when the ticket lady looked at the mound of coins with an amused smile.

"Who's going to meet you in Phoenix, young lady?"

Julia didn't like her smug expression or her tone of voice. "My father. He lives there."

"Well, now, that's fine, but I'll need an adult to buy your ticket and put you on the bus. Where's your mom?" Her concerned expression reminded Julia of Mrs. Howard's.

"She's home, but she says it's okay for me to go."

"You better go get her, hon, and bring her here. I can't sell you a ticket by yourself."

Julia frowned as she decided what to do. There was no use arguing with the lady. She'd learned that adults rarely let her win arguments. She needed a better plan.

"Okay," she said at last. "I'll be back." She swept the money into the palm of one hand and stalked away.

She thought about waiting inside the terminal for someone her mother's age and asking her to buy the ticket, but she knew the ticket lady was watching. So, she left the building and stood near the entrance where she was hidden from the lady's view. At first, there was little activity, but as the sun slowly rose in the violet sky, more people began to file past her into the terminal. Most looked too young or too rugged in appearance for her to consider asking them for assistance, but at last, a grandmotherly woman approached carrying a large shopping bag. She looked a little old for a mother, but Julia liked her kind face and stepped in front of her.

"Excuse me ma'am," she said politely. "Could you please help me?"

"Depends on what you want, I guess." The woman stared at her with slightly crossed eyes that unsettled Julia and nearly caused her to lose her nerve. But she thought about her father waiting in Phoenix and pressed on.

"They won't let me buy my own ticket, and I need to get to Phoenix to see my father. Will you buy it for me?" She withdrew the handful of coins from her pocket and held them up for inspection.

"I don't want to get in no trouble." The woman shifted her feet and cast a furtive glance around her to see if they were being watched.

"You won't. I promise." Julia summoned up a smile that she hoped would ease the lady's concerns.

The woman hesitated a moment longer, then scooped the coins from Julia's hand. "Oh, all right," she agreed. "As long as you wait right here." She patted Julia on the head. "Give me a little time to make sure nobody's watching. Then I'll come back."

Julia sat down on the curb and began to think what she would say to her father. She hadn't quite figured out how she would find him, but she assumed he'd be in the phone book under Rice. It dawned on her that she'd need coins to call him, but she'd given everything to the woman. Hopefully, there would be some change left over from the ticket. She wondered how long the trip would take. Not too long, she hoped. She'd left the house without breakfast, and she was already getting hungry.

Julia didn't know how much time had passed, but she knew it was long enough. Worry lines creased her forehead. Where was the woman with her ticket? She got up and peeked through the doorway. A few dozen people milled about or sat in the rows of blue, plastic seats bolted to the floor, but nobody looked familiar or grandmotherly. She saw the ticket lady was busy, so she slipped inside and headed for the bathroom. She needed to go, and she thought the woman might be doing the same thing. Graffiti and a few curious stares greeted her, but not the grandmotherly woman. After using the toilet--it was so icky she couldn't bring herself to sit on it--she returned to the waiting room. There was still no sign of the lady. Desperation clutched her throat as she hurried to the loading area. None of the busses displayed PHOENIX in their little window signs, and the woman was nowhere to be found.

Rain-drop tears rolled down Julia's cheeks. She plopped down on a small bench and glumly watched passengers boarding busses while she considered her situation. She had to face the fact that the kind looking lady had taken her money and disappeared. Now, she had no way to find her father, and she was late for school. She also knew when she returned to the Howards, she would face another session in the cellar. Her day, which had started with such bright promise, had turned abysmally gray.

Air turbulence jostled Julia's plane and snapped her back to the present. The unexpected rocking motion reminded her of just how much she disliked flying. She knew it was caused by her fear of heights, but that couldn't prevent her from gripping the arm on either side of her aisle seat until the bobbing motion subsided. When the pilot announced their approach into Portland, her relief was palpable.

Portland was bathed in a fine mist that glistened on the buildings and sparkled on the streets in the reflective light of the city's street lamps. She grabbed a taxi and hurried downtown in hopes that her father hadn't closed his office for the day. A band of pressure had been building in her chest all afternoon at the thought of seeing him after so many years. Now, the pressure had reached the point where she could hardly breathe. How would he react to her, she wondered? How would she to him? What would she say? The questions peppered her with stinging blows.

In the end, she needn't have worried. The address shown in the advertisement proved to be a one-room office occupied by a run-down-looking man who said he was a claims adjuster.

"Never heard of a Poppy Investments." He chewed on an unlit cigarette and squinted at Julia over the rims of his reading glasses. "Place was empty when I saw it."

Julia's heart sank as she looked around the cluttered room. She'd imagined a grand office with a mahogany desk and secretary, but this place had the tart smell of an old shoe. Documents littered the frayed carpet and scuffed desk. A fan whirred in the far corner, teasing and shifting the papers as it rotated back and forth.

She realized the advertisement for Poppy Land Investments was old and should have already been purged from the internet. CONDAD had skipped town, again.

When she told the man she was looking for her father, he pawed through one of the many stacks of papers on the floor behind his desk and handed Julia a file folder he had found in the bottom of a drawer. Julia glanced inside and saw several documents that looked like contracts. She thanked him and took the papers to a nearby coffee shop, where she could study them more closely.

Most of the documents *were* contracts, each signed by one of CONDAD's victims. Below their signatures, in meticulously inscribed handwriting, was CONDAD's flower name, Roger Poppy. She marveled at the perfect lettering and sweeping style of his penmanship. The signature portrayed an image of someone who was fastidious in his conduct. She pictured her father in a three-piece, dark suit and silk tie similar to the one worn by Detective Rodriguez, with freshly-trimmed, graying hair and a generous smile. He wouldn't have invited his "customers" to that shabby office. He would have gone to them, bearing his confident demeanor and offers of wealth. His car, a rented Lincoln or

Cadillac, would have proclaimed success without seeming overly pretentious. He would have presented an image that conveyed self-assurance and elicited trust.

A list of names had been neatly folded and inserted among the contracts. Each name had an address and telephone number typed next to it. Several had small check marks scratched beside them in dark, blue ink matching the names on the contracts. Julia looked at the first name on the list, a Mrs. Warren who had invested $50,000 in Poppy Investments. She paid for her coffee and went in search of another taxi. She hadn't come all this way just to turn around and go home. She needed to learn more about CONDAD, and the best way to do that was to visit his victims.

Mrs. Warren lived in a three-story apartment building on a quiet street in Portland's suburbs. It was the kind of neighborhood inhabited by hard-working, middle- class families. Blue-collar cars sat in driveways. Children's toys spilled off porches onto casually maintained lawns. Unpretentious families lived there, families who understood the value of a dollar and lived on tight budgets.

It was dark by the time Julia knocked on the apartment door indicated on the address sheet. Aromas from cooking meat, baked potatoes and steaming gravy mingled in the hallway, reminding her she hadn't eaten since that morning. A child shrieked her displeasure from a unit somewhere down the hall, followed by a mother's scolding voice. More than one television set blared the evening news.

Julia heard feet padding to the door, but no one answered. She could feel an eye appraising her through the peephole.

"I'm not buying anything. Go away," a woman's voice commanded.

"Sorry to trouble you. I'm looking for a Mrs. Warren who had some dealings with a company called Poppy Land Investments. I flew in today from San Francisco to learn more about the company. Can you help me?" Julia fidgeted with the file folder in her hand and tried not to stare at the eye she knew was watching her.

Television voices filled the silence between Julia and the door.

She shifted her weight uncomfortably and waited for a response. The child's voice wailed again. Seconds passed. They seemed like minutes. She was beginning to wonder if the woman had understood her. "I'm a reporter," she added in desperation.

The door sprang open a few inches, prevented by a chain from widening further. Gray eyes crowded by wrinkles and framed in silver-white hair glared at her.

"Do you know where the son-of-a-bitch is?" The woman's voice crackled with rancor. Her whole head trembled as she spoke.

"Roger Poppy? No. I was hoping you could tell me something that would help me locate him." Julia assumed CONDAD was too smart to leave any clues to his trail, but she wanted to talk to this woman, to see what kind of person would fall for his charms and believe his lies.

"Nothing to tell." The voice lost some of its edge. "He took my savings and disappeared. You want information, talk to the police. I already told them everything I know." The door slammed shut, and Julia knew the interview was over.

It was the same with the others checked on the list. They were mostly older people living on limited incomes, who, in a moment of insanity, had believed CONDAD's golden-tongued tales of riches at the end of his real estate rainbow. They were bitter and scarred, people who now faced a bleak financial landscape because of him.

Julia flew back to San Francisco in a state of depression and anger. Her father had abandoned these people, just as he had her and her mother. He'd stolen their dreams and their hopes for a brighter future. He'd stolen Julia's chance to have a father who would watch over her and give her the love and support she so desperately needed. What, she wondered, had he stolen from her mother? Her sanity? Had she slid into her confused world because of her father's broken promises?

CHAPTER SIX

When Julia returned for her next appointment with Mr. Andersen, he greeted her at the door without his cane or any sign of a limp. His energy and charm had been miraculously restored, casting aside the images of the old, tired man Julia had carried away with her the previous morning. Her own mood, on the other hand, was less upbeat. She had heard nothing further from Romeo, and she was becoming worried. Still, it was hard not to be caught up in Andersen's buoyant mood. There was something in the old man's demeanor that drew her to him, and she had to suppress a sudden urge to hug him. She was glad to see him looking so chipper.

"Come, come, Julia. I have something to show you." He led her to the couch and pulled several photos from one of his file folders. A laughing, impish woman stared back at Julia from the snapshots, a woman filled with so much life her spirit reached out from the pictures and drew Julia into them. The woman reminded her of her absent soul mate! Julia's cheeks grew warm and moist.

"The woman you were hired to observe, Kathy Griffith." It was all she could think to say. "She's lovely."

"More than lovely. She was a celestial body shining in the heavens. Tonight, I shall introduce you to her."

He resumed his position in his favorite chair, gathered his thoughts, and picked up his story as if they had only paused moments ago.

****

Whoever Kathy Griffith might be, she was an unusual woman. She moved through her day with such charm, the sun seemed to shine on her wherever she went. Her spirit brightened everything around her. People loved to talk to her, especially children. She performed her auditing jobs with vigor, but she blossomed when she picked up her camera. The children she photographed delighted her and she them. It made her photo sessions sparkle with a magic I had never seen before. Her graceful movements bewitched me; her energy invigorated me. When she moved with her camera, it was like watching Swan Lake. I was quickly becoming enthralled by her, not a good state of mind for a separatist.

There was only one problem. Kathy Griffith remained an enigma. Whoever this woman was, she had fabricated a life for herself that began as an adult and hid a past she wanted to banish from her kingdom. I instinctively knew that whatever lurked in that other world held the key to my objective. Uncover her past, and I would find the secret to separate her from Liu Kwong. Almost a week had passed, and I had not heard from Kwong. I took this as a good sign, but I did not want to try his patience. I needed to make some progress, and it seemed the only way to do that was to get to know Kathy Griffith personally. I had to capture her attention, but not in a way that would arouse suspicion. I could only think of one solution. It was time to face my demons and play poker.

Tourists saw Chinatown like an artist's canvass, filled with broad brushstrokes depicting crowded boulevards, colorful restaurants and local markets. But the real Chinatown was a labyrinth of back streets and alleyways feeding off the main avenues. Hundreds of singsong voices filled the air with the cacophonic sounds of bargaining, gossiping, and arguing among the merchants, customers, and neighbors who lived there. Laundry hung on poles from windows, along with sausages left to cure in the sun. Live chickens, fish, and fresh vegetables spilled out of open markets onto the streets. Buildings and humanity were pressed so tightly together, there was hardly room to breathe. If Chinatown had been a theater, it would have had a large Sold Out sign hung on its door each night.

I followed Kathy into that warren of side streets. She glided through the throngs of people as naturally as a bird in flight, smiling and greeting passersby just as she did her neighbors. They acknowledged her with smiles. By contrast, I skulked along the crowded walkways like a common criminal and was eyed with suspicion. At last, I found myself standing in front of the Golden Moon Restaurant Kwong had mentioned to me. Kathy had disappeared inside, and I plunged in after her.

I say "plunged" because that was exactly how I felt. The siren call of the cards was already tugging at my sleeve, beckoning me to my fate. I had no idea what my level of tolerance would be, whether I could survive the ordeal that awaited me. So, I leapt into the chasm. By the time I stood inside the entrance looking around the crowded restaurant for Kathy, my hands were trembling like a recovering alcoholic's. The place buzzed with hungry energy. Dozens of families were bent over their meals, their chopsticks moving in a blur from bowls to mouths. There was no sign of Kathy. A waiter approached, and I pantomimed dealing a deck of cards. He nodded and pointed to a red door in the back of the room. Sweat beaded my face as I walked towards that door. The room was suddenly hot, and despite its cavernous size, the walls and ceiling were closing in on me. I paused in front of the door, whose gleaming red color cried out to me to stop. It was not too late to change my mind. All I had to do was turn on my heels and walk away. But Kathy was in there, and I desperately wanted to save her from Kwong's clutches. I had no alternative but to enter. After taking several deep breaths, I swung the door open and stepped inside. I was greeted by the crisp, clean sounds of shuffled cards and tossed chips. My breathing returned to normal. My pulse rate slackened. I had just taken the alcoholic's equivalent of a shot of strong whiskey. I was home.

Instinctively, I surveyed the room. Five tables were in action, each with a dealer and six to eight players. Dealers sat at two other tables with decks of cards fanned out on the green felt covers, waiting for customers. Nearly all the players were men. I immediately spotted Kathy seated at the far end of the room and wandered to the bar near her table and ordered a scotch. My fingers itched to hold those plastic cards, to feel their ebony smoothness stroking my fingers, but I forced myself to sit down on a barstool and assess the action. Most of the men looked like two-bit players who stayed with the percentages and never won or lost more than a few hundred dollars. I had milked the likes of them for a steady income in my prime. No matter how hard they tried, most of these players betrayed themselves when someone challenged their comfort level. They changed the way they held their cards, touched their chips, did something that told me whether to raise or fold.

I saw at once that Kathy's table was different. The bets were larger and the gamblers more polished. Three of them were Vegas players I had known in my heyday. Alaska Jack--so called because of his colorful stories about the state's unbridled wilderness--once won $15,000 from me while we waited at the airport for flights home after a tournament. He still sported a wild mane of dark-brown hair that was just as untamed as his namesake. I raised my drink to him when I caught his eye. He nodded and returned his attention to his cards.

Diamond Hank always wore a five-carat diamond earring when he played. He also wore silk shirts and $500 shoes. I noted that he had added a diamond stud in his tie. He was as meticulous in his play as he was in his attire. Most players tossed their betting chips onto the table with a casual air. Not Hank. I watched him remove a dozen chips from his pile to call a bet and set them on the table like golden eggs.

Blades, who was the third member of my little trio of past

acquaintances, carried a stiletto. He once stuck it through the hand of a man he caught dealing from the wrong end of the deck. Blades puffed endlessly on Italian cigarettes while he played, hiding his shifty eyes behind a veil of smoke. When I inhaled the smoke's familiar aroma, memories stampeded through me. I heard murmuring voices calling and raising bets, cards snapping in fidgeting hands, while someone fiddled with the loose change in his pocket. My body twitched as I tried to assess people's bets. I didn't know how much longer I could sit there watching.

A seat opened up across the table from Kathy, and I decided it was time to test my mettle. I sat down with a nod to Jack, Hank and Blades, who greeted me as if I had just gone to the restroom, instead of disappearing for ten years. They weren't bad people, I knew, until someone got in their way in a poker game. Then, they became totally ruthless. Their secret to winning was their indifference to losing. The pile of chips in front of them didn't represent a mortgage payment or a new car, merely the tools of their trade. Nothing changed in their demeanor when they looked at their cards. They could drop $10,000 in an hour and think nothing of it.

I had often walked away from the table after twelve hours of calculating odds and reading opponents' faces with no idea how much I'd won or lost. Drop $50,000 one night, get it back the next. It was like playing Monopoly without the get-out-of-jail-free card. None of us ever got away from the game, unless we quit cold turkey, as I'd done.

Kathy's eyes examined me, but I deliberately avoided hers while the cards were dealt. When I did meet her gaze, I was surprised to see a cold, appraising stare that had nothing in common with the sunny woman I'd been following for the past week. She was just as ruthless as Blades and the others.

I won't bother with the details of the hands played that night, except to note that it was a high-stakes game that should have been out of Kathy's league. Yet, she kept a pile of chips in front of her worth well over $20,000 and never backed down from a raise if she thought she could win. Her play was precise. She didn't take unnecessary risks, and she wasn't easily bluffed. I learned that on the third hand when I tried to take her out by bidding aggressively with only a pair of tens. She faced me down and won with a pair of queens.

My own reaction to the game was a revelation. In the old days, I was strung tighter than a piano wire, but tonight I found myself relaxed and enjoying the game. The source of my newly discovered serenity was the woman seated across from me, the woman I had only seen from afar until now. She had delightful little habits, such as biting her lower lip while studying her cards, or crossing one arm across her chest, propping the elbow of her other arm on it, and nibbling her fingertips after a bet.

At first, I failed to see any pattern to her routines, nothing that gave her hand away. But as I continued to observe her from the corner of my eye, something struck me. She made a bet, leaned back in her chair and struck her familiar pose, only this time she nibbled the tips of her nails instead of her fingers. A distinctive pattern slowly emerged. When she thought she had a winning hand, she chewed the nails. When she was unsure, she went back to the fingertips. I watched the others to see if anyone else observed the pattern. Kathy had been holding her own, but during the next hour she went down $8,000 to Alaska Jack and $5,000 to Blades. I had no doubt they had seen the same thing.

I tried to decide what to do. In poker, everyone played their own. If I helped her, I broke a silent code, but I didn't care. I wanted to let her know.

We had played without a break for nearly four hours, so I decided to cash in my chips and stretch my legs. As I did so, I looked Kathy square in the eyes and nodded, giving her an open invitation to follow. I wandered out into the restaurant, now dark and empty except for the shadow of a man guarding the front door. It felt good to walk away from a card game without shaking all over. My compulsiveness was gone, at least for one night. I felt no need to return, except for Kathy.

"You're new." Her voice startled me. I had been so wrapped in my thoughts, I hadn't heard her enter the room. "But you knew some of the other players."

"From another place and time," I replied cautiously. "Walk with me. We should talk."

I nodded to the guard to unlock the door, and we stepped into the cold night air. Our footsteps echoed in the narrow street. It was after 1:00 a.m., and the merchants and tourists had renounced the night in favor of their beds. A heavy fog had settled over the city, making street lamps blur. I enjoyed sharing the silence with Kathy for a few moments as we walked.

"Why should we talk?" she asked at last.

"You're telegraphing your hands."

Silence. We continued walking until we reached a main street, where a few people and cars still explored the misty night. We stopped and faced each other. Passing headlights revealed intent eyes studying my face. "Why are you telling me?"

"I don't know. I guess I got tired of watching Jack and Blades take your money."

"And you? How much did you take before you decided to tell me?" It wasn't hostility I heard in her voice. It was more like curiosity.

"Sometimes, when you bet, you chew . . . ."

"I don't want to know." She snapped her response off like a dead tree branch. "The only reason you're telling me is because I'm a woman. That's chauvinistic, and I don't like it. I can take care of myself." Her tone was brisk, unyielding.

"Chivalry is dead, I suppose." I was so taken aback by her response, I nearly stuttered my words.

"Chauvinism is dead. If you want to spread your cape over a puddle for me, I'll gladly step on it, but I won't accept handouts."

More car headlights revealed tight lips. She was angry, but I didn't care. I wanted to stand there with her until dawn. I feared if she left, the fog would swallow her, and I would never see her again. It was time to take a different tack, to raise her interest level in me.

"I took a great risk entering that card club tonight, but I wanted to meet you." I could tell by her silence that I had surprised her. "I've seen you enter the restaurant before, and I've been quite taken by you. I knew about the poker game, but I haven‛t played for years. It nearly ruined me." My lies were hidden in half-truths. I felt shameless and guilty at the same time. I would say anything to keep her there.

"You're a good player." Her voice softened. Passing lights caught an expression of curiosity. My new approach was working. "You came tonight because of me?"

I nodded, although I wasn't certain she could see my gesture in the gloom left behind from the fading headlights.

"Then I owe you an apology for my rude behavior just now. The men I meet at these games generally see me as an easy target, in more ways than one. I have to keep my guard up at all times."

"Maybe we could make a fresh start, over dinner tomorrow night. I'm told the Fior d'Italia is quite good." I was playing with fire, inviting her to her favorite restaurant, but I couldn't help myself. I was a gambler again, and I thrilled at the risk I was taking. It put an edge to my mood that I hadn't experienced in years.

A silence darker than the night filled the air. I took a deep breath and waited for her response. My senses crackled with the excitement of aces over kings, wondering how my opponent would answer my bid.

"I'm not sure that would be a good idea." Hesitation hung in her voice. A good sign? I couldn't tell. "Now, I'd better get back to my game." She turned and walked away.

"I'll be there tomorrow night at eight, in case you change your mind." I watched her disappear into the fog, listened to her shoes clicking in the darkness. Had I won or lost my last bet? I would find out tomorrow night.

****

Julia was learning the signs by now. A heavy sigh followed by silence told her the old man was through. Each time they met, each time she listened to him spin his tale, she became more entranced. It was like listening to the bedtime stories her mother had read to her before she became too ill. Julia never wanted them to end.

"Will you return tomorrow evening?" he asked. "Seven is a good time."

It was all Julia could do to keep from following Kathy down that fog-filled alley. The more she learned about the woman, the more she thought of Jackie. They both had the power to enthrall those who entered their lives. Listening to Mr. Andersen's story was like peeling layers of skin from an onion. Each layer led to a deeper mystery which held Julia spellbound.

"Yes. Tomorrow at seven." She would count the hours until she could return.

Julia tried not to think of Jackie all the time, but after listening to Mr. Andersen's tale, she couldn't help recalling the events that brought them together. After her mother died, Julia relocated to San Francisco where she landed a reporter's position at the Chronicle. She was quickly consumed by the city's vitality. The air crackled with so much vigor, she thought she had been swallowed by a tornado that was twirling her around. The city succored her while she struggled to adjust to her new, motherless life, and she surrendered to its healing powers. San Francisco became her suitor, her lover, and its magical essence was never more seductive than after dark, when the city's heart thrummed in its restaurants, bars, theaters, and nightclubs. San Francisco bustled during the day, but at night it blossomed into a Cinderella dream of enchantment and desire.

It did not take her long to find her element in the city's social life. Hard work was rewarded by evenings that centered on workmates and casual acquaintances. They gathered in restaurants for culinary feasts and in bars for flirtations and romantic interludes that exploded with sexual energy, if only for a night. As time passed, however, she realized her world had more in common with Alice in Wonderland than it did Cinderella. She found herself running on a treadmill, and she had to sprint faster and faster just to stay in place. She began searching the eyes of her lovers for some insight into what they needed from her and she from them, but all she saw were the glazed looks of too many scotches or the fear of being alone. The idea that someone could be alone in the midst of so many people shocked her, but when she looked around, she realized she was just as afraid as the others, and despite her busy social life, she *was lonely.*

Her career as a newspaper reporter had progressed in fits and starts. She graduated from covering social events to front section news, but she still hadn't had a breakthrough story, the kind that made headlines and put her star on the journalistic map. She decided to try her hand at writing a book about her experiences and the people she knew, but the effort lacked depth, and she set the project aside.

It was during that unsettling period that she met Jackie at the Buena Vista. Julia had arrived after work and was slowly working her way through the noisy throng of accountants, lawyers and office workers towards a knot of newspaper reporters huddled around a table near the back. She could already taste the chilled, nutty flavor of the chardonnay she would order, but when she spotted a young woman standing with a group near the window, she stopped. Julia gazed at the woman with the wonder of a child watching her first parade. The woman laughed at a comment made by a tall, blond man and tossed her dark, thick mane with the carefree gesture of a wild mare. Julia tried to move on, but her feet wouldn't respond. All she could do was stand and stare. She estimated the woman to be in her mid-twenties. She was shorter than her friends, no more than five-foot-four, but she was the Fourth of July, bewitching those around her with a boundless energy and playful charm. Her skin had an ivory cast that told Julia she spent little time in the sun. It reminded her of the white lilies her mother used to grow. Despite her short height, the young woman never seemed to look up at her companions. The trick was in the way she held her chin, high and firm. It gave her a look of confidence that Julia both admired and envied. She had never felt such a powerful attraction for a woman, and she had to suppress an urge to walk over and introduce herself.

Julia's relationships with women had always been distant. Nor had she ever been interested in someone younger than herself. Yet, there she stood with her heart racing and pulse-rate rising. A voice inside her head frantically tried to analyze what was happening. Perhaps, the voice reasoned, it had something to do with her thirtieth birthday--a date that was speeding towards her with the subtlety of a freight train--or with her frustrations concerning men. Or her career, which was proceeding at a ponderously slow pace. She was vulnerable. She was searching for a way out of the emotional canyons that boxed her into repeated cycles of highs and lows in her work and her affairs.

In the end, the reason didn't matter. Julia saw something in the bouncing brunette that shook her life's tree. She blushed at the thought of approaching her. What would she say? How would the woman and her friends react? She took a step forward and stopped, unable to bring herself to do it. She could only stand and gape like a silly schoolgirl.

The young woman laughed, again, and flicked her cat-green eyes towards Julia, catching her gaze and holding it for less than a heartbeat. Before Julia could react, the cat's eyes were gone, but their memory lingered on her skin. Julia's face had become flushed by their quick exchange. Her body shook, and even though she was standing in a crowded room, she felt naked and alone.

Before Julia could think what to do, the woman excused herself from her friends and began walking towards her, slipping through the throng of bodies with the grace of a sailor at sea. Julia wanted to turn around and flee, but the crowded room and babbling voices held her in a fist that imprisoned her. Her face grew hot and damp. She could smell the warmth of the bodies pressing around her. A knot formed in her stomach as she stood, paralyzed, and stared at the bold woman who had now stopped in front of her.

"You've been watching me," the woman declared with a hint of amusement that teased the corners of her mouth into a slight smile. Her creamy-white face brightened with delight at Julia's obvious discomfort.

"I haven't." It wasn't a very convincing denial, but Julia didn't know what to say or do. She fumbled with her hands and looked down at them in confusion.

"It's okay. I've been watching you, too. I'm Jackie Orvieto. My grandparents grew wine by that name in Italy." She pressed closer. Julia caught the scent of rose petals on her skin. She inhaled deeply and blushed once more. She glanced toward the reporters at the back of the bar to see if they were watching. No one gave her so much as a passing glance. Julia smiled at herself for having such a guilty reaction. They were only talking, after all.

"You smile beautifully," Jackie exclaimed. "I already know who you are, by the way. Julia Rice. I've read some of your articles in the paper. You're good. I admire what you do. It must be a very hard profession for a woman."

Julia basked in Jackie's unexpected recognition and approval. The words tasted like chocolate, rich and sweet on the tongue. She longed to hear more.

There was a moment's awkward silence while she searched for her voice. "And what about you? What do you do?"

"Commercial artist for an ad agency," Jackie made a face. "Not the sort of thing that will get me hung in galleries, but it pays the bills."

"Do you want to be hung in galleries?"

"Yes. I paint every minute I can. I'm told I have talent, but so do hundreds of other painters in this city. Multiply that across the country, and you can see my chances aren't very good."

Julia was struck by Jackie's adult demeanor. She didn't boast or try to impress Julia. She seemed quite at ease with herself, with who she was. It wasn't something Julia expected from such an effervescent, young woman. Julia felt an instant kinship with her. They shared similar creative frustrations and desires: one a writer, the other a painter. It was heady stuff. Julia sensed a coming-of-age bond between them.

"I'd like to see your paintings sometime," Julia blurted out before she could stop herself. Her impulsive suggestion disconcerted her and she looked away. *What must this woman think?* When she looked back, Jackie's green eyes were fixed on hers.

"Why not now?" Jackie asked in a quiet voice that was almost lost in the room's din. "My loft and studio are only a few blocks away."

The invitation wrapped Julia in its gravitational pull and drew her along twin paths of longing and apprehension. There was something so sensual in Jackie's invitation that Julia found it difficult to breathe. Visions of two naked bodies tumbling in a sea of sheets jolted her. As badly as she wanted to lose herself in Jackie's embraces, she didn't think she could share this woman's bed. Yet, she wanted to hold onto her, not let her go. How could she explain herself without chasing this sparkling woman away? How could she explain how much she wanted to share her world with a woman she had only just met? "I've never been with a woman," she said in a hushed voice. "I'm not sure I could do that."

Jackie's face lit up like daybreak. "I'm not trying to seduce you," she cried out loudly enough for those standing nearby to hear. Heads turned briefly, and Julia cringed at the amused faces. Jackie took her hand. "Come on, I won't bite you."

Julia allowed herself to be pulled through the crowd and out into the brisk night. After the heat of so many bodies, the air was as crisp as chilled lemonade, and she wanted to sip it through a straw. Jackie's hand, which was unexpectedly large for someone so small, enveloped hers in a feverish mist of moist skin. Julia welcomed its hot touch, despite her misgivings. They walked briskly up inclines and around corners until they stood panting before a building that loomed above them in the dark street.

"Home," Jackie announced simply. She unlocked a bulky front door and flipped a switch that produced such feeble light, Julia could hardly see her feet as she followed her companion up a flight of stairs. Jackie stopped abruptly before a smaller door. More keys rattled in her hand, but she didn't open the door. Instead, she slowly faced Julia and kissed her firmly on the lips, sending shock waves bursting through Julia's body.

Before Julia could respond, Jackie turned her back and flung the door open, revealing a room the size of a basketball court. A 10' by 10' easel commanded the room's center, and large canvases stood stacked against two walls. Julia saw brilliant colors and random patterns she couldn't understand, but she sensed the power in the bold brush strokes that filled the room. They merged with the tiny explosions bursting inside her head. She hesitated in the doorway, her mind spinning from the effects of Jackie's kiss, and tried to decide what to do. Entering the room might signal her complicity in what had just happened. Refusing to enter would imply that she was rejecting the most vibrant person she had ever met.

Jackie walked over to her easel and touched the canvas with loving fingers. "That's the first time I've ever kissed a woman." She stood with her back to Julia, studying her work. "Sorry if I frightened you. It frightened me too. I don't expect it to happen again, so it's safe for you to come in." She turned and faced Julia with a pinched expression that said she was quite anxious about Julia's reaction. "I like men. Always have, but there's a magnet pulling us together that I can't explain. If you think I'm crazy, just say so, and we'll forget tonight ever happened." She picked up a brush and fiddled with its soft fibers, but her eyes never wavered from Julia's. The air between them danced with fairies and leprechauns. It was as if a magical curtain had been lifted on a secret garden filled with charms and spells. It prompted Julia to think about her mother, about the magic she had weaved into Julia's life in spite of her illness. And her father, who was nothing more than a shadow in her memories. Her life was filled with shadows.

Hot tears rolled down her cheeks as she continued to stare across the space between them. Jackie suddenly looked small and lonely, and Julia wanted to comfort her. She moved with hesitant steps across the room and tentatively put her arms around the shorter woman. Jackie leaned into her until they both became lost in the soft folds of a warm embrace.

"You're not. Crazy, I mean. I feel it too. We'll be friends for life."

They stood like that for a long time, rocking in each other's arms and wondering at the strange forces that had brought them together.

The next few months were filled with sharing and touching and exploring their relationship. They did kiss again. They caressed each other's hair and touched one another's skin. They aroused emotions neither had experienced before, but they kept themselves from falling into the abyss of intimacy. Such a leap would redefine their relationship in a way neither wanted. They were two blind women using the incredibly sensitive nerve endings in their lips and fingers to try to understand their feelings for each other.

Julia's reaction to her new friend was much like her response to San Francisco. She reveled in her discovery and snuggled into their relationship with the delight of a mother with a newborn child. She was fascinated by Jackie's artistic fervor and often sat in her companion's floppy, comfortable couch with a glass of white wine, watching her friend thrust and parry in warrior fashion with her paint brushes. Jackie worked with a paint-spattered passion that aroused Julia's hunger for her own personal fulfillment. She admired Jackie's courage and her willingness to make artistic statements that attacked the boundaries of commercial art. Julia drew inspiration from it and vowed not to give up her own creative desires.

Unlike Julia's previous explorations of San Francisco, when she played the tourist, her forays with Jackie were more intimate. They ate in small cafes frequented by local residents, walked less traveled paths, and spent much of their time in quiet conversation. Jackie described a gypsy life in New York with artistic parents who never bothered with cars or mortgage payments, or the other trappings of society, but who saw to it that Jackie went to art school and encouraged her to test her own wings in California. Julia spoke of her mother's flower gardens, the growing madness, and Julia's futile attempts to find her father. They took turns crying and comforting one another. They kissed away the tears and laughed with giddy relief that each had found a soul mate with whom she could share her life.

But six months after they met, Jackie shattered Julia's world with a single sentence. "I've been transferred to New York." She said this while they walked arm-in-arm in a small park overlooking the waterfront near Fisherman's Wharf. The sun was an orange-red balloon hanging just above the mists of an approaching fog bank that would soon obscure it and turn day into premature night. Jackie's words echoed in Julia's head, but she refused to believe them. They were repugnant words that spoke of an alien world. A world without air to breathe or affection to warm her soul. Any world would be bleak without Jackie in it.

"You can't go." She gripped Jackie's arm with fierce denial, her nails digging into her companion's warm flesh. The ground swayed beneath her feet, rocking back and forth in boat-like fashion until a feeling of nausea rose in her throat.

"I wasn't given a choice. The client is shifting its advertising account to the New York office. The entire account and creative teams are going." Jackie took Julia's trembling hand and kissed it. "It's either that or starve."

"Or paint."

"Yes, of course, but that doesn't pay the bills." A plaintive tone crept into Jackie's voice, a tone that cried out for understanding.

"I can pay your bills."

Jackie squeezed her arm. "You are the most wonderful person I will ever know, and I love you. But, no, you can't. I couldn't live with that, and it would damage our relationship. It would come between us. Not at first, but eventually. I could never let that happen."

The pain searing through Julia's heart was more than she could bear. Her flower-sated world was being devastated before her eyes, but she knew instinctively that Jackie was right. Jackie understood life's intricate patterns better than she did. It was one of the things Julia found so appealing about her. One of many things. She would do anything to keep from losing Jackie, even if it meant letting her go.

"Then, I'll have to learn to breathe again without you. I don't know if I can." Julia shuddered as a chill swept through her.

Jackie pressed her face against Julia's shoulder. Her hair smelled of chestnuts and apple cider. "We'll always be together, no matter how far we're apart. We'll write each other and visit, just like we do now."

When they returned to Jackie's loft, they quietly curled up together on Jackie's bed. Like so many aspects of their relationship, nothing needed to be said. They understood that they would allow themselves to lie together this one time, exploring the heat pouring off each other's skin. They understood that while their need for each other was emotional, not physical, they needed to feel the other's body, to draw upon each other's life force for survival.

Jackie was gone within the month, and Julia wandered through her days in a fog. She died small deaths each time she remembered a touch or a smile. Each time she saw a familiar place they had shared together. Each time she heard a laugh that reminded her of Jackie's. They did write each other, but the aching loneliness wouldn't go away. Her only remedy was to throw herself back into her nightlife, but the drinks tasted like mouthwash, and the conversations sounded out of tune.

It eased her loneliness, however, and set the stage for Phillip. When they shared drinks a few months later and ended up in her bed, Julia knew it was her own desperate loneliness that drove her there. It helped ease the pain, however, and it helped her find her footing again in the world of other people. Slowly, she returned to life.

CHAPTER SEVEN

"Give me an update on your Chinatown story." Morning sunlight slipped like stray cats through the mini-blinds into Phillip's office. He had started calling it the "Chinatown Story" ever since Julia told him about Li Chang. Phillip was munching on sesame seeds while editing the copy of a young reporter. His red marker flew across the sheets of paper, ruthlessly lining out sentences, moving paragraphs with violent arrows, deleting phrases with the force of an angry czar. She had dreaded entering that office, until two years ago when he stopped tearing her work apart, a sign that she had been elevated to a higher status.

"Romeo won't return my calls. I don't know whether to be angry or worried. Either he's decided to take our money and run, or he fears for his own safety." Romeo and Li Chang had been her best leads. Without them, she was back to square one, a fact she wasn't ready to admit to Phillip just yet.

"Be angry. We don't have time for worry. Get back down to the docks and find the S.O.B." He hunched back over the papers. Their discussion was over.

Julia spent a frustrating afternoon combing the waterfront for Romeo. A temporary injunction had brought the docks back to life, and the workers were busy unloading the ships backed up in the port. Crane engines clanged with purpose. Voices shouted out commands and warnings. The aroma of men's sweating bodies mingled with the slightly caustic odor of briny, sea air. She had already spoken to some of these sweating men while collecting information about the strike, but they no longer wanted to talk or be seen with her. A curtain of silence had fallen over them.

By the end of the day, Julia had accomplished nothing, and she returned to her car in low spirits. When she spotted a piece of yellow notepaper fluttering under the wiper blade on her windshield, she grabbed it eagerly, expecting to find some word from Romeo. Her momentary hopes fled before the wintry chill that swept over her when she read the block letters: STAY AWAY FROM THE DOCKS. Was it a threat? A warning? She could feel someone's eyes stinging her skin, and she had to fight the impulse to turn around and look for her tormentor. She kept her chin high and her eyes forward, determined not to let anyone know how badly the message had shaken her.

Julia was in no mood to return to the office, so she decided to head straight for her appointment with Mr. Andersen. That meant arriving before seven, but she hoped he would be ready for her. When she arrived, her knock was greeted by silence. She tried the doorbell. It chimed loudly, but elicited no response. Julia began to wonder if the old man had fled from her as well.

Without a watch, Julia couldn't be sure how long she waited on the porch, but she knew it was well past seven. Dusk was descending, and the city's lights winked and danced in the streets below. She could taste the spicy tang in the ocean air as she stood looking at the sparkling city. An earlier shower had washed the pavements, producing glistening images that shimmered in the reflections of streetlights and neon signs.

The scene made her think of Jackie. As much as she enjoyed the city's youthful energy and sophisticated charms, she wondered if it could ever yield someone, man or woman, to replace what she had shared with Jackie. Despite the crowded streets, dazzling theaters, and boisterous taverns, she was lonely. She thought about the parallels between the Kathy Griffith described by Mr.

Andersen and herself. She was friendly enough and had many acquaintances. But she didn't have anyone with whom she could tell her deepest secrets, not since Jackie had moved to New York, anyway.

Waiting on the porch was making her melancholy. She shifted her feet impatiently and rang the doorbell again. Still no answer. Julia began to consider the possibility that something was wrong. She tried the door, but it was locked, so she stepped off the porch and walked cautiously around the house, peeking through windows. The curtains were open, but there was no sign of life inside. The house was becoming darker and more foreboding by the minute. When Julia tried the back door, she discovered it was unlocked. After a moment's hesitation, she pushed the door open and stepped inside. Her hands trembled much like Mr. Andersen's had when he entered that poker room, but no shuffling cards or clicking chips greeted her.

Only silence filled the rooms, a stillness that mocked her attempts to walk undetected on the hardwood floors. The echo from her high heels reminded her of birds pecking at a window. She abandoned her attempts at stealth and strode through the murky rooms looking for any signs of Thomas Andersen. A casual shirt and jacket hung in the downstairs closet, but their style suggested someone much younger. The kitchen was well stocked with plates, glasses, and utensils, but all were put away in their proper places. Two cans of soup stood on one shelf. The refrigerator was empty. She moved upstairs, where she found empty closets and drawers. The two bathrooms were as void of personal items as the rest of the house. There was nothing to prove Thomas Andersen had ever been there.

Julia sat down on the bed and pondered what to do. Technically, she had just committed a crime, breaking and entering, and her instincts told her to leave at once. But she feared losing contact with the man who had so surreptitiously entered her life.

She thought of the things he had said about her during their first meeting. It still upset her to know that Mr. Andersen had spied on her and continued to do so. But, he had been right. Her only meaningful relationship had been with Jackie. Julia knew she wasn't as beautiful as some women, but she did exude a sensual charm that attracted men, especially those who wanted sex but no commitments. She could feel a depressing mood descending on her, accompanied by a feeling of intense loneliness and inadequacy. When that happened, she became convinced men only found her attractive at night when the lights were off.

The muted echo of footsteps in the rooms below snapped Julia out of her funk. Mr. Andersen had returned at last. She rose from the bed and nearly called out to him, before realizing the steps were too quick for a man who had to muster all his strength to avoid walking without a cane. And they were much too quiet. Whoever was there was moving with stealth, just as she had when she first slipped into the house. She could hear the intruder making his way towards the living room, and a rush of adrenaline surged through her at the thought that she might be in danger. Her mind became as light-headed as a cloud. *Why didn't I leave when I had the chance? What do I do now?* Julia remembered Mr. Andersen's comment at their first meeting about learning to fly. If only she could fly away and escape whoever was searching the rooms below! Suddenly, a beam of light bounced off the upstairs hallway wall, and a mouse-like squeak on the bottom step betrayed the weight of someone mounting the stairs.

Julia frantically removed her shoes and swiveled her head around the room looking for some place to hide. The empty closets mocked her in the gathering gloom. She would be discovered there in seconds, if anyone bothered to look. She slid to the floor and found the bed just high enough for her to wedge underneath it. Quickly, she pressed her back against the unyielding floorboards and worked her way under the swaying mattress. A musty odor and dust particles assaulted her, making it difficult for her to inhale without sneezing. She pinched her nose and lay as still as possible, trying not to breathe above a whisper.

The footsteps were working their way methodically up the stairs, their echo building with the thunder of an approaching storm. A throbbing noise beat inside her ears, and she realized it was her heart pounding like a great, base drum. It seemed impossible the intruder couldn't hear it. The man stepped into the bedroom and halted. Julia bit her quivering lip to keep from crying out. Sweat gushed from every pore in her body. She closed her eyes and willed herself not to move or make a sound. The silence lasted for an eternity before the feet turned and moved away. She nearly cried with relief when she heard the man's footsteps echoing down the stairwell to the floor below. A door opened and closed, and the house became still again. But try as she might, Julia couldn't find the courage to move from her sanctuary. She wanted to stay there forever.

At last, she slid from under the bed and tiptoed down the stairs in her stocking feet. The city's lights cast a surreal glow about the living room, creating vague shadows and turning familiar objects into alien monsters. She hurried to the back door, put on her shoes and embraced the chilly, evening air as she hurried to her car.

Julia drove home in a state of shock and despair. Her close encounter with the intruder had wilted her courage. She'd never experienced real fear before. It made her feel vulnerable and foolish. It made her wonder what she'd hoped to accomplish by entering an empty house at night. She wasn't normally so impulsive, and tonight's impetuous behavior had exposed her to a frightening encounter. In spite of her shaken confidence, however, she couldn't stop thinking about Andersen and how much she wanted to continue her talks with him. But how to find him, again? It seemed pretty obvious the house had been abandoned. Her best bet was the Italian restaurant where they first met. If she didn't hear from him tomorrow, she would return there. It was a long shot, but the waiter might know his schedule or how to get a message to him.

Julia's mind was still in a haze when she pulled into the carport beneath her apartment. A reserved parking space was a luxury in San Francisco, and she had gladly paid the premium demanded by the owner so she wouldn't have to circle the streets at night looking for a place to leave her car. She beeped the door locks closed and started to reach in her purse for her electronic key to the building. In that brief moment, a space of time that could be measured in the blink of an eye, she sensed movement behind her. Panic, the same panic she had experienced in that empty house, streaked through her body. Her hand frantically searched for the small stun gun she kept in her purse for protection, but it was too late. A powerful arm pinned hers to her sides, and a foul-smelling cloth clamped over her nose and mouth. She squirmed and kicked, trying to reach her assailant's groin, but he was standing too close and was too strong.

"Be quiet my little bird," a harsh voice whispered in her ear, "or I'll clip your wings."

Julia's ear burned from her assailant's hot breath, and nausea welled up in her throat, making it difficult for her to draw a full breath. Fuzzy images spun wildly through her fading consciousness. She could feel her legs buckling beneath her, her body sagging in the man's grip. The last thing she remembered was a loud grunt and the arm releasing her. She collapsed to the pavement like a pile of unwashed laundry.

Mark Hansen had parked his car two blocks away and slipped through the shadows towards Julia Rice's apartment building. Her third-floor window was dark, telling him she hadn't come home, so he stood in a doorway half a block down the street and waited. The street was poorly lit, which made it easy to hide but difficult to see if others were doing the same. A car flashed its headlights on her empty carport as it passed, but he saw nothing to arouse suspicion. A dog barked somewhere in the night as a chatting couple strolled past on the other side of the street. They entered a nearby building, and all was quiet again. Time ticked slowly past eight. He stood patiently, unmoving.

At last, Julia's small, blue roadster pulled into the street, slowed and swung into the carport. He tensed and watched intently. He heard the beep of her electronic locking system just as a figure emerged from behind the car next to hers and grabbed her. Mark was already sprinting across the street as the two scuffled, his eyes scanning the parked cars and buildings for other attackers. He approached the pair from behind and delivered a swift punch to the man's kidneys, causing him to grunt and let go of his prey. Mark caught a glimpse of a scowling, Chinese face as the man swung his arm in a furious blow that would have taken his head off if he hadn't ducked. Mark countered with a punch to the groin and heard a pained gasp of escaping air. But instead of doubling over, the man raised his foot and kicked Mark in the stomach, sending him stumbling into Julia's car. Mark was amazed at the man's strength and agility. By the time he regained his balance, the man was hobbling down the street to a waiting car, which roared to life and disappeared around the corner.

Julia was asleep, floating in a pool of bright light. She wanted to continue sleeping, but the light seeped past her eyelids with the tenacity of a lighthouse beacon. No matter how tightly she closed her eyes, it refused to go away. Reluctantly, she opened her eyes and tried to focus on her surroundings. The room was a blur, but she recognized the pastel colors around her and realized she was lying on her own couch. As her head began to clear, she became aware of a pair of feet under her glass coffee table, and she snapped awake. A stranger was seated in the couch's matching chair, watching her! Harsh images of brutish hands pinning her arms and smothering her face with a pungent cloth flashed through her mind. The images throbbed inside her head as she frantically tried to understand her situation. She wanted to sit up, but the room whirled madly about her. She was riding a merry-go-round that was turning too quickly for her to get off.

"You'd better lie still a little longer. You were heavily drugged." A man's voice, firm, yet concerned. She tried to focus on his face, but her brain refused to cooperate. A wave of nausea swept over her. Was she being kidnapped? Or worse? She gripped the edge of the couch and pushed herself upright, her body sagging into the cushions behind her. The nausea rose in her throat, but once she'd settled into an upright position, the urge subsided. Her mouth tasted like dry cotton. She thought about asking for water but feared what it might do to her stomach.

"Why did you attack me? What do you want?" Julia tried to sound self-assured, but she heard the plaintive tone in her voice and knew she was at this man's mercy.

"It was a Chinaman who grabbed you. I hit him and drove him away, although frankly, if he'd wanted to make a fight of it, I'm not sure I could've stopped him." The man leaned forward but made no effort to rise.

At last, the merry-go-round slowed enough for Julia to concentrate on her intruder. He was clad entirely in black: pullover shirt, pants, even his shoes and socks.

"You're dressed like a thief." She eyed him suspiciously.

The man glanced at his clothes and smiled. "I suppose I am. This is pretty standard for surveillance work at night. Let's me move around unnoticed."

She estimated him to be in his mid-thirties. He had the narrow hips and slender legs of a dancer, but his upper body had the hardened look of someone who spent time in the gym. His dark brown hair lay tousled about his forehead. Julia wouldn't have described him as handsome, but she was struck by how pleasing his long, pronounced nose and square jaw were to look at. It was his sympathetic smile, however, that captivated her and calmed her fears. It wasn't the smile of a rapist or murderer. It comforted her and told her she was safe, something she desperately needed to believe at that moment.

"Who are you, then? And how did I get here?" She gestured to her apartment.

"My name's Mark Hansen. I do operational assignments in the field. Used to work for the CIA, but I work for myself now. Mr. Andersen hired me to look after you, in case of trouble. I carried you here from the carport."

Her remaining cobwebs were whisked away at the mention of Andersen's name. She remembered the empty house. "What happened to Mr. Andersen? Why didn't he show up tonight?"

"He has a powerful enemy, Liu Kwong, who has learned he's back in town. He mentioned Kwong to you, I believe."

Julia nodded. "Someone searched Mr. Andersen's place tonight."

Mark blinked in amazement. "You were there?" She nodded again. "That was me. I was looking for you, to let you know about the change in plans. When you didn't show up, I left and came here."

"You scared the shit out of me. I hid under the bed."

Mark laughed at the news. "The only place I didn't look."

Her memories of cowering under the bed didn't strike her as very amusing, but his laugh was infectious, and she smiled despite herself. She grew serious again. "What happened tonight? How much danger am I in?"

"Tonight's incident may have been an attempt to use you to get at Mr. Andersen. It's likely Kwong knows you two are meeting. But it might also be associated with your own investigation of the port authorities. Liu Kwong is involved in drug smuggling and slave trading."

Now it was Julia's turn to blink in amazement. "The story Mr. Andersen told me is connected to my investigation?"

"In a curious way, yes."

Julia sat quietly, trying to absorb Mark's news. Mr. Andersen had known about her appointment with Romeo. What else did he know? "I was supposed to meet a woman called Li Chang two days ago. She didn't keep our appointment, and she seems to have disappeared."

"She was the daughter of one of Liu Kwong's concubines. She's dead."

The news slammed into Julia, forcing the breath from her lungs. She felt like a ruptured balloon gulping for air. Dead. He meant murdered! She began to shake uncontrollably, and before she knew it, Mark was seated beside her with his arm draped around her shoulders, comforting her. The warmth of his arm reassured her, but she couldn't stop shaking. Things were moving too fast. She wanted to crawl back under the bed and close her eyes.

"Why are you helping me?" she managed to ask.

"My father worked with Thomas Andersen many years ago, before I was born. They were very close. He told me wonderful stories about their escapades together, before Mr. Andersen disappeared. My father's dead now, but he told me Mr. Andersen might contact me someday. Asked me to help him, if he did. A few months ago I got a call from a man who asked me to meet him at the Fior d'Italia Restaurant. Said he knew my father. When I discovered it was Mr. Andersen, I was dumbfounded. It was like visiting the world where my father once lived, the world he'd told me about."

Julia looked at him skeptically. "You're here because of your father? It seems a lot to ask."

Mark nodded. "It's more than just loyalty to my father. Mr. Andersen hired me. Assignments like this one are what I do for a living."

"Like spying on me," she declared in an accusing voice. She knew it was unfair to be angry with this stranger. He was only doing what Andersen had hired him to do, and he'd just saved her from a very unpleasant situation. But she couldn't help it. She was both angry and embarrassed. What must he think of her after learning about her affair with Phillip and her intense friendship with Jackie? Not that she had anything to hide, but it infuriated her to know this stranger had pried her life open the way one would a can of tuna fish.

Mark smiled with chagrin and stood up. "My apologies for that. I was helping Mr. Andersen learn about you, but I was also watching out for you. I hope tonight proves that."

She had to admit that after the violent encounter in the carport and the devastating news about Li Chang, she was glad to have him watching her. And what about the connection between her investigation and Liu Kwong? Julia remembered Mr. Andersen's comment at their first meeting about making use of each other. She was beginning to understand what he meant. His story was intertwined with hers. She wasn't sure why, but she sensed they needed one another.

"What do we do now?" she asked.

"Mr. Andersen hopes you can meet him Monday morning at the arboretum in Golden Gate Park. He'll be just inside the main entrance at nine. As for me, I hope you don't mind if I tag along with you for a while. I'll stay out of sight, of course."

Julia studied Mark's face. As frightening as tonight's episode had been, she knew she shouldn't let it deter her. She had to continue pursuing both stories.

"Tell Mr. Andersen I'll meet him Monday morning." She shivered and hoped she was making a wise decision.

CHAPTER EIGHT

The morning sunlight was dimmed by wispy clouds. It cast a light so pale, no shadows lingered among the exotic flowers and plants that comprised San Francisco's famous arboretum. Julia stood just inside the entrance and waited. Only a handful of people were wandering along the trails at this early hour, and none of them displayed the slight shuffle that was so characteristic of Mr. Andersen. No one held a cane.

The arboretum's fragrances released a flood of memories of her mother's nursery, and she half-expected to see her emerge from the nearby shrubs.

A year passed before Julia's mother finally came home from the psychiatric ward with opened arms and warm kisses. Julia danced with the delight of knowing the familiar patterns of her life would blossom once more, but things were never quite "normal" again. Her mother stole away for long periods of solitude and went places at night that Julia could only guess at. The house became cluttered and the nursery assumed a wild, unkempt look. At home, dirty clothes piled up and dishes went unwashed. Dinner became abstract affairs where a peanut butter sandwich or bowl of soup was as likely to be offered as beef stew and green beans.

Julia was sure her father could help them, but when she raised the subject, her mother raged and shouted until spittle flew from her mouth, and Julia retreated to her room, where she trembled with fear and indignation.

She was fourteen when she discovered her mother's reading glasses in the refrigerator. "Oh my God," her mother exclaimed with a laugh, "I've been looking everywhere for those. How did they get in there?" She walked away shaking her head.

Other personal items soon joined the list of missing objects. Car keys became an obsession, and they would scour the house together like scavengers. For her mother's birthday, Julia bought a key chain with a beeper that was activated by clapping one's hands. After that, her mother walked around the house banging her hands together as if she were killing flies until she tracked down the chirping noise. "Best gift I ever got," she said each time with a broad smile.

Her mother's nocturnal habits worsened. When she stayed home, she prowled the house at night drinking wine or reading in the den until she fell asleep in her chair. Then, she woke late and rushed to open the nursery without changing her clothes or combing her hair. Julia saw the nursery's books scattered in the living room one evening and scanned them. She knew little about keeping ledgers, but she could tell things weren't right. Entry dates were irregular, and columns weren't totaled. Unpaid bills, some of them months old, were stuffed inside the check book.

Income was eroding and so was their close relationship. Julia watched helplessly as her mother paid less attention or grew angry for no apparent reason. Home was no longer the safe haven it had been. If she tried asking what was wrong, her mother waved her away with a vague flapping motion. Julia's bewilderment slowly turned to anger, and she stayed away as much as possible. She discovered a growing interest in journalism and became the lead writer for the high school newspaper. She loved interviewing fellow students and covering news events. Most of all, she enjoyed seeing her articles in print and knowing others were reading them. It was the one bright spot in the gathering storm clouds of her life;

it was a brief and wondrous ride.

The hammer fell one afternoon when she went to the nursery after school and found it closed. She raced home to an empty house and frantically searched the neighborhood for some trace of her mother. An anxiety-ridden hour passed before a police car pulled into the driveway. Mother sat in the back seat with a blanket pulled up to her chin. The officer explained that she had gone to the supermarket dressed only in her pajama top. No charges were being filed, but he strongly urged her mother to see a doctor. Not knowing where else to turn, Julia asked the Howards for help, and they took her mother to a local clinic. The doctor's diagnosis was Alzheimer's. Julia had never heard of the disease, and she had a difficult time understanding it. She only knew that it was ravaging her mother's mind, and nothing would ever be the same again.

The crunch of feet on the stone footpath behind her snapped Julia back to the present, and when she remembered where she was, she shivered and glanced around, half-expecting to see the Chinese assailant from two night's ago. It was only an elderly woman taking a morning stroll, but Julia's eyes darted nervously about, and she pulled her coat more tightly around her to ward off the chill.

She assumed Mark Hansen was close by, although she couldn't see him. The idea of having a personal bodyguard had been unsettling at first, but she was quickly getting used to the idea. The carport's episode hadn't dimmed in her mind. She could still feel those rough hands on her body, and it gave her comfort to know Mark was watching over her. But where was Mr. Andersen? Julia began to fear something had happened.

"I thought this would be an innocuous place to meet until other arrangements could be made." The unexpected voice behind her made Julia jump with fright. She whirled around to find Mr. Andersen standing a few feet away.

"You startled me," she gasped, trying to catch her breath.

"My apologies. I've been watching for signs of unwanted visitors, but we seem safe enough. Come, there's a bench nearby that captures what little sunshine there is this morning. We can sit there and talk."

He led her along a gravel pathway to a wooden bench, where the thin light struggled through an opening in the surrounding trees.

"Events have progressed more rapidly than I expected," he mused once they were seated. "It raises some issues we must consider. Liu Kwong is a dangerous man, and he's central to our discussions. However, I fear your port investigation may be the real reason you were accosted. You've stepped into a dangerous quagmire. Last night was not an idle gesture, although I don't think he meant to actually harm you. At least not yet. I believe he intended to give you a good scare, then let you go.

"But, you must ask yourself if your investigation and our meetings are worth pursuing. Kwong will do whatever is necessary to prevent your inquiries from reaching fruition. Li Chang's demise is proof of that. If you wish to continue, there will be risks and rewards. I can bring you information that will be helpful, and you're in safe hands with Mark. He's quite good at this sort of thing. Trained as a secret service agent. Of course, if you would rather not go on, I will understand completely."

Mr. Andersen spoke softly, but his words blazed in the morning air with the heat of a dozen suns. Julia's world had always been insulated from violence. Murders and mayhem were things she wrote about but never experienced first-hand. All that was changing. She remembered her helplessness while lying under that bed in the empty house, and when she was seized in her carport. She thought about a woman named Li Chang, who she never met, and Romeo, who had disappeared. This was no longer about bedtime stories; it was about life and death. The idea of facing such an ordeal made her shudder. She pulled her coat around her body just as she had earlier, but this time it was a symbolic gesture, one meant to ward off the menacing forces of evil encroaching on her world. It didn't help.

She could feel Andersen's eyes on her as she sorted through her feelings. What risks was he taking, she wondered, and why? In the end, it didn't matter. She was facing a moment of truth about herself: whether she had the courage to confront a peril that threatened her comfortable life. She was being tested. If she gave up now, she would relegate herself to the backwaters of reporting for the rest of her career. She would live her life as a coward. If she proceeded, she sensed her trials would redefine her as a person.

And when it came right down to it, she had to admit that curiosity held her firmly in its grip, and it wasn't about to let go no matter how hard she struggled. She had to hear the rest of the old man's story, which had drawn her into a whirlpool of hidden card rooms and misty streets. She was dying to know if Kathy went to the Fior d'Italia Restaurant. She could only pray that this time curiosity wouldn't kill the cat.

"We continue," she said with as much firmness as she could muster.

"Good." He slapped his hands on his knees. "I knew you had the spirit. We shall make a good team, you and I. Together, we shall persevere."

His enthusiasm lifted her spirits and gave her hope that she had made the right decision.

The sun finally broke through the clouds, producing a hazy glow that warmed Julia's body despite the cold air. Mr. Andersen settled back on the bench, and she realized he intended to continue his story with the whole world watching them. She leaned back as well, ready to become a time traveler, once more.

****

I had never been more tightly strung than when I prepared to leave for the Fior d'Italia and what I hoped would be a memorable dinner with Kathy. It was already dark outside when Godzilla walked through the door.

"My boss is downstairs," he said matter-of-factly, making it sound midway between a point of information and an order. I was beginning to wonder if they had telephones in Chinatown, but I was ready to leave anyway, so I followed him downstairs to the waiting limousine. This time, there was no overhead light when I got in. Only darkness.

"I hear you visited the Golden Moon last night. I keep an office there," Kwong said in a confiding tone. "I thought it was time we talked. What progress have you made in solving my problem?"

"These things usually take time. Her background is vague, but I believe that's where the answer will be found." I wondered how he knew of my visit. Had someone seen me there, or was I being followed? I could see his shape seated beside me but not his face. I thought of the musical, The Phantom of the Opera. Kwong was the phantom. He could appear whenever he liked, but I never got a good look at him.

"So, you have decided to make contact with her. Do you think that will help?"

"Yes, I believe it will. But you must trust my methods." I wasn't sure I could trust them myself. Not after last night. I knew I couldn't explain them to Kwong.

"How much longer will it take?"

The question I had been anticipating. I had to stall him. I shrugged my shoulders. "Hard to say. A few weeks, perhaps. We're just starting the hard digging now."

"A few weeks may be too long." It was an innocent statement, but it had an ominous ring to it.

"You hired me to do a job. Let me do it. I expect to know more in the next week." This was a complete fabrication. I had no idea what I would know by then. I had no idea whether Kathy would even show up tonight. I just knew that I had to keep Liu Kwong's dogs away from her as long as possible while I figured something out.

"I will be in touch next week, then, unless you know something sooner."

Once again, Godzilla opened the door, signaling the end of our meeting, and I wondered how he knew when to do that. If there was a signal from Kwong, it was too dark for me to notice.

I hurried to my car and arrived at the restaurant shortly before eight o'clock. I parked across the street beside the quaint little park that filled the adjacent block and stared through the windows of the restaurant. Several people stood or sat at the long bar, which led to the dining rooms in back. There was no sign of Kathy, however. It seemed more appropriate to wait inside, so I entered, sat down at the bar, and ordered a scotch. The Fior d'Italia was one of San Francisco's classic establishments. I learned later that the man who poured my drink had tended bar there for over twenty years, and one of the waiters had worked there even longer.

Eight o'clock came and departed with the speed of a brief snow flurry. No matter. I wasn't going anywhere. I settled on my bar stool with as much trepidation as any schoolboy on his first real date and watched the well-dressed patrons stream past me to their waiting tables. San Francisco had always had a certain elegance and panache about it, even in the days of the Wild West. I remembered reading stories about wealthy residents hanging chandeliers in their horses' stables and fighting the fire following the 1906 earthquake with champagne. Many of the city's dwellers still dressed for social occasions, such as dinner and the theater. My own attire included a wool, herringbone suit and cuff-linked silk shirt. I hoped to make a fine impression.

Mind you, I had not forgotten the purpose of my rendezvous, to learn this woman's secrets and to spin my web. Neither had I forgotten about Liu Kwong's veiled threats. My professional integrity was still intact. I just hadn't expected to find my quarry so damned beguiling. Watching her was like listening to a symphony. No, it was more than that. It was like seeing musical notes floating in the air. I was beginning to wonder who was spinning the web and who was becoming ensnared.

It was a quarter-to-nine when I saw her step from a cab out front, and my heart rate jumped several notches. My gamble had paid off better than any poker hand I had ever played. Her entrance was pure Kathy Griffith. She greeted the maitre d' like an old friend and waved to the bartender as she approached me. Her simple, black dress expressed the understated elegance of someone with extraordinary taste, and her face glowed with so much vitality, I hardly recognized the woman I had faced across last night's poker table.

"You came." What a stupid opening remark! I had never felt so foolish in my life. Her late arrival had put her in control of the evening's events, and we both knew it.

"I almost didn't." She smiled at a passing waiter who greeted her.

"We've lost our reservation," was all I could think to say.

"Taken care of. Peter has a table for us."

No sooner had she spoken, before the waiter who had just greeted her returned with menus and led us to a small side room filled with black-and-white, autographed photographs of Tony Bennett, a well-known singer from the seventies and eighties. Half-a-dozen tables filled the room. Only one was empty. It had obviously been reserved for us. No, that was incorrect. It had been reserved for Kathy. I was just extra baggage.

Peter, our waiter, treated her more like an old friend than a customer. His familiarity didn't surprise me. It was the same with everyone, and I could see why. She was Santa Claus distributing happiness the way others give gifts. I ordered my second scotch and told myself to make it last. Kathy ordered a bottle of a very fine chardonnay.

"Peter already knows this dinner will be billed to me. If that bothers you, we can enjoy our drinks and leave." She said this without umbrage, her face suddenly masked and aloof. It felt as if we were playing poker again, and I suppose in a way we were.

"After all," she continued, "I do owe you."

This caught me off guard. "Why?"

"You told me I was telegraphing my bets. It didn't take me long to figure it out. Once I did, I played your two friends like cats with string. When the night was finished, they were out nearly $20,000 between them."

I laughed outright at this news, and my outburst softened the hard exterior she was trying so hard to maintain. "It couldn't have happened to two more deserving old buzzards. I'm sorry I missed it."

After the drinks arrived, Kathy became steely-eyed again. "Now, tell me. Why am I having dinner with a man whose name I don't know, in my favorite restaurant at his invitation? What are the odds of that, do you think? A thousand to one?"

"Five hundred, perhaps. It would depend on the number of good restaurants in the city," I smiled.

She didn't. "Our evening together stops at drinks if you can't explain it to me."

It was time to spin more half-truths hidden in lies. "I'm a private investigator. I was hired to watch someone you were seeing, and I learned a little about you in the process. I very much liked what I learned."

"Harry Webster."

"Pardon?"

"You were investigating Harry Webster. He's a slick con artist. Nearly took me for a great deal of money. I hope you nailed the bastard."

I still couldn't get used to the poker playing, swearing side of this woman. It simply didn't fit the cover girl image she portrayed most of the time.

"Let's just say my client was pleased, and in the process I became quite enamored with you. You made enough of an impression for me to risk playing cards last night and to invite you to your favorite restaurant."

"Why did you do that, invite me here?" That impish smile I had seen in her photograph was starting to play at the corners of her mouth.

"So you would come. If I'd asked you to join me anyplace else, you would've declined."

She thought about that a moment and smiled. "Yes, I suppose you're right." Her smile made me want to dance on the table. The ice had been broken.

"I rest my case. And my name, by the way, is Tom Person." I held out my hand, and she shook it. Touching her skin was like caressing a Stradivarius violin. I could feel a century of music flowing through my fingertips. I had never touched anything so precious or refined, and my heart did summersaults.

I lifted the menu to my face to hide the deep red that had seeped to the surface of my skin and tried to concentrate on the choices before me. The Italian dishes swam in confusion. I chose the veal scaloppini as though I were a drowning sailor grasping a life raft.

"Try the Caesar's salad," Kathy suggested. I could feel her eyes surveying me, trying to decide whether I was made of a valuable mineral or fool's gold. "It's very good here."

Kathy ordered the salad and halibut. I followed her advice about the salad. Dinner was a delicious affair. I was bewitched before the main course was served and besotted by dessert. I was in real trouble, and I knew it. All objectivity was lost. All I could think about was how to save this enchantress from the evil that lurked beyond our little room, and how to interest her in seeing me again.

"Tell me what you learned about Harry Webster," Kathy commanded as we delved into our meals. She tossed the name on the table as casually as the ace of spades. An awkward silence followed as I tried to think how to respond to her question. Was she testing me or merely curious about my investigation? Had she seen through my earlier white lie?

"As you said, he was a con artist. Beyond that I'm not at liberty to say. Client confidence and all that." It was a lame answer, but Kathy accepted it without complaint. I cringed when I saw how quickly my lie was taking root.

"And what were your impressions of me?" Her eyes danced with teasing humor as she sipped her second glass of wine. I was still nursing my second scotch but was sorely tempted to order another.

"That you are terribly smart, wonderful with children, and a heck of a poker player." I raised my nearly empty glass to toast her.

There was another awkward pause. We both knew there should be more to the story of Kathy Griffith: where she grew up, what frightened her and made her happy as a child, what happened to her parents, why over half her life was missing. I chose not to confront her past, however, which was quite out of character for me. As I said, I had lost my objectivity. I broached the subject of Liu Kwong, instead.

"Of course, I have stayed abreast of current events. I know you have been seeing someone new."

The magic faded from her eyes, and I feared I had ruined the evening. But her expression became pensive rather than angry, making her look like a little girl who had suddenly become lost.

"Those gossip columns are awful." It was all she said, and I hadn't the courage to pursue it.

We parted that evening without touching each other again. No more hand shakes. No brushing of cheeks or kiss. I made a tactical decision not to press her for another date. Something told me I would do better if our budding relationship retained some mystery, at least for a while. So, I thanked her for dinner and told her I would see her again. She gave me an odd smile that I interpreted as uncertainty about what to do with me. Then, she got into a cab and disappeared into the city's endless night.

I decided to check for messages at the office on the way home, but I hardly needed my car. I could have just as easily floated there on the waves of happiness that enfolded me. The evening had gone better than I had dared hope, and I looked forward to seeing Kathy again. The only blight on my glorious evening was the sealed envelope I found waiting for me under the office door. *Death will come to you* was once again neatly pasted in newsprint letters across a single sheet of paper. I thought about installing a surveillance camera outside the office, but decided not to waste the time or money. It was most likely a cry for attention by some demented soul who needed therapy. One of the Arnold Grants of the world. But I would keep an eye out.

My first two meetings with Kathy had been bewitching, but they had not brought me any closer to solving my riddle. I had to find out who she really was, and fast, before Kwong lost patience. The next step was obvious--search her home for clues to her hidden past--but I dithered. I told myself it was because of her unpredictable schedule. If I were caught there, any chance of seeing her again would be sacrificed. But I knew the real reason for my hesitation. I dreaded what I might find. The Kathy Griffith I was beginning to know was as perfect as that Stradivarius violin. Every time she spoke or smiled or brushed her hair back was like listening to a performance by a great virtuoso. I didn't want to tarnish that image with whatever she was hiding. So, I procrastinated and waited for the right opportunity to see her again.

For the next two days I trailed her with great caution, certain she would try to catch me doing so. But she went about her business without so much as a backward glance. This worried me more than being spotted; I began to fear I had made no impression on her at all. Her friend, Emily, joined her after work the second evening, and they talked endlessly together in a small tavern near Kathy's home. They looked like sisters with their similar hairstyles and clothing, although Emily was much plainer and a few pounds heavier.

I was seated in my car watching them through the tavern's window. It was a dark street, making it difficult to see anything beyond the reach of the streetlamps, but when a car's headlights suddenly flared down the street, I saw a hint of movement in the alley behind me. It was nothing more than a shift in the shadows, a mere impression of motion in my rear view mirror, but it was enough to tell me I wasn't alone. I pulled out the gun I kept under my seat and disconnected the interior light so it wouldn't come on when I opened my door. Then I slid out of the car onto the pavement. As long as I kept the car between the alley, and myself I remained out of sight. I estimated the alley to be less than a hundred yards away, a distance I could cover in a few seconds on the run. I crept to the rear of the car, gathered myself and sprinted towards the alley. My unexpected assault trapped the intruder before he could flee.

"Stay where you are and show yourself," I commanded, my pistol braced in both hands.

"Easy does it, Tom," a voice replied. The man stood up from his hiding place and walked towards me until a nearby streetlight revealed the flushed face and owlish expression of Patrick Parker. His eyes shifted furtively from my face to my weapon. "No need for the gun."

"What the hell are you doing here, Parker?" I demanded. I had never cared much for him. He called himself a private investigator, but he spent much of his time doing less reputable tasks, such as intimidating people and collecting money owed his employers. He was known to beat those who couldn't make their payments on time. There had always been an undercurrent of jealousy and rivalry between us--on Parker's part, not mine. He saw himself as my competitor, as someone with the potential to become a separatist. In truth, he had neither the brains nor the talent for it and was, at best, a mediocre investigator. He wanted my respect, but I found it hard to feel more than sympathy for him. Now, I had caught him watching Kathy or me or both, and I wanted to know why.

"We have a mutual client, although I've been working for him a lot longer than you," he replied with an attempt at bravado. I frowned at him but suspected my look of displeasure was lost in the dim light. I only had one client at the moment, and I didn't relish the idea that Parker might be involved with him, as well.

"That still doesn't tell me why you're spying on me."

"I'm not watching you, well indirectly maybe, but only because you're following the Griffith woman." He said the name like it was spoiled goods, and I had to resist the urge to hit him.

Every fiber in my body was screaming a warning to me. If Liu Kwong had Patrick Parker trailing Kathy, she was in real danger. I had understood that from the beginning, of course, but now the danger had a name and face attached to it, a face I wanted to obliterate. I was teetering on the edge of violence, and I could feel my finger tightening around the trigger of my gun. My anger frightened me. The gun trembled in my hand as I took deep breaths and tried to bring myself under control. I thought wildly about rushing to the tavern and warning Kathy, but that would be a futile gesture. It would only confuse her, and it would betray myself to Liu Kwong.

No, what I had to do was deal with Parker. He had never struck me as the sort of person who could commit murder. He didn't have the backbone for it. Bottom line, he had more bully in him than courage. My anger subsided as I assessed the situation more calmly. Perhaps, I could make use of my colleague.

"It wouldn't do to work at cross purposes." I put my gun away and suppressed a smile as I watched the tension ease from Parker's body. "Why are you following Kathy Griffith, when I'm the one working a contract on her?"

"Mr. Kwong likes to cover his bets. He often uses me to keep an eye on his projects. See that things are going as expected."

"Like reporting on my progress?"

The way he nodded reminded me of a schoolboy caught smoking behind the gym.

"Then, why don't we help each other? Two-heads-better-than-one. That sort of thing."

Parker's eyes blinked rapidly, telling me I had caught him by surprise. "How could we do that?" Curiosity mixed with apprehension in his voice.

"I keep you informed on how I'm doing. Makes you look good with Kwong. In exchange, you stop shadowing me, because I'll know if you do, and I'll put a stop to it." I let the threat hang in the air for a few heartbeats. "And you share anything you think I should know."

"Like what?" Suspicion replaced curiosity in his voice.

"Hard to say, but you're an experienced investigator. I'm sure I can rely on you to use good judgment." My praise spread over him as smoothly as honey on toast. He couldn't resist such glowing words.

"I can't do anything that would jeopardize my position with Kwong." His tone was plaintive.

"Understood, but, Kwong's a dangerous man. Someone to be wary of. We'd just watch each other's back, is all. Make sure there are no nasty surprises."

Parker's face twisted into a smile that told me we had a deal. Trusting him was the last thing I could do, but I needed to gain an edge while I figured out how to help Kathy. I was making a pact with the devil, but I didn't care if it kept her out of harm's way.

The following day, Kathy skipped lunch and rode her bicycle to the park. Twice, I doubled back on my route to confirm that Parker wasn't following me, then hurried to a nearby deli to order a picnic basket filled with fresh fruits, cheeses, and sourdough bread and stopped at a liquor store for a bottle of their finest champagne. When I returned to the park, I found her seated in her favorite meadow reading a book and eating a raw carrot. The sunshine revealed red highlights in her hair, something I hadn't noticed before. The lemony aroma of freshly cut grass drifted up from under my feet as I slipped up behind her.

"Can I buy you lunch?"

Kathy closed her book but didn't turn around. "I'm dieting. Too much dinner the other night." Her voice had a lilt to it that sounded like music.

I plopped the basket down in front of her and joined her on the grass. Her eyes twinkled with amusement, as if she had been expecting me to surprise her, and I had succeeded.

"A nibble or two should be safe enough. Perhaps a strawberry in champagne." I grinned at her foolishly and began working the stopper from the bottle. It popped dramatically, spilling bubbly all over my shoes while I tried to pour the champagne into two plastic glasses.

Kathy laughed at my performance. "I should be quite upset, you know. This proves that you are following me. How do I know you're not a stalker?"

"Stalkers don't bring champagne. Only admirers. Are you angry with me?

"Complimented, but I hope in the future you'll use more conventional methods."

"Like telephones and such."

"And such."

I decided to play my rakish role to the limit and held a strawberry to her mouth as I handed her the champagne. She clamped her teeth around the red fruit, and I felt the caress of her lips on my fingers. It was like touching a doorknob after walking across thick carpeting. Tiny shock waves shivered through my fingers and up my arm.

"Tolstoy's War and Peace." I nodded to her book. "Impressive reading."

"I love Russian authors. My third time around for this one." She shielded her eyes with her hand to study my face. "What do you like to read?"

"Nothing so intellectual. An occasional novel. Depends on the dust jacket." Not the sort of answer to impress the lady, but for once I was being honest. She made a face at me, then opened her mouth for another strawberry. I complied with pleasure.

"Will you come to the card club again?"

My palms grew sweaty at her question. "Not sure. Not to gamble. That would finish me. If it's the only way to see you, I might."

Her expression lost its twinkle and became serious. "It's not. Please don't do that because of me. I'll gladly meet you elsewhere." Her words had the ring of church bells.

"But not Saturday night."

She laughed. "There are six other nights in the week, you know."

"I want them all," I shouted to the sky. People stared. "But I'll settle for tomorrow."

"Can't. I'll be out of town. Back Friday."

"Friday night, then. Six o'clock. Shall I pick you up?"

"I'll meet you. Tell me where."

"Fisherman's Wharf, in front of Alliotto's. Try to be on time for a change." I grinned at her and got another smile.

We sat quietly, nibbling the fruits and cheeses and drinking champagne. Neither of us touched the bread. Children's voices whooped with delight from a nearby meadow. Birds called to one another. A mother scolded a child. It was heaven, and I never wanted to leave.

"I have to go now." She stood up abruptly.

"Did I bore you?" I was only half teasing.

"No." She thought for a moment. "It was lovely sharing such a peaceful moment. Not something I've been able to do with many people." She touched my cheek with her hand. More shivers. "You're a very different sort of man. I'm glad you took the risk to meet me. See you Friday."

I watched her mount her bicycle and ride away. I was rooted to the spot and might have remained there indefinitely, if a wayward Frisbee hadn't skimmed past my nose. I retrieved it and tossed it back to the apologetic couple, gathered the remnants of our picnic, and walked away on a cloud.

****

Julia had fallen into a dreamy trance, and it took her a minute to realize it wasn't her in the park. She blinked and saw the arboretum, instead. Something significant had been revealed in that park, however. A name. Tom Person. It danced in the air as lightly as an autumn leaf twirling towards the ground. When she glanced at the man beside her, however, she couldn't visualize Tom Person, the man in the story. All she saw was Mr. Andersen. It was as if they were two different people, and Tom Person had lived in another lifetime. If he *had* existed, there would be data files on him. Mr. Andersen had just given her a window into his past.

"Mark will bring you some papers tonight that should prove helpful in your investigation. In the meantime, I'll be arranging a new meeting place. He'll tell you where. Shall we continue tomorrow evening?" Mr. Andersen rose to his feet and stretched to rid himself of the discomfort of the hard bench.

At the mention of Mark's name, Julia glanced around, half expecting to see him watching them, but there was no sign of him. "Tomorrow night will be fine," she replied.

"I will take my leave, then. Perhaps you should wait a few

minutes before following."

Julia stared after the retreating figure as he leaned on his cane and performed his familiar half-shuffle along the pathway. She didn't know how long she sat on the bench. She was vaguely aware of a light breeze rustling the leaves above her head and the sound of feet crunching along the pebbled path behind her. When she was certain he was gone, she left the arboretum and hurried to her car. She wanted to get to her office as quickly as possible. She wanted to learn all she could about Tom Person.

CHAPTER NINE

Julia didn't think she could ever face Thomas Andersen again. Not after the stomach-wrenching information she learned about Tom Person.

The databases revealed an uneven childhood. When he was eleven, his mother left his father and dragged him around the country for three years while she did odd jobs. An uncle took him in about the time he was starting high school. Tom did well in school: excellent grades, lots of friends, and football running back. He'd received a scholarship and played college football, but he blew out the right knee junior year, ending his football career. He married his college sweetheart and went to work as a salesman for an insurance company.

Tom started gambling a few years later and quickly developed a passion for poker, often playing in the big games in Las Vegas. His downfall came when he lost all his money and his house in a high-stakes game that lasted for three days and nights. His wife divorced him, and he drifted from job-to-job, working just enough to feed his poker habit. He began drinking too much and living out of his car.

Then, he met a private investigator, Eddie Randal, in a poker game in San Francisco. Eddie took him under his wing and hired him on the condition that he stop gambling. He made Tom visit a counselor who worked with him on his poker obsession for more than a year. It proved to be a good investment. Tom quit gambling and became Eddie's best investigator. When Eddie retired, Tom took over the firm and built it into a lucrative business by becoming a separatist.

But none of these facts mattered. They were merely words describing the events in one's life. It was the last item that reached out and smacked her in the head, the entry that said *Tom Person was wanted for the murder of Kathy Griffith!* Julia read the line over and over, until her stomach rebelled and she had to rush to the bathroom. She stood over the sink, retched, and stared in horror at the train-wreck image in the mirror: face beaded with moisture, hair scattered in damp disarray about her forehead, cheeks streaked like dirty windowpanes, red veins bulging in her eyes.

How could he have murdered Kathy, someone he obviously loved? Or had he only been obsessed with her? Was Andersen's story a fabrication? Then, why reveal his true name? Julia stared at the mirror, demanding answers. There had to be answers.

She studied herself more closely. The shock of her discovery had ravaged her far more than it should have. It wasn't just the knowledge that Tom Person could have done something so horrible to someone he cared about. It was the realization that she had begun to identify with Kathy, had begun to feel a kinship with her. Kathy had filled the black hole left by the departure of Jackie. Julia knew it was a silly notion, but she couldn't help it. She felt the loss of Kathy deep inside her. In an odd sort of way, she felt that she, too, had been murdered.

She splashed cold water on her face, fixed her disheveled hair, and gathered the strength to return to her computer. She had to read the rest of that terrible, final entry. Kathy's body was never found, but her bloody bedroom offered stark evidence to her fate. DNA samples proved it was her blood. The murder weapon had Andersen's . . . Person's fingerprints on it. Traces of her blood were also found in Person's car and on clothing in his apartment. Kathy's neighbors had seen them together on numerous occasions, until one day when a loud argument seemed to end their relationship. Kathy reportedly threw him out of the house, declaring she never wanted to see him again. A week later she disappeared, and so did he. A wealthy, Chinese businessman, Liu Kwong, offered a large reward for information leading to Person's arrest, but he vanished as mysteriously as a puff of smoke. The case was still technically open, although no one had worked it in years.

Julia was still reeling when she got home that night. Nothing in Andersen's demeanor or story had prepared her for what she had discovered. She walked around her apartment in a stupor, her head too fuzzy to think about fixing dinner. Her stomach was far too upset to eat, anyway. She settled for a stiff drink, which helped calm her nerves, then poured a second one and sat glumly on her couch trying to decide what to do. Mark was supposed to bring her documents that would help her investigation. Originally, she had thought about inviting him to stay for dinner. Now, she wasn't sure she could face him. The idea of seeing Andersen again seemed even more absurd. There were legal issues to consider, such as reporting him to the police. She wondered what the statute of limitations was on murder.

By the time her door-entry voice system informed her that she had a visitor waiting downstairs, she was lightheaded and in a state of deep melancholy. She didn't bother checking the monitor to verify if it was Mark before letting him in the building. Being kidnapped suddenly seemed very appealing. It would take the responsibility for making decisions out of her hands. The terrifying memory of her helplessness in the grip of the Chinaman's powerful arm and the sinister smell of the chloroform quickly dispelled that idea, however, and in a moment of panic, she looked around her apartment for a place to hide. All she could think to do was to crawl under her bed. I'm tipsy, she thought giddily. One more drink, and I won't care about anything at all.

Mark's expression when she opened her door told her just how bad her mental and physical state had become. He took her arm and guided her to the couch. *Why do I always end up on the couch when he's around? Must be something Freudian.* Her thoughts were vague, confused. She wanted to sleep but didn't think her mind would let her.

"What happened?" he asked anxiously.

"I know about Tom Person." Her words were slurred, but she wasn't sure if it was the effects of the alcohol or her brain shutting down. "I know what he did."

Mark laid a folder of papers on the table, sat down next to her, and took her hand. His brown eyes gazed directly into hers, penetrating her skull and pushing away the bewilderment that had wormed its way into her mind.

"He gave you his name."

She nodded.

"Do you think it was by accident? He wanted you to research his past. I believe he's testing you. He wants to see if he can trust you."

"And what about you?" she asked angrily. "You work for him. Why should I trust *you*?"

Mark's eyes narrowed. His face mutated itself to a steely expression, and the muscles tightened along his jaw. "I work for myself, not Andersen. He hired me to protect you. I think I proved that the other night." The hard edge to his voice told Julia just how incensed he was. She immediately regretted her accusation. He *had* saved her, and she desperately needed to believe in someone.

"I can't think about it anymore tonight." She flung her arms around Mark and nestled her head under his strong, square jaw. She smelled musk mingled with the odors of a man who had put in a long day. She inhaled his pleasing aroma and closed her eyes.

A warm finger of sunlight caressed Julia's face, awakening her. She covered her eyes with her forearm and willed herself back to sleep, but the metallic clang of a frying pan and the fragrance of cooking bacon swept away her drowsiness. Someone was rummaging in her kitchen. For an instant, she feared the Chinaman had returned, and she sat bolt upright on her bed. The sudden movement set off an explosion of fireworks inside her head. She sat very still, waiting for the pain to subside, and discovered she was still in her street clothes. Why hadn't she undressed before going to bed? The clatter of dishes added to the noise coming from the kitchen. No intruder would make that much racket, or cook bacon. Then, she remembered Mark, and yesterday's unhappy memories swarmed over her. She recalled drinking but not eating. As she sat there, the pounding in her head subsided to a dull ache, but an angry stomach joined it.

Julia desperately wanted a cup of coffee, but she couldn't face Mark in her condition. Her skin felt like week-old bread, crusty and stale. She fled to the bathroom to repair herself, but the reflection in the mirror looked beyond hope. After a few feeble attempts to do something about the red mark where her cheek had been pressed against the pillow, the smudged eyeliner, and her cactus-shaped hair, she gave up and headed for the kitchen. It was no way to greet a man in the morning, but she was beyond caring.

"I've fixed some breakfast," Mark announced brightly. "Hope you like it."

Eggs, bacon, and toast sat on the kitchen table. And coffee. She reached for the coffee as if she were seeking absolution. They sat facing each other across the oak table. She watched Mark remove the crust from his toast and eat it dry. No butter or jam. She was pleased to see that he looked almost as disheveled as she did. The stubble on his face was dark. It wouldn't take him long to grow a beard. The file folder he had brought last night rested between them.

"Where did you sleep?" Julia cringed at the idea that she might have had sex last night. Not that the thought of "doing it" with Mark didn't appeal to her, but she couldn't remember a damned thing. The idea that she might have done something she should remember, but couldn't, made her feel foolish.

"On the couch. A bit small for me, but I survived."

"Sorry." She smiled inwardly at the news and silently thanked the fates for watching over her.

Mark shook his head. "I've slept in worse situations." He

paused. "We need to talk about Mr. Andersen, when you're up to it."

"He murdered the woman he loved." Her voice was melancholy. She needed an explanation, some kernel of reason to relieve her agony. "I don't know how I can continue with any of this: the story, the investigation, or the meetings." Julia toyed with her eggs, but discovered her stomach wasn't ready to handle food just yet. She settled for more coffee and a piece of dry toast.

Julia found it hard to imagine Mr. Andersen as Tom Person. She'd begun to like Andersen, but now the shadowy face of Person loomed before her when she thought of him. Person was someone from another place in time, someone who murdered people, but he was linked to Andersen. It was impossible to separate the two.

"If you don't, you'll always regret not knowing the entire story." His eyes shone in the morning light, and Julia suddenly wanted to devour him. She decided that was a good sign. It told her she could trust this man and that her emotions were returning to normal. She was starting to feel in control again. Julia particularly liked the fact that Mark was nearly her age. It gave her hope that she might eventually have a more normal relationship with a man. She watched him over the cup's rim while she sipped her coffee. His rugged, unshaven face was oddly appealing. The caffeine was doing its job of reviving her. Julia felt her curiosity about Andersen returning.

"You could tell me the story," she said at last.

"Don't know it all. Only pieces." He munched on his dry bread. He nodded to the folder. "You should take a look at this."

Julia hesitated. Opening the folder would signal her continuing commitment to Mr. Andersen. She fought her desire to see what was inside, but she knew Mark was right. She *would* regret never learning what happened and why Mr. Andersen had exposed himself to her. She sighed, flipped open the cover, and began reading the documents. There was a list of ships with containers arriving from China that had been cleared without inspections. Daniel Edwards, Port Authority Manager, had signed off on each of them. She had interviewed him during her initial coverage of the pending labor strike. He was a heavy-set man in his fifties, bald on top with thick, silver hair around the sides and back, the kind of man she might have found appealing. But the way he'd leered at her had made Julia squirm in her chair. She'd felt his eyes violating her, making her feel dirty and used. When they were finished, she'd rushed home and scrubbed herself, just as she had done after being with Phillip. Edwards had given her the usual platitudes about management's need to contain costs and the union's demands for more job security. In effect, he had been non-committal and uncooperative.

She looked at the last entry in the shipping lists. "There's a ship due in port today with three containers that have already been cleared by Edwards." Excitement bubbled up inside of her and her fingers tingled. "I have to see those containers when they're unloaded." She leapt up from the table and rushed back to the bedroom to wash up and change.

"Let me take you," Mark called after her. "It's easier than following you. But, first, what about your meeting with Mr. Andersen tonight? I think you should keep it."

"I still don't know if I'm up to it." Julia wanted to tell Mark to cancel, but she hesitated. Why *did* Mr. Andersen let her know who he was? He had invited her to discover his terrible secret. It made no sense, unless he was seeking forgiveness. Her reporter's instincts told her not to let go. Whatever the explanation, there was a story behind it that she must pursue. But she didn't want to face him on his own turf.

"Tell him if he wants to see me he can come here," she said at last.

By the time Julia re-emerged from the bedroom, she had washed away the eyeliner and managed to bring her unruly hair under control. She was pleased to see approval in Mark's smile.

The docks were an anarchism of noise and motion. Engines roared. Cranes whirred. Voices shouted. Sweating workers and giant, spider-shaped haulers glistened in the sun as they muscled shipping containers around the yards. Ships sat bow-to-stern in the harbor, caught in the backlog of the work stoppage, and everybody was laboring under the stress of unloading them during the cooling-off period. Julia worried that they wouldn't locate their ship in such a jumble, but Mark pulled a pair of binoculars from his satchel and began checking ship registration numbers against the log he had shown her that morning.

"There it is." He pointed to a boat resting by a side pier well removed from the confusion of the main docks. "I'd say from the way it's riding so high in the water, its cargo has been emptied. Wonder why it hasn't been moved to make way for another ship."

Julia stared at the black hull. It reminded her of a vulture waiting for an unsuspecting prey. There was no sign of activity. The ship had an abandoned look about it. It was a ghost ship, unseen in the midst of the boisterous activity along the waterfront.

Mark approached the warning signs for the electronic fence guarding the docks and produced a device that reminded Julia of the old hand-held computers she had seen in classic movies.

"If we break the beams in the fence, it'll alert the guards," he explained, "but I can bend the beams and create an opening for us without raising an alarm." He activated the device, and a band of light illuminated the previously invisible blue beams in front of them. Julia watched with fascination as he rotated a convex dial and began to bend the beams downward. He maneuvered a dozen beams in this manner, until he had created a 10'x10' "hole" in the shimmering barrier. Mark stood back and looked at his work with satisfaction. "That should be large enough for us to slip through undetected."

The idea of casually walking through an energy field powerful enough to fry her hair gave her pause. The opening glowered at Julia with an evil eye, and she hesitated in front of it. Mark took her hand and gave her a reassuring smile. "It's safe. Just don't touch anything."

She could hear the electrons snapping at her as she followed him through the fence, but the warmth of his hand gave her confidence. She sighed with relief, however, when they were safely on the other side. At first, the random chaos of so many workers and containers seemed to defy any order, but on closer inspection, they found a sequence of letters and numbers that followed an orderly pattern. The containers were stacked five high in rows running the length of several football fields. The rows were identified by letters, and the containers by numbers. They slipped into the canyons of giant metal boxes and began working their way forward. Julia tried to remain calm, but her dry mouth and shallow breathing betrayed her nerves. Voices echoed around them, startling her, but no one appeared. One of the spider-shaped haulers roared past the end of their row, and they pressed themselves against the metal wall until it was gone. They proceeded without further incident, but when they reached the row they were seeking, they found a gap in the numbers. The containers they wanted were missing.

"They've been stored someplace else," Mark concluded. "My guess would be somewhere out of sight. Maybe in the warehouse by the side pier." He pointed in the direction of the ship, but Julia could see nothing over the skyscraper walls surrounding her.

They turned to retrace their steps when a small skip loader entered their aisle. The driver glared at them and jumped down from his rig. "You don't belong here," he said in a challenging voice as he strode towards them. He was a strapping man who looked like he was used to handling trouble.

Mark smiled and withdrew a badge from his pocket. "We're with the agricultural department. We got reports of a beetle coming in from Asia. Could ruin our tomato crops. Can you point us in the direction of the produce containers? We kind of got turned around in here."

The man eyed them suspiciously. "You come with me. I'll take you to the foreman. He'll straighten you out." When the man turned back towards his rig, Mark stepped forward and delivered a single blow with his hand to the back of the man's neck. It was over so quickly, Julia wasn't certain what had happened. One moment the worker was standing there looking like a menacing guard dog, the next he was lying on the ground. She put her hand to her mouth and stared at the fallen body. It was her second encounter with violence in the last three days, and she found both incidents alarming.

"Will he be all right?" she asked nervously.

"He'll be fine, other than a headache when he comes around." Mark dragged the fallen figure behind the loader. "We better move fast, before someone realizes he's missing."

They walked at a brisk pace towards the warehouses, but when they reached the last row of containers, Mark raised his hand and stopped abruptly. Three black vans were parked in front of the warehouse, guarded by men with gleaming laser guns. It was impossible to get closer without being spotted.

"Best to wait here. See what happens." Mark knelt down so Julia could see over him. Her heart still pounded from their encounter with the driver. She drew in a deep breath and crouched down next to her companion. She could smell the slightly acrid odor of his sweat mingling with aftershave lotion and hair oil. It was an appealing combination. When she looked at his muscled back, she wondered how he looked without a shirt. The thought made her cheeks blaze in embarrassment.

A commotion in front of the building caught her attention, and she quickly looked back towards the warehouse. A door swung open and several men emerged leading three groups of young, Chinese women. Julia realized they must be the smuggled women Romeo had told her about. She stared at them in disbelief. It was hard to imagine anyone in this day and age selling women into bondage, yet there they were, dressed in the kind of grey, baggy pants and shirts Julia associated with prison inmates. The distance was too great for her to see their faces clearly, but she could tell from the way they hunched their shoulders and bowed their heads that they were afraid. She grabbed her satellite communicator from her pocket and began photographing the scene with the system's built-in camera. As the women were herded to the vans, one stumbled and was immediately smacked with an open hand by a guard. Julia flinched at the blow, her feelings swirling in a mixture of sympathy and rage. She had to turn her head away to keep from shouting an obscenity at the abusive man. Just as the doors of the vans were opened, an alarm blared across the docks in a series of loud, steady beeps. The lookouts swept the grounds with their eyes, and then ran to join the others at the vans. The women were grabbed by their necks and arms and shoved inside. Engines roared to life as the doors closed, and the caravan sped away towards an exit gate at the far end of the yard.

Mark sprang to his feet. "They found the driver. Time to go." He took Julia's arm and guided her back the way they had come. They had covered less than fifty yards when she heard dogs barking.

"Guard dogs. They'll find us in no time." Mark signaled to Julia to stop. "We're going up top." He pointed to small handrails forming ladders up the sides of the containers.

Julia glanced up at the stacked containers and quickly looked down at her feet. Mark wanted her to climb to the top of those things! Just the thought of it caused a familiar pressure to start building behind her eyes. She knew the signs: nausea, cramps burning in her stomach with the ferocity of hot coals, and fever-induced sweating. She experienced those symptoms anytime she faced an altitude of more than a few feet. The walls loomed above her head and taunted her.

Her hands had already grown moist at the idea of clinging to those tiny handrails, but before she could protest, Mark grasped her by the waist and lifted her up to the rails with surprising ease. "No time to waste. We've got to go."

His unexpected action gave her no time to think. She grabbed the rails and started to climb, keeping her eyes focused on the shiny metal surface just inches from her nose. She could hear Mark climbing below her, and she prayed he would catch her when she fell. The dogs' barks grew louder until they rebounded off the container walls around her. She tried to move faster, but her right foot slipped, causing her shoe to flip off and disappear into the chasm that hungrily waited for her below. The dogs yapped and howled with the unbridled excitement of fox hounds closing in for the kill. Stupidly, she glanced down at them, and her world spun off its axis. She gripped the rail above her head so tightly, she could feel her nails digging into her own skin.

But there was no time to gather her thoughts. Mark's hand was already pushing her upward again. "Can't stop now. We've gotta get to the top before the guards see us."

A fresh wave of nausea slammed into her stomach, but Julia refused to let her panic defeat her. She refocused her attention on the wall in front of her and started climbing again. Her bare foot felt more comfortable, so she kicked off her other shoe. She knew the dogs would pounce on it the moment it hit the ground. She imagined herself falling into those growling fangs and, for one terrifying moment, felt the dogs' teeth ripping her apart. *Get a grip*, she scolded herself. *Don't lose it now.* Each step seemed like her last. The sweat pouring down her face stung her eyes, and her wet hands slipped on the tiny rails. But her bare feet were surprisingly firm, and she urged them to propel her higher and higher.

She had read books about the elation climbers felt when they reached a mountain's summit. Julia had never experienced it, never reached the top of anything higher than a footstool, but when she finally grasped the ledge of the top container and pulled herself onto its hot, metal surface, exhilaration swept over her in a wave of joy. She sat on the fiery surface gasping for breath and looking up at the sky. The clouds were so close, she wanted to reach out and touch them. Around her, rows of containers spread away in every direction in a series of peaks and canyons. She forgot about the dogs and the guards as she surveyed the scene. It was so majestic! She was on top of a world she had never known before, and it took her breath away.

When Mark clambered alongside her, however, her mood dissolved and she returned to reality. They were trapped atop a row of shipping containers and surrounded by angry dogs. She was about to ask him what they should do when he pulled a tiny canister from his pocket and tossed it over the edge.

"Produces an offensive odor," he explained. "It will ruin the dogs' ability to track our scent. Lasts for about fifteen minutes, long enough for us to get away."

No sooner had he spoken, than the dogs stopped barking and began to whine. Mark hastily surveyed the surrounding containers. "It won't be long before a guard climbs up here looking for us, but with the dogs neutralized, we should be able to follow this row to the end and climb down before they find us."

Julia had been so elated to reach the top, she hadn't considered climbing down again. She wanted to sit there and enjoy her triumph, but Mark calmly took her hand and pulled her to her feet. He stood close enough for her to inhale that wonderful, manly odor she had smelled earlier. Was it her imagination, or was there a current running between them? Her mind and heart were racing out of control from the excitement of the climb, but her body was also vibrating with a sexual tension that surprised her. The energy she sensed pulsating between them was as powerful as the fence they had breached, and before she had time to consider what she was doing, she raised her head and kissed him. Mark's lips tasted like salty peanuts; their touch sent shivers down her arms and legs. It was over in a heartbeat, nothing more than one might expect between cousins, but it held her frozen to her spot. As she watched, an embarrassed smile played at the corners of his mouth. It was the only indication he gave that something unexpected had happened. Nothing seemed to confound the man. His gazed absorbed her, until Julia felt drained of all her fears. She drew strength from his unwavering courage, and despite the sweating hands and hot coals in her stomach, she was determined to do whatever it took to make him admire her, even climbing back down those containers.

"We'd better go," she said quietly.

Mark turned without saying a word and led the way along the ribbon of gleaming metal. The hot surface burned her feet, but she didn't mind. Mark's salty kiss lingered on her lips, and her euphoria at climbing so high carried her aloft as lightly as a feather. At any moment, she expected to take wing and fly away.

Shouting voices broke through her reverie. They echoed in the canyons below and mingled with the dogs' unhappy whines. A cry went up indicating the guards had discovered her shoes. In less than a minute, someone would climb the rails and spot them. They raced to the end of the row, and Mark slipped over the edge in an effortless motion. There was no time for Julia to consider what lay beyond that edge, no time for queasiness or tremulous hands. She squeezed her eyes shut and plunged after him. Once she had a firm grip on the rails, she opened her eyes and saw a figure emerge on top of the containers where they had stood moments earlier. She ducked her head and focused on the surface in front of her, just as she had done during the ascent. She could smell the sticky sweat pouring from her body. Her lungs were filled with air that refused to be expelled. She was drowning in a sea of oxygen. Her mind was spinning, but it didn't freeze the way she feared it would. Gaining the summit and kissing Mark had bolstered her courage. She ignored her fears and willed herself down each step with a new sense of confidence.

When her feet touched ground, she exhaled the stale air from her lungs and breathed in the sweet exhilaration of freedom. She was lightheaded with relief. It was only a stack of shipping containers, but she might as well have scaled Mt. Everest. Then a man's voice barked at them from above, and the spell was broken. Mark grabbed her hand, and they sprinted through the canyons of steel towards the fence's perimeter. The ground bit at her feet. Warm air rushed past her, brushing back her hair and exposing her forehead to the sun's warmth. A tangy smell of ocean water greeted her as they slipped back through the electronic gap in the fence. By the time they reached the car, Julia's sides ached from exertion, but she ignored the pain. She had gathered important evidence on the smuggling operation Romeo had told her about. She had climbed her own version of Mt. Everest. And she had shared a heady kiss with the man beside her. All in all, it had been an intoxicating day.

Once in the car, Julia retrieved her sat-com and replayed the photos she had taken of the Chinese women being led to the waiting vans. She touched the images with her fingertips. What must have been going through their minds? Torn from their families. Kidnapped, most likely, or lured by promises of a better life, then pressed into the hold of that ugly ship, and held prisoner

113

in a musty warehouse. Julia couldn't begin to fathom their pain and suffering. The warehouse's number was clearly visible. Dates and times were automatically recorded with the images. It should be possible to blow up the images enough to I.D. the guards and women. The evidence was clearly documented.

Julia's feet ached from running across hot metal and uneven pavements in her bare feet, but she asked Mark to drive her straight to the newspaper. He waited while she marched barefoot and disheveled into the newsroom and plopped the photo disk and file folder down on Phillip's desk. Annoyance at the unannounced interruption ruffled his brow. His eyes absorbed the details of her untidy appearance--wayward strands of hair falling across her face, a blouse and skirt that looked like they had been trampled by horses, no shoes--but he said nothing. Julia ignored him and pointed to the evidence.

"I nearly got torn apart by dogs getting these pictures," she announced in a voice intended to impress him. "Once you've reviewed them, put them in the safe with the file."

Phillip whistled when he read the documents. His annoyance vanished in a fluttering of raised eyebrows. "Where did you get this?"

Julia was pleased to hear the admiration mixed with curiosity in his voice. "Can't say, but I should have more shortly. When I get through with this story, you'll owe me more than a raise."

She turned and strode triumphantly from his office without looking back. She didn't have to. She could feel his eyes boring into her. Julia had never been so assertive with Phillip before. Climbing those containers had set her free in more ways than one. From now on, she was going to be someone to be reckoned with.

Mark said little during the drive home, and Julia wondered if her impulsive kiss was to blame. Not that he talked a lot in any case, but his silence at that moment made her feel like a misbehaved child. When they reached her apartment, he put the car in park but kept the engine running.

"Julia, I hope you'll understand, I'm under orders to protect you." He fiddled with the steering wheel, his eyes focusing on the dashboard. A siren wailed in the distance, and a dog answered it with a howl. "I don't want to do anything that might compromise that responsibility, such as becoming personally involved with you."

"Andersen's orders." Julia wasn't asking a question. He turned his face to her, and she looked him in the eye. Her heart was pounding the way it had when she looked down at those snarling dogs, but she maintained her composure. "Did you like our kiss?"

Mark's eyes evaded hers. "That's not the point."

Julia's stomach muscles tightened. Had she misread that magical moment atop the world, that moment when their lips briefly touched? She wanted to flee to the safety of her apartment, but she had to know. "I believe it is the point. Did you like our kiss, or not?"

The dog's howl had stopped. Silence permeated the car. "Yes, I liked it," Mark said at last. His voice was low, almost hushed. A hint of a smile broke through his stern expression. His eyes met hers. They were filled with a mixture of uncertainty and desire. "Then the hell with it." She leaned across the seat and kissed him full on the lips. It was no cousinly kiss this time. It was filled with hunger, and she could feel him responding with equal passion. Salty peanuts again. She loved the taste. "Good," she gasped, breaking away. "That's all I wanted to know."

She got out of the car without looking back and marched into her building. When she reached her apartment, she was grinning from ear to ear. It had been quite a day. She had never been so adventurous or brazen in her life, and it was wonderful.

The day's only drawback was the image of those women leaving the warehouse. Their bowed heads and shuffling feet haunted her. She tried to imagine squatting for days or weeks in the sightless hold of a yawing ship and shivered at the idea of it. She thought about the gun-toting guards who had herded them like cattle. What sort of men would do that? What sort of men would force women into bondage and sell them to the highest bidder? She knew who their leader was: Liu Kwong.

The name left a sour taste of lemons on her tongue, but so did

Mr. Andersen's, and if she continued meeting with him, she would be conspiring with a murderer who might be no better than Kwong. Well, he had said they could make use of each other, and she intended to use him long enough to bring down Liu Kwong.

CHAPTER TEN

Thomas Andersen was breathing heavily when Julia opened her door. "The lift is out of order. I do hope your landlord intends to fix it soon." He stepped inside and paused to catch his breath.

"It's an old building," she replied without compassion. "We don't mind the stairs." A room full of bats had been beating inside Julia's chest for the past hour in anticipation of Mr. Andersen's arrival. Her angry mood was mixed with apprehension. Mr. Andersen might be old, but he could still be dangerous. Was she taking a risk inviting a known murderer into her apartment? Not that there was any place to hide from him. There was no bed to crawl under. If he wanted to harm her, there would be little she could do about it. Mr. Andersen remained in firm control of their relationship. The fox still lurked in the shadows just beyond her view.

Julia decided to throw caution to the wind and confront him. Her lovely image of Kathy Griffith had been bloodied, and she wanted to know why. "Tell me why you murdered Kathy," she demanded.

A sad smile played across the old man's face. "I cannot tell you why, unless you honor our agreement to hear my entire story." With the help of his cane, he plopped down in the chair opposite her couch and sank into its cushions. Had it only been four days since Mark had sat in that chair? Mark had disappeared since their passionate kiss in the car, but she could feel him close by, watching over her. She seated herself on the sofa and gave Mr. Andersen an accusatory stare. Mozart serenaded them from the apartment above hers. Normally, she liked the classical music her neighbor played so loudly, but tonight it jangled her nerves. Andersen nodded his head in cadence to the violins. He looked quite relaxed. Not at all like a murderer about to confess his crime.

"Then, let's proceed," she finally responded with a little too much irritation.

He rested his head against the back of the chair, as was his custom, and closed his eyes. His head swayed a few measures longer, before coming to a rest.

****

I knew I could no longer put off searching Kathy's house, but my growing relationship with her made it difficult. Now that I had crossed the line and broken the first rule of the separatist, now that I had become involved with my mark, my decision made me feel underhanded. Guilt poured down upon my head, but I rationalized my actions. It was for her own good, I told myself. The sooner I found some clue to who she really was, the sooner I could remove her from Liu Kwong's clutches. She was gone until Friday. It was the perfect opportunity.

Her house was typical of so many in San Francisco, a tiny, two-story, wood-framed Victorian, with a bay window above the garage and two sets of smaller windows wedged under a peaked roof on the second floor. It was painted in pastel green with a creamy trim, and its walls nuzzled against its neighbors' on either side, leaving no space for trespassers such as myself. It reminded me of a doll's house surrounded by its bigger brothers. A trestle covered in jasmine vines bordered the front of the house on the left, partially covering a set of wooden stairs leading to a small porch with a stained-glass door. The only way in was through the front door or garage, and I needed to make my search during daylight hours when I could examine the place without turning on lights. I needed a disguise, one that would let me come and go without attracting the attention of nosy neighbors, so I chose to be a utility repairman. They were a common sight and rarely raised suspicion.

I entered the following afternoon--picking the old lock only took a matter of seconds--and found myself in a home filled with lush plants, hardwood floors, and area rugs. Kathy's scent filled the rooms with a mixture of roses and jasmine, and I savored it the way one does a fine wine. A deep-cushioned, white sofa and chairs and a sleek, black piano graced the living room. Photos of ballet dancers hung in the short hallway. A bookshelf showed a preference for literary writers over best sellers. Her CDs told me she liked classical music, particularly Bach and Chopin, but she also enjoyed older jazz bands and other groups, such as Dave Brubeck, Chicago, and Simon and Garfunkel.

I could feel Kathy Griffith in everything I saw and touched: the beige sweater hanging over the banister at the bottom of the stairs; a cup and saucer turned upside down by the sink; unopened mail on the hallway table. My fingers caressed her world as I wandered through the house gathering a picture of her. She was a cultured and successful woman who enjoyed music and literature, but there were no signs of the girl who came before her, or the poker player who swore when angry.

Her upstairs bedroom had a pitched ceiling and crown molding. A large, ceiling fan hung above her poster bed. I opened drawers and searched the closet shelves, discovering a penchant for frilly undergarments and silk blouses, but no old photographs, letters, or other memorabilia. The house was as empty of her past as the computer files I had searched. The only item that suggested any sort of childhood was a battered teddy bear seated in a rocking chair by the window. It looked old and loved, but uncooperative.

I sat on her bed and tried to think what to do. I needed something to show Kwong that I was making progress, but Kathy remained an enigma. It was quite enchanting to sit there in her bedroom with the afternoon light streaming through her lace curtains. I could smell her delicate scent everywhere: in the clothing in her closet, the bedspread underneath me, the hairbrush on her nightstand. I wanted to curl up and stay there forever.

Out of curiosity, I reached over and picked up the teddy bear. It wasn't a pretty sight. One ear was tattered, and a button eye was missing. Its coat looked like it had the mange. Not the sort of thing one puts on display. It had to be a childhood keepsake, a link with her mysterious past. As I prodded it with my fingers, I felt something hard in its back, and when I turned it over, I discovered a pouch hidden under the matted fur. Suddenly, my nerves were exploding like fireworks on New Year's Eve. There was something inside the pouch! My fingers dove eagerly into the opening and removed an old charm bracelet and two photographs. The first showed a girl of eight or nine in a ballet dancer's tutu standing on her toes, her arms raised delicately above her head, a joyful smile upon her face. The second revealed a woman in her forties standing in front of a house surrounded by hillsides and trees. A note had been scrawled on the back: *To my dearest Katie, with love, always. Deidre.*

Katie! A child's name that would become Kathy somewhere along the path to adulthood. I looked more closely at the photo. Numbers were visible on the house: 10832. And a large, white letter "H" could be seen through the trees on the right. My hands trembled. My mind whirled with a dozen questions. I was holding something which had survived the black hole that had swallowed Kathy's past. Her name had been Katie. But, who was Deidre? A family friend, a relative, her mother? And where was the picture taken? What did the letter H stand for? I stared at the photo, begging it to reveal its mysteries, but the woman only stared back at me. She was as uncooperative as the teddy bear.

I carefully replaced the bracelet and pictures in the bear and returned it to its chair. At least I had a starting point. I could run the databases looking for matches between Katie and Deidre, but it would be a big undertaking. It would help to know where the photo had been taken.

I was about to leave the bedroom when I heard the front door click open then close with a soft thud. I froze in the center of the room, listening intently. A woman's footsteps tapped across the hardwood floor and into the kitchen. Kathy was home a day early! A bag of groceries rustled noisily in her arms. She hummed a familiar melody that I tried to remember, but failed. Mad thoughts dashed through my mind. My worst nightmare had become reality. It wouldn't be long before Kathy discovered me lurking like a common criminal in her house. My credibility would be ruined and her trust in me destroyed. What were my alternatives? I couldn't explain myself, and I couldn't hide. I had to find a way out of the house undetected.

The upstairs rooms were carpeted, making it easier for me to move about. The bedroom window offered no way down. Then, I remembered the trellis with the climbing vines and hastily tiptoed across the hallway to the guest room. The trellis ended just below the window. It looked so flimsy, I hesitated. If it gave way, I would break my neck on the pavement below. There was little choice, however. I opened the window and tested my weight on the top rung. It held. I pulled the window shut behind me and started down the trellis. A small boy wearing a cowboy hat and dragging a red wagon behind him appeared below. He stopped and stared up at me with suspicion. I put my forefinger to my lips and winked at him. He continued to eye me doubtfully until I reached the ground.

"What're you doing mister?" he asked in a challenging voice.

"Playing a trick on the lady who lives here."

"Like Jack and the Beanstalk? Did you take the goose that lays golden eggs?"

The boy had a vivid imagination, and I feared he might raise the alarm. "I didn't take anything. See?" I held out my empty hands.

The boy didn't respond. I glanced behind me and saw movement in the kitchen window. I had to get out of there before Kathy spotted me. The boy looked confused about my story and uncertain what to do. On impulse, I reached into my pocket and pulled out a quarter. "Here," I said handing it to him. "Now you can buy your own golden egg." This seemed to satisfy him, and I quickly walked away. As soon as I turned the corner, I ran to my car and fled the scene with all the grace of a two-bit burglar.

I called the office from my mobile phone and told Patti and Carl to start searching the databases for a match between Katie and Deidre. When I described the photograph to Patti, she solved the mystery of the photo's location in a heartbeat. The answer was so simple, I was dumbfounded I hadn't thought of it.

"A large, white letter H on a hillside?" She laughed. "That's easy. It's the first letter in the HOLLYWOOD sign. Your picture was taken somewhere around Hollywood!"

I was ecstatic. "Okay, then. Focus your search on the Los Angeles/Hollywood area and cross-reference any matches against a house address with the numbers 10832. We may finally have something." My Kathy had become Katie, and with a little luck, she would soon reveal herself.

Carl found the match in less than two hours. Katie Livingstone, daughter to Raymond Charles Livingstone, who lived at 10832 Littlerock Drive, Hollywood, with his second wife, Deidre. Katie had gone to Hollywood High School, where she earned straight A's but had a record of erratic behavior. She picked fights with other girls, destroyed school property, and was booked twice for shoplifting. She was also caught numerous times ditching school. She was sent to a school psychiatrist who reported that she was crying out for help but wouldn't say why. During her senior year, Katie ran away from home and dropped out of school. She had no known address and was presumed to be living on the streets. Six months later, she surfaced at a strip joint in Van Nuys, where she became such a popular performer, two newspapers published articles on her. Then, she disappeared a second time. Katie Livingstone vanished and was never heard from again.

Kathy Griffith magically appeared in San Francisco a few months later, complete with a new social security number and a high school diploma. She got a job helping a photographer in his studio and took her college entrance exams, scoring near the top of her group. The next fall, she enrolled at U.C. Berkeley.

I tried to reconcile the images of the little ballerina and the street-smart stripper with the woman who had shared my champagne and strawberries, but I couldn't do it. When I thought of Katie roaming Hollywood's streets and taking off her clothes in front of a crowd of riveted voyeurs, Kathy faded from view, and if I put Kathy foremost in my thoughts, I saw no one else at all. Well, almost no one. Her poker playing temperament emerged from the shadows with greater clarity. I was beginning to understand that part of her character.

Once we had the key to begin building our web, I normally sat down with Carl and Patti and brainstormed possible strategies. This time, I hesitated, and they both knew it. Patti gave me one of her librarian looks that said "what the heck are you doing crossing the line," while Carl just sat behind his desk staring out the window. They made me feel guilty as hell.

"Let's wait until after Friday," I suggested feebly. I was procrastinating. I wanted to see Kathy again before plotting her downfall, to see which woman would emerge in my psyche: the Kathy I had come to adore or the Katie who strutted naked in front of men and raged at the world.

I stood on Fisherman's Wharf watching the merchants selling their crabs and lobsters and searching my soul for guidance about my conflicting emotions. The prospect of seeing Kathy again raised my spirits to levels I had never experienced before, but I feared my joy would be tempered by visions of Katie. I needn't have worried. The moment I saw Kathy walking towards me in dark pants and the beige sweater I had seen hanging on her banister, my fears melted faster than ice cream left on a hot sidewalk in the sun. I found no sign of Katie in her vibrant energy and devastating smile.

"On time as ordered," she said with ironic humor.

"And just as captivating as when I last saw you." Our dialogue continued without missing a beat.

"Where are you taking me?" She glanced curiously at the row of restaurants lining the Wharf.

"These are too commercial. I have something more memorable in mind." I led her to one of the excursion vessels docked among the fishing boats behind the restaurants.

A man in a white serving jacket stepped forward with a formal bow. "Good evening, Miss Griffith. I am your host, Jonathan, who will be waiting on you this evening. We've been expecting you." I took her hand to help her into the boat and felt an electric current rippling through me at the touch of her skin. Her hand lingered in mine a little longer than necessary, and my head began to spin. Two lounge chairs rested on the back deck. Inside, a table covered in white linen and lighted by large candles held two place settings that included a dizzying array of glasses and silverware. Several covered tureens sat on a sideboard, warmed by small burners.

"Tom, your imagination never ceases to amaze me." She gazed at the setting with a smile that told me she was delighted with my surprise.

The ship's captain introduced himself and announced that we were ready to depart. When the boat backed out of its slip, the movement caused Kathy to lean against me. I could smell the same, heady scent that I had enjoyed so much in her bedroom, rose petals and jasmine, and it carried me aloft on the evening's summer breezes. I no longer cared who this woman was. Kathy or Katie, it made no difference. I wanted them both.

The sun had slipped below the horizon by the time we motored out into the bay, and the lights of San Francisco rose up before us. Alcatraz loomed in the gathering darkness. It's shape reminded me of a great whale that had beached itself on the rocks. The Bay Bridge formed a garland of winking lights above our heads. We sat outside in the lounge chairs sipping champagne and enjoying the views of the city parading before us. I wanted to say a million things, but ended up saying nothing at all.

"You don't have to keep dazzling me with your inventiveness, you know," Kathy said, breaking the long silence. "I'm already quite charmed by you."

"Yes, but I'm enjoying this courtship even more than you are. There's no end to the things I want to do to delight you."

She reached out and took my hand. "Try not to expect too much from me. I'm not a very good finisher." She noted my quizzical look in the city's lights. "I'm much better at starting relationships than sustaining them."

Her unexpected admission confounded me. She had just opened a small window on herself, and I mulled my words carefully before replying. "Freud would say it has something to do with your childhood." I held my breath. My whole evening, maybe my entire life, hung on how she reacted to my bid to crack open her shell. She sat so still I feared she might jump up and leap over the side. Little, choppy waves slapped against our boat. A car's horn blared angrily from the bridge. A bird screeched in the darkness overhead. I was sitting on the edge of a volcano, and I didn't know if it was about to erupt or remain dormant for another hundred years.

The suspense was broken by Jonathan offering one of the world's most timeworn invitations. "Dinner is served."

Dinner wasn't just served. It was produced with all the drama and pleasure of a fine stage play. Lobster bisque soup, oil and vinegar salad, lightly broiled swordfish, and baked Alaska were complemented by a series of red and white wines that excited the palate and stirred the soul. I took my first bites of food with the apprehensiveness of a thrill seeker who had tossed gasoline on hot coals and was waiting for them to ignite. They never did. Kathy remained unflappable as we toasted to silly things with each new glass of wine, shared bits of food, and enjoyed the lights on our journey across the bay to Sausalito and back.

Jonathan gave us windbreakers, and we sat in the deck chairs on our return run to the harbor. The sea breezes revived me after so much good food and wine; the bobbing motion of the boat in the increasing swells made me feel reckless and wild. I decided to press my luck and push the boundaries of our newly formed relationship. I needed to find a pathway through the minefield of defenses she used to keep people at bay. I wanted into her world.

"You said earlier that you're not very good at sustaining relationships. Can you tell me why?" I tried to keep my voice casual, but it sounded like a tin drum in my ear.

"How much have you investigated me?" She answered my question with a question.

"Enough to know you are a woman without a past." More half-truths hidden in lies. I held my breath, something I did a lot around this woman.

"I might be in some trouble."

Her calm voice belied her declaration and caught me by surprise. I had expected anger or accusations about prying into her personal life. Instead, she ignored my dubious confession and opened a new door for me. Something told me to enter it cautiously.

"Can I help?"

"Perhaps. I stumbled onto some disturbing information during an audit, and I've been trying to decide what I should do. There are ethical issues. As an auditor, the information I see is supposed to be kept confidential. But there are legal issues, as well. The company may be a front for criminal operations. I accidentally accessed computer files showing shipping schedules that had no connection to the business. They listed business inventories, but the contents were only distributed to men in Chinatown. When I researched the names, I came across a number of criminal records, many for selling drugs. The records also included names of port authority and police officials who have received large sums of money.

"Surely no one knows you saw them." The damp air nipped at me, and I pulled my jacket tighter around my neck.

"My client walked in the office as I was closing the file. He might have seen something. I'm not sure."

"What makes you think you're in trouble?" A chill was worming its way down my back, despite my efforts to deflect it.

"I did something stupid. When I saw those files, my instinct was to copy them, so I took two blank computer disks from the credenza and made duplicates. If my client realizes two of his disks are missing, he will be suspicious.

"But that's not the worst of it. Someone broke into my house while I was away. My friend, Emily, often house-sits for me while I'm gone. She came home yesterday afternoon and saw a stranger talking to a neighbor's boy in front of my house. Later, she discovered an unlocked window upstairs. I asked the neighbors about the incident when I got back. The boy, Aaron, said he saw a man climbing down from my window. He kept talking about Jack and the Beanstalk."

"Was anything stolen?" More breath holding. I was beginning to feel like a scuba diver running out of air.

"No. That's what scares me. A few of my belongings were not quite as I had left them. Personal items in my drawers and in the closet, but nothing was missing. I think it has something to do with what I saw and those disks. I thought about taking the disks to the police, but is that safe? Some of the police are being bribed." She looked at the skyline as she spoke, then turned to me and took my hand.

"I don't usually trust men, Tom, but I trust you. You said you're an investigator. I hoped you might help me. I would pay you, of course."

For someone who hid her past and held the world at arms length, Kathy could be very direct. I savored her words. Kathy made me feel like a commoner who had just been crowned king. I tried to ignore the fact that I was really a Judas betraying my queen.

"I would do anything for you Kathy, but not for money. Who do you fear?"

"Liu Kwong."

The name stabbed me like broken glass from a shattered window. Guilt, anger, and jealousy swirled through me in a bewildering array of emotions. I was consumed by images of a face I had never seen kissing this woman and devouring her. The face was a shadow with menacing eyes that loomed over me. I wanted to strike at it with my fists.

"Your lover." There was pique in my voice, but I couldn't help it.

"Never." She spat the denial out. "He invited me to be his

127

escort for a few social events. I admit I found him fascinating, but I never went to bed with him. Once I learned about his other activities, I stopped seeing him. I thought that would be the end of it, but now that my house has been searched, I'm not so sure. I worry that he knows I copied his files."

Either Liu Kwong had lied to me about their relationship, or Kathy was now. I chose to believe it was the former, and my spirits rose. The thought of him possessing her had awakened a primeval urge in me to shake my antlers and challenge him. Now that I knew he was not a rival for Kathy's affections, my anger slipped away on the evening tide. I wanted to shout with joy at her declaration of needing me, but my happiness was tempered by my own duplicity. Liu Kwong presented a threat to both of us, but for different reasons. He suspected something, and he wanted Kathy silenced. Dead if necessary. And if I failed to fulfill my contract, I could lose her forever.

"I'll see what I can learn," I said as earnestly as I could.

One thing still bothered me. Liu Kwong hadn't told me the truth about his reason for hiring me, his motivation. He didn't want me to compromise Kathy to hide an affair. He wanted to stop her from revealing what she might have seen in those computer files. Such reasoning had a much more ominous ring to it, and it worried me. Had Kwong truly hired me to keep Kathy from talking, or did he have a more sinister plan in mind?

It was after ten o'clock when we docked, but crowds of tourists still haunted the waterfront restaurants and souvenir shops. I helped Kathy out of the boat with all the shyness of a schoolboy on a first date: nervous and unsure how it would end. Not wanting it to end at all.

"No cabs," I said at last. "I'll drive you home."

She took my arm and nodded, and we wandered slowly along the gaily lighted street. Her body radiated the warmth of an open fire where it brushed against mine. The dynamics were changing between us; our courtship was maturing. If I had crossed a line, so had she. I prayed I wouldn't let her down.

****

Mr. Andersen stared at Julia without blinking. "Still no answer to your question. The answer will come, but you must have the whole story, if you are going to write it properly."

"Perhaps, I no longer plan to write it," she replied. Julia wanted to lash out and hurt him, and words were the only weapons she had. If they had any effect on him, he didn't show it.

"Oh, you do, more than ever. Besides, there is still the matter of your investigation. I understand your visit to the waterfront was most productive. The next step is considerably more dangerous." He handed her a single sheet of paper. "These are codes for the drug distributors who work for Liu Kwong, along with the names and addresses of their drops. Also the contacts for the abducted women. But there is a problem. The cipher to unlock the codes is in an electronic file kept in Mr. Kwong's safe in his office in Chinatown."

"The Golden Moon." Julia took the paper from Mr. Andersen and stared at the jumbled letters.

"The very same. Mark can help you steal it if you like, but, of course, that is against the law." His smile reminded her of the wolf in the Little Red Riding Hood fairytale.

"I'll talk with him about it," she replied grudgingly. No matter how hard she tried to resist this man, he always managed to pull her back into his web. She was nothing more than a fly waiting to be devoured by his spider.

"Good." He stood up. "Now, I must go. Oh, one more thing. I'm much too old to manage these stairs. Let us conduct our future meetings at a safe house I have arranged. Mark will bring you and return you home. He's expert at losing anyone who might try to follow. You can let him know when. I'll be waiting."

Julia jumped up as well. There was one more item she intended to discuss before Mr. Andersen got away. "Where's my father?" she demanded as he turned to leave.

Mr. Andersen stopped in the middle of the living room and combed back his hair with his fingers while he pondered her query.

"A good question. One I cannot answer yet, but I believe we may be getting closer to him. Be patient a while longer."

She watched him lean on his cane and hobble out the door while she replayed his vague words in her mind. "May be getting closer" didn't tell her much. Once again, she couldn't shake the feeling that he was moving her about on puppet strings. Well, she had little choice but to dance to his manipulating fingers a little while longer. It was more than the prospect of finding her father that connected her to him, however. His story still had her spellbound, and the information he possessed was priceless. She only hoped that in pursuing the information she wouldn't end up like Kathy. Julia sighed and closed the door.

CHAPTER ELEVEN
Kathy's story . . . .

Katie raced out the door and down the stairs from her ballet class. Other eight-year-old girls squealed with laughter behind her. Dozens of little footsteps peppered the stairwell with their staccato beats. It had been an exhilarating day. Her teacher, Mrs. Perrot, had singled her out for special praise. "Look how she extends herself on her toes, girls. How she expresses the dance with her body." The girls were jealous of her, but she didn't care. She loved to dance, thrilled at performing a difficult step well, and she hungered for Mrs. Perrot's attention. Some of the girls didn't like their teacher, and called her Mrs. Parrot behind her back, but Katie found her stern manner and sharp commands challenging. Mrs. Perrot's demands made her want to do better.

She couldn't wait to tell Daddy. He would be so pleased and proud of her. She would sit in his lap and play with his hair when they got home. They played a lot together, now that Mommy was gone. Katie missed Mommy and wondered what it was like in heaven. Was it really filled with white, fluffy clouds and sunshine, like in the picture her father had shown her? It didn't seem real, walking on clouds and stuff. But it didn't matter as long as Mommy was safe, and as long as she had Daddy.

There he was, standing on the sidewalk, all smiles and open

arms. She rushed into her father's warm embrace. He smelled of Old Spice and slightly musty clothes. She loved those smells.

"I was the best today," she announced. "Mrs. Perrot praised me in front of the whole class."

"Of course she did," he responded. "You *are* the best. You're a special little person."

He hugged her, and she held his hand as they walked to the car. She was still dressed in her tutu but carried her ballet slippers in her free hand. The sun warmed her legs and arms. She wanted to pirouette in the middle of the street for her father, to show him just how high she could stretch on her toes. But she would wait until they were home alone to show off her fine footwork. She would dance only for him.

The house was drowsy quiet when they entered. Only the rhythmic ticking of the grandfather clock in the hallway let her know the place was still breathing. She thought of their house as something alive, a giant animal that kept them safe from the world. The excitement of her big day had worn off, and she was sleepy. She rested her head on her father's arm as he lifted her up and carried her to his favorite chair in the den. She listened to the tick-tock of the clock and pretended it was the house's heart beating in time with hers.

He sat her in the chair and turned on the radio. Light, airy notes of music lilted through the room. Daddy told her it was a concerto by Mozart. He picked her up again and settled in the chair with her nestled on his lap. His soft hands caressed her as she dozed in his arms. Slowly, he removed her arms from her costume and pulled it down to her waist. His hands rubbed her back, her arms, her small breasts and nipples until her skin glowed. Next, he pulled off her tights and worked his hand up her naked thighs until his finger touched the magic place. The feelings filling her body always confused her. They made her feel warm and tingly, but the sensations frightened her, as well. She closed her eyes and waited for her father to stop. She knew he would as soon as he was finished with himself. Then, she would run to her room and cuddle with her teddy bear. She would tell it her secrets, and it would listen without complaint.

Katie couldn't remember exactly how long their games had lasted, but they stopped when her father married Deidre. At first, Katie was jealous at the way her new stepmother stole her father's attentions, and she pouted around the house. Somewhere deep inside, however, the discomfort she'd always felt when her father touched her gave way to a gusher of relief. When she told her teddy bear that she no longer had to worry about pleasing her father in that special way, it smiled in agreement. She still craved her father's attentions, but she was glad they no longer went beyond big hugs and pats on the head.

Over time, Katie came to realize that Deidre wasn't so bad. She had a large, round face filled with smiles and kind words. When she hugged Katie, the smell of kitchen odors wafted over her. Katie couldn't remember what her mother had smelled like, but she thought it must have been similar. Deidre's hugs reminded her of Mommy's. Deidre was a nice substitute for Mommy. Katie was old enough to understand that her mother was dead and that it wasn't Deidre's fault. Deidre wasn't Mommy, never could be, but Katie basked in her warmth.

Katie was a young teenager when her father lost his job and Deidre went to work to pay the bills. Father tried to find another job, but couldn't. After months of frustration, he gave up and stayed home. He began drinking "pre-dinner cocktails" in the afternoon, and he was often on his second drink by the time Katie got home from school. That was when the games started, again. Classical music would be playing when Katie entered the house, and her father would be sitting in the den in his favorite chair, waiting for her. He began asking Katie to sit in his lap, just as she'd done years before. Katie wanted to say no, but couldn't. She loved her father and wanted to please him. At first, he only caressed her arms and legs, but he soon progressed to her budding breasts. Katie's confusion intensified. Angst churned inside her. She knew they were doing something that was wrong, but she felt powerless to stop it.

It wasn't long before her father began taking Katie's hand and leading her up the stairs to her bedroom. The games quickly advanced to things Katie couldn't talk about. She began to shake on her way home from school. By the time she reached the house, her hands often trembled so badly she couldn't unlock the door. Twice, she stayed away until she knew Deidre was home, but this only made her father angry. He stalked around the house while poor Deidre tried to figure out what she'd done to upset him. Deidre didn't understand the unnatural dynamics of the family.

Guilt weighed heavily on Katie. She knew she had become dirty and impure, not someone with whom the other girls or boys wanted to associate. She began to spend an hour or more each day in the shower trying to cleanse herself, until Deidre put her foot down about the water bill and placed a timer in the bathroom. When the bell rang, she turned off the water, sat on the tiled floor, and continued scrubbing herself with her washcloth. It was never enough.

Katie had always dreamed of dancing Swan Lake on the great stage at the Dorothy Chandler Pavilion in Los Angeles, but she gave up ballet her sophomore year in high school. Her teacher urged her to continue, but she no longer had the strength for it. Her life's forces were slowly being pulled out of orbit by her father's attentions. It was only a matter of time until she plunged into the searing heat of the sun.

Katie felt certain the girls at school knew about her and were laughing behind her back. When she saw a girl smirking in her direction, she would fly into a rage and pull the girl's hair. Soon, the girls *were* talking about her, and they gave her a wide birth. She took her rage out on lockers and desks, until she was sent home for disciplinary action. Her father's lack of sympathy shocked her. He whipped her and sent her to bed without dinner. It was Deidre who came to her and tried to understand. Katie fed off of Deidre's warmth with the despair of a flower that had mistakenly bloomed in wintertime. Deidre became her sun, and she reached towards her stepmother's light just as she had once stretched for Mrs. Perrot's approval. She regretted never calling

Deidre Mommy.

Surviving high school was all Katie thought about. Surviving until she could graduate and strike out on her own. But one afternoon at the beginning of her senior year, Deidre came home early with the flu and discovered her husband in her stepdaughter's bed. Katie hid in the closet while a storm of screaming and shouting raged through the house. She cried and wailed at what she had done, at how she had destroyed Deidre's love. There was no longer any reason to stay home.

Katie locked herself in her room and waited for the house to calm itself. After some time, she heard Deidre bang out the front door. Uneven footsteps told her that her father was stumbling around the house. At last, he went to his bedroom, and there was silence. Once she was certain he was sleeping, she crept into his room and removed all the money from his wallet, a total of $50. She took a backpack filled with clothing, toiletries, and her teddy bear and fled into the night.

Sparkling lights, cruising traffic and late-night revelers greeted her. Hollywood Boulevard pulsated with an energy she had never known before. Prostitutes beckoned to customers. Moviegoers sat in coffee shops carrying on animated conversations about the films they had seen. The city was speaking in dozens of languages. She walked the boulevard and surrounding streets aimlessly while she tried to decide what to do. She knew Deidre would never forgive her for ruining their family. How could she? And now that her awful truth had been exposed, she never wanted to see her father again. It was best to disappear, but where or how were concepts beyond her imagination. All she could think about were the basics: where to sleep and eat. Fifty dollars wasn't going to last very long.

Katie saw two bums asleep among a pile of trash bags in an alleyway and decided to join them. She curled up among the bags with her teddy bear and listened to the street noises surrounding her. After awhile, they became melodies that eased her mind into sleep.

The boulevard wasn't nearly so attractive in the harsh light of morning. Drunks relieved themselves in doorways and threw up in the street. People looked tired, haggard, and drugged out. Two girls younger than Katie flirted with passing men, trying to find a customer who would pay for their breakfast. A boy did the same. Trash littered the sidewalks. Car fumes filled the air.

Katie sat in a coffee shop hungrily devouring pancakes and watching the passing parade of characters outside the window. Her memory reeled through yesterday's horrid pictures: her father's despairing look, Deidre's tortured face, the angry house. She tried to rid her mind of the images, but they kept repeating themselves like a bad movie. She desperately wanted to clean herself, to scrub her skin until it was raw, but that meant renting a room, a luxury she couldn't afford. She asked the waitress about a YWCA, but the woman didn't know of any nearby.

Katie spent the day looking in shop windows and sitting on bus benches, her mind too dull to think or plan beyond the moment. People went about their busy days, making everything look normal, but she knew nothing could ever be normal again. She ate candy bars to save money, but when dinnertime came, she could no longer resist the thought of food and returned to the coffee shop for a hamburger and fries. She had less than forty dollars by nightfall.

Fear began working its insidious way into her mind. Survival on those hostile streets didn't seem possible. She wasn't tough enough. Leaving the area was her best option, but she had no idea where to go. There was an uncle in Chicago, but that was planets away, and making contact with him would only bring her father. Thinking about her father made her tremble, again. She wanted to leave Hollywood, but something held her back. Things were familiar there. It had been her home for the past ten years. If she stayed, however, it would only be a matter of time until somebody recognized her and word got back to her father. She had to go. Tomorrow, she would find a Greyhound station and take a bus to another city or state. She would go north where it rained a lot and the streets were clean.

This idea comforted her. She decided to return to the alleyway for one more night, then get the hell out of there. The two bums were already in their allotted places drinking from a small bottle when she joined them, but they didn't seem to mind her company. She pulled her teddy from her backpack and curled up amongst the trash. Soon, she was fast asleep.

She dreamed Deidre and her father were fighting. The shouting terrified her, and she pressed her hands over her ears to shut out the sound. Something bumped her, and she awoke with a start. A shadow was leaning over her. Another was kicking the two poor bums, who had curled up into balls to ward off the angry blows. The shadow pulled her face into the light and shouted triumphantly that he'd found a girl. Hands pawed at her, ripping off her clothing and grabbing at her breasts. She tried to scream, but a fist slammed into her face, knocking her half senseless. Rough hands pulled down her pants. She closed her eyes and gritted her teeth as she felt a body urgently mounting her. Images of her father flashed before her, an angry father who whipped and sodomized her. Suddenly, the shadow on top disappeared. She heard an enraged voice and blows to someone's body. Then, it all went dark as she floated away from the violence into a world filled with dancing and love.

Katie opened her eyes and found she was laying among purple satin sheets on a large, round bed in a room covered with mirrors on the walls and ceiling. She thought she was at a carnival, until she remembered the ugly voices and grasping hands. Her head throbbed, and her jaw ached. Someone, she recalled, had hit her. Where was she, she wondered, and how had she gotten there? Her clothes were gone, replaced by a snow-white robe. She pushed herself off the bed and stood on unsteady legs in the middle of the room. Her bare feet tingled with pleasure in the deep, maroon carpet that covered the floor. But when Katie looked at herself in one of the mirrors, she was shocked by the filthy, bruised face staring back at her. Her image had the appearance of a frightened animal whose hair had risen in anger and become frozen.

Her reflection made her think of her teddy bear, and she rushed back to the bed, nearly colliding with a man standing there. She squealed in shock and stopped in front of him.

"Don't be afraid." The man smiled. His smile pulled the right half of his upper lip upwards, making his face slip off center. Black hair framed a narrow face with pronounced cheek bones. It wasn't a handsome face, but something about it calmed Katie and she breathed easier.

"Where's my teddy bear?" she asked. Her need for her childhood companion overrode her initial fear.

"Over there." The man pointed past the bed to where the bear lay with her backpack on a velvet chair. She rushed over and scooped it up.

"Who are you?" she asked, her concern regaining the upper hand.

"People call me Angel. You were in trouble last night. If I hadn't come along, no telling what would've happened. The street's no place for girls late at night." Memories of angry hands ripping off her clothing rushed back to her. She distracted herself by looking around the room at all the mirrors and brilliant colors.

"This place is weird," was all she could think to say.

"My palace. Make yourself at home. Much safer than living on the streets."

She studied him. He was at least ten years younger than her father, but any comparison ended there. Angel wore a flowing, silk shirt and pajama-style pants. Gold chains and jewelry adorned his neck, arms, and hands. Matching diamond earrings glittered in the morning light.

"Are you queer?" she suddenly asked.

He laughed--it was more of a grunt with a smile attached to it--and shook his head. "No, but some of my customers are."

Katie's head began to spin, and she sank down on the edge of the bed. Last night's brutal encounter and the shock of her new surroundings were taking their toll. "My head is dizzy. I want to lie down."

"Wait a sec." Angel disappeared and returned moments later

with a glass of water and a pill. "Take this. You'll feel much better."

Katie looked up at his outstretched hand with suspicion. She knew it was dangerous to trust a stranger, especially after last night, but he *had* saved her from those nasty men. Maybe saved her life. And his lopsided smile reminded her of her teddy bear.

"It's just a mild sedative. It'll make you sleep.*"

After a brief hesitation, she accepted the pill and water and lay back against the satin sheets. Before she knew it, her threatening world was gone, replaced by a glowing feeling that spread through her body in rushes of pleasurable warmth. She dreamed of pirouettes and smiling bears. Fingers tugged at her robe and roamed her flesh, but they offered caressing touches, not violent hands. Passions she had never experienced before stirred in her, and her body rose up to greet the magical hands.

When Katie awoke, Angel's arm was draped across her naked body. She tried to sit up, but her head was too woozy, so she lay back and stared at her image in the ceiling mirror. She remembered a sensuous dream, but when she studied herself in the mirror, she realized it hadn't been a dream at all. She'd had sex with Angel! At first, the idea repulsed her, but the more she thought about it, the better she felt. It had been incredibly exciting. Far better than her guilt-ridden relations with her father, or those awful hands in the alley. Katie decided that sex wasn't so bad after all. She rolled over and went back to sleep.

It became clear that Katie was expected to continue sleeping with Angel if she wanted to stay in his "palace." She thought about heading for the bus station, but Angel seemed nice enough, and his offer was a better option than facing the streets, again, so soon. So, she climbed into the round, silky bed with him and stayed. The arrangement suited her just fine. Angel was a much more skillful lover than her father, and she soon learned many new ways to give and receive pleasure. In return, Angel took her shopping for new clothes, including seductive nightgowns and sexy undergarments. She was never allowed out of the house alone, and it was impossible to go anywhere on her own. All the doors were kept locked, and bars covered the windows. The house was like a prison.

She learned that Angel's home was high in the Hollywood hills. His living room upstairs was just as bizarre as the bedroom. The same thick, maroon carpeting covered the floor. Green, velvet couches and chairs lined the walls. The lamps were all covered with pop-art shades that looked like the covers of comic books. In the center of the room stood a large pool table.

Three boys ranging in age from twelve to fifteen lived upstairs in separate rooms. They were called Bali, Star, and Aya. A bulldozer of a man with a shaved head and brutish glare lived downstairs across the hall from Angel's room. He reminded her of a schoolboy who had tormented her. His name was Alex, but she called him Bully, and he seemed pleased with the name. His official purpose was to guard the place, but Katie soon got the idea that his duties were to keep her and the boys in, as well as unwanted visitors out. Visitors came at all hours of the day and night. The doorbell only rang downstairs, and the boys were under strict instructions never to answer the door if someone knocked. They couldn't have opened the door anyway. It was locked from the inside, and they had no key. Only Bully or Angel had access to a key.

One day, she realized the oldest boy, Bali, was gone. She asked Angel about it, but he only shrugged. Had he run away, she wondered? If so, the boys must know, but they weren't talking. She couldn't imagine how he had escaped from the house.

After several weeks, Katie thought about leaving. "I think it's time to go," she announced one morning after Angel had finished shaving.

Angel wiped his face with a towel and stood looking at himself in the mirror for several seconds before turning around. "You owe me money for room and board, and all the clothes I bought. You can't leave until you pay me." He gave her his crooked smile, only this time it had a sinister look Katie had never seen before.

A chill crept up her spine as she stared at Angel. Dread gnawed at the back of her mind. "You never said anything about paying you money," she declared. "I would've left if I had known."

"And gone where?" He arched his eyebrows. "You were being raped the night I found you. How much longer do you think you could've survived on the streets?"

"I only have about thirty-nine dollars. Here, take it." Katie grabbed her bag and fumbled inside for her money.

Angel gave his imitation of a laugh. "You owe me a lot more than that, but I'll make you a deal. I have customers who like young girls as well as boys. With curled hair and a little makeup, we can make you look five years younger. After a few months, you'll have paid your debt and can go."

"No," she cried dismay. Her mind raced through a prism of images triggered by Angel's words. She could feel the dirty hands of loathsome men snaking over her body while they played out their ugly fantasies, their disgusting breath hissing in her ears, and their flabby bodies pressing down on her until she couldn't breathe. "You can't make me. I'll tell the police." The threat sounded hollow in her ears. Tears cascaded down her cheeks at the realization that she wasn't free to go. She was trapped, and Angel knew it. She thought of Star and Aya in their rooms upstairs waiting for customers. How long had they been caught in Angel's web? More than a few months, she guessed. And what about Bali? Had Angel really let him go? A dark voice in the recesses of her mind told her no. A primordial scream rose in her, but it became trapped in her throat. What good would it do to scream when no one could hear her?

Months floated by in a haze. Men came and left, but she remembered little about them. When they lay on top of her grunting like pigs, she let her mind drift away into a world of dancing. It was a wondrous world that blotted out the odors of their unwashed bodies and their animal sounds. The music built a protective wall around her, a glass wall that prevented anyone from touching her.

She no longer slept with Angel. He locked her in a room next to Bully's, where she spent her idle time watching television and reading the dirty novels left strewn about the house. When the bell rang, her mind scattered into fragments filled with fear and loathing. By the time the key turned the lock in her door, she was already dancing ballet in a grand music hall before an applauding audience. Only her dreams kept her from losing her sanity.

She rarely saw the two boys anymore. They ate at different times and were usually in their rooms when she was allowed upstairs. Once or twice, she saw them playing pool in the living room when she passed through on the way to the kitchen, but they never looked at her. She began biting her fingernails, and when they were gone she gnawed on her fingertips like a mouse worrying about a piece of rope.

There was no way to keep track of time, but she knew it had been long enough to repay her debt. When she asked Angel about leaving, he struck her so hard her legs wobbled, and she crumpled to the floor. A searing white light spread behind her eyes. Her ears roared with angry noises that drowned out the words pouring from Angel's distorted face. Later, when she looked in the mirror, she saw a ragged, blackish-blue welt the size of a baseball smeared across her cheek. When her hearing returned, Angel swore at her and told her never to question him again. She didn't need to. She already knew the answer. Angel would keep her there until his customers tired of her. When he had no further use for her, she would disappear like Bali, and nobody would ever find her.

Katie shuddered and drew a deep breath. She had to find a way to escape while there was still time. She began paying closer attention to the routines of the house. Bully was always in the house during the daytime but went out once or twice a week at night. Most of the time, Angel stayed at home managing his business and enjoying the company of young prostitutes, but once every week he left the house after breakfast and didn't return until noon. Her only hope was to make her move while he was gone. He was too smart to be fooled by her. Bully, on the other hand, seemed slow-witted, and it was clear from the way his hungry eyes lingered on her that he wanted her. Particularly when she wore her red lingerie. It was like waving a red flag. Seducing Bully seemed her best chance.

Katie waited seven long days for Angel to leave the house again, during which time she prepared her plan. She noted the locations of the three telephones in the house. One was in Bully's room, and two were in Angel's, in the bedroom and bathroom. There were none upstairs. She coaxed Angel into giving her a desk lamp to put on her nightstand so she would have better light when she read. She stopped wearing her red lingerie for customers and watched Bully fidget a little more each day as he waited for her to don it again.

When the morning of truth finally arrived, Katie was beset by such a powerful attack of nerves, she thought she was ill and nearly cancelled her plans. Waves of nausea wracked her shivery body. She heaped her clothes and blanket on top of her and rolled into a ball until the quivering subsided. Then, she paced the room muttering to herself. *You can do this! It's your only chance.*

She chewed on her fingers while Angel gave orders to Bully about schedules for her and the boys. At last, he departed. A customer was coming in an hour for her. She would have to act fast. She put on the red negligee and banged on her door.

"Bathroom," she yelled.

It was all she needed to say. The lock clicked, and the door opened. Bully stared at her with his mouth agape, his desire drooling from the corners of his puffed lips. She strutted past him and down the hall, knowing that his mind was churning with the possibilities. Now that her plan had begun, an icy calm settled over her. Her heart thudded in her chest, but her nerves and mind were composed. In a few minutes, she would either be free or most likely dead. Either option was preferable to staying there one day longer.

Katie slipped one strap off her shoulder, revealing nearly all of her left breast, and emerged from the bathroom. Bully's eyes scorched her skin. She stood in the doorway and curled her lips into a smile.

"Bully, how about we help each other?" As soon as she said this, she stepped around him and started toward her room. Bully hurried after her. She could feel his eyes burning her back. She stopped near the bedroom door and turned to face him, letting her filmy gown slip a little further. "I can give you favors, if you let me spend more time out of my room while Angel is gone." She looked at him seductively. She'd been practicing that look all week in her bathroom mirror. "It gets pretty lonely in there."

"Angel would get mad." His lower lip trembled anxiously, and his left eye began to twitch. His face was dancing with conflicting emotions.

"Angel won't know." She lifted her negligee, exposing her lower body.

Bully grabbed her so quickly she nearly fell. She feared he would take her there in the hallway and ruin her plan. "Not so fast," she gasped. "No need to hurry. Come to my room." She took his hand and led him to her bed. He nearly ripped off his clothes in his rush to be with her. Her heart boomed in her ears, but she forced herself to lie there quietly. *Be patient. Remain calm.* She had to wait until he was inside of her. Then, he would be vulnerable.

When the moment came, she picked up the lamp on the nightstand and bashed it over his head. He blinked in surprise and started to rise. A fury rose in her throat like bile, and the primordial scream she had suppressed for so many months escaped. She cried out like a wild animal, while she struck him a second and third time. He slumped on top of her and lay still. She shoved him off the bed and jumped to her feet. Blood covered the upper part of her gown. The blows had been heavy enough to kill an ordinary man. She hoped they had killed him.

Katie rifled his pockets, but only found her bedroom key. Where were the others? She ran to his room and frantically scanned his nightstand and bureau. The keys sat in a small, wooden bowl along with his watch and some money. She quickly counted it. Less than $50. She took it all, then searched Angel's room for more money and her backpack while she ripped out the

144

plugs to the telephones. All she could find were two gold chains on the dresser. Katie scooped the chains into her pocket and sprinted back to her room. To her relief, Bully hadn't moved, but there was no time to waste looking for stuff. If she wanted to escape, she had to go now. Once she was dressed, Katie grabbed her teddy bear and raced up the stairs.

"Star. Aya." She called the boys names. "I'm leaving. Do you want to come?" They both started yelling from their rooms, pleading with her to release them. She unlocked their doors, and they ran past her like fleeing mice.

It took her a few anxious moments to figure out which key worked the front door. When it finally opened, the boys flew into the breathless sunlight of freedom, shouting with joy and jumping up and down. She locked the door and raced after them down the street. Eventually, the boys turned a corner and became lost in the maze of winding lanes. She ran as quickly as she dared down the steep pavement. She ran until her sides ached and she had to slow to a walk to catch her breath. The morning sunlight warmed her body. She marveled at how glorious the sunshine felt on her skin. When she heard an approaching car, however, terror gripped her throat. She ducked behind a row of bushes and trembled uncontrollably. The car passed harmlessly, but it was several minutes before she could bring herself to leave her hiding place. She progressed down the rest of the hill that way, running, walking, and hiding, until she found herself back on the streets of Hollywood.

Katie stared at the traffic in dismay. She was back where she had started months before, with less than $50 and no idea where to go. All she could think about was getting away from that evil place as fast as possible. When a city bus hissed to a stop in front of her, she jumped aboard, curled up in the back row of seats, and closed her eyes. The rumbling noise of the bus engine soothed her nerves. It was the sound of freedom. It told her that she was leaving Hollywood and would never return.

CHAPTER TWELVE
Kathy's story continued . . .

"End of the line." The announcement jarred Katie awake. Confused, she looked about her. She was sitting in an empty bus. Nothing looked familiar.

"Where am I?" she asked the driver.

"Van Nuys."

The bus had delivered her to the San Fernando Valley. Katie glanced at the watch she had taken from Bully. It was nearly four o'clock in the afternoon. She disembarked and looked around her in despair. The reality of her situation was unchanged. Months had been stolen from her, and she was just as alone and lost as when she'd slept next to those bums in Hollywood. Katie walked along a busy street until she spotted a cheap motel. The manager wanted $20 for a night's lodging. The room was a sorry looking space with stained carpeting, a squeaky bed, and sagging mini-blinds, but it was safer than the streets. The room would protect her for the night, but what would she do when Bully's money was gone? There would be no choice but to return to the streets. Images of dark shadows and grasping hands swarmed inside her head, and her body shook as badly as when she'd hid in the bushes that morning.

Her stomach rumbled, as well, reminding her she hadn't eaten since breakfast. Food would have to wait, however, until she'd washed. When she looked at herself in the bathroom mirror, she found traces of blood caked on her fingers, and she hastily washed them off. Next, she got in the shower and performed her scrubbing ritual.

The sun was setting when Katie ventured onto the streets. A McDonald's beckoned her, and she devoured a double hamburger with fries. She wanted more, but when she looked at her dwindling supply of money, she resisted. The scrubbing and the food made her feel better, however, and she decided to look for someone to buy the watch and gold chains. Kids were cruising the boulevard in their cars. Two guys in a souped-up Chevy whistled at her. She looked at them with detached fascination. They looked so young to her, so immature. She had aged at Angel's. Her youth had been snatched from her, leaving a residue of pain and torment in its wake. She would never be young again.

Katie began asking passersby if they wanted to buy her treasures. People averted their eyes and hurried past. Bright lights up ahead announced a bar or club of some kind. When she got closer, she saw that it was a strip joint called Buffy's. Throbbing music fought its way out the closed doors to the street. She stopped and looked at the photos in the glass display by the entrance. They showed nearly nude women striking provocative poses. She looked at the women more closely. The challenging expressions and heavily made-up faces made two of the women look hard, but the third looked younger, softer, and more vulnerable in her pink ruffles. Her smile was sweeter, her pose more refined. Katie was drawn to the young woman. She made her think of her dreams about dancing before a great audience.

She continued walking and asking passersby if they wanted the watch or gold chains. A young man finally offered $20 for the watch, and Katie took it. No one wanted the jewelry. The night air chilled her, reminding her that she had no jacket. She returned to the motel dejected and still hungry.

The next day, Katie checked out of the motel, took her teddy bear, and returned to the main street, where she began begging for quarters and dimes to buy food. The sun was high overhead when she saw a girl not much older than herself in a pullover sweater, jeans, and sneakers walking down the street. Her brown hair was pulled back in a pony tail and she wore no makeup except for a hint of red lipstick, but Katie knew instantly that she was the girl in the poster at the strip club.

"I know you," she said. The girl hesitated, then stopped and looked at Kathy with a curious expression. "You're the one in the poster." Katie pointed towards the strip club in the next block.

"Crummy shot, huh?" The girl made a face.

"I thought you looked awesome." Katie felt foolish and looked down at her feet. Her heart pounded like someone meeting a movie star.

"Thanks." The girl smiled. "I'm Jenny. Who're you?"

"Katie." She looked at the girl more closely. Without makeup, Jenny was rather plain, yet in the picture she'd looked glamorous. There was something in her frank gaze and the way she held her head that told Katie she was street smart beyond her years. But there was something warm about her, as well. Katie felt drawn to her, just like when she saw Jenny's photo on that poster.

"I saw you asking people for money." Katie stiffened at the accusation. "Don't be embarrassed," Jenny continued. "I did that, too, before I started working at Buffy's. You got someplace to stay?"

Katie shook her head no and scuffed the sidewalk with her shoe. Tears glistened on her cheeks without warning, and she lowered her head. Silence enveloped them.

"You want to crash at my place for a night or two?" Jenny asked suddenly. "It's only a one bedroom apartment, but there's a comfortable couch in the living room, and I could use some company."

A wave of relief washed over Katie. For the first time in months somebody was offering her refuge, a place to hide from the storms that had been pounding her. She nodded and smiled.

Jenny lived three blocks away in a small apartment. It was simple, but much nicer than Katie's motel room. And unlike the sterile room she had stayed in last night, this one had dishes in the sink, clothes hanging in an open closet, and magazines strewn across a bruised coffee table. Somebody lived there. It was Jenny's home.

Jenny made sandwiches and Katie devoured them. "Man, I remember being that hungry," Jenny said with a smile. "Nothing worse than that. Buffy's saved my life."

Katie studied her over the remains of her second sandwich. "What's it like to…you know…undress and stuff?"

Jenny assessed Katie before responding. "It's okay. You interested?"

"No," Katie exclaimed. She waved her hands palms out, as if she were trying to shove the idea away. "I could never do anything like that."

"I thought that, too, at first. But you'd be surprised. There's not that much to it. You dance around on a stage, and the money's great. Last night I made $200 in tips."

Katie's eyes widened in disbelief. Two hundred dollars for a night's work? That was more money than she ever dreamed of making. But she shivered at the thought of men leering at her, or worse. "Don't you have to do more than dance for that kind of money?"

Jenny laughed. "Heck no. Oh, some girls do tricks on the side, but I sure don't. You dance good enough, men will give you lot's of money just to watch. You're always in control. You tease the men, play them along, but you never let them touch you."

Visions of dancing in front of an audience flitted through Katie's head. She found the idea both repulsive and intriguing. For months, she had escaped into a dream world filled with ballet and music, but she had always known it was just a fantasy. She thought about the poster. What she'd seen in it reminded Katie of her fantasies, but without the groping hands or smelly bodies. Two hundred dollars for one night! It seemed incredible.

"I have to get ready for work. Why don't you come with me? See what you think?" Jenny smiled and held out her hand like a big sister. Katie was surprised at how small it felt when she took it.

The hand made her feel safe, but for how long? Jenny had said she could crash for a night or two. After that, what were her alternatives? The same as before, she thought glumly, which meant no choices at all. The idea of entering a strip joint made her skin crawl, but if she went with Jenny she could face it. And she *did* want to see her new friend dance.

Katie followed Jenny into a cavernous, dark room that smelled of spilled beer and stale cigarettes. Two spotlights illuminated a stage to her right, where a lonely figure bounced and tossed her naked breasts before a handful of men seated in front of the raised floor. The dance looked ugly, and Katie knew it wasn't for her. But she was curious to see Jenny, so she sat at a table in the back while Jenny went to change.

A waitress in a cocktail dress that showed more of her body than it covered approached. "You old enough to be here, honey?"

Katie looked into a set of tired eyes that spoke of too many nights on her feet and too many men in her bed. "I'm older than you could ever imagine," she replied in a defiant tone. Her response surprised her. She never would have had the courage to speak like that a few months ago.

The waitress looked her up and down. "What you want?"

"A Coke."

"It's five bucks, whether you have a Coke or a drink," she said in a friendlier voice.

Katie blanched when she heard the price. "I'm with Jenny. Maybe I'll just have water."

The waitress looked at her knowingly. "You a friend of Jenny's?" Katie nodded. "Coke's on the house, then. Just don't tell the boss."

Katie watched another woman bump and grind her way through her performance, while the men whooped and called to her. She still found the scene repugnant, but it wasn't nearly as bad as what she'd been through. She sipped her Coke and waited.

Jenny finally entered the stage, and Katie's world turned upside down. Jenny was clearly not a trained dancer, but she swayed and swirled with the power of an ocean tide. She was bold and sensual, yet she expressed the vulnerability Katie had noticed in the poster. Katie watched her with fascination. The two previous women had been strippers. Jenny was a dancer. Katie felt connected to her, and she suddenly wondered what it would be like to step on that stage and dance with her.

"Jenny said you might be looking for work." A heavy-set, balding man with a chewed up cigar in his mouth plopped down in a chair opposite her. The man's pallid skin said he spent too much time inside, and his narrow set eyes gave him an unsavory look.

She was too surprised by his unexpected appearance to answer him. Her mind and heart raced at what he was suggesting. Memories of coarse hands and hot tongues snaking over her body at Angel's romped through her head. Her body shook so violently, she nearly jumped up and fled from the room. But then she remembered other hands ripping her clothes off in a dark alley and knew she never wanted to live on the street again. Katie hid her trembling hands beneath the table and tried to decide what to do.

She looked back at Jenny, whose naked body glistened in the spotlight. Jenny's performance had a grace that reminded her of the ballet dancing she'd done for so many years. Strip teasing wasn't that different from ballet, she told herself, if you did it right. Both were sensual and revealed the body. Jenny's movements might lack polish, but she turned what she was doing into an art form. And she played the men like they were on puppet strings, just as she'd said. She was always in control, something Katie found oddly appealing after being Angel's prisoner. What she liked best, however, was the money the men showered on her. Two hundred dollars was a fortune. She tried to imagine earning that kind of money.

Katie thought about all these things in a matter of seconds: the money, the dancing, and the power over men. Maybe stripping wasn't so bad, if it kept her from facing her street demons.

"I can dance circles around your girls." Katie blinked in surprise at her impudent remark, but she suddenly felt bold and reckless.

"Dancing ain't what they want baby. They want big tits and a tight ass. Let's see your tits." He looked at her expectantly.

The man's audacity raised the hairs on the back of Katie's neck, and the urge to flee rose in her chest once more. Jenny was finishing her number, however, and Katie saw the beauty in her steps. She didn't know what to say. It was one thing to think about dancing in front of a faceless audience. It was quite another to expose herself to this fat, ugly man. She felt the same wild anger rising in her throat that she had experienced when she struck Bully with the lamp. It took all her self-control to keep from picking up the ashtray on the table and throwing it at him.

His demand crystallized her thinking, however. She didn't have a work permit or any kind of identification, so finding work would be hard. And she couldn't expect Jenny to look out for her. She had to take care of herself. Facing a room full of men was far better than facing the street.

"If you want to see my tits," she responded coldly, "you'll have to put me up there." She pointed her finger towards the stage.

He studied her with greater interest, his mouth chomping furiously on the weathered cigar. "Okay," he said at last. "I'll give you a tryout tomorrow night. No pay. Just tips. If you're any good, we can talk about a regular gig."

"I'll need a ballerina's costume."

His eyes widened. She couldn't tell if it was from interest or surprise. "You're responsible for your own outfits. There's a costume shop in the next block. My name's Benny. Be here at six." He clamped down on his cigar and left.

She sat watching another stripper begin her bump and grind number, while she tried to get her mind around what she had just agreed to do. The idea of undressing in front of a room full of sexually aroused men made her stomach churn, but the idea of dancing again sent a shower of meteor sparks streaking through her body. Here was her chance to dance ballet, even if it meant taking her clothes off.

She finished her Coke and left.

There was only one ballerina outfit at the store, and it was a size too small. She managed to squeeze into it and decided she could make it work with a few alterations. If anything, it made her look sexier, and she knew that wasn't a bad thing. But when she thought about taking it off in front of those men she nearly ran from the store. She grit her teeth, instead, and suppressed the panic swelling inside of her. One night's rental was $20, the amount for selling Bully's watch. There was no turning back. She had to make this work, or she would be broke.

The club was quiet when she arrived with Jenny the next evening at six. Only one table was occupied by three young men, none of whom looked twenty-one. Jenny directed her to the door at the back of the stage. "I've got to drop something off in the office. I'll join you in a minute."

The two, hard-boiled looking women she'd seen the day before were already seated in the dressing area when she entered.

"Well, look what they brought us. A kid. You here to sweep?" The woman who spoke had long black hair, dark eyes, and a small, pouting mouth that was painted bright red. She was naked to the waist, showing off a well-proportioned figure. Katie estimated her to be in her late twenties or early thirties. She acted tough, but Katie was unfazed. This woman couldn't begin to intimidate her after what she'd just been through.

"I'm here to dance." She returned the woman's mocking stare without blinking.

"Dance!" The other woman guffawed. She was taller and heavier, a bleached blond with red highlights in her hair. "You're in the wrong club, honey. The dance club is across town at Arthur Murray's." Both women howled with laughter.

Katie pressed her lips together and said nothing. She stood in the middle of the room holding her costume and trying to figure out where she should sit. Neither woman looked ready to help her.

"Leave her alone," Jenny said as she walked in. Katie was relieved to see her and smiled. Jenny returned the smile. "Put your stuff over here next to me." She indicated a separate dressing table from the others.

"Oh, God, I'll bet she's a virgin." This was from the woman with the red highlights.

"That's Betty Sue," Jenny said. "The other's named Lori Lee. Don't mind them. They did the same thing to me when I first got here. I was a virgin too. Just remember, stripping fulfills a man's fantasies. He wants to believe you're only there for him, and you'll do anything he desires. Always focus your attention on the customers, but do it one at a time. Look at them and seduce them."

Lori Lee peeked through the curtains. "The place is filling up. Lot's of money out there. It's gonna be a good night."

"Let's put the virgin on first, see how she does." Betty Sue chuckled at the suggestion.

"Not a chance," Benny responded as he stomped into the room. "I'm not going to risk losing customers right off the bat if she bombs. Follow your normal rotation. The new girl goes last. We'll call you princess," he said turning to her. Katie realized he didn't even know her name.

"Here." She handed him a CD of Swan Lake she had purchased that afternoon. "I want you to play this." He looked at it skeptically, shook his head, and left.

By the time Katie squeezed into her costume, Lori Lee was already on stage warming up the crowd. Cheers and rowdy remarks filtered through the curtains. Katie separated the fabric just enough to survey the room. Her heart pounded as she watched first Lori Lee, then Betty Sue go through their routines. She thought about how she would perform. She wanted to combine the beauty of ballet with the seductiveness of strip tease, but now that she saw the two women interacting with the audience, her confidence disappeared as quickly as Star and Aya after she opened that front door. Each woman's sexuality was powerful, and the audience hooted its approval. The sexual energy pouring off the men blanketed Katie in a steamy shroud that burned her lungs. The music booming in her head mingled with the roars of the men. What had possessed her to think she could perform such a shameless act? She had no business being there. She had to get out before it was too late.

But when Jenny appeared on stage, Katie stood rooted to her spot. What a contrast she was to the others! Lori Lee and Betty Sue had pounded through their programs. Jenny glided through hers. The others had worked their bodies in a bump and grind fashion that Katie found repugnant. Jenny undulated so seductively Katie was entranced. She chewed her fingertips and watched intently. Jenny's act restored some of her self-assurance. She observed how the young woman blended her more artful routine with the sexual innuendos of her naked body. Just what Katie wanted to do, but could she?

The music ended amidst lusty cheers and a shower of dollar bills. Jenny had finished. It was Katie's turn. Her skin was hot and moist to the touch, her body sticky with sweat. She pushed loose strands of hair off her face as she fought the demons inside her head. How could she go out there like that? Those men would find her ugly. They would laugh at her and pelt her with their drinks. The desire to run nearly overwhelmed her, but when she looked behind her, she discovered Lori Lee and Betty Sue blocking her path.

"Bet she's ready to take her skinny legs and dog it outta here." Katie recognized Lori Lee's snickering voice.

"Yeah, she looks like a runner to me." Betty Sue chuckled.

Their hot bodies pressed against Katie's back, pushing her forward. She heard Benny introducing her over the speaker system as the virgin princess, but his voice was far away. The crowd roared its approval. She didn't know if they thought she was supposed to be a real virgin or understood this was her first time on stage. Before she could consider the question further, the two women shoved her through the curtains into the glare of twin spotlights. She squinted against the harsh light at the forest of faces leering up at her. The bar was filled with male voyeurs, and the realization that she was about to take off her clothes in front of that mob destroyed her few remaining fibers of confidence. She fidgeted, ready to turn and run.

But when the first notes of Swan Lake drifted across the room, the audience quieted. Katie closed her eyes and drank in each note with the thirst of a lost soul. The music rose around her, forming the same glass wall she had erected so many times at Angel's. She swayed quietly, ignoring the coughs and grunts of the men. Her body floated with the music and stirred with excitement. She visualized the choreography she had learned, sucked in a nervous breath and pirouetted once, twice, three times, finishing with a graceful leap across the stage. Her movements were met by silence. Even the coughing had stopped. Jennie had warned her that she only had a few precious moments to win over her audience, but she thrust that thought aside and concentrated on what Mrs. Perrot had taught her. As she raised herself onto the tips of her toes and stretched her long arms towards the ceiling, Mrs. Perrot's words echoed in her ear. "Look at how she extends herself on her toes, girls. How she expresses herself with her body."

More silence. *They don't like me.* Her mind froze in panic. *Why did I ever think I could do this?* The hot lights boiled her skin, causing rivulets of moisture to trickle down her arms. The smell of hot bodies assaulted her, and for a moment she was back in that vile room lying under the oppressive weight of some man's flesh. She drew in a ragged breath, pushed the memory aside, and began to unzip the back of her bodice while she tiptoed across the stage. The music was building inside of her, and she twirled through a series of intricate leaps and steps. With each movement, her body grew more seductive and more sensual. She could feel herself evolving from ballerina to stripper, and the room was coming alive with sexual energy. She ended her steps with her bodice pulled down to her tutu and her naked back facing the audience.

"Oh man, turn around," a male voice shouted. "Turn around, turn around," others chanted.

Her fear vanished. A moment of brilliant clarity flashed through her. Every one of those men wanted her. She could feel her power energizing them. It was an incredibly heady experience, and she prolonged the moment as long as she dared, swaying with her back to the audience and spinning too quickly for them to see her clearly. When she finally turned and bared her breasts, her breathing was coming in quick bursts of excitement. By the time

156

she had shed the rest of her costume, she was flying through the air, and the room was howling with shouts and whistles that bathed her body. She looked into the face of each man, just as Jenny had told her to do, and they devoured her with their eyes. Money floated onto the stage floor like snowflakes.

Benny was waiting for her when she returned back stage. "You're hired," he said without preamble. "See me after the show. In my office. We'll talk." Lori Lee and Betty Sue looked at her with grudging respect. Jenny beamed.

She performed until two in the morning, until exhaustion crept into every muscle in her body, and her costume reeked of sweat, and beer, and cigarette smoke. Her fatigue couldn't spoil her jubilation, however.

The atmosphere had been so different then she'd expected. Ballet was performed on a stage far from the audience. At Buffy's, the crowd sat within touching distance. She'd quickly learned just how close she could come to them and still avoid their groping hands. She'd learned to tease them, to play hide and seek with what they wanted to see and touch. Her power over them had been absolute.

By the time she'd changed, the club was nearly deserted, and a moment of doubt crept into her joy. Benny was waiting for her in his office, and she remembered the way he'd looked at her when they first met. She feared she was about to face another Angel.

"Do I need to worry about Benny?" she asked Jenny anxiously. Lori Lee and Betty Sue were already gone.

"You mean are you safe with him? Don't worry. He's okay. Better than a lot of men in this business, or so I'm told. He never messes with the girls. Gives you a fair shake."

She was relieved to hear that and pleased to see that Benny was all business when she entered his office. He gave her the standard employee agreement to read and sign. The wage was low. The real money came from the tips. That depended on how well the girls pleased the audience. She would perform six nights a week, Tuesday through Sunday. He advised her not to "date" the customers and to stay clear of drugs. "Those are your two worst enemies in this business," he told her. "You have a natural way with the men. Keep your nose clean and you can make good money."

Katie gulped the night air into her lungs when she reached the street. It had been one hell of a night. She was amazed at how much pleasure she had derived from dancing in front of those men. She'd enjoyed arousing them and fulfilling their fantasies without having to face them in bed. It may not have been center stage at the Dorothy Chandler Pavilion, but it had its own hypnotic appeal. Best of all, she had earned $150 in tips.

Months flew by. Katie moved into a small apartment and started a savings account. She quickly became the star at Buffy's, and her savings grew rapidly. Men approached her, but she kept them at arm's length. The glass wall she'd built at Angel's rarely came down, now. Lori Lee and Betty Sue were making extra money on the side by "dating" customers, but she never wanted to put herself in that position again. She drew strength from Jenny, who never left with a customer. Their friendship grew.

Only once did she yield to the advances of a customer, a young man named David who kept pestering her for a real date. There was no offer of money or expectation of sexual favors. They went to an afternoon movie, and she invited him back to her apartment. She gnawed the ends of her fingers as she tried to find pleasure in his ardent attentions. It was no good. She couldn't rid herself of those grunting men, and she floated away in a series of leaps and pirouettes. She didn't go out with David again.

Katie was in her second year at the club when her popularity suddenly exploded beyond the fraternity of local voyeurs. Her unique style of combining ballet with strip tease caught the attention of a reporter, and before she knew it, her name and picture appeared in the entertainment sections of two newspapers. At first, she was pleased with the attention, and Benny was delighted with the extra business she brought him. But her growing notoriety bothered her, as well. She feared her father would discover her whereabouts and try to contact her. She imagined looking into that sea of faces surrounding her stage one night and seeing her father's eyes slithering over her naked body. Her body convulsed involuntarily.

When other writers tried to interview her, she declined, much to Benny's chagrin, but the damage had already been done. It wasn't her father's face that emerged from the crowd one Saturday night; it was the baleful stare of another familiar predator, the unsmiling face of Angel. Katie nearly missed her step when she saw him seated at a table near the back, and she moved through the rest of her routine in a daze, her mind reeling from the shock of discovering him there. In less than a heartbeat, her nightmares reclaimed their old territory, and she shook so violently, she had to flee from the stage without gathering her tips.

Jenny saw her terror and swooped Katie into her arms backstage. "Those are her tips," she yelled at Lori Lee, who was strutting onto the stage. "Katie, what happened out there?"

Katie began to sob. "There's . . . there's a man out there who wants to kill me, or worse."

"What could be worse than being killed?"

"There's much worse. I've got to get out of here, now." Her trembling subsided and she thought about her alternatives. "Look out the back door. Tell me if you see anyone in the alley."

Jenny complied and returned with a worried look on her face. "There's a big guy standing right outside the door."

"Is he bald?" She nodded. "Bully. He's alive." In a strange way, Katie was relieved to learn she hadn't killed him, although she had no doubt he would kill her if he got the chance. "Jenny, you've got to help me. I need to borrow your pink outfit."

Jenny handed it to her without question. She was two sizes larger than Katie. The costume hung loosely around Katie's waist and shoulders, but it would have to do. Tears welled up in her eyes when she looked at her friend. She knew she would never see Jenny again.

Lori Lee's number was in full swing when Katie sauntered over to the bar for a drink. Angel sat two tables away, but he hardly noticed her. His rapacious eyes were focused on the stage where he expected her to reappear. When he curled his upper lip into that familiar smile, she had to clench her glass to keep from spilling her drink. The music throbbed inside her head. Memories of clammy hands fondling her body tormented her. It was all she could do to keep from screaming.

When a man in a leather jacket offered to buy her a second drink, she accepted, then excused herself to use the bathroom. According to newspaper accounts Katie read, he told police that she walked out the front door without looking back, hailed a passing cab, and disappeared into the back seat. Investigators discovered she'd withdrawn a considerable sum of money and closed her bank account the next morning. Clothing was strewn around her apartment, but there was no evidence of a struggle.

Katie Livingston vanished without a trace. Foul play was suspected, and the police scoured the San Fernando Valley for the popular dancer, but her body was never found. Eventually, people forgot about her, except for Jenny, who knew she was alive and kept her in her prayers. And Benny, who bemoaned the loss in business after she was gone. No one ever performed ballet at Buffy's again.

CHAPTER THIRTEEN

It'd been an hour since Mr. Andersen had left, but Julia couldn't decide what to do. She wandered around her apartment with thoughts swarming through her head in staccato beats. *The girl Li Chang dead. Romeo missing. An odorous hand smothering her. Kathy murdered by Person . . . Andersen . . . no, Person. Snarling dogs snapping at her shoes. Kidnapped girls. Mark's worried face. Mark's handsome face. Mark.*

Julia fought off the panic that threatened to send her mind into a tailspin. She stood in the middle of her living room, her emotions swinging back and forth between hope and apprehension. The list of coded names Mr. Andersen had given her weighed heavily in her hand. Things were slipping beyond her control; danger was lurking outside her door. Its precise nature was unknown to her, but it was there. Her only comfort was the knowledge that Mark was close by. She needed to see him. He was the only person who could chase away her demons.

Julia grabbed her Sat-Com and sent a message to Mark's, asking him to join her. She'd already given him access to the building in case of an emergency, and when she heard his light steps moving up the stairs, she flung her door open. Mark stopped at the threshold. Julia sensed his hesitancy and felt the sexual tension simmering between them. Their passionate kiss in the car still burned her lips, and she shivered at its implications. Did he feel it, too? Julia searched his face for a sign, but his expression remained reserved, non-committal. *God, what am I doing? All the poor man wants to do is protect me, and I'm charging after him like a mare in heat.* But she had never felt this way about anyone, before. Not even Jackie.

"We can talk more comfortably if you come in." She gave him a half-smile that showed she was as uncertain as he was. He grinned sheepishly and stepped inside.

"Drink?" It was all Julia could do to keep from throwing her arms around him.

He shook his head no. "Coffee, if you've got it."

"Sit down. It'll just take a minute." Julia nodded towards the kitchen table. "Mr. Andersen gave me a list of names and addresses for Kwong's drug distributors and the contacts for the kidnapped women, but it's in code," she called over her shoulder while she poured water and started the coffee maker.

"I know. I'm making arrangements to gain access to Kwong's computer files, so we can decipher the codes. I should have the information by tomorrow night."

Julia sat down facing him while the coffee perked in the background. Now that they were talking business, his face had become more relaxed, more confident. "To do that, you'll have to break into Liu Kwong's office in Chinatown. I'm going with you." She said this with all the conviction she could muster, but her nerves quivered. Images of menacing dogs and falling shoes were still fresh in her mind.

"Not a good idea. It could be dangerous." Mark's furrowed brow signaled his concern. Was he worried professionally, she wondered, or personally?

"I can't let you take the risk by yourself." Her voice softened. "I want to be there with you, to be a part of it." Julia fiddled with the paper Andersen had given her.

"You've got courage, I'll give you that. Most people would bail after that incident at the docks." He reached out and took her

162

hand. Julia jumped at the touch of his skin. She was on the verge of erupting. One spark was all that was needed to ignite the pressure building inside of her. She threaded her fingers through his and gripped his hand.

"I couldn't live with myself if anything happened to you while I sat at home." A wave of heat flashed through her body. She disengaged his hand, jumped up from the table, and busied herself with coffee cups to hide her shaken nerves. When she looked back, she saw Mark studying her intently.

Why am I acting so scattered? So stupid?

"About the other day . . . ." His voice became cautious, less self-assured.

"If you're going to say something patronizing, I *will* throw you to the sharks." Julia gave a high-pitched laugh that sounded like fingernails on a blackboard. She was relieved to see Mark smile.

He stood and walked to where she had withdrawn in the kitchen. "It was quite wonderful." He touched her cheek with his fingers.

The sparks flew. He knew all about her, and he still wanted her. Tears clouded her vision. She didn't know whether they were tears of joy or absolution. It didn't matter. Her spirit was rising from the ashes of too many failed relationships and blossoming.

Before she knew it, they were in each other's arms, and Mark was searing her mouth and neck with an unbridled passion that threatened to devour her. Julia tasted the damp, night air on his skin, smelled the tanginess of his desire. She grasped his hand and pulled him into the bedroom, where they fumbled like teenagers in their haste to undo buttons and open zippers. Julia loved the feel of his hands kneading her skin. When he touched her breasts, her body exploded as if it were dry tinder touched by a match. When he began to explore her body, she soared into the heavens, her temperature rising higher and higher, consuming her.

They clung together afterwards in a tangle of sweaty arms and legs. Every nerve in Julia's body jumped at Mark's touch. She marveled at how someone trained in violence could be so gentle.

She knew almost nothing about the man lying beside her, yet she'd just given herself completely to him. He was a mystery, a puzzle she had yet to solve. Julia yearned to ask him questions, but an attack of nerves held her back. She turned her attention to obtaining the codes, instead.

"How do you propose to get into Kwong's office?" Julia rolled over on her stomach and stared at him. She was fascinated at how his facial muscles tightened when he talked business. He could shift gears in a heartbeat.

"Kwong's office is located on the top floor of the four-story building housing the Golden Moon. There's no access to it from the street. Kwong has installed an electronic alarm system that's state-of-the-art. Much too sophisticated for a restaurant."

"What can we do?"

"There's a tenant building across the street with on old fire escape. I suggest you stand guard on the street. I'll climb the fire escape and ferry myself by wire across to the roof of Kwong's office. I believe I can gain entry from there."

Julia had told Mark about her fear of heights, and she knew he was protecting her. She could feel her heart rate accelerating as he described his plan. Fire escapes and high-wire acts reduced the magnitude of those shipping containers to a Sunday stroll. She would be crazy to consider such a venture, yet . . . . She sighed and set her jaw the way she had as a child when she was determined to get something.

"There's no way you're leaving me behind, Mark. I'm going up on that roof with you."

He propped his head on his hand and contemplated her. The silence between them lengthened into shadows that filled the room. Julia liked the silence. It said they were comfortable together. They could understand one another without the need to talk. She leaned forward and kissed Mark's shoulder, then his neck, then his lips. Mark touched her breast, gently pinching her hardening nipple. The conflagration had begun, again.

A full moon suspended in the western sky bathed the narrow

streets with unwelcome light and etched Chinatown's ghostly buildings against the sky. Julia tried to suppress the flurry of tiny wings beating in her chest. Only Mark's calm presence kept her from bolting. They were both dressed in vampire black, but the unwanted moonlight made Julia feel as though she were standing in the center ring at the circus. Everywhere she turned, she saw eyes peering out at her from the shadows. It was nearly 4:00 a.m. They had waited patiently for two hours, until the last of the poker players exited the card room that still operated in the back of the Golden Moon restaurant, and the staff had gone home.

Julia stared at the small clamp attached to the belt at her waist and wondered how she was going to manage it. Scaling the shipping containers at the docks had been exhilarating, but it paled in comparison to climbing a fire escape and flying over the rooftops of Chinatown on a wire.

Julia was lost in these thoughts when Mark touched her arm and told her it was time to go. The tiny wings beat more furiously as she followed Mark down the street to an alley that ran alongside the tenant building. Mark moved like a stalking cheetah, silent and unobserved. Julia felt clumsy as she hastened to keep up. He stopped beneath the fire escape and hoisted a thin rope with an attached hook to the bottom rung of the metal ladder. The hook gripped the rung, and he quietly pulled the ladder down to them.

Julia went first, just as she had on the cargo containers. The ladder's rungs felt familiar to her, and she found herself listening expectantly for the sharp reports of barking dogs. All she heard was the night's heavy breathing as it sucked at her hands and feet. The night was a living entity that disoriented her. She could feel it inhaling and exhaling, trying to wrest her from her perch and cast her into the moon-washed cavern below. Julia's hands trembled on the railings. Her feet stumbled on the steps. She silently raged at the demon night and steeled her mind, then grasped the railings more firmly and kept climbing.

Reaching the roof brought none of the euphoria Julia had experienced when she climbed atop the containers. She knew a much harder task lay just beyond the roof's edge. She still had to fly over the rooftops. Mark moved as quietly as a shadow. He produced a harpoon-shaped device filled with a small, explosive charge and fired it at the roof of Kwong's building across the street. It struck with a soft thud and held. He secured the attached wire to the top rung of the fire escape, tested its stability, and clamped a mechanism with two, small wheels to the wire. Julia's body froze as she stared at the tiny wheels. If she wanted to reach Kwong's office, she would have to attach the clamp at her waist to that roller and fling herself into the abyss between the two buildings. The tenant building was one story taller than Kwong's. Gravity would pull her down the wire to the other side. Julia had bullied herself into believing she could do it, but now, the moon pressed down on her head, reminding her just how high she had ascended into the sky. An unexpected breeze raised goose bumps on her flesh. Julia knew it wasn't nature's wind. It was the nocturnal breath of the night waiting to send her crashing to the ground.

Mark sensed her dismay and pulled her trembling body to his. "You can do this. All you have to do is believe in yourself."

His warmth flowed through her with the magic of a sorcerer's potion. The demon night retreated, and a finger of hope restored a few threads of her confidence. Julia buried her face in Mark's shoulder and nodded.

She watched Mark set the clamp on the rollers. He cast himself into space without hesitation and slid down the wire with the ease of a trapeze artist. A pulley string attached to the roller allowed Julia to retrieve it and attach it to her belt. The moment had come. The wings beat so furiously in her chest, she feared her heart would fail. Julia closed her eyes, said a small prayer, and stepped off the roof. The wire yielded slightly under her weight, and for a terrifying moment she thought she *would* plummet to the ground. Her eyes flew open, but the wire held. Wind chilled her face as she rocketed down the silvery, metal strand; moonlight framed her in its stark brilliance, making her feel exposed and vulnerable. She focused her attention on Mark and tried to ignore the gaping chasm filled with jagged shadows beneath her. At last,

Mark's arms engulfed her and pulled her onto the roof.

A cry of relief escaped her tense lips. Her legs wobbled, and she grabbed Mark's arm to steady herself. She had survived the second stage of her ordeal, but there was still no feeling of triumph. There was only the knowledge that she faced one more horrifying challenge. She pressed herself into Mark's reassuring embrace and let his strength succor her.

The final stage required her to rappel down the side of the building. Mark set the line and lowered himself to Kwong's office window, being careful not to touch the glass. When he activated his laser light, Julia saw why he was being so cautious. A force field of electronic beams similar to the ones at the shipping docks glowed menacingly in the dark. Mark bent the beams in the same manner as before. When he was finished, he climbed back to the roof and attached Julia's waist clamp to his. Oh *God, let me endure this.* She clung to him.

Mark gave her no time to think. She gasped as he quickly swung them both over the roof's edge and began walking down the side of the building towards the open window. Julia's insides rose and fell with the adrenaline rush of a roller coaster ride, but her experience with the shipping containers came to her rescue. She controlled her breathing and focused on the wall in front of her. *All I'm doing is floating down the wall one step at a time.* By the time they were inside, Julia felt as limp as a boxer pinned against the ropes, but she'd made it! She'd flown over the rooftops and rappelled down the wall. Nothing could ever terrify her again. Ecstasy swept aside her jitters.

Mark scanned the room with his sensor, but there was no signal from an electronic safe. They checked the obvious places in the floor and walls but found nothing. The drawers in the desk held files and accounting ledgers on the restaurant, but nothing more. Puzzled, Mark stood in the middle of the room. Julia looked at the desk. On impulse, she began running her hand under the desktop, just as she had watched detectives doing it in old movies. Her fingers touched a switch. She flipped it and watched in awe as a portion of the wall behind the desk slid away, revealing a 5'x5' room filled with weapons, files, and a computerized safe that looked like a flat-panel wall screen. The walls of the hidden room shined in the moonlight streaming through the window.

"The walls are lined with an alloy designed to block electronic signals," Mark commented. "That's why my scanner failed to detect anything."

He gave her hand a congratulatory squeeze and activated the computer screen on the safe. Next, he attached a digital readout box to the panel's controls and pressed a sequence of buttons. Numbers began to flash in rapid sequence on the box, until a seven appeared. Mark pressed the buttons and started the process again. While he worked the combination sequences, Julia wandered to the window and looked down. The moon was getting lower, but it still cast enough light for her to see the dark outline of a figure slipping through the alley below. It reached the corner of the building and disappeared. Her first thought was a local resident on his way home, but the figure's movements were too catlike. Her pulse quickened. She rushed back to Mark.

"I think someone's coming," she whispered.

Mark nodded and kept working the buttons. "Listen at the door but don't open it. It's wired. Here, take this." He pulled a laser gun from his bag and handed it to her.

The weapon was much heavier than the little stun gun she carried in her purse. She stood stock-still and stared at the black metal object in her hand. This one killed people. Mark had said there could be danger, but the idea had been abstract. Danger meant scaling fire escapes and flying through the air. Not firing a weapon. Not killing someone. Or, worse yet, feeling the hot beam of a laser searing through her chest.

Julia's happy mood dissolved in the fading moonlight. A new reality slid with serpentine cunning underneath her skin. Her perspiring hands were already making it difficult to hold the deadly weapon, but when she thought about the shadowy figure she had just seen slinking towards the building, she quietly admonished herself. Julia gripped the gun in both hands and hurried to the door.

She pressed her ear against the varnished wood but could hear nothing over the blacksmith hammering of her heart. *Take a deep breath. Calm yourself.* She listened more carefully but was greeted by an endless silence. The gun was growing heavy in her hands. It was an anchor dragging her to the bottom of a misty world where nothing existed except empty space. She remembered a line from an old movie: in space no one could hear you scream. Was that true? Perhaps nothing existed beyond that door but the silence of deep space. Where nothing could be heard? Where sound didn't travel?

Then, a dull thump echoed just beyond the door, and Julia knew in that terrifying moment that it *was* possible to hear things in space . . . and that they weren't alone. Before she could warn Mark, the door crashed open, knocking the wind from her lungs and sending her tumbling to the floor. She sat there in dazed confusion and watched as two bodies collided in the center of the room. The moonlight was nearly gone, leaving the room too dark for her to know which one was Mark. Other than a loud grunt when one of the men was slammed into the wall, they fought in silence.

Julia grabbed the weapon that had spilled from her hands when she fell, but she didn't know where to aim it. Remnants of moonlight outlined the two struggling figures, but which one was Mark? A burst of light flashed across the room, followed by an explosive bang in the wall near the door. The momentary light revealed one figure holding a weapon and the other gripping the arm that controlled it. Then, it all went blank as the momentary light robbed Julia of her ability to see anything. She stood up and groped for a light switch but couldn't find one. Images began to re-emerge from the darkness. Her weapon trembled in her hand. She pointed it at the men, uncertain what to do.

"Julia," Mark cried out, "I don't have the gun."

He wanted her to shoot the man with the weapon. Her heart pounded like a piston in her chest. She watched in horror as the gunman struggled to shift his weapon in her direction. Holding her laser as steady as possible, she squeezed the trigger. She heard a man cry out just before a brilliant light slammed into her shoulder and a searing heat spread through her chest. Then, there was silence. She saw one figure standing over the other, and for a paralyzing moment feared she'd shot Mark.

"He's dead." It was Mark's voice. He sounded pleased. "Good shot, Julia. Julia? Are you hit?"

His voice floated to her in a fog. The room was spinning so fast, she couldn't hang onto the gun. It slipped from her hands and clattered to the floor. Strong arms lifted her as she fell into deep space. Space, where no one would hear her scream.

Julia awoke in the soft folds of her sheets and blanket. Her right shoulder burned so hotly, she thought her arm had been amputated. She wiggled her fingers and was relieved to feel movement. The room was dark. She remembered the flash of light and Mark's voice telling her she had killed the horrible man who attacked them. But why did her body hurt so much? Had he shot her, too?

"Mark?" she called out in a rusty voice. The effort sent a fresh wave of pain shooting through her body.

Her bedroom door opened immediately, and she was pleased to see Mark's familiar figure framed by the light streaming through the doorway. He was at her side in three strides, holding her hand and brushing the hair from her forehead. "You're finally awake." There was a happy tone in his voice. When he flipped on the lamp beside her bed, she saw a haggard, unshaven face.

"What happened to me?" she asked as quietly as she could. She didn't want to feel that jarring pain, again.

"You both fired at the same time. His clipped your shoulder. You hit him dead center. You're quite a shot." She heard admiration in his voice. She soaked it up. Wanted more.

"I was lucky," she admitted. "How long have I been like this?"

"Just a day, but I'm in the doghouse. Mr. Andersen is very upset with me for letting you tag along."

"What do you mean, tag along? I *saved* you." Her indignation triggered another bolt of pain. She winced and lay still.

"Yes, you did, and that fact was not lost on Mr. Andersen. But he doesn't want you taking unnecessary risks. Anyway, you won't be climbing cargo containers or fire escapes for a few weeks." He laughed. She liked his laugh. It was strong and sincere. "He's anxious to see you as soon as you're ready."

Memories of Kathy Griffith's murder and dinner on the Bay streamed back into her consciousness. She wanted to see him too, to learn what had happened. When she thought about what he'd done to Kathy, though, her anger boiled as hotly as her shoulder.

"Maybe later. I'm pretty groggy."

"That's the medication. Mr. Andersen had a doctor who specializes in weapon wounds attend to you. It was too risky to take you to a hospital. Liu Kwong would be watching for that. You'll feel fresher tomorrow after the medicine wears off a bit. Sleep now. I'll be in the next room if you need anything."

"Why not in my bed?" she asked impishly.

"Too many temptations. Not good for the patient."

"Maybe I should decide what's good for the patient."

He smiled, kissed her on the lips, and closed the door behind him as he left the room.

CHAPTER FOURTEEN

Mr. Andersen came to see her two days later. Julia continued to think of him as Andersen. She had to keep the old man separated in her mind from Person the murderer. It was the only way she could deal with him, at least for now. She was sitting up in bed, and her shoulder had graduated from burning coals to a dull ache.

"I see I must contend with your stairs awhile longer," he said as he puffed into her bedroom and sat down in the chair Mark had put there for him. "I'm very relieved to see you are all right. I gave Mark hell for being so irresponsible."

"I forced him to take me. And if I hadn't been there, he might have died. I couldn't have lived with myself if that had happened because of me." She looked him straight in the eye and challenged him to question her actions. He smiled benignly and let it pass.

Julia was still trying to come to terms with the knowledge that she had killed someone. Every time she thought about it, she became agitated. She had a picture in her mind of fire searing through flesh, opening a gaping hole in the shadowy man's face. Since she had closed her eyes at the moment of impact, she hadn't actually seen anything, but her imagination filled in the blanks in a most disturbing way.

Phillip had been beside himself when she spoke to him on the phone. "What are you trying to do, for God's sake, get yourself killed?" He sounded genuinely concerned, which touched her. There was a human side to him after all. He cared what happened to her. Not too long ago, that knowledge would have unnerved her and sent her straight into his arms. Now, she had Mark, and she found her emotions calmer than they had been in years. Her newly discovered self-control felt wonderful, and she thanked Mark for entering her life.

"While you've been healing, we decoded the list," Mr. Andersen continued. "Found some very interesting information. You'll be able to make good use of it in your investigation."

"I want to hear about Kathy," she replied with irritation. She wasn't prepared to feel beholden to this man for lists or information. She still wanted to know why.

"Yes, of course. Kathy." His face became so dreamy Julia had a hard time disliking the man for what he'd done. He clearly loved the woman, even now.

****

With mixed emotions, I took Kathy home after our dinner on the boat. My duplicity with Liu Kwong weighed heavily on my mind. I wanted to be with Kathy as much as possible, which only made my dual role all the more damning. Guilt sat on my shoulder like an accusing raven crying "nevermore." I also sensed some hesitation on her part about letting me get so close. In spite of her warmth, she kept that protective barrier around her. It insulated her from the world, and that included me. Knowing that made me hesitant. As much as I wanted to be near her, I feared if I appeared too eager I might undermine her growing affection for me. My guilt was exacerbated by the knowledge that I was returning to the scene of my own crime, her home. My only comfort was the knowledge that it was late at night and I need not worry about the little boy pointing an accusing finger at me.

"Come in for coffee," she offered when we arrived at her door.

I was parked in her driveway looking at the dollhouse I had so recently invaded. It was a remarkably warm evening for San Francisco, one that spoke of held hands and soft caresses. Her body glowed next to mine with the warmth of a summer day.

I followed her into the house, a familiar house that I knew would betray me if it could. I had to be careful not to do or say anything that would defrock me in the eyes of this spellbinding woman. So, I stood in the hallway admiring the ballet photographs on the wall while Kathy brewed coffee. When she was done, we sat in the living room, side-by-side on the white sofa.

"You like classical music," I observed. I was increasingly nervous and felt the need for small talk. "The piano and the photographs in the hall."

"How much do you know about me, from your investigation?" She looked at me curiously. It was the second time she had asked for any information I might have gleaned from my supposed inquiries into Harry Webster.

"I knew you played the piano. I didn't know about your interest in ballet." Again, half-truths hidden in lies. How long could I keep it up? Sooner or later I was going to trap myself, no matter how careful I was, and the deceits were driving me crazy.

It was time to change the subject. "You mentioned computer disks that you copied at Liu Kwong's. I take it they're not here or weren't found."

"No, I've put them where they're safe. But I don't want to talk about that tonight. I want to talk about you and me." She gave me a smile that wilted my resolve about not appearing too eager. "You look nervous," she continued. "It's the first time I've ever seen you less than a hundred percent sure of yourself. Am I doing that to you?"

"Yes," I blurted. "Forgive the cliché, but I'm ready to jump out of my skin."

She laughed and then her expression grew more serious. "It's the same for me. I told you before that I'm not very good at lasting relationships, not a good finisher. I don't want that to happen with us. I hope you'll be patient with me, if I ask you to take things slowly."

I put down my coffee, cupped her face in my hands, and kissed her with so much passion, I feared I would be consumed on the spot and blown away in a whirlwind of ashes. Our tongues explored the delicate tastes of each other's mouths; our bodies scorched one another where they touched. I was telling her I loved her in the most poetic way I knew how, and she was responding. That moment has stayed with me forever.

"Tell me what to do." I was nearly breathless from our embrace.

She hesitated and brushed back loose strands of hair that had become unmoored. "I want to ask a favor. Yesterday's break-in scares me a little. I worry the intruder might return. Please, stay with me tonight." She touched my lips with her fingers before I could reply. My lips still burn from the memory of that touch. "Only, I don't want to have sex, not now." Her eyes pleaded for my understanding.

She was asking me to protect her from *me*. What irony! Her fear was warranted. I did threaten her, but if I didn't fulfill my agreement with Liu Kwong, she would be in much greater danger. Images of Patrick Parker's sinister smile lingered in my mind. I had to protect her, even at the risk of losing her.

Kathy interpreted my momentary lapse as hesitation. "Don't feel you have to, if you find my request awkward."

"It would be my honor. I can sleep here on the couch, or in a guest room if you have one." I pictured the room with the trellis by the window.

"I would like you in my bed, if you don't mind." An impish half-smile played across her lips, and I wanted to kiss her again but dared not. "Do you think you can do that? Sleep with me without sex?"

It was the most extraordinary proposal I had ever encountered, and I found the idea incredibly arousing. I feared I wouldn't sleep a wink, but I couldn't deny her. Not when I was the cause of her fears. So, I followed her up the stairs to her bedroom, where I had to endure the accusing, single-eyed stare of her teddy bear. We curled up on the bed together fully clothed. I inhaled the rich scent of her hair and tried to imagine a world without her. Lying there beside her, I faced the awful truth of my predicament. My web of deceit and lies had trapped me like an animal, and I might have to chew off my own foot in order to escape. Without her, I would never be whole again.

I slept. I know this because I dreamt that Kathy's delicate hands roamed my body during the night. In my dream, I lay very still, listening to her breathing and relishing the stimulating sensations streaking through me. I felt her passion in those elegant fingers, but I didn't move. I dared not move, for fear I would destroy the dream. She kissed me lightly on the lips and settled back down beside me. Her breathing became slow and regular. She snored. My dream ended.

I awoke in the morning to an empty bed, and for a moment I feared it had been a dream after all. Then, I smelled the aroma of brewing coffee and heard humming coming from the kitchen downstairs. I followed the sound and found Kathy seated in the dining nook smiling radiantly. She had changed out of her clothes into a large, yellow bathrobe, and I wanted to ravish her on the spot. I poured coffee, instead, and sat down opposite her.

"Hi," was all I could say.

"Hi, yourself." Kathy tossed her head to one side, shifting her hair off her face. She looked as natural and beautiful as a morning flower.

"No more burglars?" I asked.

"None."

"You seem happy this morning. No, you look pleased with yourself." She had a smug expression on her face that made me think of the cat and mouse analogy. I was the mouse.

"I'm pleased with *you*. You're a gentleman, someone I can trust. I value that highly." She took my hand and rubbed her thumb against my palm, sending shivers up my arm. And endless waves of guilt. The raven had returned to my shoulder and was mocking me.

"You're incredibly lovely in the morning." I shrugged my

shoulders and the raven flew away. "The most beautiful woman I've ever seen, in the morning or any other time."

"Have you seen many?" Her voice teased me. The corners of her mouth lifted into that familiar half-smile I loved so much.

"None that mattered until now." I hoped I was not overstepping my bounds. Her smile said I wasn't.

We ate croissants and drank more coffee. It was Saturday, but I knew Carl and Patti would be waiting for me at the office. I had put them off as long as possible. It was time to spin the web that might destroy my life and save Kathy's.

"I have to go into the office this morning," I said at last.

"Good, because I have a photo shoot in the afternoon."

"And Saturday is poker night."

She nodded. That meant I couldn't see her again before tomorrow. I wasn't strong enough to face my gambling demons. We agreed to meet for Sunday lunch at a local Vietnamese restaurant she liked. I left in a cloud of confusion, uncertain if I was Sir Galahad or Benedict Arnold. I felt like both.

The office was a mess when I arrived. The outside door had been forced. Papers were strewn everywhere. My small safe had been opened, and the five hundred dollars I kept there for expenses was gone.

Patti was busy trying to put things back in order. "The police have already come and gone. They think it's just petty thieves looking for money to pay for drugs. So far, nothing important seems to be missing. Just the money from the safe."

I looked around the room with suspicion. Thieves or vandals, either one was fine with me. Little harm done, as long as there wasn't a Chinatown connection.

"Where's Carl?" I asked.

"Went to get coffee. They broke the coffee pot. Oh, and there's an envelope on your desk. Marked personal. I found it on the floor by the door when I got here."

I walked into my office and saw the familiar white envelope lying on my desk. The previous three simply had the flap folded inside. This one was sealed, which gave it an ill-omened countenance. I reached for the miniature samurai sword I used as a letter opener and saw it was gone. Stolen. The loss of the sword bothered me more than the money. It had been given to me by one of my first clients, a Japanese businessman who had introduced me to the delicate art of separatism. The sword had sentimental value.

I ripped open the envelope. The message, still pasted neatly on a single page, was longer: *Death will come to you where you least expect it.* It was time to install a hidden camera system in the hallway.

Carl returned, and the three of us sat down in my office to sort through our options. I had dreaded this moment, and now that it was here, I fidgeted in my chair with the guilt of an unruly child waiting in the principal's office. Normally, I began our brainstorming sessions with a background summary, but today I was silent.

"We could connect Kathy to her past as a stripper," Carl suggested, trying to get the ball rolling.

"Not strong enough," Patti responded. I agreed. Liu Kwong was going to want something more damning than taking clothes off in front of a few bawdy men.

"What about an accounting scam?" Patti continued. "We could arrange an audit and implicate her in a fraudulent scheme to 'cook' the books. Hide expenses or bribes. That sort of thing."

Still not bold enough. Kathy was tough. She would fight the charges and probably win. "No," I said softly, "her weakness is the children. We must betray her through her photography." Even as I said it, I regretted spawning such a satanic idea. It struck at her soul.

"Child molestation charges?" Carl reached for the miniature samurai sword but saw it was missing. He liked to play with it while we talked.

"Pornography." Patti spoke matter-of-factly, but the word resounded in the room with the force of an explosion. I stared at her accusingly. She avoided my eyes. "Set up a bogus photo assignment with partially clad children," she continued. "A theatrical setting. After she photographs, we arrange some dummy pornographic scenes. Insert them into her portfolio when you deliver them to Kwong."

It was brilliant. A simple device, but precisely the instrument needed to keep Kwong away from Kathy. It would devastate her, and me.

Carl and Patti left to begin working on the arrangements while I sat in my office in a state of despair. Could I face Kathy after unleashing such a diabolical plot? I doubted it. Could she face me again, if she knew? Never. The message in the latest threatening letter rang in my ears: *Death will come to you where you least expect it.* Patti's plan would sign *my* death warrant with Kathy, and I would know its source, me. My head was starting to coil and uncoil like a rusty spring in an old mattress.

Patti buzzed to inform me that Mr. Parker was in the outer office to see me. My black mood immediately worsened.

"Tell him to come in," I said without enthusiasm.

Patrick eyed the mess as he wandered in with his hands in his pockets. The toupee he wore to cover his thinning hair was carefully combed back and slicked down in the fashion of a '30s gangster, and his brown sports coat and slacks had a slept-in look about them that I found annoying. To me, clothing reflected a man's breeding and his ability to pay attention to details. Patrick's clothing told me he had neither.

"Looks like somebody doesn't like you."

"You wouldn't know anything about this, would you?" I shot back angrily.

"Nothing to do with me." He removed his hands from his pockets and held them up like twin stop signs while he sat down. "Which was it? A burglary, or an unhappy client?"

I ignored his question. "What brings you here?"

"I need to give Liu Kwong an update. Was hoping you could help me out, as we discussed." He gave me a benign smile that was meant to put me at ease, but it only succeeded in making the spring in my head coil and uncoil faster.

"Tell him we're ready to proceed. I want to meet him tonight. I'll be in front of my office building at seven." I didn't care if

Kwong had other plans. I wanted to get this over with.

Patrick must have called Liu Kwong as soon as he left me. Fifteen minutes later, I got a call from someone at the Golden Moon Restaurant confirming our meeting.

By afternoon, Patti had things well in hand. A local theatrical agency would provide a stage that was between productions. Finding subjects to pose wasn't a problem. There was a thriving market for photographs of underage boys and girls. Carl would arrange for some stage backdrops and for a second photographer to take the more damaging images once Kathy was finished. A dummy company we often used for our operations would contact Kathy and make the arrangements.

I asked Carl to have a camera system installed outside the office on Monday and left for the nearest bar. I needed a stiff drink, maybe two, before my meeting with Kwong.

****

Mark interrupted them when he opened the front door with the key Julia had given him. It allowed him to come and go without disturbing her, but she could see by Mr. Andersen's frown that he wasn't pleased with her and Mark's growing familiarity. She didn't care. She expected Mark to keep the key when she was better.

"Romeo's still missing," Mark announced without preamble. "Word on the water front says he's either hiding or left town. Nobody knows for sure."

Julia thought about the street-tough man she had met at the Buena Vista. He had been a vibrant individual, one who exuded a strong sexual energy. Li Chang was dead and Romeo was missing. Everyone connected to Liu Kwong seemed to disappear one way or another. She thought about the skeleton of Patrick Parker lying for so many years in its earthen grave. Had he also met his end at the hands of Liu Kwong? Death was a cheap commodity in Kwong's world. Julia hoped Romeo was safe.

"I made our break-in look like a robbery," Mark continued,

"but I doubt Kwong was fooled." He looked at Julia. "If he gets his hands on Romeo, you can bet he'll learn everything you discussed with him."

"What about the police?" she asked. "What have they learned?"

"The police haven't been called," Mark replied. "Chinatown takes care of its own problems. Which means we've got to be careful. Kwong won't hesitate to eliminate anyone who threatens him."

Memories of brutal hands grabbing her and the acrid smell of chloroform made her shudder. She had no doubt he would kill her, too, if necessary. "Maybe, it's time for me to start writing. Expose his operation in the newspaper. It'll be harder to keep murdering people if I take him public."

"A little more patience would be useful," Mr. Andersen replied. "You still don't have the hard evidence you need to put Liu Kwong away, and there are other big fish you want to catch in your net. I have some interesting computer disks that might help." He produced two antiquated disks from his pocket that looked like they belonged in a museum.

"Kathy's disks," Julia said in a solemn voice.

"Yes, Kathy's disks." His tone was reverent.

"I don't know where I can find a computer to run them." She hadn't seen disks like those in years.

"Try the Technological Institute. They have a display of old computers in their visitor's room that are still operational. Mark can take you there."

Julia mended for two more days before the doctor pronounced her well enough to move about. She promptly asked Mark to return to her bed. "Or I'll report your break-in to the police."

Marked laughed and began caressing her in places she had forgotten about during her recovery. She stuck her tongue in his mouth and tasted the sweetness of his passion. Soon, her whole body felt like hot coals, and her wound became a distant memory.

"It's not fair that you know all about me, and I know next to nothing about you." Julia made her declaration while they lay exhausted in each other's arms an hour later. "Tell me about *you*."

"Maybe I like being mysterious," he teased.

Julia grabbed a handful of his chest hairs and yanked them.

"Ouch. Okay, I'll talk. Just stop torturing me." He placed a pillow against the headboard and pulled himself into a sitting position. Julia snuggled against his chest. "Pretty normal childhood. Mr. Andersen's told you about Carl. He was my father. By the time I was old enough to remember anything, Mr. Andersen--Tom Person in those days--had disappeared, but father told me about some of their escapades. It made me want to find my own adventure, so I volunteered for the marines and joined special operations, where I learned to do a lot of useful things."

"Like swinging across rooftops and climbing down walls."

"Yeah, like that. After fifteen years I decided I'd had enough of the marines. I needed more room to breathe. When I was discharged, the CIA approached me about working for them. I didn't want to get involved in another bureaucratic organization, but I agreed to work for them on a freelance basis. That's what I've been doing ever since. I was between assignments when Mr. Andersen contacted me, so the timing was good."

"That explains the Spider Man stuff, but what about girlfriends?" She raised her head and gave him a threatening glare. "I better not find out there's anyone else."

Mark hesitated and grew more serious. "Not anymore. There was someone, but it's hard to keep a relationship going when you're given twenty-four hours notice and disappear into some country for months at a time. My only friends now are the guys I work with, but we're all pretty independent. Have to be. We work well together on assignments, but we try not to bond too closely, in case an assignment gets messy."

Julia sat up and kissed him. She loved looking at his naked body and letting him see hers. Touching his skin sent shockwaves through her. Caressing his muscled arms and legs felt like climbing oak trees. It left her dizzy and panting but ready for more. "I guess I should say I'm sorry, but that wouldn't be totally honest. If there were somebody else, I wouldn't be here with you now. I want you for myself. Pretty selfish, but that's the way it is." Julia touched his lips with her fingers and felt the fire building in her again.

After making love for the third time, Julia sat up and begged for a ceasefire. "I never thought I'd say it, but I've had enough!" Her body was covered in a film of perspiration that gave her skin a silky sheen she found pleasingly attractive.

Mark rolled onto his side and propped his head in his hand. "When Mr. Andersen asked me to research your background, I learned about Jackie. You seem very close. Were you lovers?"

The question crashed through Julia's reverie. She shot a nervous glance at Mark, looking for signs of disfavor or jealousy, but his smile suggested neither. Just curiosity.

"Spiritually, yes, but not physically. Not like you and me. It's hard to describe in words. We have a very deep attachment for each other, one I know will last our entire lives. You might call us soul mates, but that doesn't explain it adequately. It's more physical than that, more loving. Does it bother you?"

Mark laughed. "Not really. I can share you with Jackie. I hope to meet her sometime. She sounds special."

"She is."

"Just don't expect me to share you with other men." Mark gave her a mischievous look that turned to mock horror just before she belted him with a pillow.

The next morning, they visited the Technological Institute and got permission to run Kathy's disks on an old IBM machine. Julia marveled at how antiquated and slow the computer was compared to modern technology. Commands had to be typed in since there was no voice recognition, and the lack of nonvolatile memory meant they had to move through a series of start-up options before opening the files. When they finally accessed the data, they found detailed records of names, transactions, and payoffs to city officials. They were all retired or dead by now, and Julia began to wonder why Andersen thought the disks had value. Then, she saw the bank account numbers. They were all recorded at the Asian

Bank of Chinatown. The balances ranged from a few hundred thousand to several million dollars. A series of company names were shown on official bank documents, but behind each account was the name of a city official or employee at the port.

"These were dummy accounts, weren't they?" Julia commented. "Used to transfer bribes to Kwong's accomplices. But how did he manage it?"

"Kwong owns the bank," Mark replied. "Always has. Mr. Andersen checked the accounts. The numbers used to deposit money and transfer bribes were changed after Kwong became suspicious of Kathy, but he had to document the changes by law. He did his best to hide them, but I have a source who can trace the original numbers to the current accounts."

"My God, Kathy was sitting on a time bomb. Did Kwong know about these?" Julia pointed to the disks.

Mark shrugged. "Kathy never knew, but she feared that he noticed the two missing blank disks she used to copy the files."

"Mr. Andersen mentioned her concern when he told me about the dinner cruise. So why didn't Kwong have Patrick Parker or one of his thugs just kill her?"

"Murdering her was messy. Kathy wasn't some local thug or criminal. She was a respected member of her community, and he was associated with her professionally and socially. He needed to use a more discreet way to silence her."

"Tom Person." A sad note crept into her voice. The irony was nearly too much for her. The man Kwong had hired to neutralize Kathy so he wouldn't have to kill her had murdered her anyway. What had triggered Person's anger? What had driven him to take the life of the woman he loved? Every time Julia thought about it, she wanted to pummel Tom Person with her fists. But he no longer existed. There was only a pathetic old man who still professed his love for a woman he had killed over forty years ago.

Images were zigzagging through Julia's mind, again. She closed her eyes and forced herself to return to the present. "If we can trace these numbers to current users, we can blow the lid off Kwong's operation."

Mark nodded. "Exposing Kwong is your job. Mr. Andersen wants to keep a low profile."

"He doesn't want to be arrested for murder, you mean." Anger rose in her voice despite her effort to control her emotions.

"That's part of it, yes, but not the whole story." Mark touched her hand.

"Just when do I *get* the whole story? I'm tired of his games." She shook his hand away and immediately regretted it.

"He works in strange ways, I know. He and Liu Kwong are enemies. He not only wants you to know his story, he wants you to bring down Kwong. He's trying to achieve both goals and keep you safe. He cares about you."

Mark's words surprised Julia. She reached out and took his hand again. It felt warm and strong in hers. It was a hand she wanted to hold onto for a long time, perhaps forever. "And what about you, Mark? What happens to you when this is over?"

Julia sensed people around her. Voices echoed off the bare walls. Footsteps clicked on the marble floor. Old computers hummed busily in the background. Yet, at that moment, she was alone with the man in front of her. The world stopped turning, except for the two of them. She studied Mark's face, looking for a tightening of his jaw or some other sign that would tell her not to expect too much. She waited for him to withdraw his hand, to look embarrassed or uncomfortable. Instead, he smiled, took her in his arms, and kissed her in front of the curious onlookers. "We can talk about that later."

Her body trembled with a rapture she had only known with Jackie. She suddenly became aware of the sunlight warming her shoulder where it streamed through the institute's windows. She returned his kiss with passion, not caring who saw them. She wanted the world to know that she was in love.

CHAPTER FIFTEEN

The man walking towards Julia wore a double-breasted suit and broad-rimmed hat that covered the upper portion of his face, making it difficult for her to see his eyes. He strode effortlessly along the sidewalk, arms swinging freely at his sides, hips moving in rhythm to his feet. It was the walk of a self-assured man, a man who knew what he wanted and how to get it. It took some time for Julia to realize it was her father. She bounced up and down, waving to him, but he didn't notice her. His eyes were focused on a woman standing under a noisy overpass. Her long, black hair and steadfast chin were unmistakable. It was Jackie! Julia called out to her, but Jackie couldn't hear her over the thrumming traffic. Jackie threw her arms open, welcoming Julia's father. Welcoming CONDAD. Julia's stomach wrenched with fear. *Stay away from him, Jackie. Stay away.* But Jackie just smiled and swept CONDAD into her embrace.

Julia's arms were flailing when she woke up. The image of Jackie and her father in each other's arms floated like a ghostly apparition in the dark. She sat up shivering and fumbled for the lamp on the nightstand by her bed. The image scuttled away before the lamp's white glow. Julia pulled the blanket around her and rocked back and forth in the bed. She'd been thinking a lot about them both, so it was reasonable to dream of them, but seeing them together, intertwined in each other's arms, sent chills through her body. It was an unnatural image, an abomination that tasted like rotting flesh on her tongue. She wanted to cast the memory aside.

The dream reminded Julia how much she missed her friend. It had been nearly a year since Jackie left, and her soul mate's eccentric behavior only exacerbated Julia's frustration. Jackie refused to use sat communicators, computers, or even a telephone. Jackie was the only person Julia had ever met who couldn't be contacted electronically. She wrote letters, instead. Long, passionate letters that enthralled Julia whenever they arrived in her mailbox.

New York is a forest of glass and steel. The buildings are so tall and so close together, the sun disappears by three every afternoon, leaving the city awash in premature dusk.

Communicating with Jackie was like slipping through a time warp into another century, a time before electronic devices had been invented.

Energy oozes from every surface, a frenetic kind of vitality that zings through the crowds, touching one person, then another, in a chorus of shouting voices and honking horns. People don't converse as you and I do. They curse, hiss, squeal, howl, and complain.

Julia had to admit it made their correspondence special. She treasured Jackie's letters and responded with notes of her own. But her writing was a blunt instrument compared to Jackie's, and she ached to hear her friend's buoyant voice. Yesterday's letter had sparkled with so much news, Julia felt compelled to retrieve it from the nightstand and read it again.

Dear Julia:

Fortune is smiling on me! Where to begin? My art has turned a corner and soon will be seen by the world. I have discovered a new force inside me, a new way to express myself. Before, my paintings were very linear with lots of angles and corners. They drew the eye through sharp turns to a specific point. Now, my compositions have become more indirect, more roundabout in their paths across the canvas. The eye is allowed to wander and follow circuitous routes to their destinations. And people want to see them! I've found a gallery, The Whitman Gallery. They are going to show my work complete with caviar, champagne, and press clippings. I'm told it has a very upscale clientele with lots of money to spend. It opens in a month, and I'm frantically producing more pieces for it.

I've just learned that my building is being converted into condominiums, and I can buy my loft at a very good price. With my income from the advertising agency and projected sales from my show, I should have enough to put down the required twenty percent. It will be my first home. A place that belongs to me. Visit me soon, Julia. I miss you terribly!

My last news is even more wonderful. I have a lover! He's a fellow artist, very emotional and excitable. His moods swing with his creativity, but he's tender and giving. I met him at an art exhibition and felt so drawn to him, I immediately thought of you! Isn't that strange? My love for you has set a very high bar for others. Raul, that's his name, is the first person I've met since coming to New York who meets the test. It feels so good to have someone to share my life with again, but it still isn't complete without you.

If you don't come to me soon, I'll forsake my art and my lover and come to you! You are my inspiration.

Love and kisses,
Jackie

A pang of jealousy raced through Julia each time she read about Raul. Which was silly, of course. She and Jackie were *not* lovers, at least not in the physical sense, and she now had Mark, about whom she had not yet told Jackie. She knew she was being selfish, but she couldn't help it. She found the idea of sharing Jackie with someone else disconcerting. The letter brought her joy, as well. Jackie was about to enjoy her first artistic triumph, and Julia wanted to be there. Perhaps, the investigation would be through in time for her to join her friend.

Julia's thoughts turned to Mark as she put the letter back in its envelope. She had wanted him to stay with her, but he had declined on the grounds that he needed to maintain some space between them until they were finished with Liu Kwong. His caution was understandable, but it confused her. One minute, Mark was warm and responsive, everything Julia could want in a lover. The next, he became distant, more professional, as if he, too, were confused. She sighed and turned out the light. Worrying wouldn't help, and she had another meeting planned with Andersen in the morning. She needed to sleep.

Mr. Andersen puffed his way into Julia's apartment the next morning and sank into a living room chair. "Now that you are better, Julia, it is time to think of an alternate location for our meetings. Otherwise, I may not last long enough to tell you my entire story. That would be regrettable for both of us." He set his cane aside and wiped his brow.

Julia clenched her jaw at the sound of her name. In spite of Mark's warm remarks about Mr. Andersen's concern for her, she still found it hard to think of them as being on a first-name basis. She was tempted to ask him to call her Miss Rice but thought better of it. There was no sense stirring the pot when she was getting so close to the truth about this man. She offered coffee, instead, and sat on the couch, waiting for him to compose himself and begin.

****

Kwong's limousine pulled to the curb at seven sharp, and I let myself in the back seat before Godzilla could step from the car. The light was back in my eyes. I had the feeling I was being inspected for flaws in my character or my proposal. I wanted to look confident, but I squirmed in the light's hot glare.

"Don't suppose we could turn that thing off." I tried to sound business-like.

"The light gives me information, Mr. Person. Whether someone is too nervous. Whether they are lying. You're not planning to lie to me, are you?" Kwong's voice was smooth and pleasant, but I detected a menacing undertone that told me to be very careful.

"In a few days, I'll deliver photos showing Miss Griffith taking pornographic pictures of underage children. If they were ever made public, they would ruin her career. You'll have the leverage you need to be rid of her, as you say."

Silence. Tiny beads of sweat formed on my forehead, revealing how anxious I felt. Was it enough to stay Kwong's hand? To save Kathy's life? I looked out my window and saw Godzilla's shadowy figure looming close by. There was violence in the air. I felt it all around me.

"I'm impressed, Mr. Person," he responded at last. "You have surpassed your reputation. Exactly when can I expect these photographs?"

"By Friday. I'll deliver them to the restaurant, if you want."

"No, here will be fine. Friday at seven. I will have the balance of your money with me."

I knew it was time for Godzilla to open my door, and he was right on schedule. I would have gladly discounted my fee by $5,000 just to know how he did that.

"By the way," Liu Kwong added as I stepped out of the car. "I have explained to Mr. Parker that his participation in our arrangements is at an end. You will not hear from him anymore." His choice of words stabbed at me, opening small wounds behind my eyes where the rusty coils resided. "Explained" was too refined a word for the treatment Patrick might expect from this man. I suddenly felt remorse for my unwitting competitor and hoped he would be all right.

I stood on the street trying to decide what to do. It was Saturday evening, but I wasn't in the mood to go anywhere. The idea of joining Kathy at the Golden Moon tempted me, but I discarded the thought as foolish. Kathy would wonder why I was there, and I was certain I wouldn't have the strength to control my passion for poker as easily as the last time. On a whim, I strolled across the street to my favorite bar and ordered a scotch.

I'd been sitting at the bar for less than ten minutes when a man wandered in and sat down on the stool next to me. I paid no attention to him until he spoke.

"You ever get a guilty conscience in your line of work?"

"Pardon?" His question startled me, and I looked at him. It was one of my marks! From several years ago. I had to stop and think who he was. Frank something. His business partner had hired me to ruin his reputation so the partner could buy him out ten cents on the dollar. They'd had a real estate investment firm, and I arranged a scam that cost the firm one of its largest clients. Frank had taken the fall for it and left the business. His partner became rich. One of Frank's trademarks had been a gleaming two-carat diamond ring on the little finger of his right hand. I noticed it was still there. Times couldn't have been too bad.

The man ordered a vodka tonic. "I work across the hall. Couldn't help noticing your business. I always wondered about you private eyes. That's what you call yourselves, right, private eyes? I always wondered how you guys felt about what you do. Nosing around in other people's lives. Digging up dirt. That sort of thing."

I studied the man more closely. His face was fuller, and his complexion had become blotchy, suggesting too much booze. Also, his hair had thinned considerably. He looked like life had beaten him over the head, and I supposed it had, with my help. I didn't detect any hostility in his remarks, and it was highly unlikely that he knew I was the one responsible for his downfall. Still, he put me on edge. He seemed genuinely curious, but his questions were a bit abrasive, and I wished he would go away.

"Across the hall? That would be the life insurance company."

"Cosmopolitan Life. I sell insurance, now. Used to be in real estate." Frank made circles on the bar with his glass.

"Do you ever sell a policy to someone who doesn't really need it or can't afford it?" I couldn't resist parrying his sword and mounting a counterattack.

"Everyone needs life insurance," he responded defensively. My foil had struck home.

"I expect we both do things that make us uncomfortable from time to time. Goes with the territory and pays the bills." I nodded at the ring.

He didn't respond, and we finished our drinks in silence. I didn't want to spend the evening exchanging philosophies about work with Frank something, so I paid for my drink and left. Back on the street, I watched with envy as people hurried past me on their way to dinner or some other social occasion. The night was young, as they say, but I had no idea what to do. Kathy's gravitational pull still tugged at me, luring me back to the Golden Moon. Visions of a full house, aces over kings, made me shiver with hunger, but I set my jaw and resisted the primeval urge to destroy myself. I shifted my thoughts to tomorrow's lunch date with Kathy. My whole world revolved around that date, but first, I had to get through the night.

A different shock jolted me when I glanced up at my office windows and saw the lights were on. Had my tormentor returned with another message or to steal more of my belongings? I raced across the street and up the stairs, ready for any signs of trouble, but when I opened the office door, I found Carl working at his desk.

"You're puffing like a steam engine," he observed as I entered.

"Guess I'm out of shape. I thought you were our visitor returning to the scene of his crime." I sat down across from him. No one could ever accuse Carl of being out of shape. He worked out regularly, and his hefty body had a hard edge to it that reminded me of Godzilla on steroids. As I said before, Carl was not only a work associate, he was also my friend, and I had a sudden need to purge my soul to him. "I think I'm in real trouble on this case."

"Kathy Griffith?"

I nodded. "Love is too drab a word to describe what I feel for her. It's more like watching a new star system being born. I'm surrounded by fireworks with no safe place to land. And now, I'm about to pillage her reputation. It's tearing me apart."

"Maybe, we should drop the case. You'll only compromise yourself with her if we continue."

"Can't. If I don't deliver the goods, Liu Kwong will have her murdered."

Carl sat upright at my comment. "Do you really think so?"

"He all but said so the first time we met. He doesn't strike me as the sort to make idle threats. I have to protect her, and the only way I know how is to ruin her."

We sat in silence. My mood was becoming more morbid by the minute, and talking to Carl wasn't helping. It was time to change the subject. "By the way, do you remember a case we worked on about four years ago for that real estate investor? We scammed his partner so he could get rid of him."

"The Cochran case."

"That's it. Frank Cochran sat down next to me at the bar across the street tonight. Didn't seem to know my connection to his past but asked some eerie questions. Claims to work for the insurance company across the hall. Check him out, will you? Maybe, he's the guy sending me those love notes."

Carl agreed to look into Frank first thing Monday.

I was about to leave when the phone rang. My first thought was to let the answering service take a message, but I changed my mind and picked it up.

"Tom, we need to talk." I recognized Patrick's raspy voice and was pleased to learn that he was all right.

"Kwong suggested you were off the case," I replied in a neutral tone of voice. I didn't want him to think I was happy to hear from him.

"That's what we need to talk about. But not over the phone. Can you meet me at my office, say in thirty minutes? It's important." The last thing I wanted to do was waste my Saturday evening with Patrick Parker, but there was an urgency in his voice that got my attention. Something had him spooked.

"Okay," I agreed. "Thirty minutes." I hung up.

Carl gave me a quizzical look. "Who was that?"

"Patrick Parker." Carl made a face, and I nodded in agreement. "Says he's got something too important to tell me over the phone. Something to do with Liu Kwong."

"Want me to come along?" Carl disliked Patrick even more than I did.

"No. He's harmless enough. And since I don't have any plans for tonight, I might as well find out what's got him so riled up." On impulse, I went to my desk and retrieved my gun. Patrick might be harmless, but Liu Kwong wasn't. I stuck the gun in my waistband and headed for my car.

Twenty minutes later, I pulled up across the street from Patrick's office in time to see him being escorted by two Chinese men to a waiting car. The streetlight on the corner revealed a half-wild look on his face that worried me. I didn't need to be a detective to know Patrick was in trouble. The black Cadillac roared away from the curve, and against my better judgment, I followed.

The driver stayed in the left lane and drove at a moderate pace, never changing lanes or altering speed. It was the kind of lazy, inattentive driving that told me he wasn't worried about being tailed. My gun bulged uncomfortably in my waistband, and I removed it and placed it on the passenger's seat. Why I bothered with it, I didn't know. A separatist's work required grace and polish, not violence. I had never discharged my weapon, except on a firing range when I practiced for my license many years ago.

My quarry took the Bay Bridge and rolled across the water towards Oakland. I followed at a comfortable distance. When we exited on the other side of the bay, the Cadillac headed for the shipping docks, where there was less traffic. This made my surveillance harder, and I had to stay farther back to avoid detection. Eventually, the car turned onto a dark road that ran behind the shipping yards, making it impossible for me to continue with my lights on. I turned them off and drove as fast as I dared on the unlighted pavement, while I tried to keep the Cadillac's red taillights in view, but they grew fainter. Just when I thought I would lose them completely, the red lights flared, telling me the car was braking.

I pulled onto the road's shoulder, grabbed the gun and started forward on foot. Headlights in the distance revealed three figures moving across an empty field towards the fence behind the docks. Their pace was leisurely, like their driving. Only the figure in the middle gave any indication that things weren't right. Patrick Parker was being dragged across that field against his will. He stumbled, lost his footing, and kicked up dust, giving the appearance of a sulking schoolboy pulled along by angry parents.

My heart beat faster with each step they took. What should I do? I looked at the gun in my hand as if it were an alien object. Confronting them or starting a firefight would be foolhardy. I had no doubt that they were far better marksmen than I. But, if I didn't do something, what would happen to Parker? Perhaps, I could distract them and give Patrick a chance to run for it. Yes, that was it. I would fire my gun but stay out of sight. That might confuse the men long enough for Patrick to escape. I raised the gun in the air, but before I could pull the trigger the sound of a gunshot burst across the field, tearing the night asunder with its deadly message and telling me I was too late.

My mind churned as I tried to assimilate what had just happened. The gun's report exploded in my head, causing my breathing to splinter into shards that fought unsuccessfully to escape my lungs. I gasped spasmodically and watched in horror as the two men bent over Parker's fallen body. If I needed evidence to justify what I was planning for Kathy, if I needed proof of Liu Kwong's deadly intent, it had just been delivered to me with the sharp, crisp sound of a murder.

The ground began to seesaw beneath my feet. I pressed my free hand to my chest to slow my ragged breathing. The message in the last #10 envelope briefly flashed through my mind. *Death will come to you where you least expect it.* Was this what the message had meant? Was this its warning? No, I told myself. Whatever that message had in store for me, it had nothing to do with Patrick Parker. What message had *he* wanted to deliver? I would never know.

As I came to my senses, I realized I was still holding my gun in Statue of Liberty fashion above my head. I jerked it down and thrust it back into my waistband. The gun served no purpose, now. Nor did I. A need for self-preservation took hold of me. I flung one more look across the field and retreated to my car.

I had always enjoyed my apartment by the Marina, but when I awoke the next morning, it looked like it had been blighted by a plague. Books and magazines were strewn about where I had tossed them when I returned home. An empty scotch bottle lay tangled with the telephone cord on the floor, offering bleak evidence to the little binge I had taken in an effort to rid myself of Patrick Parker's memory. But the image of him stumbling and falling to the ground was still pressed against my skull, which added to my morbid mood. The only thing that stopped me from opening a fresh bottle was the thought of seeing Kathy. Lunch seemed a lifetime away, however. I thought about calling the police, but that would alert Kwong, which was the last thing I wanted to do at the moment. Parker had died by the sword, so to speak, and there was nothing to be done about it. So, I nursed my hangover, read the Sunday paper, and dawdled over my coffee in anticipation that time would march forward, which it did.

Kathy was already at the Vietnamese restaurant when I arrived. "You're late," she teased with a smile that was brighter than the sun. I took her in my arms and pulled her warm body against mine. It was a protective gesture that was meant to reassure me, not her. Kathy's hair brushed my face, and her aroma filled my nostrils. It was wonderful to be in her orbit once more.

She gave me a funny look as I let her go.

"Did you win last night?" I quickly asked to deflect her curiosity at my demonstrative greeting.

"Some. Your friends weren't fooled anymore, but I held my own."

We sat towards the back of the restaurant. I was used to people greeting her by now and was unfazed when the owner took our order personally. I *was* surprised when Kathy ordered in French. Her list of talents continued to lengthen. Soon, a dish of noodles and prawns appeared on our table.

"You're quiet," she observed as she used chopsticks to deftly maneuver a prawn into her mouth. I was content to stab at my food with a fork.

Images of frozen headlights and Parker's inert figure haunted me, but I couldn't share them with Kathy. "I spent last night fighting the urge to come see you at the Golden Moon. It wore me out." I smiled sheepishly. "Does my silence bother you?"

"On the contrary. I like it. I *am* glad you stayed away, however. You shouldn't tempt fate too often."

Large bowls of beef and noodle soup in a russet-colored broth arrived, followed by a plate of crepes accompanied by been sprouts, lettuce, mushrooms, and shredded chicken. Kathy sprinkled the items on a crepe and rolled it like a tortilla. I made a clumsy attempt to mimic her, resulting in chicken and vegetables spilling everywhere.

Kathy laughed at my embarrassment and gave me a bite of her crepe before continuing. "I had a strange call yesterday afternoon about a photo assignment next Wednesday at a local theater. They want me to shoot half-naked children!" She took a small bite of her crepe and shook her head slowly while she ate. Furrowed lines in her forehead tarnished her smile. "I've never done anything like that before, and I must admit it makes me nervous. It has something to do with a new stage production. They assured me they were only interested in very tasteful poses to be used for publicity. I almost turned them down, but they were quite insistent. Said they needed me because of my reputation. In the end, I accepted, but I'm still not sure."

My insides went to war with the vegetables and chicken. Every fiber in my body screamed at me to warn her, but I couldn't bring myself to utter the words. What could I possibly say to her? Take the assignment or die? It sounded so simple when I played it in my head, but the choices were far more complex. Living or dying had little to do with the emotions vaulting through me. After last night, I knew I was doing the right thing, but my guilt-spewing blackbird had returned to my shoulder, and I had the feeling it would never leave again.

I reached out and took her hand. It was so warm and alive. I never wanted to let it go. "I think you'll do something wonderful. Artistic even."

The frown lines in her forehead disappeared; her smile returned. "What a lovely thing to say. Yes, I suppose I should think of it as art. Perhaps, it will elevate my photography to a new level."

Or drag it down to the depths of despair, I thought ruefully. I returned her smile but said nothing. I was getting quite good in my role as Judas.

****

Julia was no closer to learning what had happened to Kathy. What she heard, instead, was Mr. Andersen's struggle with his conscience all those years ago. The pain in his words was evident even now, but she wasn't going to offer him absolution, no matter how charismatic he was. She wanted answers, but she knew from his behavior that she was going to have to wait a while longer.

Silence weighed heavily in the room. Mr. Andersen sat in his chair and stared at Julia. His gaze was so stark, she worried something might be wrong. It was as if the story he told was a part of him, and each time he shared a portion of it, he shared something of himself. He was growing weaker before her eyes, and she feared telling his tale would finish him. Was she worried that he might not have the strength to complete it, or was she concerned about his well being? Both, she thought with chagrin. *Despite everything, he still has the power to beguile me.*

"I have some news for you," he said in a solemn tone. His eyes gleamed at her across the coffee table, causing Julia to sit up straighter.

"What is it?" she asked.

Mr. Andersen hesitated and fiddled with his cane. His eyes

darted away from hers and returned just as suddenly. "I have found your father," he said in a soft voice. "He lives in New York at the present, but he no longer uses flowers for names. He has turned to non-deciduous trees. Evergreens, I believe they call them. Currently, he is known as Roger Pine."

Julia wasn't sure she'd heard him correctly. She sat as still as a totem pole. His words pressed down on her chest with the weight of a great boulder, making it impossible for her to move. She slumped against the cushions and tried to assimilate what she had just been told. *How did he find my father in New York?* Her heart palpitated in ragged, uneven beats. It didn't matter how he knew. Mr. Andersen had an uncanny way of learning things, and Julia was suddenly faced with the reality that, after so many futile years, she might finally confront her father.

"There is more," he continued. "Your father knows who you are and where you live. He knows about Jackie. I must warn you that he is totally unscrupulous. He not only steals his victims' money, he steals their lives, and he gains great pleasure from it. I should be very careful of him, if I were you."

With that, Mr. Andersen heaved himself out of the chair, clutched his cane and started for the door. "Mark will bring you the cross files on those bank account numbers as soon as he has them. You can arrange out next meeting at that time." He stopped at the door and looked back at her. "Remember what I said at our first meeting about letting go of your past, Julia. You won't be free unless you do."

Julia was trembling by the time Mr. Andersen left, and she still couldn't move. All those years of looking, and her father knew where she was! *But he never tried to contact me. Why? What did I do that was so awful he wouldn't want to see me?* Julia's upstairs neighbor began playing the heavy music of a Beethoven symphony just as a cry of anguish escaped her lips. The two sounds blended together in a duet of pain and fury.

Julia paced back and forth by her desk at the Chronicle while her computer searched the databanks for a real estate firm under the name Roger Pine in New York. The din of ringing telephones and clamoring voices surrounding her receded into a fog of muted echoes. Julia's mind was focused on the information scrolling onto the screen in front of her. Her bat wings were back, beating frantically in her chest as she quickly scanned the growing list of names. Then, a listing for Pine Real Estate Investments, Roger Pine, Managing Partner, scrolled onto the screen and slammed into her with the force of a derailed locomotive. There he was. Her father. The man who had haunted her dreams for three decades, reduced to a single line of type on a computer screen. This time, she wasn't looking at an out-of-date advertisement. This was real-time data. He was there, *now*.

An address and phone number were included, and she nearly snapped up the phone to call him. That would be a mistake, she realized. He would just disappear again. *I must go there. And Jackie's there. I can see her. See her show.* The joy at seeing Jackie crashed headlong into her dread at finally meeting the man who had abandoned her and her mother. Images unexpectedly flashed through her mind, images of her father and Jackie in each other's arms. Last night's dream! She stared at the screen in a hypnotic trance. Had it been a premonition? Julia had never believed in such nonsense, but she began to wonder. A sharp voice calling her name snapped her back to the present. Phillip's voice. She quickly wrote down the address and telephone number and bolted for his office. Whatever he wanted would have to wait. She intended to be on the next flight to New York.

CHAPTER SIXTEEN

Julia could feel Jackie's warm smile radiating across the terminal even before she saw her. She flicked her eyes through the throngs of airport travelers, and there she was, tossing her head of thick, dark hair, just as she'd done that first evening at the Buena Vista. Julia's legs nearly gave out, but before she could make a spectacle of herself by fainting, Jackie's sturdy arms were wrapped around her, and their bodies were crushed together in a fervent embrace. Julia felt the frank stares of passersby reproving them for their public display of affection, but all she cared about the sweet fragrance of L'Oreal shampoo in Jackie's hair and Jackie's soft fingers caressing her cheek.

"How I've missed you," Jackie declared when they separated. "I'm so happy you came, even if it did take your wayward father to get you here." Jackie flashed a reproachful look. She took the handle of Julia's carry-on bag and began rolling it towards the main concourse.

Julia fell in step beside her. Loudspeakers blared flight arrivals and departures. Voices babbled along the busy corridor. Unapologetic shoulders brushed past her. The antiseptic odor of scrubbed floors mixed with sweating bodies rushing to boarding gates. There was a purpose in everyone's stride, an urgency that suggested the last grains of sand were flowing through the hourglass. Julia hadn't traveled to New York before, and the frantic energy of Kennedy Airport amazed her.

"It's a good thing you told me about the Whitman Gallery, so I could get a message to you." Julia was already starting to breathe heavily as she kept pace with Jackie's quick strides. "Otherwise, I would have just shown up on your doorstep. When are you going to join the twenty-first century and get a telephone?"

Jackie laughed. "Maybe never. Why ruin such a wonderful surprise? I'm sorry I told you about Whitman's. Imagine opening my door and finding you standing there. It would be like Christmas."

In some ways, New York's skyline reminded Julia of San Francisco's rows-upon-rows of buildings surrounded by water, but New York was so much bigger, so much taller. And flat. There was no crown of rolling hillsides to provide a backdrop to New York's stage. Not that the city needed one. The endless array of skyscrapers sparkling in the night provided all the backdrop any city could want.

Jackie's studio sat atop a warehouse building that had been converted into large apartments near Manhattan's waterfront. The vastness of the place reminded Julia of a cathedral. The ceiling rose in arched splendor high above her head. Three skylights revealed a panorama of stars. Four immense windows filled the wall to her right with views of Manhattan. Canvases were stacked against every available wall. An island counter at the far end of the room partitioned a kitchen area from the rest of the room. Julia recognized Jackie's oak dining table and chairs by the far window. A week's worth of unopened newspapers was piled on the table. Nearby, two leather couches faced each other across a glass coffee table stacked with mail. The chaotic setting spoke of furious days and nights spent in preparation for the show about to open at the Whitman Gallery.

Julia saw at once how much Jackie's art had changed. The sharp lines were gone, replaced by misty swirls that reminded Julia of tropical fish frozen in a vast aquarium. She stood entranced in front of them. Jackie slipped her arms around Julia's waist and rested her chin on her shoulder.

"They're breathtaking," Julia whispered. "Like Fourth of July mixed with cotton candy. I want to lick them." Jackie's warmth enveloped her until she could hardly breathe.

"I've met someone," Julia said in the hushed voice of sinner taking confession.

Jackie's grip loosened for a heartbeat, then tightened again. "A man I hope. If it's another woman, I shall be livid with jealousy."

"There could never be any woman but you, silly." Julia squeezed her companion's hands. How good it felt to be together again. It was as if they'd never parted. "His name's Mark. I love him, but in a different way." She held her breath. Confession over.

Jackie turned Julia around and gazed into her face. "I'm jealous anyway, but happy for you." A tear materialized in the corner of her eye. She wiped it away.

Julia hugged her fiercely. "I was jealous of Raul, too, you know. We can't ever let men come between what we have." They stood in silence, rocking in each other's arms. Julia became conscious of a ship's horn bellowing somewhere on the Hudson and the sounds of faraway traffic. The astringent odor of oils and paint thinners floated through the room. Water plopped relentlessly into a bowl of water in the sink.

Jackie took Julia's hand and led her through the rest of the rooms. Only the bedroom was free of canvases. "I bought a waterbed," she announced and jumped on the sloshing bed like a delighted child. Julia knelt on the undulating surface. The motion reminded her of a boat tossing at sea.

"I don't know if I could sleep on this. I might get seasick."

"Then, we'll sleep on the floor." She bounced back to her feet, again. "In another few months I'll own this place." She made a sweeping gesture with her hands.

"How will that work?" Julia asked as she followed Jackie back into the studio.

"An investment firm has arranged with the city to convert the entire building into condominium units. It took awhile, but everyone in the building has agreed to the conversion and made deposits. Now, it's just a matter of paperwork." Jackie nodded to the couches. "Sit down. I'll make tea."

Julia plopped down on a couch and watched her friend pour water in the copper kettle she always kept on the stove and reach into a cabinet for cups. She idly glanced at the opened mail on the coffee table in front of her. When she saw a letterhead in familiar gothic type, she looked at the name and froze: **PINE REAL ESTATE INVESTMENTS, ROGER PINE, MANAGING PARTNER.** A siren wailed somewhere in the night. The high-pitched scream bounced off the inside of Julia's skull in stabbing blows that left her momentarily blinded. *My dream of Roger and Jackie was no dream. It was a Goddamn nightmare.* Mr. Andersen's cautionary words snapped at her. *My father knows about Jackie. He takes pleasure in hurting others.* But why would he want to hurt Jackie? Memories of a hand holding Julia upside down by her foot when she was a little girl streaked through her consciousness. Once again, she heard her father laughing at her terrified screams, and for the first time, she understood that laughter. He had enjoyed frightening her. *By hurting Jackie, he's hurting me!*

She wanted to shriek in dismay, but the siren in her head held her in its manic grip. She looked up and realized Jackie was standing over her with a wrinkled frown.

"Julia? Are you all right? You look so pale." She sat down and grasped Julia's hand.

Julia's shoulders shook as she fought to regain her self-control. She opened her mouth, but quickly closed it for fear the siren's scream would escape. She pointed at the document lying on the table and tried to speak. "The . . . the company . . . arranging the conversion of your flat. Please tell me it's not him." She indicated the paper.

"Roger Pine, yes. A very smart businessman. Why?" Jackie's dark eyes shone with the intensity of black star sapphires in the room's low light.

Julia sighed and sank back into the leather cushions. A wave of fatigue swept over her, robbing her limbs of their strength and making it difficult to hold her head upright. All she wanted to do was crawl into her friend's waterbed and sleep.

"How much money did you give him?" she asked in a colorless tone.

"Twenty thousand dollars. Why? What's going on?" A note of alarm crept into Jackie's voice.

Julia gulped in air. She felt like one of Jackie's paint swirls frozen in time. "That's the man I've been looking for all my life. That's CONDAD."

Jackie's grip tightened on Julia's hand. "Your father?" The question discharged with the hiss of air escaping a punctured tire. Julia nodded.

"Oh my God. He's got my money!"

"Not for long he doesn't." Anger boiled inside Julia. She pictured the desperate faces of the people she had met in Oregon. How their eyes had looked at her with despair. If CONDAD had his way, Jackie's face would soon be added to that group, along with hers. This trip was no longer about finding her father, no longer about connecting to someone who had never been there when she needed him. It was about atoning for the losses of all those people. It was about atoning for her mother, and, yes, even for herself. It was about preventing him from hurting the most wonderful friend she had ever known. It was time to put an end to CONDAD.

Julia fought down a sudden urge to spit up the hot cereal Jackie had fixed her for breakfast. She was standing in front of a two-story, brownstone building with tall, narrow windows that reminded her of slits in a castle's walls, slits used by archers to fire arrows down on their enemies. Today, *she* was the enemy, and she half-expected to hear the whine of arrows whizzing past her head. Jackie had been beside herself with worry about what Julia intended to do. "Forget the money," she'd pleaded. "It isn't worth $20,000 if anything happens to you." Julia had calmed her and told her everything would be fine; told her to be patient until tomorrow. Tomorrow had arrived, and Julia was about to put her plan into action. She prayed the heavy makeup and wig of long black hair she had purchased that morning would be enough to keep her father from recognizing her.

Pine Real Estate Investments was listed in small, neat letters on the building's directory. Room 216. Second floor. She climbed the stairs and walked down a carpeted hallway to a frosted glass door that announced its occupant in those familiar gothic letters. Julia stopped in front of the door and straightened her skirt and blouse. The brief bout of nausea had passed, and she was amazed at how calm she felt. The bats wings in her chest had disappeared, as well. Her pulse rate was normal. Only the cold remnants of last night's rage still shifted inside of her, leaving the taste of ashes on her tongue. She pressed her skirt one more time, opened the door, and entered.

A hint of pine-scented air freshener greeted her, and she smiled inwardly at the irony of the smell and name. An attractive brunette sat behind a receptionist desk in the middle of the room. The fullness of her face and crows feet around her eyes told Julia she was at least forty, but her lustrous black hair and creamy skin showed how careful maintenance could slow the aging process. Julia idly wondered if CONDAD had seduced the woman, or vice versa.

"May I help you?" The receptionist raised her penciled eyebrows in a manner that said Julia wasn't expected.

"Just tell Roger Pine that someone is here about a $20,000 deposit on the condominium project." Julia's voice had a hard edge to it. She had no intention of letting this woman play gatekeeper.

The brunette hesitated while she appraised Julia, then she buzzed the inner office and conveyed the message. Now, Julia's heart did begin to flutter. She gripped the sat-communicator she held in her right hand and tried to breathe evenly. Moments later, the door to the inner office swung open, and thirty years of wondering and searching were washed away.

The man standing before her was over six-foot-six. He had the build of an aging basketball player who had begun to put on extra pounds. His hair, speckled gray and white, was cropped short. Thin lips were pressed into an expectant smile. Blue eyes framed by heavy eyebrows and puffed cheeks bore intensely into Julia's, searching for some explanation as to who she was and what she had to do with a $20,000 deposit. His right hip swayed slightly when he walked, and Julia suddenly visualized a limp she had carried in her subconscious memory all those years. Its re-emergence now nearly caused her to swoon. She blinked her eyes to clear them and forced the demons whirling inside her head back into their hole. Sentiment would not stop her now.

Julia searched his face for any sign of recognition, but there was none. She stepped forward and thrust out her hand. "Hello, Mr. Pine. My name is Robin Orvieto. I'm Jackie's sister."

A quizzical expression crept into her father's face. "I don't recall Miss Orvieto having a sister."

"I'm visiting from Portland, Oregon, and have some money to invest. Can we talk?" Julia opened her eyes wide to show her innocence, just as she had practiced in the mirror the night before. She noted how the muscles below his eyes twitched when she mentioned Portland, but that was his only visible reaction.

"Please, join me in my office." His thin lips were transformed into a charming smile. Julia saw why he could ensnare people. All he had to do was smile.

The inner office was nothing like the rental space she'd seen in Portland. This desk had a rich, teak color and was varnished until it glowed. Plush, beige carpet cushioned her steps. Two blue leather chairs with serpentine-shaped armrests faced the desk. Julia sat in one while her father stepped around the desk and lowered himself into a larger, matching chair that he swiveled into position in front of her.

"Now, how can I be of service to you? The units where your sister lives are already spoken for. Were you looking for something similar in New York? I could probably arrange it." The charming smile remained, but Julia saw sharp teeth and a twitching tail. She was a goldfish about to be gobbled by the cat. How many people had he swallowed over the years, starting with her mother? Julia thought about the little girl who had run away to the bus station in hopes of finding the man who sat before her. She remembered the dreams she'd carried for so many years about this meeting. How her father would renounce his unlawful ways and devote himself to her. How they would share a life together. She sat in front of her father and knew there were no dreams, only the reality of CONDAD.

Julia took a deep breath and discreetly pressed a button on her sat-communicator. "Actually, I'm here to collect my sister's $20,000. She no longer wants to participate in your venture."

CONDAD's bushy eyebrows bunched together in the manner of gathering storm clouds, and the smile slid back into neutral. "I'm afraid that's not possible. The money is already in escrow, and the title transfers were completed today. Loan documents and final closing papers will be delivered tomorrow."

His words fanned the ashes of rage that had burned in Julia's gut last night, whipping up the embers and rebuilding an inferno inside her. "You don't have until tomorrow," she replied with a fury that pushed CONDAD back into his swiveling chair. She slammed the sat-communicator down on the teak desk, scratching its pristine surface. "See this sat-com? The moment I touch that button," she pointed at the send button, "the police will be on their way. I've already told them to expect my call. If you'd rather sort this out with them, I'll press the button." Her hand wavered over the instrument. CONDAD's eyes widened, much as Julia's had earlier, but not from innocence. "If we can resolve our little problem, however, you can keep the sat-com, and I'll be gone from your life forever."

Julia knew one of the basic tenets of effective interviewing was to guide the conversation to a critical juncture, then keep quiet until the interviewee responded. Inevitably, the respondent would speak, but the intervening silence could be nerve wracking. That was how Julia felt now as she sat back in her chair and let the silence build between them. An old fashioned clock tic-tic-ticked on the wall to her right. The phone rang once in the outer office, and Miss Brunette scurried to answer it in a hushed voice. CONDAD scowled as he tried to wait out Julia's silence, but before long, telltale signs of moisture appeared on his forehead, and the neutral smile slowly faded. Julia knew she had him.

"I don't keep that kind of money just lying around." His words broke the quiet like a sonic boom.

"Bullshit." He flinched at the word, telling Julia that her harsh response had taken him by surprise. A tiny muscle near his left eye began to twitch, again. "You keep most of your dirty money in cash, so there's no way to trace it. There's well over $20,000 in your safe right now." Julia knew her accusation was risky. If she were right, it would unnerve CONDAD even more, but if she was wrong, it could undermine her credibility. Either way, there was little to lose. If the cash wasn't on hand, she doubted she would ever see it.

"You seem to know a lot about my business," he replied almost defensively. If she hadn't known better, she would have felt sympathy for him.

"I have my sources." CONDAD's body tensed. It was time to go for the kill. Time to bring closure to the pain that had tormented her most of her life.

She placed her hand on the sat-communicator. "Give me $20,000 from your safe now. Otherwise, we talk to the police." CONDAD blinked as he watched her fingers moving restlessly over the device.

"Okay, you win. Wait in the reception room for a minute, and I'll get your damn money."

Julia eyed him with suspicion. "You don't leave my sight until I have the money." She picked up the communicator to emphasize her power over him. "Just get the $20,000. I'm not interested in knowing where your safe is. You'll be gone by tonight anyway."

CONDAD hesitated. His eyes darted back and forth between Julia's face and the sat-com in her hand. She set it back on the desk. Satisfied, he swiveled to the wall behind him and pushed aside a narrow credenza, revealing a small safe. Julia saw it was one of the new electronic models without combination dials. It required a coded card, which he produced from his pocket and slid into a slot in the safe, and a series of numbers. Moments later, the door popped open, and CONDAD piled two stacks of $100 bills wrapped in sleeves on the desk.

"There's $10,000 in each packet. Count'em if you want." His voice was terse.

Julia's hands tingled as she picked up each stack and fanned the bills to make sure they were real. She'd done it! She'd beaten CONDAD at his own game. But her elation subsided when Julia looked at her father's irate expression. Danger lurked in his face. If she showed any sign of weakness, he would pounce. She suppressed her joy and faced him across the desk. This wasn't her father. This was CONDAD, a man who had ruined countless lives, including her own. *But today is judgment day. Today, I set myself free.*

Julia shoved the money into her bag and stood to leave. "I believe everything is in order, Mr. Pine. Goodbye."

She walked out the door and down the stairs to the street in a trance, her mind buzzing with conflicting emotions. Images of her mother puttering in the nursery showered down upon her. Memories of her previous attempts to find her father blurred her vision. She squeezed her eyes shut in an unsuccessful attempt to prevent tears from flowing down her cheeks. Julia stood on the sidewalk, lost and bewildered, until she saw the flashing lights of a police car racing down the street. The lights wrenched her back to reality. CONDAD was probably gathering his money and files in a frantic effort to escape the trap she had set for him, but he was too late. Two officers were already entering the building, and an unmarked detective's car joined the scene. All the years of lying, stealing, and abandoning others had finally caught up with CONDAD.

Julia inhaled a deep breath of crisp, morning air and quickly walked away from the crowd of curious on-lookers who were beginning to cluster along the sidewalk. Eyes forward, head held high, she strode down the street without a backward glance. There was nothing for her back there. Just a blank wall where one world stopped and another began. Her life was ahead of her, a life she hoped included Mark, and Julia was eager to pursue it.

Only one person stood in the way of her happiness, and she instinctively knew that he was far more dangerous than CONDAD. He was a diabolical man who hid in the shadows and struck with terrifying force, but she would have to ignore her fears and face him. It was time to uproot him from his lair. It was time to put an end to Liu Kwong.

CHAPTER SEVENTEEN

"We're being followed," Mark told Julia matter-of-factly as he drove down Van Ness Avenue. Julia whipped her head around and spotted a black Mercedes switching lanes three cars behind them. They had just left a computer firm where one of Mark's associates agreed to start the convoluted process of tracing the bank account numbers from Kathy's old computer disks to their current users. As soon as Julia had those names, she could write her story. That would have to wait, however, until Mark did something about the Mercedes. She could see two men in front and a third seated behind the driver. The car looked like a black cat waiting to pounce.

"How do we get rid of them?" she asked.

"Shouldn't be too hard. Lombard Street's coming up."

Mark turned right on Lombard and drove at a leisurely pace until they reached the cobblestone, switchback lane for which the city was famous. It was only a block long and bordered with so many flowers Julia thought she was back in her mother's nursery, but its notorious charm lay in the fact that it snaked back and forth down a very steep hill. Tourists loved to line up and drive down the one-way Street. Julia had never had the nerve to try it, and even with Mark behind the wheel and her new confidence in dealing with heights, the winding decent made her feel as though she were tumbling through a series of rapids.

To keep her mind from losing control, she focused on the Mercedes, which was four cars back. Mark had just rounded a curve halfway down the hill when he dropped a handful of tiny metal objects out the window. The car behind them suddenly stopped in the middle of the lane with a flat tire, blocking traffic. There was no way for the Mercedes to get around the stricken car, so Mark continued his leisure pace to the bottom of the hill while their pursuers watched helplessly.

"What did you do to that poor car?" Julia couldn't help laughing at the sight of the black car stranded in the instant traffic jam.

"Razor-edged jacks. They're murder on tires. I feel bad for the driver behind us, but it's better than trying to outrun that Mercedes. We often use them in situations like this. Is there any reason why you have to return to your apartment tonight?"

"No," she responded more soberly. "What should we do?"

"Join Mr. Andersen. He's renting a house nearby in Presidio Heights and has plenty of room. Liu Kwong doesn't know where he is. It might be a good idea if you stayed there for a day or two while my associate traces those bank numbers. It'll give you a chance to hear the rest of his story. Then, you can decide what to do."

Julia stiffened at the idea of staying with a murderer, although she knew she would be safe. Mr. Andersen had always been a perfect gentleman, and he was too feeble to present any physical danger, but Julia still recoiled at the idea. "I want you to stay with me," she said quietly.

Mark hesitated. Because of Andersen, she wondered? Or was there another reason? "I can't," he replied. "I have to be somewhere else."

Mark's announcement surprised Julia. "Aren't you supposed to protect me?"

"Yes, but not every minute." There was mild irritation in his voice. "You'll be safe until tomorrow."

Julia slumped in her seat and stared at the passing traffic in disappointment. She was suddenly aware of all the cars jockeying for position in the lanes around her and the angry trumpet of car horns. It had been three days since she returned from New York, and they hadn't spent a night together. Mark blamed it on his work for Mr. Andersen, but Julia was starting to wonder. He seemed more distant, no longer touching her face with his hand or brushing his body against hers. Julia had ignored the signs, certain they would soon be together again, but now she sensed a barrier growing between them, and it seemed every bit as daunting as the electronic fence protecting Oakland's docks. If she got too close, it would burn her.

"It's Mr. Andersen, isn't it? He knows about us and doesn't approve."

"Mr. Andersen has made his concerns known to me. It's got nothing to do with you, but he worries about anything that might compromise our situation." The words came out in a rush. Julia could tell Mark was relieved to be rid of them.

"Then take me home," she responded firmly. Her anger at Mr. Andersen boiled with the same fury she had felt when she confronted CONDAD. She had no intention of letting Andersen dictate her behavior.

"That wouldn't be wise, Julia." Mark's tone became conciliatory. "I can't be two places at once. Please stay with him, at least for tonight while I'm gone. I promise you'll be safe there." Mark took her hand. The unexpected contact sent sparks flying. Heat from his touch radiated up her arm until it warmed her cheeks.

Her thoughts flew back to New York and her tearful farewell from Jackie. Jackie had been ecstatic when Julia plunked the stacks of money down on her coffee table. They had celebrated their triumph over CONDAD with wine and steamed clams at a local bistro, then walked along the waterfront arm-in-arm. Julia regretted not staying for her showing at the gallery, but she'd wanted to get back. Despite her joy at being with Jackie, she hadn't stop thinking about Mark. Guilt had wormed its way into her happiness when she realized the time had come to share their intense friendship with others. The two women had clung to each other at the departure gate. Then, Julia had boarded her afternoon flight and flown home to Mark.

Now, she sat beside the man of her dreams and wondered if he had been waiting for her at all. Perhaps, she'd misjudged his interest, read too much into their passion. He was no different than other men. Great sex and then goodbye. Only Jackie had remained steadfast. Maybe she should've stayed with her, instead. *Except, I don't love her in that way. I love Mark.* But he was pushing her away. Why? Julia's thoughts were in danger of running away from her, just as they nearly did back there on Lombard Street. Her earlier delight at outwitting their pursuers had spiraled into despair.

One decision became clearer, however. She had to regain her composure and stay the course on her story, even if that meant putting herself under Mr. Andersen's control. She gritted her teeth and calmed her nerves.

"All right. Take me to Mr. Andersen." You win, she thought, fighting back tears.

Mark used secondary streets to be sure no one followed them and worked his way into a residential area lined with elegant homes overlooking the famous Presidio. They pulled into a small, circular driveway hidden by trees and stopped in front of a wood-sided, two-story house with a broad veranda. Few California homes had real front porches like this one. The home's style and setting had a distinct east coast flair.

Mr. Andersen opened the front door and greeted them with a broad smile. His eyes had that sparkle Julia had noted at their first meeting. "I'm pleased to see you, Julia. Welcome to my new domicile." Despite her anger, she was glad to see him moving about without his cane.

Golden yellows and rust reds resonated on the painted walls in the hallway and den; large, floral patterns bloomed in the wallpapers in the sunken living room. Beige couches with fluffy throw pillows surrounded an octagonal glass table supported by brass swans. It was a setting from a designer magazine, except for the absence of photos, plants or other personal effects. Thomas Andersen didn't live in those homes. He occupied them and could be gone at a moment's notice.

"Let's go to the den where we can be comfortable." He guided them into a room filled with leather furniture and striped wallpaper. Paintings depicting English horsemen in red coats, eager hounds, and fleeing foxes decorated the walls.

"We had to shake a tail on our way here." Mark remained standing. "Julia has agreed to stay with you for a day or two."

She could see he was anxious to be gone. Her mood grew darker.

Mr. Andersen chuckled. "This will be rather like the old gangster days when warring gangs holed up in hideouts. I believe they called it 'going to the mats.' Are you comfortable doing that, Julia?" Andersen's expression became stoic, reminding her of the dangers they faced.

"I would be more comfortable if Mark stayed with me, but he has business elsewhere." Julia resisted the urge to look at Mark and kept her focus on Mr. Andersen, who reacted with the hint of a frown.

"Yes, I see. I'm sure Mark has told you my concerns about your personal relationship. My reasons are purely pragmatic. It brings to mind the problems ancient armies often faced when troop members developed emotional attachments for each other. If one fell in battle, the other often tried to rescue him, resulting in broken ranks and further losses of men. I hope your emotional attachment will not cause broken ranks in times of trouble."

"It's a risk I'm willing to take," she replied coolly. She looked at Mark and was pleased to see him squirm under her gaze. He gave her a smile but said nothing.

"So be it then." Andersen slapped his hands on his knees and turned to Mark. "As Julia says, you must be elsewhere. We shall see you off and settle in."

Julia was tempted to remain seated, but she rose and followed the two men to the door. Where was he going that was so urgent?

Why wouldn't he confide in her? Something was wrong, but she couldn't figure out what it was.

Mark interrupted her thoughts. "I expect you'll want to call your editor, tell him what's going on. Just don't mention the disks or say where you are, in case his line is tapped. And don't stay on for more than a minute. Kwong may try to trace your call. This phone has a scrambler, but it wouldn't take long to get a fix on the satellite connection."

Julia watched Mark drive away, then followed Mr. Andersen back to the den. She detected the aroma of brewed coffee. Mr. Andersen disappeared and returned with a pot, cups and cream. He poured two cups and sat down in his chair.

Julia studied Mr. Andersen for any hint of suspicious behavior, but he settled comfortably in his chair and nodded to her. "Let's continue our story for a little while before dinner."

He leaned back and closed his eyes while Julia hastily retrieved her notebook and recorder from her purse.

****

I tried to maintain a cheerful face for the next two days, but I dreaded each minute counting down to Kathy's Wednesday photo session. My destiny was rushing towards me. I was an inmate on death row whose final appeal for clemency had been denied. All that remained was the walk to the execution chamber.

Kathy was busy during the day, but we spent time together in the evening. My growing discomfort showed in my behavior. I was distancing myself from her in subtle ways. There was less physical contact between us, and our conversations lost some of their earlier sparkle. Kathy interpreted this as a good sign.

"Thank you for being so sensitive to my request about taking things slowly," she said Tuesday evening as we sat in a café near her house having a light dinner. "It makes me appreciate just how wonderful you are." Her smile dazzled me, and for a moment I forgot what a base character I was. I took her hand and basked in her glow.

"It's working, by the way," she added. "I've never felt closer to anyone in my life." She laughed. "I'd better stop before I get all teary eyed."

I wanted to say something profound, but the words caught in my throat. Instead of pleasure, I felt pain, but I bravely returned her smile and ignored the burning sensation in the pit of my stomach.

Wednesday was announced by a thunderstorm that suited my mood perfectly. I didn't have the fortitude to oversee the photo session and put Carl in charge. It was a simple operation, and Carl knew the routine as well as I. A hidden photographer would take pictures of Kathy during her shoot and take the damning images after she left. The two sets of photographs would be ready in time for my meeting with Liu Kwong on Friday.

I was relieved to learn that Kathy was leaving town Wednesday evening for an audit and wouldn't return until Saturday, in time for her poker game. It was only a temporary reprieve, not a stay of execution, but it meant I didn't have to face her right after the event. I had no idea how Kwong would handle the photos, but I assumed samples would be given to Kathy when she returned, along with a message to keep her mouth shut if she didn't want to see the images made public.

I spent Wednesday in the bar near my office getting quietly drunk. If Frank Cochran had joined me, I believe I would have told him everything about the scam that unplugged his real estate career. I was ready to bare my soul in a desperate bid to save my sanity. Frank didn't appear. I toyed with the idea of joining Kathy at the poker table Saturday night and surrendering myself to the game. There were worse fates than returning to a life of gambling.

When I stopped by the office on my way home, I was disappointed not to find another #10 white envelope waiting for me. I would have welcomed its promise.

The next two days slipped by in a haze of meaningless activities that did little to keep my mind off my approaching Armageddon. Carl showed me the new camera system outside the

218

office. It was discreetly hidden behind a false wall panel above the door and commanded a sweeping view of the hallway in both directions. Carl had it installed at night so that nobody would know about it, not even our fellow tenants.

Patti joined us and we discussed prospects for future cases. One involved a married man who feared being blackmailed by his mistress. He was giving her money, and she expected the arrangement to continue if he stopped seeing her. Another offered a new twist to the traditional love triangle. In this case, the wife knew about her husband's affair and wanted him to end it, but he refused. The wife wanted to hire us to get rid of the mistress by threatening her reputation. The third prospect had a more chilling request. He was a mobster who needed to "get the goods" on his boss to prevent the boss from "whacking" him. We instantly agreed to decline that job. One Liu Kwong in our lives was enough.

I thought a good deal about my life during those two days. My work was taking its toll on me. It wasn't so much the long hours and unseemly tasks we often had to perform. It was the emotional cost of living with the deceptions and lies that had woven themselves into the fabric of my life. Watching so many relationships dissolve at my hands had left me bereft of any hope for my own life. My career as a separatist had forced me to slowly push people away in order to survive. Carl was my only friend, and I had not loved a woman for years, until Kathy. I had forgotten what it felt like to hold hands and share caresses. I had lost my soul, and Kathy had returned it to me. Now that I was about to throw it all away, I realized I was throwing myself away as well. My life as a separatist was finished. My life was finished. All I could think to do was to get as far away from San Francisco as possible and bury myself in a world where I could live without human kindness or love.

When the photos were delivered on Friday, I refused to look at them. Patti was conspicuously busy doing God knows what to the files. Carl reviewed the portfolio and confirmed that everything

219

was in order. He put the pictures in a large manila envelope and placed it on my desk without looking at me. There were three more inquiries about new work, but I was in no mood to review them. I sat in my office and did nothing.

At seven that evening, I was standing on the sidewalk when the limousine pulled up to the curb. It was the last time I would meet with Kwong, but that didn't make me feel any better. I decided to go to my execution in style and deliberately waited for Godzilla to come around and open my door. The interior light was off, for which I was thankful. I didn't need Kwong scrutinizing my face. It would tell him more than I wanted him to know.

"Good evening, Mr. Person. I presume you have something for me."

I handed him the manila envelope without comment. The overhead light snapped on, and a gloved hand removed the photographs from their refuge. I averted my eyes, no longer caring what Kwong thought. "Excellent, Mr. Person." His voice purred with the controlled malice of a large cat. "You have delivered just what I need. I must compliment you on your fine work. Here is your second payment, as promised. You are welcome to verify it, if you wish."

A briefcase slid onto my lap, but I didn't open it. "As you said, Mr. Kwong, a man's word in Chinatown is worth more than a contract."

Mr. Kwong grunted with pleasure at my remark, and I knew it was time for Godzilla to open the door. He was right on schedule.

I stood on the sidewalk and watched the sleek car slither away for the last time. My world went with it. I had handed my head to the executioner, saving him the bother of lopping it off.

****

Silence. It was the end of another chapter and still no hint about Kathy's fate. Julia desperately wanted Mr. Andersen to continue, but when she saw how his face sagged under the weight of his sadness, she held her tongue. She would press him for more after dinner.

Mr. Andersen showed her to a spacious bedroom on the second floor with lace curtains and mini-print wallpaper. *My home for the next few days.* It reminded her of a hotel room: clean, comfortable and practical but as void of personal items as the rest of the house. She took out her sat-communicator after Mr. Andersen left, sat down on the bed, and called the office.

"Where the hell have you been?" Phillip growled. He was trying to sound gruff, but Julia could hear the worry in his voice.

"Can't say. Just wanted to let you know I'm okay and working on the story. I need to be out of the office for a day or two, but I'll keep in touch."

"Why don't I drop by and see you tonight? We can talk." Julia heard the sexual undertones in his voice and smiled. Her independence from Phillip continued to grow as she dug deeper into Liu Kwong's world. It was her story, and she was running with it. He sensed it, and it stimulated him like a buck during mating season.

"Better if I call you." She hung up the phone over his protests and checked her watch. Less than a minute. She was pleased with the way she'd handled Phillip. Rappelling down buildings and "shooting it out" with criminals had given her a new outlook. Julia Rice sensed she was being reborn in the heat of battle.

Dinner was a surprisingly simple affair. Food was delivered from a nearby delicatessen, and Mr. Andersen opened a bottle of dry red wine. "You will find the food from this particular deli quite tasty," he commented.

Julia suspected he was apologizing for ordering food rather than preparing it, but when she tried the bean salad and roast beef on onion roll, she found it scrumptious. If this was what it was like to "go to the mats," she was impressed.

Julia could hardly contain herself after dinner. She wanted to pursue Kathy's story to its conclusion, even though it meant facing the awful truth about her death. Mr. Andersen looked tired, but she didn't care. "I want to hear about Kathy."

"Yes, we're getting to the seamy part of the story. It becomes harder for me, but perhaps we can cover a bit more this evening."

He led her back to the den, and they resumed their familiar places.

****

Kathy was scheduled to return from her audit in time for her Saturday poker game, and I feared if I didn't chain myself to my desk, I would rush to Chinatown to join her. I no longer cared about my gambling addiction. I only wanted to comfort Kathy when she saw those lurid photographs, and to console her for my cowardly act. But who would console me? I knew the answer to that question: no one. My office confined me like a prison cell, and I fled outside, where I wandered along Market Street ignoring the homeless people asking for handouts and observing the numerous couples on their way to dinner or the theater. I looked for glimpses of Kathy and myself in their festive behavior but saw only strangers. The night air made me shiver, and I pulled my head down into my jacket's collar much like a turtle hiding in its shell. I wandered past O'Farrell and Geary Street. Walking wasn't something I did a lot. Carl liked to walk; I liked cabs. But tonight walking helped me cope with my demons. I couldn't purge them, but I managed to shove them into my subconscious where I didn't have to confront them.

Forces were tugging at me, pulling me along the pavement with a magnetism I found irresistible. I turned left at Montgomery and strode with more purpose. A momentum was building in my stride. By the time I reached California Street, I was breathing in quick rhythm to my steps and a tropical warmth was spreading through my body. I no longer had a choice in what I did. Fate had intervened. My feet moved of their own accord, carrying me towards my Waterloo. Unlike Napoleon, I already knew the outcome of my confrontation with destiny, but I could no more ignore it than he could have ignored his.

A few more blocks, and I was in Chinatown.

The Golden Moon Restaurant buzzed with the same

gluttonous energy as before, but I hardly noticed the crowded tables as I marched towards the beckoning door in the back. I trembled with each step, only this time my apprehension had little to do with aces and kings. I was about to throw myself into a black hole of emotional torment, and its gravitational forces were whirling around me in a great storm of fear and angst. I paused before the door to gather my courage and entered. The room's serenity had an immediate calming effect. My trembling stopped and the merry-go-round gyrations in my mind subsided. My reaction surprised me. I had rarely walked into a card room and felt so at ease. Everything proceeded in slow motion. It seemed an odd way to meet one's fate.

My eyes skipped across the room to the one table that mattered, only to discover a stranger seated in Kathy's chair. My eyes darted from face to face around the tables, but there was no sign of her. I was perplexed by this unexpected development. Panic replaced my momentary repose, and my feelings of guilt were quickly replaced by concern. Had she seen the photos? Was she ill? I knew it would take a catastrophic event to keep her away from her Saturday night game, and I worried that something was amiss.

The bartender was kind enough to lend me the house phone, but when I called her home, there was no answer. Which was odd. The message machine wasn't picking up. My concern escalated. I hurried back to Montgomery Street and hailed a cab.

I could see the downstairs lights from a block away. Their cheery glow had a chilling effect on me, however. It was too much of a coincidence to think she had just gotten home. Why hadn't she answered the phone? Why wasn't she playing poker? The questions gnawed at me as I paid the cabbie and raced up the steps to her porch. My eyes burned with dread when I saw a thin beam of light slipping through a crack in the front door, telling me it was ajar. I cautiously pushed it open and entered.

I was greeted by the stillness of an empty house, but that was an illusion. The house wasn't empty. A foot in a nylon stocking peeked around the corner at me from the living room floor. The foot lay on its side, motionless. I stared in dumbfounded silence, not certain what to make of it. I suppose I was in denial. As long as I remained rooted to my spot, I could refuse to embrace the terrifying reality that confronted me. When I could no longer stand it, I stumbled into the living room and found Kathy lying face down in a carpet-soaked pool of blood. Nothing could have prepared me for this sight of her. Her face was so badly battered, I couldn't find any sign of the beauty I loved so much. I sank to my knees and sucked in the desperate breath of a drowning man. How long I remained like that, swaying on my knees and moaning like a wintry storm, I do not know. All I could think about was my failure to save her. Despite my willingness to betray her, I hadn't been able to stay Liu Kwong's hand. I knew I should feel anger, but the pain of my loss was too great. It burned inside of me until I couldn't breathe.

I reached out to her but couldn't bring myself to touch her lifeless body. It was no longer Kathy who lay before me. Her spirit was gone, and all that remained were the shards of shattered dreams. I was moaning so loudly, I thought at first the gasp I heard was my own. Then a sob burst forth, and I wheeled around to see the porcelain skin of Kathy's face twisted into an expression of horror as she stood in the hallway behind me. I stared at her with joy and disbelief, not certain if it was really her or only my desire to see her alive.

"Emily," she cried out in a child-like voice. "Why have they killed Emily?"

I leapt to my feet and threw my arms around her. "Liu Kwong," was all I could bring myself to say. She burrowed her head against my chest and convulsed uncontrollably.

"I thought it was you," I mumbled in a barely audible voice.

We stood for an eternity swaying in each other's arms. I breathed in the moonlit scent of her hair and marveled at how wildly my emotions were flying about the room. A dead woman lay behind me, but it didn't matter. I was basking in the warmth of the woman I thought I had lost. I knew instinctively that I must never lose her again. No matter how excruciating my guilt, I must hide my betrayal from her. There was no place on this earth for me without her.

We sat on the outside steps and waited for the police. A chilling wind whispered in our ears, but we couldn't bring ourselves to go inside. We clung to each other with the desperation of mountain climbers lost in a storm.

"Why were you here?" she asked at last.

"I went to the Golden Moon and got worried when you didn't show up. The door was ajar when I got here. I thought it was you. I thought I'd lost you." Her grip tightened on my arm.

"My flight was delayed. I knew Em . . . Emily would be worried." Kathy gulped for air when she said her friend's name and started crying again. I gave her my handkerchief to stem the flow of tears. "I tried calling her, but there was no answer." Her body heaved with a heavy sob, and I pressed her against me.

"We need to talk about Kwong," I said at last. "What do we tell the police?"

Kathy sat twisting my handkerchief into a knot with agitated fingers. "Are you sure it was him?"

Her question struck a chord. Kwong's aggression made no sense to me, and try as I might, I couldn't sort it out in my mind. Why did he try to kill Kathy after I had given him what he wanted? None of the damning photographs had been delivered. She was still unaware of the trap I had set. For that matter, why had he bothered with my services at all? Had he changed his mind? A hundred thousand dollars was a steep price for such whimsy. It didn't add up with the cunning man whose face I had never seen. I was unnerved by the violence of the attack, as well. It was crude and sloppy, not the kind of work I would have expected from my mysterious client.

"Who else could it be?" I asked.

"I don't know. A random attack, perhaps?"

"Seems unlikely. Still, it might be a good idea not to say anything until we know more. If it *was* Kwong, we must get your computer disks to someone with enough authority to do something.

I know a few people. I'll make inquiries."

The rest of the evening unfolded in short bursts of disjointed activity. A detective named Barnes asked us questions while the police took photographs and dusted for fingerprints. Why had I entered the house? What had I touched? How long before Kathy arrived? There were more questions, but I no longer remember them. Kathy explained about Emily house sitting and her delayed flight. We sat in the dining room in high-backed chairs and stared with dull eyes at the emerald-green wallpaper. We said nothing about Kwong.

Barnes told us a blunt instrument had been used, but no weapon was found. Time lurched along in spasms of interrogation surrounded by silence. Emily was finally taken away under a shroud, and the police officers followed. The house grew quiet. Barnes asked Kathy if she had somewhere she could go. He needed to preserve the crime scene for a few days.

Kathy grabbed her travel bag, and we headed for my place, where we sat in the kitchen drinking scotch and pushing aside any thoughts of sleep. Kwong hung over both our heads like an angry cloud. Kathy stared with lifeless eyes at her hands, at the ceiling, at the walls. She looked everywhere but at me. Less than a dozen words passed between us. I accepted her silence. I understood it. She needed to be alone with herself, but I knew she was glad I was there.

A gritty dawn transformed the incandescent glow of florescent lights into gray slabs of daybreak. Our mood remained glum, but the start of a new day gave us purpose. Kathy took a shower while I made breakfast. She returned to the kitchen looking like a wet Labrador who was about to shake water all over the place. When I grinned at her disheveled appearance, she managed to lift the corners of her mouth in a hint of a smile. I took it as a good omen. Neither of us was hungry, and we only nibbled at the edges of our food. I shaved while Kathy called Barnes and got permission to return home to gather more of her belongings. He agreed to meet us there.

Barnes and his partner were searching for more clues when we arrived. Sunshine had chased away the earlier gloom, and the day was beginning to look more promising. I stood in the front doorway and watched the men work while Kathy disappeared upstairs. A few neighbors gathered on the street with curious faces.

I didn't notice the boy at first. The boy pulling his red wagon down the street behind his mother. But, he noticed me. His face lit up with recognition, and he pointed a finger at me. "It's Jack," he exclaimed to his mother. Kathy had just come down the stairs and was standing behind me. I will always remember that moment. Time seemed to stand still for a split second. Or, maybe it was just that things slowed way down. I tried to move away from the door, but Kathy was blocking my path. The crowds' eyes were turning towards me, following the accusing finger's direction.

"Jack?" Kathy asked. "Jack who?"

"Jack and the Beanstalk. He's the man I saw climbing down your house." The boy jumped up and down excitedly as he spoke. His mother slapped his hand and admonished him for pointing at people. Voices murmured in my ears. I could *feel* Kathy's stunned silence behind me. It was like an ill-gotten wind rising from the depths of Hell. I didn't dare turn to look at her.

"Tom?" Her voice was tentative, disbelieving.

"He's got me confused with someone else." My throat had gone dry, making my reply sound as if my mouth was full of marbles.

"It's him. It's him," the boy repeated with maddening certainty. "It's Jack and the Beanstalk."

Kathy's hand grasped my shoulder and turned me around. Something blazed in her eyes that I had never seen before. It was the look of a madwoman. "It was you?" The question scalded me with its white-hot intensity. Her eyes flitted about my face looking for something to hold onto. Her mouth trembled with a frenzy that told me her initial incredulity had been replaced by fury. "All this time, you were working for Liu Kwong?" The strength of her voice grew to volcanic proportions.

I stood unmoving, trying to think what to say, but no words came to me. I felt like an animal trapped in the death grip of a predator. My systems were shutting down as I accepted my fate. I was fully aware of everything happening around me, but my mind had dulled to the point where it would no longer respond. The neighbors on the sidewalk watched the unfolding drama with mouths agape. Even the little brat who had unmasked me stopped his yelling and stared in dumbfounded silence. Barnes' partner poked his head around the corner to see what was going on.

I felt strangely at peace. My self-inflicted torment was over. Kathy's anger was purging me of my guilt, even as she raised her sword to smite me.

"Bastard." The word exploded with such force I jerked my head back. Blood coursed through my veins again. I was still alive and fighting for my survival.

"It's not what you think," I responded in desperation.

"Bastard." Another explosion.

"I was trying to *save* you from Liu Kwong," I cried.

"Get out!" She raised her hand imperiously and pointed to the street. "Get out. Get out." I took a reflexive step backwards, unable to withstand the onslaught of her wrath. I opened my mouth, but no words came out. All I could do was watch in silence as she spun around and fled back up the stairs. Her words ricocheted around in my head, making it throb. I took a step to follow her but froze at the sight of the detective watching me. It was no use talking to Kathy now. Her accusations were all too accurate, and there was nothing I could say to counter them. My only hope was to let time soften the blow enough to let me explain myself.

I threw a spiteful look at the boy and scuttled away in full retreat.

****

Julia sat in disturbed silence. This was not the turn she had expected Mr. Andersen to take, and she felt no closer to solving the riddle of Kathy's death than before. Was this the murder referred to in the news reports? Was Thomas Andersen accused of killing Emily, not Kathy? Julia knew better than that. No experienced reporter would get the story so mixed up. There was more to tell, but Mr. Andersen was finished for the evening. He sat infuriatingly still with his eyes closed, as if he knew how disappointed Julia was and refused to look at her. Anger welled up in her, but quickly subsided when she saw the fatigued frown on his face. The story was ebbing his strength.

Julia rose quietly, prepared to return to her room, when she noticed a crumpled note lying in a waste basket near the phone stand. She couldn't say why she retrieved it. A reflex action, perhaps, caused by her natural curiosity as a reporter and her frustrations at not learning Kathy's fate. She straightened the paper and looked at it as she walked from the room, then halted abruptly in the doorway, her mind unable to comprehend what she had just read. She looked at the note more carefully, certain she had been confused by the scrawled handwriting. But the words stared back at her unchanged: *Mark, call your wife, Thomas.*

Wife! The letters in the note taunted her. It was a choking word that wrapped its tentacles around her throat. Wife! The sound of it made her want to vomit and purge herself of the heart-wrenching grief that suddenly engulfed her. Mark had a wife! The unexpected news brought clarity to her mind. Painful, searing clarity. It explained Mark's behavior since her return from New York: his coolness towards her, his distance. Men with wives acted just like that. All warm and loving one minute. Remote the next. Phillip had done that. But why Mark? How could Mark have a *wife*?

Julia stood on her toes poised to flee. Flee from what? The house? Mr. Andersen? Her life? She needed to do *something*. She needed air and time to think. Fresh air would help. Walking would help. Anything but staying in that house. Julia studied Mr. Andersen's peaceful repose and wanted to throw a book at him, except there were no books. The shelves were empty, just like the house. She turned away from him and headed for the front door, uncertain if she would return again.

CHAPTER EIGHTEEN

Julia wandered the pristine streets above the Presidio. A light wind sent chilly fingers dancing up her spine. She smelled the fresh-cut grass of neighbors' lawns and felt a familiar dampness in the air that told her fog wasn't far away. A small dog yipped at her from behind a fence as she passed. Otherwise, the street was cemetery quiet. She knew she shouldn't be outside alone, but she didn't care. She needed the bite of the chilled air to clear her head. Still, the shadows did look menacing, and she instinctively wished Mark were watching her. Mark! His name twisted inside her, slashing its sharp edge into her heart. She still held the note with the damning three words . . . words that flipped her world upside down. *Call your wife.* The message burrowed into her psyche with the rapacious talons of a vulture. She shook her head to be rid of them, but the talons clung to her.

Julia's somber mood brought memories of her mother floating to the surface. She sat down on a curb and thought about the last time her life had been turned upside down, by her mother's illness. Instead of relying on her mother for emotional and physical support, Julia had taken care of *her*. That meant closing the nursery, cooking meals, and maintaining a budget. There was no time for after school activities, and she had to abandon her role as a reporter for the school newspaper. She was also growing up much faster than her friends, who soon drifted away. Not that it mattered. Julia had to hurry home every day after school.

By the time she graduated from high school and enrolled at UCLA, her mother's Alzheimer's had progressed to the point where she hardly recognized her daughter much of the time, and Julia knew the time was approaching when the current arrangement would no longer be adequate. The end came with dramatic clarity the afternoon she came home and discovered the front door wide open. A quick search of the house confirmed that her mother was gone. Julia alerted the police and drove in widening circles around the neighborhood desperately looking for a glimpse of her. It was after seven when the police finally found her wandering in a convenience store wielding a kitchen knife and babbling to herself. Two days later, Julia moved her mother into a nursing home.

Julia had to come to terms with the fact that at twenty she was still a virgin. Lack of sex wasn't what bothered her. It was the lack of a life. She roamed the house she had shared with her mother for so many years with a sense of wonder at how quickly time was flashing through her brief and uninteresting existence. She had been so wrapped up in the cocoon of her mother's gathering madness, it hadn't dawned on her that life could be any different. Now, she had to find a way to move on.

Julia had just graduated from UCLA and was tying to decide what to do about her career when her mother delivered the final, shattering blow. There was a cub reporter's position available at the San Francisco Chronicle, but she had not applied. Moving north meant separating herself from her mother, and even though Mother no longer recognized her, she could not bring herself to leave.

Then one night, Julia dreamed of lilacs and violets and roses spilling from the sky. She awoke startled and unnerved. The delicate mixture of scents from her dream permeated the room. Images of her mother flooded her, and she nearly put on her clothes and drove to the nursing home. When the call came the next morning, she bawled like a newborn child and wished she had listened to her instincts. Her mother had somehow obtained a bottle of sedatives and taken them. She had died peacefully during the night.

Julia sat in the morning sunlight streaming through her kitchen window and thought about all the beauty her mother had given the world. Even last night's dream had been beautiful. Her mother had said goodbye, and Julia would treasure the memory forever. It was while Julia sat in the sunlight that morning that she decided to seek the job in San Francisco. Her mother had given Julia her freedom in a shower of petals, and there was nothing to hold her back.

****

A foghorn warned Julia that it wouldn't be long before the city pulled a wet blanket over itself and shut out the world. She thought about Kathy and how alike they were. Kathy had held people at arms length until Tom Person entered her life. She had let Tom penetrate her defenses, and he'd betrayed and murdered her. Julia had been just as guilty of pushing people away. She'd had affairs, but not loving relationships. She had always played the chameleon in her relationships with men. She had sought out men who wanted to mold her to suit their idiosyncratic needs, and she'd fulfilled their wishes. A prostitute to Phillip, for example. What had she been to Mark? A mistress? Another ugly word, like *wife*.

Chilly fingers were playing a sonata on her spine, but it wasn't the chilled air that made her shiver. It was the realization that she must say goodbye to Mark. Her love for him didn't matter. She was through with married men, with any man who couldn't give himself honestly to her. She was through with Mark. Nausea rose in her throat, just as it had that night in the carport when she was attacked. The night she met Mark. She sat on the curb and pressed her hands against her face to quiet her sobbing.

Julia didn't know how long she sat there. A car's headlights startled her, and she looked around nervously, suddenly aware that she was exposed on a lonely street corner. She debated returning to her own apartment but realized that would be foolish. Liu Kwong might look for her there. So, she stood up with a sigh and retraced her steps back to the house with the veranda in front. There was little choice but to return to Mr. Andersen's, at least for one night. Tomorrow, she would decide what to do. The words of a long-ago hit song from a musical rang in her ears. *Tomorrow, tomorrow. There's always tomorrow. Tomorrow's a day away.*

Julia faced a dilemma the next morning when she checked her sat-com and saw two messages from Detective Rodriguez. Making contact could be dangerous. She had to be careful not to do anything that would expose where she was staying, but her instincts told her she could trust the man, and if she ignored his messages, she would be pushing away a potentially valuable ally. If she contacted him, however, she increased the risk of being discovered by Liu Kwong.

"It's dangerous to leave here unescorted," Mr. Andersen commented when she asked him what she should do, "but if you must meet him, it would be wise to stay clear of the police station. Kwong will have eyes there. Choose a public place where you can come and go safely, like a coffee shop or restaurant. But when you leave your meeting, you must be certain you are not followed."

Julia nodded. Her mood hadn't improved much from the previous night, but she had decided to stay the course with Mr. Andersen until their work was finished. If it meant facing Mark again, so be it. She would deal with him when the time came. She called Rodriguez.

"You're a hard woman to find, Ms. Rice," Rodriguez said by way of greeting. "I've been trying to reach you at work and at home. Anything I should know?"

"Just staying with friends at the moment, detective, working in the field. What can I do for you?" Julia tried to sound noncommittal. She wanted to keep the conversation short, in case the call was being traced.

"I've got some questions concerning Patrick Parker. I need to see you, this morning if possible. Can you come down?" Julia heard an undertow of urgency in his voice.

"Not at your office. How about a coffee shop?"

After another of his famous pauses, Rodriguez suggested a small diner around the corner from his office. Another rendezvous, she thought. Another risk. And this time she would face it without Mark to protect her. Her fury at him abated somewhat when she realized how vulnerable she was without him. She might be hurt and angry, but she still needed his protection. All the cloak-and-dagger precautions were beginning to wear on her nerves. She would be glad when the investigation was over.

Traffic was normal downtown, which meant it was aggravating but negotiable. Julia parked in a nearby lot and hurried to the diner. She glanced in store windows along the way, just as Mark had taught her, to see if anyone was following, but she saw nothing suspicious. That didn't quiet her jitters, however, and by the time she reached the diner, she was as twitchy as a caged bird. Detective Rodriguez was seated in the last booth facing the room. His eyelids drooped, suggesting a night without enough sleep, but he always looked tired. She wondered if it was part of his routine, his way of keeping his subjects off guard.

"Have a seat, Miss Rice." He rose long enough for her to slide into her side of the booth. "I've been digging into Mr. Parker's history, and I'm finding some disturbing information," he continued without preamble. "I'm hoping you can shed some light on things."

Julia squirmed under the detective's intense stare. She always felt like a microbe being studied under a microscope by him. She fiddled with her napkin, then thrust her hands out of sight under the table. The heat of his gaze followed her moves relentlessly, making it impossible for her to retain her composure. She decided to concentrate on a spot just above the detective's nose. It was a trick she used during difficult interviews when she wanted to avoid someone's eyes.

A waitress approached and she ordered coffee. "I know nothing about Patrick Parker. He was dead before I was born."

"But you knew it was his skeleton uncovered near the shipping docks, which makes me wonder what else you know. Do you know, for example, that Parker worked for a man named Liu Kwong?"

Julia tensed at the name and shook her head. She hoped he couldn't see she was lying. He continued to bore into her with his eyes.

"Let's try another name. Tom Person."

Rodriguez's question destroyed Julia's effort to regain her equanimity. She abandoned her attempt to avoid his unrelenting gaze and returned his stare. His eyes probed hers, reading them as one would tea leaves. Tom Person's name caromed inside her head, making it difficult for her to think. She frowned and remained quiet.

Another of the detective's familiar silences filled the space between them. It was a very effective interrogation method, she thought. It inflamed her guilt and whipped it through every nerve in her body.

"One last try, Miss Rice, how about a Ms. Kathy Griffith?" Rodriguez's sultry tone and set jaw revealed his impatience. A tropical storm of suspicions and undeclared accusations scorched the air between them.

"How do you know these people?" she managed to ask.

"Mr. Parker was required by law to make a full report of his jobs as a private investigator. It took some effort, but we uncovered old computer files and tax reports showing sources of income. He was in the employ of Liu Kwong until shortly before his death. Mr. Kwong still lives. When we contacted him, he told us Mr. Parker's employment ended when he began working with a Tom Person. Our police records indicate Mr. Person may have murdered a woman named Kathy Griffith. I say 'may have' because her body was never found. However, all evidence pointed to her death and to Mr. Person's involvement in the crime. Now, I'm wondering if he's the one who killed our friend in the morgue. It's a very messy set of relationships."

Julia knew she faced some hard choices. She could deny any

knowledge of these people and the murder, but that might lead to legal actions against her, and she would lose Detective Rodriguez as a potential ally. The other choice was to trust Rodriguez and tell him some of what she knew. Not about Mr. Andersen or Kathy Griffith, but about Liu Kwong. Considering her circumstances, it seemed a reasonable risk, and if the detective proved as trustworthy as he claimed, she could use him to shut down Liu Kwong's operation. She wished she could consult Mr. Andersen first, but there was no time. Rodriguez expected answers. It was time to play ball.

Julia took a deep breath. "How much do you know about Liu Kwong?"

Silence. He eyed her with interest. She said nothing. "Not my department, but I know about Kwong's drug trade and bribes. Been doing it for years, but no one's been able to tag him. He keeps his hands clean."

"What if I could bring you evidence that would put Kwong in jail and shut down his operations?"

A longer silence. Rodriguez stared at her with a look midway between curiosity and accusation. This time, Julia yielded to the silent treatment.

"I'm working on a story about Kwong that links the Oakland contraband operations back to him, along with the names of politicians and police officers who are taking his bribes. Did you know he's also smuggling young women from China to be used as sex objects and slaves? I have photos documenting a group being transferred from the Oakland docks just a few days ago."

Now it was Rodriguez's turn to lose his characteristic coolness. He leaned forward, his face animated with interest. "You have evidence of this?"

"I hope to have it in a day or two. When I do, I write my story and you get the files." Julia was pleased to see Rodriguez's keen expression. Her news transformed him from angry and tired to energized and upbeat. She was also relieved that Liu Kwong's name had diverted Rodriguez away from Kathy Griffith and Tom Person.

Rodriguez's mood became more pensive. "You're dealing with a very ruthless man, Miss Rice. You should let me help you."

Julia acknowledged his offer with a smile. "I appreciate your concern, detective, but I have help." She didn't bother to articulate her concern that any information given to the police would immediately be leaked to Kwong, whether Rodriguez was honest or not. It was best to keep a low profile for the moment.

"All the same, call me the moment you sense trouble. I don't need more murders to solve." He tried to retain his gruff exterior as he handed her a card, but she noted his concern. "My home phone number is on the back."

"Thank you, detective. I'll do that."

Julia left the restaurant, but instead of returning to her car, she walked to the nearest Bay Area Rapid Transit station. Most of the BART system was above ground, but in downtown San Francisco the trains ran under Market Street. Julia had to be certain that no one had picked up her trail, and Mark had told her how to use the BART system to spot anyone following her. She was about to put his plan to the test. She bought a ticket from the computerized dispenser and joined several dozen people milling about along the platform waiting area. Soon, she heard the familiar whoosh and felt the compressed air being forced through the tunnel ahead of an approaching train. A metallic voice echoing through the station announced the train's arrival and next destination. It slid along the platform and glided to a stop with hardly a whisper. Riders emerged from the cars in a flurry of warm bodies and aftershave lotions. Those boarding the train pressed forward in a scramble for empty seats. Julia followed but stopped at the door's threshold. She quickly glanced up and down the platform, looking for anyone who hesitated to board. The automated doors closed, leaving Julia standing alone on the now empty platform. Satisfied, she ran to catch up with the exiting crowd and blended into the throngs of pedestrians as they emerged on Market Street.

Julia retrieved her car and took a circuitous route back to the house, keeping a watchful eye on her rearview mirror. Thoughts of Kathy and Mark intertwined themselves in her mind like two strands of DNA. Today, she was determined to learn Kathy's fate. No more excuses. No more delays. She would pin Mr. Andersen down and wring the facts out of him. Facing Mark was a bigger dilemma. Her heart still fluttered whenever she thought about him. In the past, she hadn't cared about the marital status of a lover. She'd even been relieved when she learned of a wife waiting at home. It made it easier to keep her distance. Mark was different. He had penetrated every pore in her body, enveloping her with his luminous eyes and tropical breath. Sitting there in the car, her eyes flitting back and forth between the road and her mirror, her thighs ached to feel his skin rubbing against hers again. Needing to feel him probing her, entering her, fulfilling her. By the time Julia parked in the circular driveway, her chest was heaving to the rhythm of her heart, and she was perspiring heavily. *What am I going to do? He has a wife!*

Julia stopped at the front door, pressed her hand over her breast, and swallowed handfuls of air before entering the house. When she did, she found Mr. Andersen in the study and sat down opposite him. She was still breathing rapidly, and a film of sweat had formed on her arms and face. She gave him a stormy look, her face as tense as a bowstring pulled back to its limit. "Tell me," she said with the firmness of a child demanding a bedtime story. "Tell me the end of it, now."

The lines in Mr. Andersen's face conveyed a sleepless night, but she didn't care. She leaned forward and fixed her gaze on him. His face tightened in surprise at her insistence, but he smiled and nodded.

"Yes. It is time to finish." He followed his usual routine, closing his eyes, and taking a minute to compose himself.

****

I had just been expelled from paradise and consigned to purgatory. It was no less than what I deserved, but my misery was so absolute, I didn't know if I could survive until nightfall. It was Sunday, and I had no idea where to go. My best choices were my

238

office or a bar. It was too early to drink, so I pointed my car towards downtown. I drove along the quiet streets in a stupor, my mind as fuzzy as sheep's wool. I thought about driving to China Town and confronting Liu Kwong, but I knew that would do no good. He would deny everything and bide his time. I wanted to stay in contact with Kathy and protect her. But how? Where would she go? Now that she knew about Kwong's venomous attack, I doubted she would return to the Golden Moon. My best bet was to put surveillance on her accounting firm and pick up her trail when she returned to work.

As soon as I entered my office, I saw the white #10 envelope lying in the middle of the floor. My tormentor had given it quite a push under the door. From anger? I snatched it up and tore it open, expecting to find a message similar to the others. But the message had changed, and it put last night's events in a terrifying new light. I knew in a heartbeat that I had been wrong about Emily's murderer. Kathy had been the intended victim, but the killer was not Liu Kwong. The meticulously worded message on the lined paper told me that. *Death has found you.* Whoever sent it believed he had murdered Kathy, and that by murdering her, he had evened an old score with me. The motivation was revenge, after all.

I stared at the letters, each carefully cut from a newspaper or magazine. The letters formed words. The words a message. *Death has found you.* Not just a message. A shout of triumph. A cry of victory. I never knew Emily, but I nearly wept at the thought of her dying because of me. I don't know how long I stood there before the newly installed camera flashed through my wooly mind. Of course, the camera! My vengeful murderer had been captured on film. I rushed to the recorder, removed the tape, and inserted it into the monitoring equipment we kept behind Patti's desk. As I watched the tape rewinding on an empty hallway, I thought about the fury on Kathy's face. Her wrath was more than I could bear. I had to find her and explain my unseemly behavior. Not to get her back--I knew that was no longer possible--but to spare my sanity and save my soul.

A figure suddenly loomed on the screen, and I stabbed at the stop button with an unsteady hand. By the time I hit play, the hallway was empty. Was my tormentor a ghost? No, I told myself, I had simply rewound the tape too far. I stared at the screen, willing my assailant to appear, and there he was, slinking down the hall, his head swiveling back and forth with apprehension. I had seen his kind before: a timorous person trying to act bravely. When desperate, they could be very dangerous because they were unpredictable. Given sufficient motivation, they could become murderers.

This one was cautious. He wore a wide-brimmed hat to hide his face and dark gloves. Even when I froze the image and enlarged it, I couldn't make out his features, and the gloves eliminated any chance of a stray fingerprint. I was seized by an alarming thought. The man was going to get away, and when he learned of his mistake with Emily, he would strike again. I had to find out who he was and stop him. My hands were pressed against the sides of the monitor while I silently pleaded for him to reveal himself, and in a flash he did so. The flash came from his hand. Once he had thrust the envelope under my door, he stood up and pulled off his gloves. It was the gesture of a job well done, like mowing the lawn or laying cement. It showed his satisfaction, and it betrayed him, for I could clearly see the source of the flash . . . a two-carat diamond ring on the pinky finger of his right hand. My tormentor was my real estate mark, Frank Cochran.

I grabbed the phone and called the number Detective Barnes had given me. Barnes wasn't in, but when I explained the nature of my call, the officer on duty told me to sit tight.

My phone rang less than a minute later. I told Barnes about the notes and film and gave him enough background to understand Cochran's motivation. He assured me he would put out an arrest warrant at once. Someone would be by shortly to retrieve the tape and note. I asked him about Kathy's whereabouts, but he was noncommittal. The images of Kathy damning me before the world were fresh in both our minds, and I decided not to press him.

By the time a police officer arrived to pick up the evidence, it was late enough in the afternoon to justify a drink, and I headed across the street to the bar. I hoped Frank Cochran would show up to torment me, so I could have the satisfaction of busting a beer bottle over his head. He didn't show, and I drank in silence.

Somehow, I survived a sleepless night and was in the office so early the next morning, I arrived before Patti, which was no easy feat. She blinked with surprise when she found me there, barely shaven and wearing yesterday's wrinkled clothes. Her "library look" told me I looked like a bed sheet someone had forgotten to wash. When Carl came in, I asked him to do a computer search and look for any match of Kathy, Katie, Griffith, or Livingston in the hotel reservation systems in the greater San Francisco area. Nothing turned up. I called her accounting firm, but they said she wasn't due back until tomorrow. All I could do was sit and wait. Two hours later, we got the news of Frank Cochran's arrest. The good news swept the wool from my head, and for the first time in the past twenty-four hours I was able to think straight. Knowing Kathy was safe lifted my spirits, but they quickly plunged into another round of self-pity at the thought of never seeing her again.

Patti and Carl were running out of things to do, and the worried frowns on their faces told me I had better trim my sails and get the ship moving again. Just not today. I promised them we would sit down in the morning and review our prospective client list. Having bought a little time, I escaped the office and spent the rest of the day driving around Kathy's old haunts. Now that Cochran had been arrested, I hoped she would surface, but there was no sign of her. The yellow police tape had been removed from her house, but the drapes were closed. I tried to muster the nerve to ring her doorbell, but failed. I would have another look that night.

It was after eight o'clock when I drove back to her house. My hopes were at low tide by then, but they spiraled upwards when I saw a light in her bedroom window. Was she home, or had someone simply forgotten to turn it off? I drew closer, my thoughts whirling with apprehension at the prospect of seeing Kathy again. I could still picture the anger distorting her face. Her eyes flashing. How could I confront such fury from the woman I loved? But I had to tell her about my contract with Liu Kwong. She had to know what I had done to save her. Not so she would forgive me, but to convince her to destroy those computer disks.

It wasn't until I stopped across the street from her house that I realized something was wrong. The light in her window flickered, steadied, then flickered again. It was an unnatural light, a light filled with evil spirits and unholy acts. Don't ask me how I knew this, but as I watched it flickering behind the closed drapes, a cold dread rose inside of me. I grabbed my gun from under the car seat and ran to the front door. It was closed and locked this time, but I picked the lock in less than a minute and slipped inside. A chilly breath of air brushed my cheeks. The downstairs was as cold and dark as a cellar. Only the light from Kathy's bedroom pushed the shadows back far enough for me to see the upstairs landing. I could hear a faint squeaking noise coming from her room at regular intervals. Otherwise, the house seemed deserted. Then, a soft moan broke the silence. I gripped my gun with both hands to steady it and ascended the stairs towards the light.

The scene that greeted me was an abomination against the laws of mankind. I staggered back, refusing to believe what I saw. This couldn't possibly be happening, I told myself, but I knew it was. And in that split moment of recognition, I understood the deeply depraved mind of Liu Kwong.

Kathy hung by her wrists from a piece of rope tied to the ceiling fan above her bed, which slowly turned her around and around. Each time she turned, the fan squeaked, and she momentarily blocked the light from the small lamp by her bed, causing the flicker I had seen from the street. Blood flowed from multiple wounds in her breasts, back, stomach, and legs. Her naked body glistened in the red fluid as she turned. Dark blotches had formed on the bed covers beneath her, where the blood dripped relentlessly from her body. It gave off an odor of decaying flesh. I had never seen Kathy naked before, but even covered in blood, I saw how beautiful she was. Her head was slumped forward as if she were already dead. Godzilla stood before her wielding my miniature samurai sword in his gloved hand, the one stolen from my office. Its blade glowed red in the weak light as he flicked it at her, opening another bloody gash. Kathy briefly raised her head and moaned.

Thoughts tore through my mind with the speed of light. The break-in at my office hadn't been a robbery. It was Liu Kowng's men looking for a murder weapon with which to frame me. My souvenir sword had presented the perfect instrument. Kwong had never intended for Kathy to live, and he'd hired me to be the fall guy. I saw it all in the blink of an eye.

I moved into the room, my gun raised and a primordial scream dancing on my tongue, but Godzilla sensed my presence before I could fire. He thrust the sword into Kathy's side and whirled away so quickly, I only saw a blur. From his arm's motion, I knew he had thrown something and heard a soft thud near my head as I ducked. Before I could recover, he was gone, his cat-quick feet carrying him out the bedroom door, down the stairs, and into the night.

My body shook so violently I dropped the gun. The knife he had thrown still vibrated in the bedpost in front of me. At first, I thought the bedpost had saved my life, but I realized later that Godzilla hadn't missed his target. He had thrown the knife to disorient me long enough to escape. Liu Kwong wanted me as a live murderer, not a dead victim. I stumbled to Kathy and carefully withdrew the small sword from her body. It was a much deeper wound than the others, and blood poured from it unmercifully. I prayed it had missed her vital organs as I cut her down and tore bed sheets into strips to bind her wounds. She cried out in pain, and her eyes opened.

"Tom, it's you," she mumbled. "You were trying to protect me, but I wouldn't let you."

"Hush, now. Save your strength until I get you to a doctor." My hands trembled so badly, it was all I could do to tie off the bindings. Tears blurred my vision. I was a mess, and I had to get a hold of myself. Every second was precious. Kathy's life hung in the balance.

I wrapped her in a blanket and carried her to my car. My first instinct was to drive to the nearest hospital, but circumstances held me back. A hospital meant police reports. Liu Kwong would know Kathy still lived, and he would come after her again. The only way to save her was to convince Kwong that he had succeeded. He must believe that she was dead and that the police thought I was the murderer. I had to take Kathy somewhere more discreet than a hospital. I made a phone call to a previous client as I tore through the dark streets to his private clinic. He was a surgeon who had wanted to be rid of his partner. I had arranged it, and he had expressed eternal gratitude. I knew the clinic was staffed twenty-four hours a day and had an operating room. It was time to test my client's gratitude.

****

Julia was so absorbed in Mr. Andersen's story, she didn't realize that he had stopped. Her entire body was quivering as she tried to rid herself of the image of Kathy hanging from that rotating ceiling fan, but it wouldn't go away. A child's voice peeled with laughter somewhere on the street outside, breaking the silence.

"What happened?" she whispered. She feared if she spoke in her normal voice, it would crack.

"Oh, the rest is history, as they say." Mr. Andersen's cheeks seemed to have caved into his face, but he managed to smile. His eyes peered across the room as if he were searching for someone. "Kathy mended at the clinic, and once I had explained the situation to my client, he kept his silence. After all, he knew Kathy wasn't dead, and that I was saving her life, not taking it. Fortunately, I was able to withdraw my substantial bank balances the next day, before the police learned of Kathy's disappearance, and transfer them to a numbered Swiss account.

"The media had a field day with the bloody scene. Newspapers and news programs vilified me for my heinous crime. Talk shows speculated about my motive for taking Kathy's life in what must have been a violent manner. The uproar only lasted a

244

week, however. By then, the reporters and the public had lost interest and moved on to other sensational stories.

"But if I was to protect Kathy from Kwong, I had to let the world believe that I had murdered her. That meant living my life as a fugitive. I had to convince Kathy to leave the country with me and start over again abroad. I contacted Carl, who arranged new identities and passports for Kathy and myself. He took over the business, just as I had done from my mentor.

"Kathy and I talked at great length during her recovery. I told her everything. She admonished me for not confiding in her sooner. The sparks were still there between us, however, and she agreed to forgive me if I promised never to leave her. That was an easy promise to make. The surgeon told me many of Kathy's scars would be permanent, but those wounds never detracted from her beauty, at least not in my eyes. Once she was well enough to travel, we drove to Mexico and hopped a plane to England. We lived there together for forty years, until Kathy died last spring. Losing her caused me great pain. We never married or had children, but our life was filled with so much happiness, I wasn't sure I wanted to go on without her. But I knew that Liu Kwong still lived, and I decided it was time to bring him to justice. That led me to you, Julia, and I must say it has been a most rewarding experience."

Julia's mind had gone missing. She knew where she was, and that Mr. Andersen had just explained the police reports and newspaper headlines from all those years ago, but her mind wasn't there. It had vanished in such a flurry of images, she was lost in a snowstorm of uncertainty, and the room was spinning so fast, she couldn't think. She sank into the cushions, letting them swallow her in their smothering embrace. The air had turned thick as gravy, making it hard to breathe. Names sprang forward: Li Chang, Romeo, Patrick Parker, Kathy. How many other victims had there been in Liu Kwongs' long and murderous rule? Kathy had lived, but only because of luck and Tom Person's unceasing love. Who had been there for the others? Julia had become Mr. Andersen's cudgel to destroy this evildoer, and it seemed a daunting task. She shivered at the thought of failing and being snared by Kwong's claws, but there was no choice. Not after all she had learned. It was time to bring an end to Liu Kwong, just as she had to CONDAD.

A cave-like stillness drifted through the room. The air was hushed, as if it hadn't been disturbed for forty years. The room slowly returned to focus. Julia stared at Mr. Andersen's closed eyes and peaceful repose, and for a moment she couldn't tell if he was alive or dead. His skin had become the color of ashes. His body had slumped against the cushions of his chair. Then, she saw the touch of a smile form on his lips and knew he had slipped away into his dreams. She stood up and quietly left the room.

Julia retrieved her sat-com from the night stand next to her bed and punched the autodial to check her messages. The first two were routine, but the third one jarred her out of her pensive mood.

"This is Romeo calling for Julia Rice." Julia jumped at the sound of Romeo's nervous voice. He was alive! "I've got some papers Li Chang was gonna give you. Can't say much about 'em on the phone, but they should be worth another $500. Bring the money before two to pier forty in San Francisco. After that I'm gone. If you want the stuff, this is your only chance."

Julia was heartened to know another of Kwong's victims was slipping through his clutches, but the tension in Romeo's voice worried her. It was the voice of a fugitive. The urgent tone told her he was going to run. It was nearly one o'clock, and she had no idea where Mark was. *Probably with his wife.* Julia's stomach churned. She thought about trying to reach him but changed her mind. Romeo was her business, not his, and Romeo wanted that money. There was no reason for him to endanger her. She lifted her chin defiantly. Mark could enjoy the day with his *wife.* She would take care of business.

Her mind returned to the task at hand. It would only take a few minutes to withdraw $500 from her bank's ATM. If she hurried, she could make it before two.

Julia grabbed her bag and hurried downstairs. Mr. Andersen hadn't moved from his chair and appeared to be sleeping. He looked so peaceful that she couldn't resist stopping to observe him for a moment. She remembered her first impression of him in the restaurant, when he had roared into the room like an aging lion. It seemed so long ago. At rest, he looked more like a battered ship that had weathered too many storms. She touched his cheek with her finger tips and watched him stir. He was a good man. She knew that, now. Why couldn't she have had a father like him? *Why did I end up with CONDAD?*

Julia jotted a note explaining where she had gone and raced out the door.

CHAPTER NINETEEN

A seagull squawked unceasingly from its perch on the rail of an old fishing boat tied alongside pier forty, and the stench of decaying fish from the boat wafted over Julia as she crossed the dock's splintered planks. The pier had never been converted to handle modern ships and hadn't been used for commercial shipping in years. It had an abandoned look about it, except for the seagull. Julia covered her nose with her hand and looked cautiously about her as she approached a warehouse located half-way down the forsaken pier. Why was the pier so deserted, she wondered? Where was Romeo? It made sense, she supposed, for him to stay out of sight. An opened doorway towards the end of the dock beckoned her, but she hesitated. Something did not feel right.

A figure suddenly stepped out of the doorway and waved to her. The bright sunlight reflecting off the bay behind him made it impossible to see if it was Romeo, and the idea of entering that building with anyone else was a leap of faith she wasn't about to make. She waved back, uncertain what to do. The figure gestured again, and after a brief struggle with her nerves, she advanced a few more steps, her hand raised to shade her eyes. By the time she was close enough to see that the man was a stranger, it was too late. She looked back to see two Chinese men slipping down the gangplank from the fishing boat behind her, cutting off her retreat. Her mind reeled at the possibility that she might be in danger. Before she could think what to do, the men closed on her.

"Romeo's inside," one of them hissed in her ear, but she knew it was a lie. She thought of Li Chang, and a scream rose in her throat. But it was suffocated by a rough hand clamped over her mouth that smelled of liquor and cigarettes. She tried to wrest herself free, but more hands gripped her arms. The two men half-dragged her across the boards into the dimly lit building, where a black car crouched in the semi-darkness.

As she feared, there was no sign of Romeo. He was either dead or on the run. Alarm bells throbbed against her temples. How could she have been so stupid? She thought of Kathy, bloodied and resigned, and imagined it was *her* hanging from that ceiling fan. Soon, a knife would rip *her* skin and draw *her* blood, unless Mark could save her, much as Tom Person had saved Kathy. She could only pray he would find the note she left and think of some way to rescue her. Mark was her only hope.

Tape was slapped across her mouth and a hood yanked over her head. Someone pulled her hands behind her and bound them, then pushed her into the car and pinned her to the floor. Chinese voices and darting footsteps echoed in the darkness around her. She tried to call out, but the tape strangled her cries. The coarse fabric of the hood chafed her cheek where it pressed against the floor, but when she tried to lift her head, a heavy foot shoved her face down again.

She listened to the clatter of wooden planks as the car pulled out of the warehouse and rolled down the dock. This was followed by honking horns and cars' engines, telling her they had merged into the street's traffic along the Embarcadero. Julia tried to visualize their route but found it impossible to keep track of the car's twists and turns. She shook with the same terror she had experienced while hiding under the bed in that empty house and cursed her own stupidity for putting herself in such a helpless situation. If she had called Mark, none of this would be happening.

She prayed that her foolish behavior wouldn't cost her life.

Her cramped position and the claustrophobic hood made her feel as if she'd been thrown down a well. Every muscle in her body quivered with the desire to free herself of the rope binding her wrists, but when she struggled, the rope bit deeper into her skin and the ever-present foot pressed her head down unmercifully. Images of Emily's battered body flashed through her mind, and she nearly gave in to her growing hysteria. She was close to losing her sanity, but she knew doing so would only worsen her circumstances. Julia took deep breaths and tried to calm herself. She had to think and act rationally.

As she calmed herself, she began to assess her situation. It had to be Liu Kwong's men who had kidnapped her, but if he wanted her dead, they could have killed her at the warehouse. That meant he wanted her alive, at least for the moment. She guessed that he planned to use her as bait to lure Mr. Andersen from his hiding place. Once that happened, Julia reckoned her life wouldn't be worth anything. She had to keep her wits and hope that Mark would find her. Those thoughts didn't make her feel any less afraid, but they did relieve her panic. Her body relaxed; her anxieties subsided.

The car slowed to a crawl, and the sing-song melody of Chinese voices could be heard outside her window. They told her she was in Chinatown. When the car stopped, Julia heard a bird singing. Probably in a cage, she thought, just like me. Rough hands pulled her from the car and pushed her across a cement floor. She stumbled over an object and had to pedal her feet to keep from falling. The sing-song voices were gone; only the sounds of her captors' heavy footsteps echoing off the walls could be heard, now. Then, a door creaked open, and she was suddenly surrounded by women's voices babbling in Chinese. The door slammed shut behind her, but the voices continued to chatter like hungry birds. Hands worked at the ropes binding hers. Once they were freed, she tore the hood from her head and found herself staring at dozens of young, Chinese women. They gestured to her and spoke in a cacophony of noises. Julia rubbed her sore wrists and shook her head to indicate she couldn't understand them.

Panic tightened her chest as she gazed around the room. It looked like the inside of a giant shipping container whose metal walls rose high above her head. Heat poured down from the unprotected ceiling, making the air uncomfortably warm. There was no furniture: nothing to sit or lie down on. The girls, many of whom wore the same baggy clothes she had seen at the shipping docks, had taken extra clothing from their bags to cushion the floor where they sat. The room reeked of unwashed bodies and urine. She spied a bucket in the far corner and guessed that accounted for the ugly smell. The warmth of the girls' bodies momentarily robbed Julia of the air she needed to breathe. She slumped against a wall and thought distractedly about the girls she had seen being led away at the docks. Were these the ones? If so, they had been imprisoned there for more than a week.

When she thought about the implications of her situation, her legs lost their strength, and she slid to the floor. Liu Kwong wouldn't let her see these girls unless he intended to kill her, or use her like he would them. Julia recoiled at the idea of men having their way with her. If it came to that, she resolved to find some way to kill herself.

The girls returned to their places and settled down, but they talked in lowered voices and looked askance at her. She could tell that they were as uncertain of her fate as they were their own.

As Julia began the tortuous process of adjusting to her surroundings, she studied the room more carefully. The only light came from two florescent fixtures hanging some twenty feet above their heads, and the metal door she'd heard clanging shut was the only way out. Oil stains in the concrete floor suggested the place had once been used to store vehicles of some sort. Now, it was a prison for her and these unfortunate women. She tried to imagine what they felt and thought. It was possible they did not know their fate. She wished there was some way she could warn them, not that it would do any good. Escaping their destinies was not a likely prospect. Neither was escaping hers. She shuddered and closed her eyes against the terror that had burrowed into her mind.

A routine slowly revealed itself. Most of the girls sat in subdued silence, but she noticed three or four who made some effort to converse. When one of the girls needed to relieve herself, she walked quietly to the bucket and squatted with her back to the room. When she needed to move her bowels, however, she banged on the door, and a guard took her out. The longer Julia sat there, the more she felt the walls closing on her and crushing her will. The urge to escape the stifling room overwhelmed her; the metal door represented her only way out. She had to see what lay beyond.

Julia stood up and banged on the door. "I need to use the bathroom," she called. Her plea was answered by silence. She banged louder. "Do you speak English? Please take me to the toilet." The room grew breathless with anticipation. No one moved, but Julia could feel the girls eyes riveted on her. Their silence told her she was defying "house rules," but she didn't care. Could she hear the guard breathing just beyond her reach, or was it just her imagination? She listened intently but couldn't be certain. Minutes passed without a response. She pounded again, this time with anger. "God damn it, let me out." This outburst prompted the guard to stir. She heard muffled footsteps, but they were walking away! She stood fuming and clenching her fists. More minutes passed, but she refused to budge. Periodically, she thumped on the door with her fist, but her hand was getting sore and her energy was flagging. The girls continued to watch in silence.

Finally, she heard two sets of footsteps returning. The guard had somebody with him. The door clanged open, revealing a sinewy man dressed in western-style trousers and a long-sleeved shirt buttoned at the neck. His baby smooth face was misshapen by a venomous glare that contorted his thin lips and gave him the appearance of a witchdoctor casting an evil spell. Julia recoiled from the fury in his look and tried to retreat from the doorway, but he grabbed her arm and pulled her into a dimly lit corridor.

"You think if you make trouble you'll get special treatment?" he asked in good English as he pulled her close to him. His breath blistered her cheek. "Come with me. I'll give you all the attention you want." He twisted her arm behind her back and shoved her ahead of him. She squirmed in his grasp but could do nothing against his iron grip. The fingers of his free hand encircled her neck, and her arm was suddenly released. But before she could react, a knife was pressed against her throat. Julia cringed and tried to pull away. The fingers tightened and held her fast, while the knife's cold metal snaked up her throat to her cheek.

"Be quiet my little bird, or I'll clip your wings," the voice hissed in her ear.

The familiar words slammed the air from her lungs. It was the man who assaulted her in the carport! She nearly gagged at the memory of that foul smelling cloth covering her nose, and the floor wobbled beneath her feet. She began to quiver uncontrollably. *Oh, God, why did I make such a fuss? If only I'd used that stupid can.*

Heat from the man's body radiated through hers as she lurched along the corridor. The place was tainted by a decaying odor that reminded Julia of rotting flesh. A smudged window at the end of the corridor offered so little light, she was forced her to watch her every step to keep from stumbling over the discarded crates littering the floor. They halted abruptly in front of a foul-smelling bathroom that was more repugnant than the bucket. Julia tried to break free of her captor's grasp, but he leaned against her and licked her earlobe with his tongue, sending shockwaves of terror rippling through her body.

"You have one minute little bird, before I come for you." With that, he shoved her into the filthy room, causing her to stumble against the far wall, and stood in the doorway dissecting her with his eyes. Julia regained her balance and closed the door. She covered her nose with her hand to ward off the stench and stood trembling in the center of the loathsome room. Her eyes darted about looking for a loose pipe or some other weapon to defend herself, but she found nothing. Tears streamed down her face as she tried to think. She *felt* like a small bird, a bird at the mercy of a savage cat. The man could kill her at any time, but what could she do? She was defenseless against him. Julia had never felt so alone, and she suddenly missed the warmth of the girls' company.

The door banged open without warning, and her tormentor motioned for her. The anger was gone from his face, replaced by a mask that gave Julia no hint of his thoughts, but she was relieved to see that he had returned his knife to a sheath in his pants leg. When she hesitated, he grasped her arm, twisted it behind her once more, and marched her back along the corridor. He no longer pressed his body against hers or breathed in her ear. The cat had become bored with the bird. When the guard opened the steel door to her cell, she stumbled into the stuffy room with the joy of a child returning to its mother's arms.

Julia had just gotten settled when the door clanged open again. Large trays crammed with cups of tea and bowls of rice topped with cabbage were shoved into the room. The girls buzzed at the sight of the food and hurried forward to claim their dinners. Their burst of energy surprised her. She hung back, unsure whether there would be enough for everybody. One bowl and tea cup remained unclaimed, and the girl seated next to her gestured that she should take them. She was impressed at how considerate they were, despite their circumstances.

When they were finished eating, the girls stacked the empty bowls and cups back on the trays. Julia followed their example, and a short time later the guard removed them. The girls began to spread themselves out on the soiled floor in preparation to sleep. One of them offered Julia a coarse sweater for a pillow. She accepted it with a smile but couldn't bring herself to lie down just yet. Doing so would imply that she had given up, and she wasn't ready to do that. But when the lights snapped off and threw the room into a pit of darkness, she had little choice but to sit down. She listened to the steady sounds of breathing around her and tried not to think about what tomorrow might bring. *How did these poor girls keep from going crazy?* Her mind was already bending away from reality, much like the electrical beams that had yielded to Mark's hand-held device. The idea that she might go mad churned inside her head. *How long did it take my mother to lose herself? How long will it take me?* The questions pressed against the back of her forehead.

Eventually, the darkness took its toll. She lay down on the floor, put the sweater under her head, and curled into a ball. She had no idea how long she lay there before a black veil covered her mind and she slept.

****

Mark returned to the house with a sense of excitement that he couldn't wait to share with Julia. But something was wrong. He sensed it the moment he entered the house. It was too quiet. He saw Mr. Andersen asleep in the living room, but where was Julia? A quick look around the room produced the note announcing her attempt to meet Romeo. He knew at once it was a trap. Romeo hadn't been seen in days and was almost certainly dead or gone by now. Even if he was still in the area, he wouldn't risk telling anyone where he could be found. Not even for the money Julia had promised him. He knew the only one waiting for her was Liu Kwong.

Mark tried to contact Julia on her sat-com, but there was no response. He started to wake Mr. Andersen, thought better of it and ran for his car. He could move faster on his own, and he hoped he wasn't too late to keep Julia from stumbling into Kwong's clutches.

Pier Forty was deserted when Mark arrived. He eyed the old boat tied to the dock with suspicion as he proceeded towards the warehouse's open door. He hadn't covered more than a hundred feet when he sensed movement behind him and turned in time to see two men moving down the gangplank from the boat. Mark pulled his weapon and dived onto the roughhewn planks as twin flashes of light sped past his head. He rolled twice. The heat of more flashes burnt holes into the boards beside him. On the third roll, he came to a halt in a prone position on his stomach just as twin flashes skipped past him and charred the place where he should have been. He fired two bursts from his own weapon. The first man toppled; the second spun to his left from a glancing blow. Before the assailant could recover, Mark fired again and watched him crumple to the deck. He stood up cautiously, looking for other attackers, but there were none.

The warehouse was as desolate as the dock area, but he could see where the floor's dust had been disturbed by shuffling feet and a car's tires. They had waited for her there and taken her away. He prayed she wasn't in immediate danger. His only hope was that Liu Kwong wanted Mr. Andersen, and he would keep Julia alive as long as it furthered his plan. He wouldn't wait forever, however. There wasn't much time to devise a way to thwart Kwong and save Julia. There would be more traps waiting for him when he went looking for her, but he didn't care.

He ran to his car and drove back to the house to advise Mr. Andersen.

Stirring noises that sounded like small animals foraging in a forest and water trickling in a bucket woke Julia from a dream about her mother. It had been a pleasant dream. They were talking and laughing together in the old nursery. Julia was a small girl again. She knew this because she was holding her mother's hand and smiling up at her.

Her mother faded when harsh light flooded her half-closed eyes. She opened them and was greeted by the sight of several girls waiting their turns to use the bucket. The odor was less caustic than she remembered. *I'm getting used to it, just like these girls.* The air had become cold during the night. Julia shivered as she stood up and tried to decide what to do. She thought about banging on the door and asking the guard to let her use the bathroom, but memories of that satanic man's knife chafing her throat and hot tongue licking her ear sent fresh chills coursing through her body. She quickly discarded the idea and walked over to the bucket. The girls watched her inconspicuously when she squatted down. It was humiliating to do something so private in front of others, but oddly consoling, as well. Sharing their discomfort gave her a sense of camaraderie that she found gratifying.

When she returned to her place, the girl seated next to her smiled and touched her hand. The gesture affected Julia deeply, and she nearly threw her arms around the girl and bawled. Tensions had been building in her since yesterday's ordeal began. She had fought to keep them from getting the best of her, but the girl's touch had nearly caused her to lose her nerve. That would do no good, she knew. She had to curb her fears and be strong. Mark would surely have seen the note by now. He wouldn't let her fall in battle without attempting to rescue her. It was a slim hope, but it was all she had, and it was enough to keep her courage from failing, at least for now. She slumped back down on the floor.

The heavy metal door clanged open, again, jarring the drowsy atmosphere that hovered in the room. The sudden disturbance raised a murmur among the women. Julia tensed and pressed her back against the wall. The agitated behavior of her companions told her this wasn't a routine visit. Two men stood in the doorway with grim expressions that did little to relieve the sudden tension boiling through the room. The Chinese men were perfectly matched in height and girth. Like a pair of bookends, she thought. One of them motioned for Julia to come forward, but when she tried to move, her legs refused to respond. *No, not yet,* an inner voice cried out. *I'm not ready to die!* But, no sound escaped her lips, which were as frozen as her limbs. Her screams were in her mind where only she could hear them. One of the men stepped towards her with a menacing glare, and this galvanized Julia into action. She got to her feet and shuffled towards him, even as she tried to ignore her blinding fear. Was this how she was going to end her life, walking to her death without so much as a struggle? She looked for some sign of hope in her captors' faces, but they were void of expression. Her legs began to wobble, but her prisoners' strong hands grabbed her arms and prevented her from collapsing.

Julia floated between the two men, her feet hardly touching the ground. They half-carried her down the familiar hallway leading to the bathroom, but they turned right before reaching it and led her down a new corridor. The lighting was better there. She could see Chinese lettering on the tilted stacks of crates piled against the walls. Pages from a Chinese newspaper littered the floor. A leaking overhead pipe fed a pool of oily water that chilled her feet as she was dragged through it. Julia saw these things but didn't recognize them. Her vision was floating in and out of focus, registering one moment and sliding away the next.

They stopped in front of a frosted, glass door. Chinese voices chimed with surprising clarity beyond the door. Men's voices. Three, maybe more. They were waiting for her! Were they her executioners? She thought about Mark, how strong and fearless he was. How he never showed weakness. Thinking of him gave her strength. Whoever these men were, she couldn't let them see her fear. With a mighty effort, she straightened her back and shrugged off the offending hands. The door opened, revealing a sparsely furnished office. A cluttered, teakwood desk and chairs stood in the room's center; a zebra-striped couch sagged against the wall to her right; a row of filing cabinets lined the wall to her left. The man who had terrorized her the previous day lounged on the couch with unblinking eyes. Next to him sat another man wearing similar trousers and long-sleeved shirt. A veil of smoke rose from their cigarettes and curled above their heads in the manner of tarnished halos. Julia's heart jumped, and she quickly looked away.

Behind the desk sat the shriveled figure of an old man. His white hair, thin and wispy, floated around the deep wrinkles and folds in his face. Unlike the modern dress of the younger men, the old man wore traditional silk garments that shimmered in a rainbow of colors. He gestured for Julia to come forward and sit in one of the straight-backed chairs facing him, but she was too mesmerized by his fingernails to move. Each was inches long and shaped like an elephant's tusk. The nails transformed his wilted hands into menacing claws. She shifted her gaze to the man's face and found herself being scrutinized by a pair of cold, reptilian eyes. They were evil eyes, and she knew without doubt to whom they belonged: Liu Kwong.

One of the bookends shoved her from behind. She stumbled, regained her balance and strode to the chair with as much bravado as she could muster.

"We are delighted you could join us, Miss Rice. Please sit

down." The man's voice crackled the way old newspapers do when wadded into a ball. "These are my two sons. I believe you have already met my number one son." He waved his claw towards the couch as he spoke. The first son smirked at her with eyes as cold as his father's. The second had a more wiry build that reminded Julia of a coiled snake that could strike without warning. His expression remained impassive, but she could sense the violence stored in his thin body. In his own way, he was every bit as frightening as his brother. Tiny shivers pricked her skin, and she gripped the edge of the chair to keep from revealing her fear.

"I would like to renew my association with Mr. Person. I believe you know him as Mr. Andersen." Kwong smiled benignly. "It has been many years since we last saw each other. Perhaps, you would be willing to help me arrange a meeting, in exchange for your life." The smile broadened, revealing gold fillings and nicotine-stained teeth. "There are worse things than dying, you know, so I hope you will be cooperative."

Julia's stomach twisted sharply, and a bitter taste rose in her mouth. He was threatening to torture her. Or sell her into bondage. She sucked in her breath and held it to prevent herself from crying out. Thoughts of bravery scurried away, replaced by alarm and foreboding. She didn't know if she had the strength for this ordeal, but she had to try. Mark was looking for her. She had to believe that. Otherwise, there was no hope.

"Mr. Andersen will know something is wrong by now and have moved..." Julia stumbled over the words; her voice sounded tinny and off-key.

"You can call him." Kwong spread his hands before him, and for the first time, Julia noticed her purse lying on the desk. He lifted her sat-com from the purse and held it up. The first son sprang from the couch, took it, and handed it to her.

What should she do? Call Mark and risk leading him into a trap? She glanced around the room looking for an answer. There was none. Maybe, it was better to accept her fate for being so stupid, rather than endanger Mark or Mr. Andersen. But he wouldn't want that, and he would know better than to fall for

Kwong's tricks.

She pressed the memory button for Mark's number. He answered on the third ring. "It's me," she said.

"In some trouble I think." A husky voice. Worried, but steady.

"Yes." The warmth of his voice spread across Julia's cheeks. Just hearing him made her feel safer. She pictured his set jaw and resolute stare. He was out there, somewhere, trying to rescue her. She reached out her hand and touched his imaginary face. It no longer mattered that he was married. She loved him anyway.

Before she could say any more, the first son snatched her sat-com away and handed it to his father.

"Good day, Tom. Ahh, I see. It's Mr. Hansen . . . He's not there . . . How inconvenient. You will speak for him, then. Yes, I wish to meet with him." Amusement lifted Kwong's crinkled face into a feline smile. It was the contented smile of a predator toying with his victim. But the face suddenly darkened into a scowl, and Kwong glowered at Julia as he listened. "You have been busy, I see." His remark seemed to be directed towards Julia as well as Mark. She marveled at Kwong's self-control. His voice never wavered, never betrayed the anger that now defined his wrinkled face. "You are in no position to make demands, not if you want to see Miss Rice alive." A harsher tone. Julia recoiled at the surprising force of his threatening words. Kwong's restraint was gone, overpowered by fury, which boiled off his corrugated skin.

"I suggest you come to some arrangements today, while Miss Rice still lives." His oily calm returned. "My number one son will take care of the details."

Kwong handed the sat-com back to his son and motioned to the guards behind Julia. Firm hands grasped her shoulders and yanked her from the chair. She was half-dragged out the door and back down the corridors to her prison. When she was thrust back into the room, the girls gasped and began chatting excitedly. Hands reached out to touch her, to let her know she wasn't alone. Voices surrounded her in a sing-song melody she couldn't understand but gladly embraced. It was clear the girls were happy to see her again.

After she was settled, she realized the girl who had been

seated next to her was gone, and Julia sensed she wouldn't return. That was why the girls were so excited when she came back. When the others were taken away, they disappeared forever. It was a chilling thought, the idea of sitting there waiting to be plucked from the room and taken God-knows-where, never to be seen or heard from again. She looked at her companions with sympathy. In many ways, their fates were even worse than hers. She at least knew what lay ahead of her and still had hope of a rescue. These shattered souls didn't even know if it was day or night, much less what would become of them. The room was a graveyard of lost lives that could never be salvaged or reclaimed.

CHAPTER TWENTY

Julia endured another cycle of meals and sleep. Twice, the door clanged open at unexpected intervals, and she recoiled in anticipation of being dragged away to her doom. Each time, however, another girl was chosen and led off to a fate Julia could barely comprehend. The hours trudged by in an unbroken reel of empty frames. Her right eyelid began to flutter and her hands fidgeted constantly. The tension from waiting was taking its toll. She understood why many of the girls no longer spoke. She could feel her own mind slipping into the shadows of despair. Soon, she would be just like them, withdrawn and resigned to her destiny. She began to listen for the door, urging it to open for her. *Come for me now, before I lose my sanity.*

Her prayers were answered when the guard returned for the dishes from the morning meal. The first son appeared while the guard gathered the trays and motioned to her. Julia's trembling legs nearly betrayed her as she rose, but she forced herself to stand erect and to walk from the room without stumbling. He clamped his powerful hand on her arm and led her back down the corridors without saying a word. She sensed a tension in him this morning that hadn't been there before. His fierce anger was channeled in his long strides and his iron grip. The cat was in no mood to play, and

Julia knew that didn't bode well for the bird.

The scene in Kwong's office had hardly changed since yesterday. His second son still sat on the sagging couch blowing wreaths of cigarette smoke, while the old man pulled his silk robes around him and glowered from behind his desk.

This time, Julia wasn't offered a chair. She stood in the middle of the room, still flanked by Kwong's son, and tried to control the shivering waves of terror coursing through her body. Liu Kwong's wrinkled face remained implacable, giving no hint of her fate. *It's been forty years since he tried to murder Kathy, and nothing's changed. He still has the power to decide who lives or dies.*

"Tom Person believes your life is worth saving," he said after a protracted silence. "We have agreed on a meeting, Person and I, in exchange for you. You should feel complimented." A leering smile emerged from the folds of his face, but his reptilian eyes remained cold and unblinking.

Julia's legs sagged at the news, forcing her to grasp a chair for temporary support. A flash of giddy relief skipped across her spirit, but it quickly faded in the face of reality. She was a reporter, and she had witnessed Kwong's abominable operation. Her situation was no different than Katie's all those years ago when she was held prisoner by Angel. Kwong promised freedom, but his intentions were otherwise. He did not mean to let her live.

Kwong's son bound her wrists and pulled the hateful sack over her head. Julia thought briefly about resisting but knew the gesture would be futile. It was better to remain docile and pray there would be an opportunity to foil Kwong's plans. She was led from the office and pushed into a waiting car. A hand tried to thrust her down onto the floor once more, but she shrugged the hand away and forced herself into a sitting position on the car's leather seats. Someone grabbed her shoulders and shouted at her in Chinese, but another voice intervened, and she was left alone. She smiled at her small victory. The weight of two bodies jostled the seats on either side of her.

The car roared to life and shot out into the streets of Chinatown. Once again, she quickly lost her sense of direction.

Julia hoped someone might notice her and call for help, until she remembered how dark the limousine's tinted windows were at the warehouse. No one could see her from the street. The oppressive cloth covering Julia's head made the air clammy. Her arms tingled from their cramped position behind her back, and her heart pulsated to the rhythm of the bat wings beating in her chest. After awhile, Julia no longer heard the street noise or felt the bumps in the road. A dark world was closing around her, a world that enfolded her in a spidery web. She fought back the urge to scream.

Just when Julia thought she would surely go mad, the car lurched to a stop. The rope binding her hands was released and the offensive cloth lifted from her head, revealing the bookends seated on either side of her. She rubbed her chafed wrists and gasped the deliciously cool air, while she quickly looked around to get her bearings. They were parked at the Fort Point National Historic Site just below the first span of the Golden Gate Bridge. Early morning sunlight flickered off heavy ocean swells rolling into the bay. She could smell the salty waves dashing against the seawall that protected the Point's promenade along the waterfront. Seagulls swooped over the water with dancing wings.

The old fort standing before her served as an historical museum for tourists, but it was too early on a Sunday morning for visitors. Two cars filled with men sat alongside the limousine. She could see Kwong's second son behind the wheel of the closest vehicle. His face curled into an evil smile as he peered at her.

A small motor suddenly whined, and the dark glass separating the limo's back seat from the front slid down, disclosing the unblinking eyes of Liu Kwong and his first son.

"We are going to walk onto the bridge and meet Tom Person, who will approach from the other side. I expect your friend, Mark Hansen, will be with him, so I have brought a few of my men to assure our safety." Kwong waved his clawed hand at the two cars Julia had noted, but his small, black eyes never left hers. They jabbed at her pupils. "Whether you live or die depends entirely on you and your friends' actions. If you try to escape or raise an alarm, it will be the last thing you do. If Mr. Hansen tries to be a hero, you will be used as a shield. Either way, you will die."

A resignation settled over Julia that calmed her fears. Liu Kwong's threats still frightened her, but she knew Mark was nearby and had a plan. Whatever it was, she had to be ready for it.

Julia was escorted onto the bridge by Kwong's first son. He pressed a laser gun against her back as they walked along the pedestrian walkway. Its steady pressure reminded her that death was only inches away. Liu Kwong followed at a surprisingly quick gait, his bright robes flowing in the morning breezes. There was a vitality in his step that reflected the energy of a much younger man. The two cars carrying his men slunk along behind them.

Fog had begun to flow into the bay from the sea, partially obscuring the sun and turning the sky into a brilliant curtain of polished brass. Julia strained her eyes against the glare for some glimpse of Mark and Mr. Andersen, but all she saw were a few early joggers enjoying their morning run across the fabled bridge. A handful of cars zoomed past. Otherwise, all was quiet. Julia looked up and saw workmen high above her head cleaning and painting the top of the structure. They reminded her of ants. It seemed strange to see them working on a Sunday morning, but she knew bridge maintenance was a year 'round project because of the corrosive effects of the ocean air.

Julia pushed these random thoughts aside and concentrated on her surroundings. There was no way to escape Liu Kwong, other than to throw herself off the bridge, which would almost certainly be fatal. She had to put her faith in Mark and bide her time.

The fog was beginning to shroud the bridge, making it difficult to see beyond the middle span. But, as they walked towards it, the mists lifted just long enough to reveal Mark and Mr. Andersen less than fifty yards away. Julia nearly stumbled at the sight of Mark. His handsome face beamed at her. She could see his worry and knew he still cared for her. Their eyes locked together in a blaze of emotion that was stronger than Julia's fear of death. But even as her heart pounded in her chest, Julia faced the reality of her situation. What was it Mr. Andersen had told her? She had to let go of the past to set herself free? The words seemed so prophetic now. They told her she had to let go of Mark. Otherwise, she would repeat her endless cycle of trysts with married men and never learn to fly. It didn't matter that she loved him. She had to say goodbye. Her smile faded as Mark's face dissolved in the advancing fog.

Kwong noted her reaction with a satisfied grunt. "I see our guests have arrived." He raised his hand and signaled to the cars following them to stop.

Julia detected a glint of metal in the palm of Kwong's hand. Was it a weapon? She couldn't be sure, but she knew he was preparing to spring a trap. She swallowed hard and looked for Mark, who reappeared in the swirling mists. He had moved closer and stopped beside Mr. Andersen to survey the situation, but his view was partially blocked by an abutment between them that supported the bridge. He couldn't see the danger lurking behind her.

Kwong moved closer to Julia. "Well, Mr. Person," he purred, "we meet again, at last."

"So it seems." Mr. Andersen leaned on his cane as he replied. "I wanted to tell you that Kathy did not die. I saved her."

"Yes, I suspected that when her body was not found and you disappeared. I looked for you, of course. But that no longer matters. She took two disks of mine. They are old and useless, but I want them back in exchange for your friend." He gestured to Julia with his empty hand.

"I don't have those, I'm afraid." Mr. Andersen spoke so softly his voice was nearly lost in the heavy air. He stepped forward as he spoke. "Why don't you take me instead?"

The two old men faced each other with the countenance of duelists at twenty paces, and for an instant Julia thought she had been whisked back to a forgotten era when scores were settled by a code of honor. At any moment, she expected to hear the boom of ancient pistols. What she heard, instead, was the beep of a car horn somewhere in the gathering fog and the deep rumble of a motorcycle as it moved cautiously through the gloom. Something terrifying was about to happen, and it wouldn't be settled by gentlemen's rules.

Julia opened her mouth to warn Mark, but the pressure of the gun in the small of her back reminded her that death was only the tick of a clock away. *But I'll die anyway, if I don't do something.* A gust of wind whistled in her ears, sending shivers through her brain. She felt exposed and alone, her mind numb with dread. She heard the click of car doors opening behind her and looked back to see eight of Kwong's men emerging from the two vehicles. They advanced on foot along the railing where the abutment hid them from Mark's view. Blood rushed to Julia's head, just as it had all those years ago when she was held upside down by her foot, and she found herself fighting back the same nausea she had experienced then. Her thoughts were racing too fast for her to concentrate, and it took all her strength to keep her mind from swirling away in the fog. She had to keep her focus; she had to act, before it was too late.

Julia clamped her eyes shut and made her decision. It was better to die doing something than waiting for Kwong's son to kill her. She ignored the hard metal pressed against her back, raised her foot, and smashed her heel down on the instep of her captor's right foot. A cry of pain erupted and the pressure in her back disappeared.

Opening her eyes, she cried out, "Mark, it's a trap," but her words faltered in the damp air. Kwong's hand was quicker. He flicked his wrist, sending a jagged, metal object spinning toward Mr. Andersen. Mark leaped forward to shield his companion, but he was too late. The weapon struck home, jolting Mr. Andersen and flooding his face with pain. He swayed on his feet, his eyes locked in a death grip with Kwong's, then he collapsed to the sidewalk. Julia screamed as she watched the scene unfolding before her. Mark dove to the pavement and raised his gun, but Kwong had already stepped out of his line of sight behind the abutment. A sob escaped Julia's lips as she looked at Mr. Andersen lying on the ground. It had only taken a heartbeat for Kwong to strike. She had acted too late to save him.

Instinct took over, and Julia threw herself to the ground, her body tensed in anticipation of the withering blast of heat she expected to tear through her flesh. But nothing happened. Rolling on her back, she looked up. To her amazement, the workers she'd noticed earlier toiling on the bridge were materializing through the veils of fog above her head as they rappelled down ropes at a high rate of speed. They no longer reminded her of ants. They looked like black spiders rushing towards her, and she watched them with fascination. They weren't workers after all. They were Mark's men. Flashes of light exploded around her, forcing Kwong's troops to take cover along the railing and return fire. Julia found it difficult to keep track of the conflict. All she saw from her vantage point were bursts of light and bodies flowing around her in a blur of motion. She was surrounded by grunting men and the popping noises of laser blasts striking their targets. The flashes and sounds roused memories of the brief battle she had endured the night she and Mark broke into Kwong's office.

The bright colors of Kwong's robes flared into view, and she looked up to find his merciless eyes glaring at her over the barrel of a gun. Before he could fire, however, a body tumbled on top of Julia, its weight nearly crushing her. She sucked in her breath and waited for something to happen, but the body didn't move. The acrid smell of burnt flesh assailing Julia's nostrils told her that he was dead. His gun had clattered harmlessly to the pavement beside her.

A flash streaked past Kwong's head, diverting his attention and giving Julia a few precious seconds to defend herself. She pushed the body away, grabbed the gun, and scrambled to her feet. The weapon had felt like an alien object the night she fired it in Kwong's office. Now, it rested comfortably in her hand. The familiarity of the weapon surprised her and gave her strength. Her fear was gone, replaced by the desire to avenge Mr. Andersen. She raised the gun and leveled it at Kwong just as he turned back to her. The folds of his face twisted into a scowl filled with disdain. His expression told her she was nothing more than a bug to be squashed under his foot. Just like the girls he had enslaved, and Kathy, and Li Chang, and Romeo, and Mr. Andersen. None of them were important in Kwong's world. None of them mattered.

Anger boiled in Julia as she watched Kwong raise his weapon to destroy her. He did so deliberately, demonstrating his arrogant belief that she wouldn't know how to fire her weapon, or find the courage. But his insolent expression widened in disbelief when she pressed the firing mechanism and sent a bolt of light slashing through his body. His robes flew up as he jerked back, but instead of falling, he stood looking at her with a school boy expression of disbelief. Julia's pulse thumped in her head as she waited for him to drop. Her hands were suddenly shaking so violently, she found it impossible to keep her weapon aimed at its target. Was the man human, she wondered, or a mythical being that could never be destroyed? She fought to steady her hands and was about to fire again when he suddenly crumpled to the pavement.

Joy surged through Julia, but the continuing firefight quickly sobered her. Drawing a deep breath, she looked for Mark, but he was hidden behind the steel abutment with his men. She wanted to join him, but there was no way to do so without exposing herself to a deadly crossfire.

Her mind recoiled at the realization that she had now shot two men: the assailant in Kwong's office and Kwong himself. Either would have killed her without hesitation, but that didn't calm the turbulence churning inside her. The only thing that prevented her from rushing to the rail to be sick was the knowledge that she was still in danger.

A shout, Mark's voice, broke through her thoughts. "Julia, look out behind you!"

She whirled around and saw the distorted face of Kwong's first son glowering at her. A gun wavered in his hand, and the threat of violence contorted his face into a furious scowl. Julia stepped back in alarm, nearly tripping over the body that had fallen on her. She knew Kwong's son had seen her shoot his father, and she had no doubt that he wanted revenge. The intensity of his hatred shook her already fragile state of mind. Images in a dark corridor flitted across her memory with such realism, she could feel his hot breath on her skin, his fingers slithering around her throat, and his knife's blade caressing her cheek. A burst of light from his gun streaked past Julia's ear. Instinctively, she ducked as a second shot flew wildly over her head. Adrenaline steadied her nerves long enough to return fire. To her astonishment, Julia watched her shot strike his weapon and send it skittering under the wheels of a passing car. He scowled and drew the knife she so much feared. As he raised his hand to throw it, Julia leveled her weapon and fired again, but nothing happened! The gun would not respond. An ugly smile transformed his face from anger to expectation. He lowered the knife and started towards her. Julia saw with satisfaction that he limped where she'd kicked him, but she feared he was still too quick for her. In desperation, she threw the weapon at him and managed to strike a glancing blow off his head. He dropped to a knee, but his sullen expression told her she had only stunned him.

Again, Julia considered running towards the abutment where Mark and his men had taken cover, but twin beams of light flashed within inches of her face, forcing her to retreat. To make matters worse, Kwong's son was already getting to his feet. She frantically looked for another weapon but saw nothing within reach. The thickening fog was her only chance. If she crossed the bridge, the fog would obscure her. Julia plunged into the traffic lanes, trying to avoid the approaching cars, but headlights suddenly loomed in front of her. Brakes screeched as a car caught her on the hip and sent her sprawling to the pavement. An anxious face stared at her through the driver's window, but the car kept moving, its fumes mixing with the salt air. She knew the driver could see the flashes from the firefight through the fog and wanted to get away. Fortunately, the car was traveling slowly, which saved her from serious injury, but her body felt like a sack of potatoes when she got up, and her right hip and elbow ached from the fall. Another car's tires whined against the pavement as it rushed past at a higher rate of speed.

Julia waved to an approaching car, but the driver ignored her. Nobody was going to stop, and she couldn't blame them. Looking back, she spied the shadowy figure of Kwong's son working his way through the traffic towards her. Julia gritted her teeth and dodged through the headlights until she reached the far side of the bridge. She had hoped to cut back through the traffic and join Mark, but Kwong's son had anticipated this and was moving at an angle to cut her off.

Her eyes darted back and forth, looking for a possible escape route. Her only choice was to turn away from Mark and pray that the fog would keep her hidden, but as she limped along the sidewalk, the fog lifted enough for her to see Kwong's son gaining on her. To her right, a span of cables holding the bridge's support wires rose into the sky above her head. Climbing those cables seemed out of the question, but she didn't know what else to do. Memories of that razor-sharp knife pressed against her skin were motivation enough. She stared at the cables in dismay, but she was out of time. She had no choice but to embrace the sky.

The cables were as thick as tree trunks, but Julia soon found hand holds and began to climb. The fog immediately enveloped her in its dank arms, masking her view. At first, the ascent was gradual and the poor vision helped her control the stress tumbling inside of her. She had scaled those containers, after all, and ridden a wire between Chinatown's rooftops. Her greater fear was knowing that Kwong's son lurked somewhere behind her, clambering up the same cables with his evil knife. Julia didn't want to think about that. She knew climbing the bridge would only put off the inevitable unless she devised a plan.

The climb soon steepened, and she had to stop to catch her breath. Her hands had grown slippery with perspiration, and her stomach muscles had tightened into a hard, burning knot. The fog continued to obscure her view, which was a blessing. She didn't need to see what waited for her below if she slipped and fell. She could already envision the jaws of hell waiting to devour her. There was no turning back, in any case, for an even more violent fate awaited her in the form of Kwong's son if she didn't keep going. She began to climb, again.

Suddenly, Julia popped out of the fog and faced a sky so brilliant, she had to squint her eyes to see her surroundings. A rumpled panorama of fluffy contours lay at her feet. The bridge's second tower punched through the snowy landscape ahead of her. So did two hilltops less than a mile away. Julia was mesmerized by the dreamy scene. It reminded her of a Zen garden. She knew she had climbed to a great height, yet her equilibrium was still under control, and her head did not ache the way it normally did. Was she cured of her fear of heights, she wondered? Not likely. It was surreal world created by the fog. It didn't threaten her.

Julia wanted to catch her breath and enjoy the view, but memories of her pursuer's poisonous eyes pierced her reverie and her rapture faded. She sensed him close behind and began climbing again.

She could no longer detect any sounds below. Either she was too high to hear the battle and traffic or had the fight had ended. It did not matter. She was in a separate world, now, one beyond the reach of lasers and flying disks. A gust of wind buffeted her with an icy fist, making her shiver. She thought about Mark's expression on the bridge, the mixture of anxiousness and tenderness in his eyes. She'd seen the heat in married men's eyes, their bold passion and selfish desires, but not the warmth he'd shown. His look had left her feeling heartened and confused. She still loved him, but no matter how much she wanted him, she couldn't forget that he had a wife. The word had lost its bitter taste, but it still burned her mouth and chafed her tongue. Now that she had found Mark, she wanted nothing to do with a married man again, but *he* was married. The irony of her situation made her laugh.

A grunt from below snapped Julia back to reality. Kwong's son emerged from the fog. He had shoved the knife back into its sheath, leaving both hands free to climb the steep cables, but something in his manner had changed. He was no longer making the confident moves of a hunter. He looked hesitant, even frightened. Julia recognized his uncertainty and realized their roles were now reversed. She was in more familiar territory, now that she had scaled those shipping containers and buildings in Chinatown, whereas her assailant had most likely never scaled anything in his life that didn't involve an elevator.

Julia was heartened by this knowledge, but looking down still took its toll. It stirred the placid waters of her mind and made them swirl in her head. Her fantasy world of fluffy clouds crashed in an upheaval of nerves that blurred her vision. She looked up again and gripped the giant cable with both hands. The tower's peak wasn't far away. All she could do was focus on the cable and keep climbing. Air escaped her lungs in ragged bursts, and despite the cooler air, she felt sticky-hot.

Julia concentrated on each handhold and continued her ascent until she reached a small platform just below the span's peak. She sat down gasping for air and shaking with the realization that she could climb no farther. She didn't need to look down to know that Kwong's son was close behind her. She could hear his heavy breathing. While she'd climbed, Julia had tried to think of some way to defend herself. Only one choice presented itself: her waist belt. Her fingers quivered as she removed the belt and wrapped it around her right hand so that the belt's metal buckle dangled from one end. She swung it tentatively and grimaced. It was a wretched weapon, but it was all she had.

To ease her mind, she focused her attention on the twin, brown hills beyond the far end of the bridge. They looked solid and comforting. Julia saw two hang gliders floating gracefully above their rugged contours. How free they looked, swooping and soaring like birds! They reminded her of Mr. Andersen's words at their first meeting about learning to fly. Perhaps, she could join the gliders and fly away from the violence that lurked in her shadow. Without Mark, what did she have to live for, anyway? Life would never be the same without him. All she had to do was leap from her perch into the beckoning fog.

A scraping noise forced Julia to look down, and her head spun violently when she saw her adversary just yards away. It would take less than a minute for him to reach her, and when he did, he would plunge his knife into her heart. Julia closed her eyes. She wanted to spread her wings and float like those gliders but could not bring herself to do so. Life was precious, and she would fend off death, if only for a few more seconds. Julia turned her face to the sun's warming rays and waited.

A hand clamped onto her wrist, and Julia knew that flying from the bridge was no longer possible. Her eyes flew open and saw the leering face of Kwong's son just inches from her own.

"Be still my little bird," he hissed. "It's time to clip you wings."

Panic seized her as she tried to wrestle free, but his grip was too strong. She looked for the glimmer of his knife, but it was still in its sheath. He was holding her hand with the belt in it, but his other hand still clung to the cable. Retrieving the knife meant letting go of one or the other. She could see the indecision in his face, and the waters in her mind calmed.

Without thinking, she raised her leg and kicked him. She couldn't gather much power from her seated position, but the heel of her foot caught him flush on the nose, drawing a cry of outrage. His face screwed into a mask of anger and pain, and he released Julia's hand to reach for the knife. Julia immediately swung the belt, catching him on the temple with a glancing blow. The punch had little effect, however. Before she knew it, the knife flashed through the air and struck her right shoulder. The blade sliced through flesh until it hit bone, sending a spasm of pain down her arm. She nearly lost her grip on the belt as her arm dropped limply to her side. The speed of the attack had caught her by surprise. The knife flashed again, cutting her side just below the ribs. Her body convulsed from the shock of the pain piercing her body.

Her mind screamed at her to do something, but her shoulder was imprisoned in fire, and her arm refused to respond. Kwong's son seemed to be moving at hyper speed, just as his father had when he launched his deadly missile at Mr. Andersen. His hand was already poised to strike again, but he paused and stared at her, his face dancing with a triumphant smile. Death was only a knife's plunge away, but that wasn't what galvanized Julia to action. It was his gloating face. He was savoring his kill, and she refused to give him the satisfaction. For some reason, Mr. Andersen's words floated to her. He had said learning to fly would set her free, but he hadn't meant jumping from a bridge. He was talking about a spiritual freedom that would let her grab hold of her future. But it was up to her to grasp it. Nobody else could do it for her.

She cried with anguish, forcing her wounded arm into action, and swung the belt with all of her remaining strength. The buckle gouged into her assailant's eye, ripping through its soft tissue to the nerve centers of his brain. He jerked his head back with a roar, releasing his grip on the cable and reaching for his eye. The sudden movement unbalanced him. He dropped the knife and flailed with his hands as he searched for a fresh handhold.

Julia watched with fascination while his fingers played across the cable as if it were a piano. His body was already tilting backward, making it impossible for him to reach the handhold he so desperately needed. He hung suspended for what seemed an eternity, the dark scowl on his face widening into a look of disbelief, then he slowly cart-wheeled away from her. His body banged twice against the cables as it gained momentum and disappeared into the fog.

Julia sat on the platform dazed and shaken. The exhilaration of knowing she had escaped the venomous clutches of Kwong's son sang from every pore in her tattered body, but her elation was quickly tempered by the realization of what she had done. Kwong's son had forced her to defend herself, but that didn't ease the burden of knowing she had killed him. Her life, which had always been free of violence, had been visited by three deaths at her hands in less than a week. Her eyes blurred with tears. *I'm a killer, just like Liu Kwong.* No, she scolded herself with a shake of her head that sent a fresh wave of searing pain knifing through her shoulder. That was not true. Kwong murdered people for personal gain. He had tried to murder Kathy. *I'm not like that. I'm not a murderer.* Still, the reality of what had happened weighed on her, and she knew it would take time for her conscience to heal.

When Julia looked down and saw the blood oozing from her wounds, she realized she was still in danger. If she stayed where she was much longer, she would bleed to death. Every move sent fresh needles of pain shooting through her body, but she had to climb back down those cables.

Julia took off her sweater and bound her shoulder as best she could, then started a slow descent using only her left hand and feet. The frosty air quickly chilled her exposed body, but she braced herself against the frigid metal and continued working her way down the steep slope one foot at a time.

By the time she reached the sidewalk, her body and mind were too numb to support her, and she collapsed on the pavement. The last thing she remembered were booming voices and pounding feet. They sounded loud and distorted, as they would inside a tunnel. Was one of the voices Mark's? She couldn't be sure because of all the echoes.

When Julia regained consciousness, she found herself lying on a stretcher on the Golden Gate Bridge with Mark's jacket bunched under her head. Her right shoulder and lower abdomen were heavily bandaged, and an I.V. had been inserted in her arm. Her head throbbed in rhythm to the cacophony of shouting voices and sirens wailing around her. Uniformed figures hurried past her. A helicopter buzzed overhead. She raised her head and saw ambulances and police cars parked at crazy angles on the bridge. Several covered bodies lay near the tower's abutment where the firefight had taken place.

Julia looked up and saw white clouds bouncing across the sky in blowsy patterns that made her think of playful rabbits. The fog had been pushed out to sea by the warming sun. She eyed the bridge's elegant support cables swooping overhead with fascination. *Did I really climb them?* It seemed so improbable, she wondered if she had only dreamt it.

Mark's frowning face appeared above her. He knelt down and brushed the hair from her face. "You okay?" he asked in a husky voice. "I was afraid I'd lost you."

Julia was finding it difficult to concentrate, but she heard the concern in his voice and smiled. She remembered his worried expression earlier on the bridge. He still cared for her, and that knowledge warmed her heart.

"How did I get here?" she asked.

"Near as we can figure, you climbed down from up there." He pointed to the tower. "And we found the body of Kwong's son under it. From the looks of your wounds, I'd say you put up a helluva fight."

"He tried to kill me," she said in a pleading tone. It seemed important to justify her behavior to Mark. She didn't want him to think she was a murderer. Questions crowded her mind. "What happened to Mr. Andersen?"

Mark's face grew serious. "Mr. Andersen is dead. I think he expected Kwong to kill him. He knew it would put an end to Kwong's kingdom."

Mr. Andersen dead! Julia's mind reeled at the news. There had to be some mistake. Surely he wasn't dead. Then she remembered the ashen look on his face before he fell. Other memories swarmed inside her head, memories of Kwong's venomous eyes, beams of light exploding around her, and Kwong's son cart-wheeling into the fog.

"Kwong was badly wounded, but he survived." Mark continued. "He's in custody for Mr. Andersen's murder, and his operation will be rolled up like an old carpet when you write your story. My computer contact has completed Kathy's disks. I'll have the names on those bank accounts for you by tomorrow."

Mark's voice snapped her back to a new reality, a future that did not include him. She thought about Mark's wife and stifled a sob. Living without him was more than she could bear. Her mind was becoming fuzzy from the medication. All she wanted to do was close her eyes and sleep. Mark took her hand. Its warmth spread over her like a blanket, and the world became hushed.

CHAPTER TWENTY-ONE

"You're lucky you weren't more seriously injured," Detective Rodriguez gave Julia a grudging smile. The rough edge to his voice didn't bother her. She could see the relief in the uplifted folds of his face. They were seated at Julia's desk at the Chronicle, where she was in the middle of writing her exposé on Liu Kwong. Telephones and voices provided their usual noisy backdrop to her workplace, but that would soon change. Phillip had promised her an office as well as a substantial raise to keep her from bolting to another paper. He knew the story was big. He was holding the headline and lead columns on tomorrow's front page for her, and she was working hard to make the deadline.

Julia had spent the previous night at the hospital after being stitched up. The doctor had wanted her to stay another twenty-four hours, but she'd refused. Her body felt like it had endured a ten round title fight, but she wanted to get to the Chronicle and write her story. She had immediately called Detective Rodriguez and welcomed the break he now provided her.

"I don't know whether to commend you or arrest you," he continued. "That was a damned fool stunt you and your friend pulled on the bridge."

"You'll want to kiss me when I give you these." She laughed

at the surprised look on his face and held up several documents and computer disks. "Here are the people who are taking bribes from Liu Kwong." She handed him a copy of the list and watched his eyes widen with interest.

Mark's computer associate had successfully traced Kwong's trail of changing account numbers from Kathy's old computer disks to their current users. The numbers revealed a damning list of Port Authority and city hall officials. Bribes, bank transfers, dates and names were spread across decades of corruption. The trail led directly to five key men in Oakland's current inner circle. Julia had been pleased to see the Port Authority Manager, Daniel Edwards, among them. Her skin still crawled at the thought of his eyes undressing her.

When Rodriguez read the names, he whistled. "You can prove this?"

"The numbers by the names are for accounts at the Bank of Chinatown, which is owned by Liu Kwong. Each is a dummy account, but you can trace them to these people through the coded numbers next to the accounts." Julia was pleased to see a satisfied smile play across Rodriguez's lips. It was the smile of a detective about to make a major bust, and it told Julia she'd been right to trust him. "The disks contain detailed records of drug transactions and slave trading," she added.

Rodriguez shook his head. "I guess I'll have to commend you. You've done a remarkable job. We can finally shut down Liu Kwong's operations." He stood to leave but stopped and looked thoughtfully at Julia. "I know you've had someone helping you with this, Miss Rice. Whoever it is, thank them for me, will you?" He gave her a knowing smile and trudged toward the door. Julia marveled at how unassuming the detective looked to the casual observer, but she knew better. She was glad to have him as an ally.

When Julia finished her article, she marched into Phillip's office with it and told him to keep his editing pen in his desk drawer. "No changes," she said in a firm voice. "This story is too powerful to tamper with. It runs as is."

Next, she called Mark. He had brought the decoded banking

files to the hospital before she checked out, then left to make arrangements for Mr. Andersen's funeral. Julia couldn't stop thinking about Mark, but as badly as she wanted to see him, her heart froze every time she thought about what he would say. It didn't matter. She had to know why Mark had betrayed her. Why he never told her about his wife.

"I don't want to go home," Julia said when Mark answered. "Take me someplace where we can talk."

"You sure you're up to it?" A concerned voice. It didn't change things, but she couldn't help glowing at the knowledge that he cared for her.

She recalled observing the hang gliders soaring above the hills and fog from her perch atop the Golden Gate Bridge. There was a seaside community just beyond those hills. It was a tranquil village, the kind of setting where Julia thought she could wrestle her conflicting emotions without making a fool of herself. It was a good place to face Mark.

"Take me to Sausalito," she demanded.

Julia was in a pensive mood when Mark picked her up an hour later and said little. Her wounds ached more than she cared to admit, but that wasn't what troubled her. She knew she was about to lose the only man she had ever loved, and she wanted to postpone the moment as long as possible.

When Mark crossed the bridge, Julia's thoughts were shattered by memories of blazing laser beams and flashing knives. She flinched at the images and tugged at the collar of her sweater.

"You okay?" Mark asked, looking at her with apprehension.

Julia sucked in a breath and nodded. She thought about the first time she'd seen Mr. Andersen shuffling through the park toward the Fior d'Italia restaurant and marveled at how much had happened since then. Mr. Andersen had changed her life. Her new self-confidence, her confrontation with CONDAD, and her front-page story were all made possible by him. Every time Julia thought of his limping gait and watchful gaze, tears came to her eyes. He had died at Kwong's hands after telling her the final episode of his story. In the end, it hadn't really been a story about greed or murder. It had been a love story, a story she would cherish her entire life. Julia's only regret was not having the opportunity to thank Mr. Andersen or to say goodbye.

And what about her own love story? Could she really say goodbye to Mark, or would her determination wilt from the heat of her desire? She studied his profile while he weaved through the tight turns leading down the hill into Sausalito, his alert eyes periodically checking the rearview mirror. She couldn't help smiling at his habit. The pursuers were gone, but he looked anyway. *I love this man too much to give him up, but what can I do?* Julia fidgeted in her seat, her nerves as taut as piano wires.

They pulled into the village of Sausalito and parked on the rough planks of a small pier where the Ondine Restaurant jutted into the bay. Tourist shops strutted their merchandise along the opposite side of the street, and fashionable houses played hide and seek among the lush trees running riot up the steep hillsides.

Mark held Julia's arm for support as they entered the restaurant. The warmth of his touch had a calming effect, but it couldn't stop the bat wings working overtime in her chest. A hostess seated them by a window where Julia saw seagulls floating over the bay and sailboats skimming the water against the backdrop of San Francisco's skyline. It was an idyllic setting, one meant to fill hearts with fairytale dreams, but Julia surveyed the scene with misgivings.

"You've hardly said a word," Mark offered in a quiet voice.

Julia caught his eyes and held them. The heat rising in her cheeks told her she had abandoned any chance of appearing aloof. Her love pounded in her chest, and she had no way to hide it.

"Tell me about your wife." Her calm voice belied her inner turmoil.

Mark's face reddened, and the muscles tightened along his jaw. It was one of the few times Julia could ever remember seeing Mark caught off guard.

"You know," he said finally.

"Yes, I know." Julia's head spun as violently as it had atop that bridge tower. She feared what Mark was about to tell her more than she had feared Kwong's son, but she was determined to maintain her composure.

Mark took her hand and returned her questioning gaze. She was always surprised at how soft his hands were, considering his penchant for dangerous work. It was like holding newly-shorn lamb's wool.

He released her hand and leaned back in his chair. "I didn't want to talk about it until I had resolved things. That's why I left the other day." The waitress approached to take their orders, but he waved her away.

"Mary was my best friend's fiancée. He died during an operation that went bad. Saved my life in the process. Mary was three months pregnant at the time. She came from a small town where her father was prominent. The embarrassment overwhelmed her, but she didn't know what to do. I had gotten to know Mary and liked her, so I married her. It seemed the right thing to do, and it repaid my friend for my life." Mark furrowed his brow, indicating how hard it was for him to talk about it. "We thought we could make a go of it, but we didn't love each other. After the baby was born, I was gone most of the time on assignments. We finally separated, and she moved back home with her folks. That was three years ago. Neither of us got around to filing for divorce. There was no need, until I met you. But when I told Mary about you, she agreed it was time to settle things. She filed the divorce papers two days ago."

Only Julia's painful wounds kept her from leaping out of her chair and wrapping her arms around Mark. Her joy rocketed through the room. Had she heard him correctly? Was there hope? Mark started to say more, but she leaned forward and put a trembling hand to his lips. Her mind raced through a maze of thoughts as she fought to control a fresh wave of nerves. There were so many things she wanted to tell him. Where to start? How could she explain the torment that had haunted her for so many years?

"I need to say something before I lose my nerve," she began. She hesitated, trying to find the right words. "I've been moving through life as if I were in a trance. No, that's not it." She waved the words away with her left hand, took a breath, and started again. "It's more like I've been traveling on a train looking out the windows. I've watched the world passing me by, but I never knew how to make the train stop. Now, I do, and I love you too much to be content just looking out windows. I want to *feel* my life." She clenched her hands to emphasize her point, causing a stabbing pain to shoot through her shoulder. "I have you to thank for that, and no matter what happens between us, I'll always be grateful to you."

Julia slumped back in her chair, exhausted from her dialogue. Her body shook from exertion and her wounds throbbed, but she ignored them. Perspiration slid down her temples to her cheeks. She tried to read Mark's eyes but couldn't.

"You don't have to do or say anything," she continued. "I just wanted you to know how happy you've made me."

Mark looked at his hands, then out the window. Silence hung between them for an eternal heartbeat, and Julia feared he might bolt from the table. Then he smiled in his warm, funny way, and she nearly collapsed with relief. His smile told her everything would be all right.

"I'm not very good at this kind of talk, Julia." Mark looked at his hands again. "I've been living in my own world for too many years. I guess I've been looking out the same windows." He lifted his head and met her gaze. "But, when you kissed me on those shipping containers, I was so unnerved I nearly fled back to the CIA. Mr. Andersen was right. I could never have let you fall in battle without breaking ranks to save you.

"You mean more to me than life itself, and it scares the Hell out of me. What happens when I go back to work? I'm like those long-ago sailors in wooden ships who went to sea with no idea how many months they would be gone or where their journeys might take them. It's not a life that's well-suited for most women, and I fear it may be too much to ask of you."

Julia glowed in the aura of his words. They washed over her in velvet waves and wrapped her in their promise. "If you wanted to go to the moon, I wouldn't care, as long as you came back to me."

She grasped his hand, but said nothing more. There were times when nothing needed to be said.

Mark broke the silence between them. "There's one more thing," He reached into his pocket and removed a folded paper. "There were some things Mr. Andersen wanted you to know once we were finished, but he feared he might not be able to tell you personally. He dictated this letter a week ago, before you were kidnapped." Mark handed the paper to Julia.

She unfolded the letter and stared at the neatly typed sentences. Her eyes misted, making it difficult to see the words clearly, but she could feel their weight in her hand. Mr. Andersen's voice reached out to her through those words. She grabbed a napkin to wipe away her tears, leaned back in her seat, and began to read:

Hello Julia:

If you are reading this letter, it means we can no longer meet, which is a shame. I have very much enjoyed our times together. There are a few things I must tell you, and I hope you will not be too angry with me for revealing them so late in the game. I had good reason to wait until now.

When you researched my background, I'm sure you learned that my mother abandoned me to an uncle when I was fourteen. We have something in common, there, don't you agree? What you don't know is that she later married a man named Rice and had a son, Roger. I was twenty-five by then and had lost contact with her, but my uncle kept me informed. Roger married your mother twenty-seven years later, and you were born. That's right, Julia. I am your half uncle. Why didn't I tell you this sooner? I didn't want anything to prevent you from ending our arrangement if you thought our project was too dangerous. Knowing who I was would have placed an unfair burden on you and might have influenced your decision. As it happened, I was the one who wanted to stop everything when you were nearly killed in Kwong's office. If anything had happened to you, I could never have forgiven myself. But Mark convinced me to continue. He thinks very highly of you, as do I, and he promised to protect you.

I was already in England with Kathy by the time you were born, but I kept an eye on you over the years. I also followed your father's unconscionable career as best I could. He moved around a lot, as you know, which made it difficult. What a bad seed he turned out to be! I have often wondered if being raised by our mother had something to do with that. It gave me great pleasure to find him for you and to see you confront him the way you did.

But it was you who worried me most. I could tell you were suffering. Anyone would be who had lost her mother and been abandoned by her father. I wanted so much to help you, but I couldn't endanger Kathy. Liu Kwong still thrived and would have stopped at nothing to track me down if I had given him even a hint of our trail. And, of course, the police were still looking for me. I had to stay in England.

After Kathy died, I no longer cared about Liu Kwong or the police. My life was at an end, but I wanted to bring Kwong to justice before I died. And I wanted to help you, just as my uncle had helped me. You were still struggling to find your place in the world. I thought if I could safely guide you through Liu Kwong's treacherous waters, you could learn about Kathy and me and get a blockbuster story to boot. I hope my efforts are successful.

The most satisfying part for me has been getting to know you. What a team we have made! It has been quite rewarding. Oh, I know you are upset with me, now, because you think I harmed Kathy, but that will change when you have heard the complete story. In the process, I have discovered a wonderful partner. Your courage and steadfastness are truly impressive. But the relationship has run deeper than that. In many ways, you have become the daughter Kathy and I never had, and that discovery has given me the greatest pleasure of all. My only regret is that Kathy could not share our relationship. She would have liked you as much as I do. I will tell her all about you when I catch up with her.

Come to think of it, there is one other regret. I wish I could have met Jackie. What a spark she creates wherever she goes!

Even from a distance, I can see why you are so enamored with her. Do keep her close to you.

Well, we are nearly finished, and I suppose all good things must end. You have a new life ahead of you. If it includes Mark, so much the better. He is a marvelous young man. Either way, I know you will make your life count for something special because you are so special. Please keep Kathy and me in your thoughts. You will always be in ours.

With great affection,
Thomas Person Andersen

The words wheeled through Julia's mind faster than she could comprehend them. She tried to read them again, but they became too muddled to decipher. Had Mr. Andersen really been her uncle? It was an incredulous revelation. He was family! Her family. Why hadn't he told her sooner? How she wished she'd known in time to take his hand and feel the warmth of his arms around her. Like a daughter, he said. It was true. She did feel like his daughter. He personified all the things she wanted in a father, including warmth, kindness, and caring. And he was family!

Julia felt the tears running freely down her face. Mark was watching, but she knew he understood. She looked out the window at the sailboats on the bay. The setting had seemed so unnatural before. Now, her heart *was* filled with fairytale dreams. Her world made sense for the first time since her mother became ill. Julia had spent her adult life searching for her father, and she had found him in an unassuming old man who hobbled into her life and stripped her of defenses. In the process of making that discovery, Julia had found herself, and she liked what she saw. She looked forward to getting to know herself better.

Julia looked at Mark and beamed a smile. She said nothing, but that was okay. There were times when nothing needed to be said.